Pr

'Not many boc ... *Perpetual*
Astonishment of Jonathon Fairfax is ... omic gem.'
Francesca Brown, *Stylist*

'It cleverly combines intrigue with comic, astute observation which made me laugh throughout.'
The Bath Novel Award (2014 shortlist)

'You can't help being tickled.'
Alfred Hickling, *The Guardian*

'Shevlin was rightly picked up by the literary agency that represents the likes of David Nicholls. ... the comic hero is caught up in a murder plot that unravels into a political thriller, which is by turns absurd and engaging.'
Ben East, *Metro*

'*Jonathon Fairfax Must Be Destroyed* is funny, it's daft-yet-relatable, it's still a nerve-jangly thriller and it moves at a cracking pace. In fact, if you're stuck in a bit of a reading rut, it's just the palate cleanser you need.'
Emerald Street

In need of some absorbing comedy? ... Written with the gentle comic precision of Nina Stibbe and Neil Gaiman, you need Jonathon Fairfax in your life right now.
Stylist (reviewing *The Spy Who ...*)

The Fairfax Redemption

CHRISTOPHER SHEVLIN

ALBATROSS

Part One

Potato

Monday and Tuesday

1

The London Underground is a conspiracy for bringing you face to face with inconvenient figures from your past. If, for example, you've had a doomed and deeply wounding love affair with a person, the chances of sitting opposite them on the Tube approach a hundred percent.

This morning the vehicle of fate was a Victoria Line train. Jonathon Fairfax was on his way back from a meeting with some people who might (but crucially might not) want to pay him to illustrate a brochure. He sat, immobilised by the huge portfolio he clasped to his shins.

That was when he glanced up the carriage and saw her – in the next block of seats, on the opposite side. There were only about half a dozen people between them. He looked away quickly, stared at the backs of his hands, then read the advert opposite him a few dozen times. It was about life insurance, reminding him that he had no money and was going to die. He glanced up the carriage again, just to check it was her.

It was her.

Oh god.

If she happened to glance his way, their eyes would meet, and he would have to deal with the expression on her face as she recognised him. Or – more immediately convenient but infinitely worse – the expression on her face as she didn't recognise him at all.

The train squeaked to a halt: Highbury and Islington. This was not his stop, but he was going to have to get off anyway. He rose, smacked his knee into his huge portfolio, and shuffled off, head down.

As he stepped off the train, his eyes flicked to the right. Was that her getting up? Oh god.

He joined the flow of people walking down the platform. As he rounded the corner, heading for the stairs, he hesitated. Going upstairs would mean going through the barriers. He'd have to queue to get back in, and if she had got off and was leaving the station, she'd see him. He'd be a sitting duck.

He shouldn't stay where he was either, because she might walk around the corner at any moment and see him. He should go to the other platform. But then if she was changing trains she would already be there and would see him. Oh god, this was a nightmare. Was it possible, he wondered, for him to be instantly vaporised? That seemed the only acceptable solution to this awful quandary.

The train was pulling out. He averted his face in case she'd stayed on and was looking out of the window. Then another thought struck him: a glint of hope. If she had got off and wasn't changing trains, wouldn't she already have reached this point? After all, he'd been standing here agonising about this for so long that the staff were probably already using him as a landmark: 'Downstairs, left at the indecisive man, and next train to Walthamstow Central.'

So, that meant she had either stayed on the train which had just left, or she was waiting on the other platform to change trains. He turned, manoeuvred his portfolio out of the way, and took a decisive step back towards the platform he'd just left, ready to resume his journey and begin the long process of rebuilding his life.

'Oof,' he said. He had just walked into her.

Rachel stood back, looked up into his eyes, and – contrary to all his expectations – smiled.

'Jonathon!' she said. 'Oh my god, Jonathon. It's totally you. How are you?'

Every conceivable emotion galloped through him, laying him waste.

'I'm,' he said. 'It's. Oh. Hello. How. Rachel. Yes. Are?'

He should smile, he thought. He did, and it came out bigger than he'd intended.

'Do you mean, "Hello, Rachel. How are you?"' she asked.

'Yes. Roughly that. Sorry for walking into your, um, self.'

It was amazing, after all these years, that he still couldn't speak properly around her.

She looked the same, except that her perfectly mid-brown hair was a bit longer, and her face was somehow more definite, as though it had been carefully reproduced in a slightly more durable material. Her glasses exaggerated her large eyes, and she wore a light-grey jumper and jeans. She looked beautiful.

'I'm totally fine, thanks,' she said. Her Scottish accent had worn away a bit in France. 'I mean, not *totally* fine. Who is? But basically fine. I–'

'I–' he said simultaneously.

'You go,' she said. 'I mean, speak.'

'I can't,' he discovered. 'You should.'

'I was just going to say, I really need to get going. I'm late to meet my aunt. But will we swap numbers?'

He remembered this habit of hers – asking a question as though he had a limited power to see into the future.

'Yes,' he said – proving that, in a certain way, he did.

'Give me your phone,' she said.

He handed it over, and she tapped away.

'There,' she said, handing it back. 'I'll be in London all this week, but Wednesday's a bad day.'

'Right.'

'Bye then,' she said, and reached up to hug him, more strongly than he'd anticipated. Then she unhugged him, shifted the weight of the bag on her shoulder, and disappeared into the crowd that he now saw had been quite seriously annoyed at having to step around their reunion.

He smashed his knee once more into his inconveniently gigantic portfolio, said 'ow', and lugged it over to a bench to collect himself.

Well, he thought, staring at a huge advert for alcohol, *thank god that's over. Now I can get back to never seeing her again.*

After all, she had broken his heart eleven years ago. It had taken him a very long time to get over her.

When Jonathon got home that evening he found the whole household gathered in the narrow hallway to meet him, alerted by his telltale protracted fumbling with the lock.

The dog made her deep groaning noise of welcome and patrolled the perimeter of Jonathon's gigantic portfolio. The cat, from his perch halfway up the stairs, remarked, *'Rowl?'* And Piper gently pushed the dog aside and put her arms around Jonathon. Her long chestnut hair was in disarray, and she was wearing an old cardigan, which was, to him, exactly her most attractive mode. They kissed and she said tenderly, 'Have you ever thought of getting a smaller portfolio?'

'I saw Rachel,' he answered.

Their conversation wasn't, as a rule, absolutely crammed with talk of Rachel. And they did slightly know another Rachel, but nevertheless Piper immediately knew who he meant.

'Oh,' she said. 'Where?'

'On the Tube. At Highbury and Islington.'

'Oh, but I thought your meeting was in–'

'I got off there to try to evade her. She was on the same train and I was afraid she would spot me, so I got off and … well, hid, and then I accidentally walked straight into her.'

'Would,' she said gravely, 'you like a cup of tea?'

Once they had their teas and two chocolate digestives each, this being a moment that called for them, they sat at their favourite corner of the kitchen table and he narrated the whole thing for her.

'So, when are you going to call her?' she asked, when he'd finished.

Like Rachel's reaction to seeing him, this was contrary to all his expectations. Come to think of it, he wondered whether anything had happened the way he'd expected.

'Well,' he said, 'I thought I might, um, live out the whole of the rest of my life without ever calling her?'

Piper gasped theatrically and looked at him over the rim of her chocolate digestive, as though she were a lady at the court of Versailles regarding him reproachfully over her fan.

'But …' she said. 'I mean, I'm not telling you what to do, but you have to call her.'

'Do I?' He was alarmed by this, because Piper was absolutely always right about this sort of thing.

'Yes. Would you never call *me* again, if we broke up?'

'If we broke up I would live in a shallow hole in the ground, crying. I wouldn't call anyone.'

She stroked the back of his head with her non-biscuit hand. 'Poor Jonathon,' she said. 'Not even a deep hole in the ground?'

'I wouldn't have the energy.'

'That's sweet,' she said. 'But you really need to call her. Maxine' – this was the therapist Piper saw on Thursday evenings – 'says it's really healthy to be friends with your exes. And I feel better after getting back in touch with Ronald. Sort of. I mean, maybe he's a bad example. But they're both our first loves, who still give us a terrible pang whenever we think of them. Well, not so much with Ronald, now I know he works for Shell. But you know what I mean.'

'There's something I've never quite told you,' he said.

'What is it?'

He paused. 'You know I never quite knew where I was with Rachel?'

This disorientation had been natural. Jonathon and Rachel had got together after a sequence of horribly traumatic events, in the course of which her colossally muscular uncle had serially terrified Jonathon and had then been gravely injured and sent to prison. It had been a confusing time for both of them, especially since Rachel thought her uncle was a big pussycat who only wore a balaclava because he got a cold face.

Piper nodded.

'It just seemed so unlikely that she would like me. And mostly when I was with her I felt good, but sometimes I would get tense, because she just seemed a much better person than me. Well, I mean, all the same things as with you, really.'

Piper turned the remainder of her biscuit into a moustache and nodded gravely.

'Is it all right to talk about this, by the way?' he asked, suddenly worried. 'I mean, you know I love you, and …'

'Jonathon,' she said gently, 'we talk about *everything*. We had

7

a conversation last week about whether cows are happy. It's good to talk about this.'

'Okay, good. Thank you. It's just, I never really managed to talk to Rachel properly about any of that, the things I just said. And I didn't know how often I should call her, because I didn't want to be bothering her all the time – especially since she was doing her degree.'

'Did you ask her how often she wanted to be called?'

'Sort of? Did I? No, probably not.'

'Oh dear. And then what happened?'

'After about two months she said she was going to visit her dad in France. And no one had mobile phones then, because it was still the Nineties, and I didn't have her dad's number, and I just never heard from her.'

Piper gasped. 'Never?'

'Or only once. Anyway, after a while, I realised that we must have split up. And then I thought I'd messed up this one chance of happiness, and that I was just fundamentally not cut out for having relationships. I mean, women don't clamber over each other to be with a man who falls over things and gets his words in the wrong order and possibly wears his old green jumper slightly too often.'

'I think you're–'

He held up a finger, unable to bear hearing nice things about himself.

'You're very handsome,' was what she confined herself to.

'I'm just lucky that you have a weird eye defect that prevents you from seeing my face properly.'

'I'm lucky that you have a weird face defect that makes you handsome.'

'Anyway, I … decided to stop existing. And, well, anyway, it's still the worst I've ever felt – even after all the weird stuff that's happened to me since.'

'Oh, love.' She put her hand on his leg.

'And, um, and,' he said, 'that's why I don't really want to see Rachel again.'

'You're right,' she said. 'It probably is best if you don't call Rachel.'

2

Later that evening, Jonathon called Rachel. She came round for lunch the next day, bringing her aunt, who she didn't want to leave on her own.

'This is Lisa, my aunt,' said Rachel, as the dog shyly inspected the relative, while the cat observed them haughtily from the top of the stairs. Lisa was tall-ish and trim, with a strong, tired face and opalescent nails.

'Hello! Jonathon, is it?' said Lisa. 'Nice to meet you. Lovely place you got here. Bijou.' Lisa pronounced this as though it had been carefully graded for discerning Jewish people. Jonathon was suddenly confused about how Rachel managed to be so softly Scottish when her aunt was so loudly London.

'Thank you,' he said. It *was* a lovely place: an improbably beautiful little cottage in Hampstead, which they'd got as a result of a different sequence of horribly traumatic events. 'We got it kind of accidentally – we're not rich or anything. Anyway, this is Piper.'

'Hi, Piper,' said Rachel, and they did a little hand-on-shoulder-cheeks-nearly-touching thing.

'Piper?' said Lisa, frowning in confusion. Then she added, 'Nice name. Unusual. *Exotic.*' And then she did a big laugh to cover the awkwardness.

They all looked at each other and smiled, and then Jonathon said, 'Shall we, um…' and Piper said, '… have some lunch?' and gestured down the short hallway, to the kitchen.

They sat around the wooden table, Rachel and her aunt on one side, with Jonathon and Piper on the other.

'Rachel, what, um, what are …?' Jonathon began, losing his thread as soon as Rachel looked up.

'What am I doing in London?' suggested Rachel, speculatively, one eyebrow up.

'Yes! Sorry.'

'I'm, er, here helping Lisa out,' said Rachel. 'Basically …' She turned to her aunt. 'Can I say?'

'Might as well, love. Keeping quiet won't change it.'

'My uncle's getting out of prison, so I'm kind of here to help with that: do the driving, make sure there's enough milk, that sort of thing.'

'Ow,' said Jonathon, who had somehow managed to flip his spoon into his eye.

'Oh, which prison?' said Piper, interestedly, as though helping relatives out of prison were a thing that she did all the time.

'Flintwinch,' said Lisa. 'South of the river.'

Jonathon asked Rachel, 'Is this, um, is this the uncle who's a pussycat and gets a cold face?'

Lisa looked at Rachel. 'Is that what you said, love?'

'Is it? Totally could be. I mean, he is, kind of. And he does.'

'He does,' Lisa confirmed to Piper in a confidential tone. 'He's a martyr to that face of his.'

'I get a cold face sometimes,' said Piper. 'I wear two scarves in winter. Jonathon calls me Scarf-face.'

'Only when you call me Johnny-boy,' said Jonathon.

'How long has he been in?' asked Piper.

'Twelve years,' said Rachel.

'Eleven,' corrected Lisa, as though that made it much better. *'And* that includes the time he was in hospital custody. Ninety-five he went in. It's 2006 now.'

'And where do you live?' Piper asked Lisa.

'Fellows Road. About a mile over that way.' She gestured roughly southwards, through the kitchen wall. 'Two-bed flat. Me and our Gemma. Don't know what we'll do for space when Col comes back. And Gemma's a bit of a funny age.'

'How old?' asked Piper.

'Thirteen.'

'Thirteen's a bit of a funny age for everyone,' said Piper. 'I went through a phase of pretending to be Jo from *Little Women.*'

Lisa looked blank.

'It's an American book from the nineteenth century about some … well, some little women.'

Lisa looked a bit relieved and said, 'She's not at a funny age in *that* way. I mean, she's not weird or nothing. No offence.'

'None taken,' said Piper. 'I was objectively weird.'

'Our Gemma's always been very mature, very sensible. She don't throw nothing out, but everything's got its place, all neat. She's in the Youth Orchestra too, plays tuba. And they *was* talking about her doing her GCSEs a year early …'

'Aren't they now?' asked Rachel.

'I don't know, love. It all went downhill last term.'

'How?' asked Piper.

'They say she's got anger-management issues. Came out of nowhere. I mean, she's always said what she thinks, but she lost all her self-control. She lets herself get all upset.'

'What about?'

'What you got? Mr Lowther told her to take her coat off and she called him a pencil-neck tit.'

'Okay. Wow.'

'Told him he could shove her coat up his you-know-what. Stormed out. Had to spend the rest of the term reporting to the deputy head every day. I'm telling you, if she carries on like that when they go back in September, she'll be chucked out before you can say Jack Robinson.'

'Jack Robinson?' said Jonathon, emerging from a fear-induced trance.

'Faster than that. You say Jack Robinson really slowly, love. You all right?'

Jonathon assured her that he was fine, but continued to quake inwardly.

Once they'd gone, Piper closed the door behind them and said, 'Well that went well. She's nice, Rachel.'

Jonathon was looking pale and staring at a patch of wall with a pained expression on his face.

'Oh no,' said Piper. 'What's wrong?'

'I … her uncle's getting out of prison. You remember what I told you about him?'

'Sort of?' she said.

Piper made them both a cup of tea, and he told her about it

in more detail. He'd told her before, of course, but they quite understandably didn't bring it up all that often.

At some point Piper said, 'Oh, he's the one you call the murderer.'

'Yes,' said Jonathon. 'But his real name's Colin Slater.' Jonathon shivered as he said the words. 'I'm worried he'll blame me for what happened, and will want revenge.'

'But didn't you say he got badly injured in a fall?'

'Yes. But he must have recovered, or he wouldn't have been put on trial.'

'I see.'

'The thing is, with bumping into Rachel like that and then hearing that the mur– … that the uncle's getting out of prison, it makes me feel like this is the beginning of another sequence of horribly traumatic events.'

'Maxine says it's good to reframe things, to make them more positive. Perhaps you could think of them as … as adventures?'

'Adventures?'

'Maybe?' said Piper.

'Maybe,' said Jonathon doubtfully. 'But then that means I'm terrified of adventures. And I'm not, really. I *want* the sort of adventures normal people have – you know, like living in France for a year, or renovating an old mill, or learning to rap.'

Piper raised her eyebrows. 'You want to learn to rap?'

'God, no. That would be awful. But you know what I mean: normal adventures. I just don't want to have to start worrying again about people … trying to kill me.'

She put her arms around him. 'It's all right,' she said. 'No one's going to kill you. We'll get through this.'

And then Cess, the dog, with her instinct for human distress, came padding over and shyly laid her snout on his knee, with her cold wet nose against the back of his hand. And the cat, with his utter indifference to human distress, stared at the curtains.

Wednesday

3

The cell door clanked open.

'All right, Slate,' said Barker. The miniature prison officer bustled in, all keys and shoulders. 'Ready for big day?'

Barker was from Yorkshire, and was thus forbidden to say the word 'the', instead leaving a tiny superstitious gap to mark where it would have gone.

The murderer, who had been sitting on his bed, got himself to his feet – which took quite a while, there being so much of him – and picked up the two clear bin bags with all his possessions in them.

'Ready as I'll ever be,' he said.

'What, not looking forward to getting out, then?' asked Barker.

'Course I am. Course I am. It'll be magic. I just … you know, you hear stories, about how difficult it is … to adapt and that.'

'Come on, Slate. You adapted all right to this place, and it's a right shithole. You'll be fine.'

'Course I will.'

They both looked around the cell, at all its fabulous bounty. It was a double, made from two small singles that had been knocked together long ago, for reasons no one knew. The toilet was hidden behind a shower curtain, which was rumoured to be from John Lewis. And there was a non-prison mattress, a colour TV, a big kettle, a rug, a toaster, and – most impressive of all – a miniature fridge.

'It'll all go to McGill, won't it?' said the murderer. 'You'll make sure of that.'

'He's probably packing his stuff now,' said Barker.

'Just hope that boy steps up, keeps the peace.'

The murderer patted the wall and left the cell, followed by Barker, who locked the door behind them. They walked in silence for a while, along the familiar walkway with its scuffed cream wall, running down one side of the huge Victorian hall.

'I been thinking, about your little problem,' said the murderer.

'Oh aye?' said Barker.

'What about hiding them in one of them big sand buckets in the kitchen?'

Barker thought about it and said, 'Not a bad idea, that.'

They walked in silence for a while, down the stairs, then Barker said, 'God knows what it'll be like when you go, Slate. Been practically no trouble on this wing while you've been here. But Riley were telling us other day what it were like before you turned up.' Barker made a face and sucked air through his teeth.

'Well, I don't know about that,' said the murderer.

In his youth, he'd done violence for fun. Then he'd gone professional, progressing to larger and more spectacular acts of violence in order to feed his family and fund his loss-making gym. That had eventually landed him in prison, where he'd run a publicly-funded gym, which had freed him up to commit smaller, more heartfelt acts of violence in an entirely voluntary capacity. It had felt good to give something back.

They were now on the ground floor of the main hall, the ceiling high above them. Eventually, they came to a scuffed cream waiting room, where the murderer put down his bin liners and sat on a wobbly plastic chair. Barker shook his hand – little beefy Barker, who was at eye level with him now he was sitting down – and said, 'Cheers, Slate.'

There was no one else waiting to be released – the room was empty – but, because it was prison, the murderer still had to wait nearly an hour before the door opened and a bored voice called, 'Mr Slater?'

The murderer went through into a scruffy little office with a wooden counter. An overweight man confirmed his name, prison number and date of birth, and then left him waiting again while he went off and located the murderer's box of possessions. He plonked it down heavily on the counter and took out a brand-new eleven-year-old sports holdall, and all the items the murderer mysteriously hadn't been allowed to bring in with him, including some elderly Lynx deodorant, a biro and a watch, as well as his suede jacket and gold chain.

Once the murderer had signed for these things, he was given a travel warrant and told to mind how he went. And with that, the overweight man shuffled around the counter, unlocked a set of double doors, and ushered the murderer out into the world, a free man.

The world greeted him, as you might expect, with a featureless stretch of road and a light drizzle. The murderer turned back to the overweight man, who was swinging the heavy doors closed behind him.

'Where's the visitors' car park, boss?'

'Down the road and round the corner, mate. Not sure you have to call us boss any more.'

'Cheers, … mate.' It felt strange to say the word to someone in a prison officer's uniform.

He found the visitors' car park and trudged along the rows of vehicles – mostly models he'd only seen on his tiny cell TV – until he saw, framed in the windscreen of a red Astra, the faces of Lisa and Rachel. They looked slack-jawed and gormless, as people do when they're waiting in cars, and they were watching patiently for him to come out of the wrong door.

The murderer knocked on the passenger window and Lisa reared back as though someone had dropped a small grenade in her lap. Then their eyes met and her face was instantly one large smile. She scrabbled the door open and got a surprising way out of her seat before being hauled back in by her seatbelt. Once Rachel had helped her undo it she clasped her arms tight around him and burst into tears.

The murderer dropped his bin liners and took her in his arms, his chin resting on her head. He felt the tiny gleam of tears at the corners of his eyes. It was the most un-prison thing, hugging a woman and doing anything even remotely like crying. And it was suddenly the best moment of his life.

She looked up at him and put her arms around his neck. His neck was too massive to be held by a single pair of arms, but she did her best, grasping somewhere between his earlobes and the edges of his jaw.

'Oh, Colin!' she said.

'You're a sight for sore eyes, you are,' he said.

'Oh, Colin!' she said again. And then she couldn't say any more because she was crying again. 'Oh, love! I'm so happy to see you. You're out.'

'I'm out,' he said. 'I'm out. It's amazing to see you, love. Amazing.'

She hugged him again and put her cheek on his shoulder. He put his cheek against her hair, and they rocked from side to side. His eyes were bright and shiny, and his nose was wet, like a dog's.

'It's a lovely car park, this,' he said. 'Probably the best prison car park south of the river – but how about we go home?'

'Course, love. Do you want to go in the front?'

'I want to go in the back, with you.'

As Lisa opened the back door, Rachel got out of the driver's side and said brightly, 'Hi, Col!'

'Rach, love! Thanks a million for coming to … to help out.'

'Oh, it's no problem. I–'

'Give us a hug.'

She walked around the car, and he gave her a one-armed hug, keeping the other arm around Lisa's shoulders.

'Right then,' he said.

And then the other back door opened and someone got out. The murderer looked across the roof of the red Astra and saw a thin man with startled eyes, smiling awkwardly. His hair was sticking up at the back and he had a slight resemblance to the Cat in the Hat.

'You again!' said the murderer.

4

Jonathon was sitting in a small red car with a giant murderer. They were stuck in traffic.

He glanced over at Rachel, who glanced back with a slight smile about the eyes, which might have been reassurance or might have meant, 'I told you this was a stupid idea.'

'Gemma not around then?' asked the murderer from the back, his voice rippling through Jonathon's body as though he were a component in a huge amplifier. 'At school, I suppose.'

'It's the summer holidays, love,' said Lisa. 'But she's got a practice today. Youth Orchestra.'

The murderer let out a long breath through his nose. 'Couldn't get out of it then?'

Neither Lisa nor Rachel replied. There was one of those very loud and intrusive silences, as though someone were playing a silence solo on an invisible saxophone.

'Been three months since she come to visit,' remarked the murderer.

There was another virtuoso silence solo – intricate, nuanced and expressive.

The murderer must have looked at Lisa, because she interrupted the performance to say, 'She's at a difficult age, love.'

The murderer sighed, and this signalled a return to the normal kind of silence produced by the fact that nobody happened to be talking.

'So we got Johnny-boy instead,' said the murderer, brightly. 'What you been up to then, John?'

'Um,' said Jonathon. How do you sum up eleven years of your life – including two sequences of horribly traumatic events, a break-up and meeting the love of your life – to a man who's just got out of prison and once threatened to kill you? He could feel overthinking cranking itself up, so he turned his mouth on and it said, 'Um, I got a dog?'

'Nice. What breed?'

'I don't really know. She's white.'

'Oh, yeah, *white* dogs, lovely breed,' said the murderer sarcastically.

'Yes. She are. Um. They is.'

Silence returned, and Jonathon broke it by asking, 'So, um, what do you plan to do next, … Colin?'

'Don't worry about me, Johnny-boy. I got plenty of options. In fact, seeing you has reminded me of a job I was offered years ago.'

Jonathon quailed. He hoped the job wasn't murdering someone. He particularly hoped the job wasn't murdering him.

'What you doing for work then?' asked the murderer.

'I'm, um, I'm an … illustrator,' Jonathon said, and added quietly, 'Yes I am,' because a small voice in his head had pointed out that he was doing terribly badly and certainly wasn't good enough to call himself an illustrator.

'What, drawing and that?'

'Yes.'

'Much money in that then?'

'Not much.'

There was a ruminative silence from the back, and then the murderer said, 'What you draw then?'

'Um, mostly animals wearing clothes, in pen and ink. A bit like John Tenniel but not as good.' This was his standard way of explaining what he did, almost custom-designed to allow people to write him off as a harmless crank and move on. And since most people had never heard of John Tenniel, they tended to switch their ears off before he'd even got to the end of the sentence.

'Like *Alice in Wonderland* and that?' said the murderer.

Jonathon was so surprised that the murderer had heard of John Tenniel that he turned around. The murderer took up about two thirds of the back seat, and his shaved head was pressed against the ceiling as though the whole car were just an elaborate hat that he was wearing. His face was inches from Jonathon's, and he looked very much as he had the last time he remembered them being this close. The main differences were that he was a bit paler, a bit more trim, and he wasn't asking directions to the house of someone who would later be found murdered.

'Yes,' said Jonathon. 'Have you seen those drawings?'

'What, white rabbit with a massive clock thing, bloke with the hat, all that? Course. Everyone has.'

'Oh. Have they? When I talk about his drawings, everyone just looks blankly at me.'

Jonathon glanced at Lisa, who was exaggeratedly demonstrating this exact facial expression – almost as if John Tenniel had popped in and illustrated her.

'So you sit there and draw pictures all day?' asked the murderer.

Jonathon nodded.

'Cushy life that.'

It was a cushy life, really. How did he manage to import so much worry into it?

Jonathon said, 'It's mostly for companies and magazines and things, so I have to go to meetings to talk about what they want me to draw. And then sometimes afterwards they just go quiet and I don't get the work, or they keep changing their minds about what they want – so sometimes I spend ages on jobs that don't pay much. And then there's all the invoicing and admin. And I never get time to do the drawing I really want to do.'

All of this fell out of him, because it was constantly going around in his head and it was a relief to be able to say it, even to a man who had, apparently, once concussed him with a large ornamental palm tree.

'John, you're talking to a man who's been paid a pound an hour for the past few years for managing a busy gym in a popular prison location.'

Jonathon felt his face go red. He was so spoiled.

'So,' said the murderer, 'I'd say you have a very cushy life.' He paused, then added, 'Done well for yourself. Good lad.'

Jonathon faced forward again, looking out of the window. He had never felt so pleased. Or so terrified.

5

The murderer looked grimly out of the window as they pulled into a run-down car park. In the middle, as though parked there, was a twenty-storey tower block covered in scaffolding. Cars were scattered around – mostly old, though there were a couple of brand-new Mercedes with blacked-out windows. In a corner, a wheel-less car rested on bricks, a notice pasted to its windscreen.

The murderer struggled out of the tiny red car and looked around. For a man who had spent the last few years in a grim featureless box, this was like a home from home. Lisa was looking anxiously at him, so he smiled and put his arm around her.

'I love a nice bit of scaffolding,' he said. 'Lovely job they've done here.'

She giggled and said, 'I've made it nice inside, love.'

'I bet you have.'

The kid – Johnny-boy – had got out of the car and was lifting the murderer's two bin bags out of the boot. The murderer let him, wondering again why he was there. It was as wrong and inexplicable as a plate of chopped liver turning out to play for Arsenal's away squad. But the murderer wasn't going to make a fuss, not today.

He and Lisa walked hand in hand to the building's entrance, with Rachel and the kid a few paces behind, all under the watchful yellow eyes of the pigeons. On the building's front door there was an official notice, saying what was being done to the tower and spelling out the strict behavioural code which the workmen would ignore.

Lisa used her key fob to let them in, and they walked on dirty plastic sheets to the lift, where a wheezing old man with a little cart on wheels squeezed himself in alongside them.

'Got enough room there, mate?' asked the murderer, thrilled at coming across his first random civilian. He meant it to sound friendly, but the old man just wobbled fearfully and looked away.

On the sixteenth floor, the lift bonged and they got out onto a small landing where Lisa unlocked a door and led them into her home – and now his.

Inside, the hallway was long, dark and narrow, the ceiling only a couple of inches above his head. The first door on the left had a nameplate saying 'Gemma', above some partly peeled-off *My Little Pony* stickers. It was closed. On the right was a tiny bathroom, with a cracked washbasin and old lino, but new deep-pile mats. Lisa bustled ahead of him, explaining and excusing it all, but he couldn't really listen. He was too distracted by the non-prison normality of it all, and by how far they'd fallen.

There was a bedroom with a neatly made double bed, a dressing table and a mirror-fronted wardrobe all squeezed in. At the end of the hallway was a little kitchen, whose door had been removed to make space for a fridge, which jostled with an old oven, a slice of worktop and a sink, all knackered and spotlessly clean. Beside it was a living room that strained to accommodate a sofa with many things stored behind it, a TV, two sets of shelves and an inconveniently huge coffee table.

The murderer squeezed past the coffee table and stood in front of the living-room window, mesmerised by the sight of a distance with things in it – tower blocks, shops, warehouses, car parks, train lines, roads, and rolling hills of terraced houses. He hadn't realised he'd missed this.

Behind him, Lisa was saying, '… kept it special because I know you always liked it, in the old house, and you've got to have somewhere to put your coffee down, haven't you, love? And the shelf was from Eileen, ever so expensive – from Heal's.'

He nodded.

'Oh, the bags?' she said, talking behind her into the hallway. 'Just put them in there for now, on the bed. That's it. Ta for that, John. You are a love. What? I don't know, Rach love.'

She turned back to him, wiping her palms on her jeans. 'So? What do you think, love?'

'You done a lovely job, love. Magic.'

Lisa was standing on the other side of the room, but still he could almost have reached across and touched her. Someone was hoovering in another flat, as loud as if it were in this room, and someone else was watching Jeremy Kyle. Behind her, the hallway struggled to contain little Rachel, and the skinny kid had overflowed into the kitchen.

'What's wrong, love?' asked Lisa.

'I'm sorry, love,' said the murderer. 'I'm sorry I went away and didn't provide. And you had to get a job and … and you done well with this place.' He paused. 'But it isn't what we had before. That's all. We was just having the kitchen done. All them lights for the table things.'

'Dedicated task lighting for the worktops?'

'That's the one.'

'It's all right, Col,' she said. She came over to him – squeezing her ankles around the sides of the coffee table – and held his hand. 'I don't care about kitchens and onyx-effect worktops. And I like the job, most of the time. As long as we're okay, that's what matters. Long as you're home.'

'I'm home,' he said. 'I'm not leaving again.' Their eyes met. Then he looked at his watch. 'Except for right now. Got the probation office meeting at ten past two. Don't want to be late.'

'You got time for a cup of tea, haven't you?'

'I can't, love. Not this morning. I can't sit down inside. I need to walk up and down a street, buy a paper or something, walk past people who don't want to steal my flip-flops for the shower. Need to do that before the meeting. You all right to drive me, Rach?'

'Totally,' said Rachel. 'That's what I'm here for.'

'Maybe we can pick up another plastic bag for you to hold, Johnny-boy.'

'Um, thanks,' said Jonathon. 'Great. I ought to go now though. I've, er …' He paused for an uncomfortable amount of time, as though trying to work out what he had to do. His cheeks were red with embarrassment.

'It's all right,' said the murderer. 'You got your own plastic bags to take care of. I know.'

The probation office reminded him of his doctor's, before prison: the official posters, the old plastic chairs in the waiting area, the plastic-topped reception desk with a beaten-up computer, the lady behind it who looked like she'd been steeped in tea. Why was his heart beating so hard?

'You all right, Colin?' asked Rachel.

'What? Yeah. Fine, love. Never better. Love a waiting room, me.'

He swaggered over to the reception desk.

'Good afternoon. How can I help you?' said the receptionist in a slightly artificial way, as though she were acting out a dialogue for people learning to speak English.

'All right, love,' he said. 'Got an appointment, two ten. Mrs Stewart. The name's Slater.'

The receptionist peered crossly at her computer, which seemed to be vexing her, rapped its keys a few times as though to teach it a lesson, and then said absently, 'Please take a seat, Mr Slater.'

'Right you are, love. Don't let that computer give you no cheek.'

She glanced up at him in surprise, then smiled.

He and Rachel went and sat in the waiting area. Every so often a door would open, and someone would call a name. Sometimes a man would get up and go off with the caller, and sometimes the caller would repeat the name several times, then frown, scribble something on a clipboard and call a different name.

'So what you bring him for?' he said to Rachel.

'What?'

'Monkey boy. Mr Cat in the Hat. What you bring him for?'

'Jonathon? I just totally thought we might need an extra pair of hands.'

The murderer held up the vast expanse of his two huge hands.

Rachel opened her mouth but didn't say anything. Then she looked at him. 'Okay. He asked if he could meet you.'

'What for?'

'It's a bit complicated, but basically he was scared of bumping into you when he was least expecting it, so he wanted to get it out of the way. He's terrified of you.'

'Yeah, I spotted that: written all over his face. That boy should definitely not take up poker. Or go to prison.'

'Agreed.'

'You're not … seeing him, are you?'

'What? No! He's got a girlfriend. And I live in a different country.'

The murderer nodded and looked at the carpet tiles.

'You know I did though,' she said, 'don't you? Years ago.'

'What, before Fabio?'

'Fab*ien*, yes.'

They were quiet for a bit. A name was called and a man made his way across the waiting room, aggressive and embarrassed.

'Tell you what,' said the murderer, 'I've never met anyone like him for spreading chaos. And that's coming from someone who's shared a cell with a compulsive arsonist.'

'You don't … blame him, do you? For …'

'For the injury and the years in prison? Hadn't crossed my mind.'

'Seriously,' she said.

He sighed. 'I went to prison because I did some bad things, I had a debt to repay to society, and now I'm a new man.'

Rachel glanced at him.

That was definitely what he was going to say in his probation interview, if it ever happened. It was twenty-five past already.

6

Gemma didn't have a Youth Orchestra practice. But, having lied about it, she couldn't risk leaving her tuba in the flat. As a result, she now had to lug a huge chunk of dented brass around with her all day.

Looking for a place where no one would see her, she clanked over to the little concrete playground behind the neighbouring tower block. But as she stepped over its low wall, she saw KT and Olivia. KT was lounging like a model on a spring-mounted plastic duck, and Olivia was sitting nearby on the remains of a wooden bench.

It was a stunning piece of bad luck, because Gemma had – in an unguarded moment – told Mez that KT had funny ears. Had Mez told KT? And Gemma had wanted to be friends with Olivia, but Olivia had gone off with KT instead. In short, the politics of the situation couldn't have been worse. Gemma didn't even know whether she should talk to them.

Luckily, Olivia gave her a little wave. Gemma waved cautiously back and walked over.

'What is up?' said Olivia. It had been their greeting last term, when it had looked like they were going to be friends. They said it like they were foreigners who'd learned it from a phrasebook.

'What is up?' said Gemma. It was nice that Olivia remembered.

KT made a face but didn't actually say anything about it, so that was okay.

'Hi,' said KT expressionlessly.

'Hi,' said Gemma.

'What's with the big saxophone?' asked Olivia.

'It's a tuba.'

'What's with the tuba?'

'Me,' said Gemma, not wanting to get into it. 'I'm with the tuba.'

'God, why are you two being weird?' asked KT.

'We're not being weird,' said Olivia, and then she wibbled her finger between her lips and laughed hysterically.

After that, no one could think of anything to say for a bit. Gemma felt her face going hot, and started to feel bad.

KT ostentatiously checked the time on her pink flip-phone and said, 'I've got to go and meet my brother.'

Olivia said, 'Okay, bye!' and KT looked at her in a weird way that told Gemma that KT had wanted Olivia to walk with her. So maybe Olivia did want to be friends, now that she'd found out what KT was really like. Perhaps she'd got sick of looking at those funny ears. It was all making Gemma's head hurt a bit, so she sat down on the low wall and watched as KT walked huffily off.

'Is KT all right?' said Gemma. 'She gave me the evils when she left.'

'She never,' said Olivia. 'She's just upset because Mez found out that she fancies Robot.'

Gemma shook her head at the implications of this.

'Got any goosey jossip?' Olivia asked.

Gemma shook her head again.

'You okay?' asked Olivia. 'For seriouslies? Because, you know, tuba.'

Gemma tried to think through how much of her huge life problem she could tell Olivia. If she told her nothing they would never be friends. But if she told her even half of it, and Olivia told KT, then it would end what was left of her social life. She would have to start hanging around with Toolshed and Emma Beige.

'It's Colin,' said Gemma. 'My mum's husband.'

'Like, your step-dad?'

'No, he is my … I mean, I'm his daughter. But he's been away … in the navy, since I was two or three, and I've only seen him a few times, and now he's coming to live with us.'

'So you're carrying a tuba around. Good plan.'

'No, I told Mum I had a practice so I wouldn't have to go and pick him up with her.'

'Pick him up from where?'

'The … from the port, the navy office. Oh god, right, please swear on your life you won't tell anyone about this?'

'I swear,' said Olivia.

'On your gran's life – and your cat's?'

Olivia nodded solemnly and put her hand on her heart.

'Colin's getting out of prison today,' said Gemma.

'Really!' said Olivia. 'That is *so* cool.'

'It's not cool,' said Gemma. 'It's sad.'

'*Going* to prison is sad,' said Olivia. 'Having a dad who's *been* to prison is cool. Mine's an audit manager. He'll never go to prison.' She sighed.

They sat in silence while Gemma wrestled with her feelings.

'Why does he have to come back *now?*' she said fiercely. 'We was doing fine, me and Mum. I finally felt like I wasn't a freak, and then the closer it come, the more I'm going mad. Sev started calling me Hulk after I lost my rag with Mr Lowther.'

'That *is* funny though, Gemma.'

'Not when it's you being called Hulk.'

'No. But.'

'Plus Colin's massive. Our flat's tiny. There won't be no space, no air to breathe.'

26

'What did he do then, your dad? To end up in prison.'

'Mum won't talk about it. She just said he was trying to do his best for us and he made a mistake. My Aunty Rach says it was violence, basically. But even she won't really talk about it. She says I should hear it from him, when he's ready. But what about when *I'm* ready? Why's it all about *him?*'

'Have you asked him?'

Gemma shook her head. 'I can't. In the visitor centre thing in prison, with Mum next to me. Can't talk about nothing. He won't say much about his life there. I used to tell him what I was doing, but now I think, "What's the point?" He'll just say, "That's magic that is, Gem." Every single time. Drives me mental.'

'That's magic that is, Gem,' said Olivia in a deep voice. They laughed.

'I've been educating myself though,' said Gemma. 'I got a criminology book out of the library, and Durkheim says that crime is a normal–'

Gemma stopped, seeing how Olivia was looking at her. Olivia shook her head slowly.

'You got a *school textbook* out of the *library?*' said Olivia. '*That* is what you should have made me swear I'd never tell anyone, not the dad-prison thing. You've got your priorities all wrong, girl.'

7

Imagine the world's most handsome and self-assured man. Add tiny and precise darts of white hair at the temples to give him an air of glamorous distinction. Mix in a nice jacket and a beer, and you have Lance Ferman. Events had somehow conspired to make him Jonathon's friend, which was why Jonathon had just sat down at his table in the Flask, their local pub.

'Shark-man,' said Lance, who, by tradition, never called Jonathon Jonathon.

'Please don't call me Shark-man,' said Jonathon, still lightly quivering from his ambiguous encounter with the murderer.

The Flask had been their local ever since Lance had moved back to London from New York a few months before. It was an oddly charming pub, fighting a desperate rearguard action against the vast wave of money sweeping through the area, turning it from a gentle, arty village into a corporate facsimile of the same thing.

Outside, the pub's weathered sign showed a powder flask from the Napoleonic wars, held by a plucky redcoat with a musket. Inside, the pub was split into three rooms: one full of scuffed wooden tables, one divided into ancient booths, and one carpeted and full of old prints satirising the Prince Regent. If you were the Prince Regent, that room would have really upset you. 'It's so unfair,' you would say, emerging ashen-faced. 'I mean, I know I'm a *bit* bloated, corrupt and indolent, but there's a whole other side to me that they've completely ignored.'

Luckily, neither Jonathon nor Lance was the Prince Regent, so they sat undistracted at their scuffed table near the magnificent zinc-topped bar, and discussed the events of the last two days in forensic detail.

'So,' Lance summarised, when Jonathon had finished, 'you're afraid of another ... How did you describe it?'

'Sequence of horribly traumatic events.'

'You're afraid of another sequence of horribly traumatic events breaking out. So, to prevent that–' Lance broke off, interrupting himself. 'Maybe you need to reframe these things. I mean, I've been involved in most of them, and I think of them as adventures.'

'That's what Piper said. But then that just makes me reframe an adventure as a sequence of horribly traumatic events.'

'Okay, well then you need to change your reframing. Why not reframe an adventure as ... as an opportunity for self-growth?'

'Well, because I never self-grow. I always stay exactly the same as I was before, except more traumatised.'

'Can we reframe "more traumatised" as "wiser"?'

'Can we reframe reframing as a thing we don't have to do any more?'

Lance considered this. 'Yes,' he said, at length. 'I think we can. Anyway, you're saying that to prevent another adventure' – he held Jonathon's eye, to insist on this bit of reframing – 'breaking out, and to make sure you didn't accidentally bump into the murderer–'

'Uncle,' interrupted Jonathon. 'I'm trying not to call him the murderer any more because–'

'So now you're reframing.'

'I'm not reframing, I'm just trying not to call people murderers.'

'You say potato.'

'Only when I'm talking about potatoes. It's terrifying enough that he's out of prison and living about a mile away, without calling him "the murderer". Anyway, we used to call him that because we thought he'd murdered Sarah Morecambe all those years ago. But it was never proved at his trial, so it seems a bit unfair. He's definitely an uncle though. He doesn't deny that.'

'Okay,' said Lance. 'So, to make sure you didn't accidentally bump into this terrifying self-confessed uncle, you arranged to be in the car that picked him up from prison and took him to his flat?'

Jonathon scrunched up his face and nodded. 'I overthought it.'

'That's some overthinking,' said Lance.

'Well, I just thought that life is a huge conspiracy to play upsetting practical jokes on us. If you try to make something happen, it's guaranteed not to. In fact, it's guaranteed that your efforts will make exactly the opposite happen. So, if you're desperate to avoid something, it'll seek you out. And I couldn't stand the idea of just waiting for the uncle to loom terrifyingly over me when I least expected it, so I deliberately went out and loomed fearfully under him at a time of my own choosing.'

Lance took a drink and ate a thoughtful pork scratching. 'It's weird,' he said, 'but it almost makes sense when you say it, even though it's insane.'

'That's what Piper said.'

'You should go into politics. By your logic, people would conclude that the best way of keeping you out of office would be to vote for you, so you'd win by a landslide.'

'Oh, good.' Jonathon felt obscurely proud of this.

'So,' said Lance, 'you're desperate to avoid having another

adventure–'

'Only another traumatic adventure. I'd like to have normal adventures like normal people do, like exploring a Greek island or opening a restaurant–'

'You want to open a restaurant?'

'Jesus, no,' said Jonathon. 'That would be awful. I'd be terrible at it. But, you know, that kind of thing, where you try something new and exciting and no one tries to kill you.'

'The restaurant business is definitely not the way to go if you don't want people trying to kill you, especially in New York. Probably in London too.'

'But you know what I mean?' persisted Jonathon.

'I think so,' said Lance, still clearly reluctant to abandon his reframing. 'You don't want people trying to kill you.'

'Um, yes. I suppose that is the main bit of it.'

'And you're still – after sitting in a car with him – worried that the uncle might be … tempted to do that?'

Jonathon had been giving this quite a lot of thought. The huge man had been quite nice to him, in a way. But that's unnerving when combined with a look in the eye that bespeaks a fierce desire to pull your head off.

'A bit,' Jonathon admitted.

'Well, I guarantee I'll protect you from any further adventures.'

'Wait, doesn't that mean you've reframed adventure so that the only essential element of it is people trying to kill me?'

'Hey, I'm new to reframing – it's a thing I got from Arlene.'

'I think Arlene got it from Piper. Where is Arlene, by the way?'

'At a work thing. Where's Piper?'

'She's, um, meeting Rachel.'

Lance raised his eyebrows. 'Anyway,' he continued, 'let's not worry about the details. I guarantee something to do with protection from some definition of adventure.'

'Thanks,' said Jonathon. And he meant it, because he could see that Lance was having one of his moments of sincerity. But at the same time, he couldn't help remembering that Lance had a habit not only of reckless irresponsibility, but also of unthinkingly drawing Jonathon into life-threatening situations.

8

Rachel had called Piper late that afternoon and said, 'Look, I know this will totally sound weird, but I don't really know anyone in London any more, and I really need to … to have a beer. You probably totally have loads of things on, so–'

And Piper, to whom an invitation to spend time with the legendary Rachel was gold dust, had said, 'No, I'm doing less than no things this evening. I'm there.'

And then Rachel said she'd forgotten all her pub knowledge. So Piper, who was in town for a meeting with someone at the V&A, had suggested her favourite haunted pub, the Lamb. And that's where they were now, in that odd nook at the far side of the bar that's like a little private booth with a table in it.

Rachel had just claimed, in a slightly offhand way, that Jonathon had broken her heart, all those years ago.

'What, *Jonathon?*' said Piper.

'Yes.'

'Really?'

Rachel shrugged, as if to say, 'You don't have to believe me.'

Piper took a sip of her beer to cover her continued confusion. She was slightly thrilled to hear that Jonathon had broken another woman's heart, because – much though she loved him – she had to concede that he wasn't absolutely classically the heartbreaking type. But she also felt a bit ashamed of that reaction, because it's not good to want your boyfriend to be going around inflicting emotional pain on other women.

Rachel said, 'Sorry. Maybe I shouldn't be saying this to you. It's just that seeing him again has brought it all back. Plus, beer.'

'Beer's really good, isn't it?' said Piper. 'I'd forgotten.'

They clinked glasses, and Piper suddenly felt a bit shy. After all, they'd only met once before, and now here they were having a heart-to-heart in a pub. It was strange how suddenly it had happened.

'I mean,' said Rachel, glancing up nervously from her beer, 'obviously I'm over it now: it was a long time ago. And I would never try to ...'

'It's all right. One thing I don't have to worry about is Jonathon having an affair. Apart from anything else, he'd never cope with the stress.'

'That's true. Anyway, it was a total shock, bumping into him on the Tube. I mean, when I first recognised him it was just like seeing an old friend. But then afterwards I totally started to remember how I felt back then. It was such a strange time.'

'Jonathon has always said you broke *his* heart.'

Rachel pulled a wry face and then smiled. 'Well, he would do, wouldn't he?'

'What do you mean?'

'I mean that's what I liked about him. Everything affects him so much – and you can totally watch every emotion as it passes through him, like his eyes are a sort of emotion TV. So, yes, I'm totally sure I broke his heart. But the ... the corner shop probably breaks his heart when it runs out of milk.'

'Oh no,' said Piper, 'that makes it sound like ... well, like you're a pint of milk. And you're not. I think he was ... shattered for quite a long time after your break-up. He says ...'

Piper stopped herself.

'What does he say?' asked Rachel.

'That you suddenly, well, moved to France, married a farmer and invited him to the wedding.'

'Oh,' said Rachel, and stared into her beer, as though the events of eleven years ago were being replayed on its surface.

Piper sat for a while, waiting for an ad break.

At length Rachel said, 'Well, I suppose that's totally what did happen. It's just weird to hear it that way.'

'What do you mean?'

'So, I mean, just to rewind to the beginning, it's eleven years ago, and I'm in London at university. And for ... well, let's just say *reasons*, I was a bit anxious about relationships. And to just avoid the whole question, whenever I met a boy I would tell him I was a lesbian.'

'But you weren't?'

'No. It seemed a fine enough thing to do at the time, though I have to say it's looking a bit problematic now.'

'You think that's problematic. Our whole conversation so far has completely failed the Bechdel Test. We've been talking about Jonathon the whole time.'

'What's the Bechdel Test?'

'It's a thing for films. To pass the test, there have to be two female characters who talk to each other about something other than a man.'

Piper watched Rachel mentally replay a selection of films in her head.

'Wait a minute,' said Rachel. 'That's totally outrageous. *Every* film fails it. It's like a weird conspiracy.'

Piper nodded. 'The test was made up by a cartoonist Jonathon really likes, called Something Bechdel. Alison? Maybe Alison Bechdel. Oh, that's another thing: the female characters have to have names, I think.'

'Well, we do totally have names, so if this is a film, credit to the director for that at least.'

'Yes, thank you, Mr Director!' said Piper, waving at the ceiling. 'Thank you for giving us names!'

'Also, sorry, Alison!' called Rachel. 'We'll totally stop talking about Jonathon in a minute.'

They smiled at each other, in that conspiratorial way people have when beer is allowing them to march off together into a world of their own.

'Anyway,' said Piper, 'sorry, I interrupted you. Problematic lesbian pretence.'

'Yes. And then I totally started bumping into this boy all the time: thin, slightly cartoony face, always wore an old green jumper, hair sticking up at the back–'

'It still does that,' said Piper, 'but I give him tips to manage it.'

'But he totally didn't feel like the boys at school, or guys doing their chat-up lines in pubs. He felt kind of … comfortable, in a weird way. And then there was this night where we sort of … got together–'

'Was this at a time of extreme danger, by any chance?'

'Yes! Sort of. He thought Colin – my uncle – had sent him a threatening message. And he also thought Col had … had killed someone. And, I mean, it's totally possible. There's no doubt that Col's done some bad stuff, and he *was* tried for the murder Jonathon suspected. And he was found guilty of all sorts of other stuff. He was probably pretty lucky he got injured, because it delayed the trial and I think they lost some evidence.'

'How do you feel about your uncle now?'

'I don't know. I mean, he's the same person he's always been, in a way. Him and Lisa were always really good to me when I was in London. I don't trust him the way I did, but … well, Lisa asked me for help and I'm not hurting anyone by giving it, so that's it. It's only a few days. And I'm just trying not to think about all the moral stuff.'

'Sorry,' said Piper. 'I feel like I made you talk about all of that.'

'It's totally fine. It's good to talk about it. Why did you ask if we got together at a time of extreme danger?'

'I think it might be Jonathon's pattern. Anyway, you were telling me what happened.'

'Yes, well, after that, we were … meeting up. And I often felt really happy when I was with him, and I thought he felt the same. But if I didn't call him it would be ages before he called me. And I just felt this big tension developing, and I thought, "Why wouldn't he call, if he likes me?"'

'Fear,' said Piper. 'And overthinking. Continue.'

'And it was a weird, unsettled time. We were both living in really horrible rooms. I was trying to do my dissertation and all that, for my degree, and I knew he was thinking of going to university and didn't know where, so I didn't know how long he'd be around, but we didn't really talk about it.'

'No, you have to kind of make the conversation happen,' advised Piper. 'I mean, if you ever go back in time and have to deal with it again. Only don't, please.'

'Okay. And then after the dissertation and exams, my dad suddenly invited me to go and stay with him in France, and that had never happened before. So I went, and the room I'd been renting finished. And then I was in France and Jonathon *never* phoned me.'

'Oh.'

'And I just felt so miserable and went through this whole mourning thing. And then one day I met Fabien, who … well, he co-owns a vineyard now, but at the time he was just managing one. And he was *so* up-front and emotionally stable. It was just really easy. And we got married. He just asked me and I said yes. And I totally thought it would be really mature if I invited Jonathon to the wedding, to show there were no hard feelings.'

'Oh,' said Piper. 'Well that sounds completely different than his version, but also sort of the same. Oh dear. He's still really bad at phone calls, if that helps, even now we've all got mobiles.'

There was a silence, as Rachel stared into her beer again.

'So, you're still with Fabien?' asked Piper.

'No,' said Rachel, with one of those surprisingly joyful *I've made a gigantic mess of my life* smiles. 'We're getting divorced.'

Rachel didn't really feel up to talking about her divorce, so they talked about what it was like being in London again, and how bizarrely people in their early twenties were wearing their jeans, and – on the topic of younger people – what a lot of trouble was brewing with Rachel's niece, Gemma. And much of this passed the Bechdel test, so they thought on balance it was probably okay, especially since they both had names.

That got them onto graphic novels, which was a surprisingly diverting subject and meant they drank much more than they meant to. But they also felt quite happy about it, and it was all fine – a perspective that beer can temporarily make blindingly obvious.

And all in all they were merrily oblivious of the sequence of horribly traumatic events that was to come.

9

Just a few streets away, Horatio Brandon – Hooray to his friends – was sitting in a worn velvet chair in a darkened room, dramatically framed by the curtains and silhouetted against the dim golden glow of the London night.

He had been waiting a long time, and now his performance was about to begin.

There was the click of a key in the lock, the rattle of the door handle, the snap of the hall light. There were footsteps in the hallway. The kitchen light ticked on, the radio began muttering to itself about the government's prison privatisation programme, and then the footsteps were back in the hallway. The living room door was pushed open. A hand reached out and clicked the light switch. A sudden intake of breath was intook.

The moment was perfect.

'What the bloody hell are you doing in my house?' asked the man.

He was tall and thin, slightly stooped, with grey hair guarding the borders of his bald pate. Despite his shapeless suit and mushy beige shirt and tie, he had presence – an air of command even, given him by his disdainful gaze and hooked nose.

'Good evening, Rhys,' said Hooray. 'I'm here for your classics lesson. Translate the following: *mors certa, hora nunc etiam certa.*'

Hooray had carefully rehearsed this chilling twist on the proverb: 'Death is certain, its time is now also certain.' He was *very* pleased with it.

'Is this some kind of joke?' said Rhys. 'If so, I don't consider it a particularly funny one. Mr Brandon, I know who you are and I advise you to leave my house immediately.'

Hooray picked at one of his nails with a commando knife. It was a move he'd seen in a film, but great artists steal.

'Now I'm here, Rhys, I intend to stay for the rest of your life,' said Hooray. He enjoyed the casual menace of his tone. The performance was going well, apart from Rhys's failure to appreciate the *mors certa* line.

'I'm calling the police,' said Rhys, moving over to the telephone on the mid-century sideboard, next to a low leather armchair which Hooray had briefly considered for his opening reveal.

'Of course,' said Hooray. 'If someone threatens to kill you, even in a wittily veiled way, you are *seriously* within your rights to call the police.'

Rhys put the phone to his ear and then replaced the receiver on its hook, having heard there was no ring tone. He pulled a mobile phone from his pocket and dialled.

Hooray reached into his own pocket and pulled out a rectangular block of plastic with three lights on it.

'This is an S140 mobile-phone blocker,' he said. 'It has a range of around fifty yards. So you don't have to get *all* that far away from me before you can make the call. How are you at running? Done much recently? Difficult to fit it in with such a demanding job, I should imagine.'

'For heaven's sake,' said Rhys. 'This is a ridiculous way to react to someone writing an article about you.'

'You make it sound so harmless, Rhys. Because of you, the New York police want to talk to me – about an *extremely* sensitive matter. I've had to leave the city where I'd made my home.'

'Because you committed fraud! I didn't force you to! I simply reported the facts. That's my job. I'm a journalist.'

'You could have written about anything you wanted to, and you chose my small, victimless piece of business.'

'Insurance fraud isn't victimless. And it isn't business.'

'*And* you called me a wastrel.'

'I quoted one of your tutors at Oxford!'

'But it was you who decided to put those words into an article for everyone to read! No one forced you to give a platform to such hurtful remarks.'

Hooray was getting angry now, which wasn't part of the plan. He was losing control in a different way than he had wanted.

'You know, Rhys, you're really spoiling this,' he said. 'Typical Harrow man.'

'I'm glad I am spoiling it,' said Rhys. 'And I'm proud to be a Harrovian, rather than a spoiled and oversensitive Etonian, like you. Now please leave my house.'

'I had a whole bit planned where I was going to pleasantly suggest that you call for help. And then I was going to turn the stereo up just as you did, drowning out your cries. But I've decided to cut that bit now, and proceed directly to the main act.'

'All right, I've had enough of this,' said Rhys. 'This has gone too far, Horatio. I'm going to leave my house now, and I'm going to my neighbour's, where I shall call the police.'

'I'd run if I were you, Rhys.'

'I am not going to run,' said Rhys with dignity, though his voice shook. 'I am going to walk out of my house.'

Rhys took three careful steps backwards, into the hallway. Then Hooray heard him – contrary to his promise – run to the front door and fumble with the latch. Hooray waited until the very last moment, then sprang to his feet. He bounded down the hallway, reaching the front door just as Rhys got to the end of the path. Rhys was about to put his hand on the gate when Hooray grabbed him by the ankle and pulled him, hopping, inexorably back into the house.

There he assassinated him, with extensive classical commentary.

Thursday

10

The murderer checked his appearance in the bedroom mirror. Being set up for Lisa, this showed him what he looked like from the mid-chest down. Pretty good, he reckoned. He'd lost a bit of weight in prison. He wasn't sure how he was going to keep it off now he was back in a world where food tasted nice, but he'd try.

Lisa came in while he was admiring himself, and put her arms around him from behind, burying her face in his suede jacket and his trapezoid muscles, not far from the scar he carried from having been impaled that time.

In the hospital, a nurse had told him he'd been clinically dead for a while.

'Clinically dead?' he'd said.

She'd nodded gravely.

'But I'm alive,' he'd said. 'So I can't have been dead, can I?'

'*Clinically* dead,' she'd said.

'*Mistakenly* dead, you mean,' he'd said. 'You want to watch these doctors. They're having a laugh.'

He shook his head, bringing himself back to the present, in front of the too-short mirror.

'Looking good,' said Lisa, her face appearing in the mirror beside his upper arm.

He grunted and adjusted the thick gold chain around his neck.

'How long you going to be?' she asked.

'No idea, love. Probably a couple of hours.'

'Where was you? Last night. I woke up and you wasn't in bed.'

'Couldn't sleep,' he said. 'I just went and looked out the window, in the other room. I'd only have woken you up otherwise, turning over and that.'

'You'll get used to being out, Col. It's a big change.'

'Cheers, love. I will. I know I will.'

They kissed, and then he squeezed himself around the bed and down the hallway – once again accompanied by a voice from a neighbouring flat's TV. It was like living with the ghost of Jeremy Kyle. But he was going to do whatever it took. He was going to provide for his family.

11

Lance Ferman wasn't troubled by how to provide for his family, because Arlene, his wife, had always earned more than him and would have physically assaulted him if he'd tried to provide for her. That freed him up, now he was back in London, to launch his own private investigative agency, which he'd always wanted to do.

'How's the agency going?' Jonathon had asked him the night before, when they'd exhausted the topic of Rachel, her possibly homicidal uncle, and sequences of horribly traumatic events.

'Great,' Lance had said. 'Amazing. I just need to pick a font for my website and choose a camera. Oh, and get some clients and earn some money.'

Jonathon had predictably boggled at Lance's airy assumption that everything would turn out well, seeming to feel that even managing to choose a font shouldn't be taken for granted.

Since the agency's success was still in its pre-nascent stage, Lance had decided to sharpen his skills and get a case study for his website by taking on a pro-bono case. The pro-bono case was also secret, which made it even more glamorous and noble.

Lance had been working on the secret pro-bono case since early that morning, when he'd pulled into the car park of a medium-sized tower block covered in scaffolding. There he had sat, pretending to read the *Financial Times* while actually watching the entrance through a small pair of neatly designed binoculars. This was a follow: it was what he was born to do.

The murderer had emerged from the building twice that morning. The first time he'd just wandered around the block, looking at the sky and the buildings and occasionally shaking his head. The second time he'd got some milk. Lance wondered whether this was to flush out any potential follows. If so, a) the murderer didn't know who he was up against and b) he was clearly up to no good.

At around one o'clock, the murderer left the building again. He walked around the corner, waited ten minutes for a Number 31, then went to Camden and got on a Number 29. This was a challenging follow: buses benefit from having their own lanes and from the fact that everyone is afraid of them. But hadn't Jonathon said that Rachel was here to help the murderer? Why hadn't he asked her for a lift? It only increased Lance's suspicion. As did the fact that the murderer got off at Finsbury Park and walked into a chicken shop on Blackstock Road. No one was doing anything wholesome in chicken shops on Blackstock Road.

Had there always been this many, Lance wondered? What could people possibly do with that amount of fried chicken? Were they burning it for fuel? Lance had really lost his feel for London in the years he'd been away. He'd spent much of that time sitting in luxuriously appointed trailers, demanding increasingly obscure types of coffee and very occasionally getting out, putting on a trench coat and doing contrived pieces to camera in a fake moodily lit alleyway, wearing makeup that accentuated his cheekbones.

What he was born to do, by contrast, was sit in strategically located cars and cafes, drinking ordinary coffees and occasionally getting out, not putting on a trench coat, and busting a case wide open, possibly in a genuine alleyway, his cheekbones looking fantastic in whatever ambient lighting happened to be around.

As the murderer went into the chicken shop, Lance executed a daredevil high-speed piece of parking into a space that someone had been just about to reverse into.

'Oi!' shouted the other driver.

'London!' shouted Lance, shrugging, as though the city made

it impossible to avoid behaving absolutely appallingly.

The other driver seemed to accept the justice of this, and drifted off into what would no doubt be an endless odyssey of one-way systems in a futile search for another space.

Lance took his time paying at the meter, all the while watching the chicken shop into which the murderer had disappeared. It looked like a perfectly standard chicken shop, with a big window featuring a framed menu and a rotisserie chicken, above which was a red signboard with a logo and, in white, the name of the shop: Ken's Plucky Fried Chicken.

Lance sauntered along the pavement on the opposite side of the road, looking in the windows of the shops, many of which were also selling fried chicken. This made Lance hungry, so he ducked into a little cafe, ordered a cappuccino and kept his eyes on Ken's, hoping to see something that would bust the Fairfax case wide open.

Surprisingly enough, he was not disappointed.

12

'Ken in?' asked the murderer.

The question seemed to surprise the server, who had obviously mentally prepared himself for a conversation about chicken.

'Don't know, boss,' said the server.

'Maybe you could find out,' said the murderer, turning his burly looming up a notch.

The server nodded. 'Asif man,' he said over his shoulder to a chubby youth labouring over the fryers. 'Watch the counter, will you?'

'Fuck off,' said Asif amiably, eyes fixed on his deft swapping of wire baskets in the fryer.

'Asif man, turn around for *one* second,' said the server urgently.

Asif turned around and saw the murderer, who added a slight narrowing of his eyes to the looming.

The server said, 'I'm going to see if Ken's here for this … gentleman. Back in five, bruv.'

'Okay, but you need to be back in two, bruv. There is already more customers coming in.'

The server saw the customers, clacked his tongue and bustled out of a door beside one of the huge fryers.

'Don't worry, Asif,' said the murderer, suddenly turning off his looming. 'You do the cookers and that. I'll just write down what everyone wants, and then your mate can put it all through the till when he gets back.'

'Yeah, sick. Good. Thanks, man, sir, boss.' Asif spun around and returned to his juggling of wire baskets.

The murderer turned to the new customers and said, 'Afternoon, gents. My colleague has just stepped away from the till for a sec, so I'll write down your orders and he'll ring 'em up soon as he gets back. All right?'

They nodded.

'Lovely jubbly,' said the murderer. This surprised him, because he was not, as a rule, the sort of person who says 'lovely jubbly'. In fact, he didn't think he'd ever said it, because it made him sound like he sold fruit on a market stall. Still, it seemed to fit the situation somehow.

By the time the server came back, the murderer had six orders, each written clearly and laboriously on the back of a napkin, with the exact money piled on top.

'Ken will see you upstairs, boss,' said the server, urgently beckoning him from the door by the fryer. The murderer opened a hinged flap in the counter and squeezed himself through, manoeuvring his shoulders and arms through the cramped kitchen.

The door closed behind the murderer, leaving him in a narrow, dark hallway with a flight of stairs at one end, covered in an old carpet. The murderer walked up the stairs, angling his body so as not to get his shoulders wedged between the walls.

At the top waited a man swathed in shadow, the dim light glinting on his moustache.

13

That evening, after many coffees in the surprisingly nice Mediterranean cafe opposite Ken's Plucky Fried Chicken, Lance was lying with Arlene on the chaise longue in the artfully lit flat they shared. Like them, the flat had all its original features, plus many carefully chosen decorative touches.

'So, how was your day?' she asked.

'Pretty good,' he said. 'I started doing some pro-bono work – you know, to put on my new website.'

'Oh, you started that? Good job. Who's the client?'

'Jonathon.'

She gave him a long look, then said, 'Does he know?'

'Not exactly.'

'So he exactly doesn't know,' she said, drawing on her long experience of how Lance's exactlies worked.

'Exactly,' he said.

'This immediately sounds like a bad idea,' she told him.

'But I haven't told you anything about it,' he protested.

'You've told me one word and this whole thing already has "bad idea" pasted over it in letters a mile high. Which I could do, by the way, at two days' notice, in chiffon.'

Arlene worked in a field she described as 'couture logistics' and was proud of her ability to perform feats such as this.

'A mile? How can you see what the letters say if they're that huge?'

'I'm standing a long way away, where it's safe. And by the way, don't try to duck this by getting me so bogged down in my own metaphor that I eventually have to just pull out at any cost, like a tiny argument-based Vietnam War.'

'Good metaphor,' said Lance approvingly, regretting how well she knew his tactics.

'Thanks!' said Arlene, brightly. 'I've been– Wait. No you don't. You're trying to distract me with compliments now. That won't work either.'

He did an exaggerated pout.

'And neither will that,' she said. 'You're gonna have to walk me through this, mister, and no distracting metaphors.'

Lance knew Arlene was serious when she dropped her standard affectionate 'jerk' in favour of 'mister'. The only thing that signalled he was in more trouble was if she called him by his actual name.

'Okay,' he said, taking a fortifying gulp of wine. 'Here's what happened …' He started to waggle his fingers, as though the screen were going wavy.

'And no flashbacks!' she said.

'Okay.' He sighed. He was going to have to tell the truth.

'Right. Well, I went for a drink with Jonathon last night and he told me that he bumped into a girl – really brown hair, sort of pretty – who he was in love with eleven years ago, and who totally destroyed him when she unexpectedly went farmer.'

'Rachel. You told me about her.'

'You remember her name?'

'I'm good with names. You may proceed.'

'She came over for lunch at his house and said her uncle's getting out of prison.'

'What was he in for?'

'He got twenty years altogether for tax evasion and various different kinds of violent crime, which were probably not the worst things he'd done.'

'What were the worst things he'd done?'

'I think he probably murdered a woman called Sarah Morecambe. She was a civil servant.'

'Why?'

'She just needed a job, I think. Maybe enjoyed the prestige. Plus, it has a great pension scheme.'

Arlene gave him a look.

Lance said, 'Why was she murdered, or why do I think it was him?'

'Both, I guess.'

'I think her murder had something to do with her wanting to leak some documents. And I think it was him because Jonathon said he saw him nearby, wearing a balaclava and asking directions to her street.'

'But why would he do that if he was going to murder her? That would be insane.'

'Yes. I don't know. But I feel like if all the indications are that someone did a thing, and the most compelling defence is that it would have been insanely stupid for them to have done it, then they probably did it.'

'You mean, once you have eliminated the impossible, then whatever remains, no matter how insanely stupid, must be the truth?'

'Exactly,' said Lance.

'Okay. So you're following this guy – the insanely stupid murderer?'

'Jonathon prefers to call him the uncle. He says we can't know for sure whether he's a murderer, but he's definitely an uncle.'

'But nonetheless, that's what you're doing – following an uncle?'

'Yes,' conceded Lance.

'Who you believe to be a murderer.'

'Yes.' Again, Lance had to concede this was true.

'Tell me again why you think that's a good idea.'

'Because Jonathon's afraid that another adventure's going to break out before he's recovered from the last one. He's worried that the uncle wants revenge on him. So I'm going to follow this uncle, wait for him to put a foot wrong, get evidence of it, show that to his parole officer and get him sent back to prison to finish his sentence.'

'I'm confused. Did he not finish his sentence? How come he's out of jail?'

'In this country you do half your sentence and then get let out on parole for the other half. So there are conditions he has to stick to, and I bet he doesn't.'

'Conditions like what?'

'I'll find that out in the next phase of my investigation,' said Lance, as though the question had occurred to him long ago.

'And what happens if he was never going to commit another crime, and you get him sent back to prison for some little violation of the rules? Does he have a family?'

'Maybe.'

'Meaning yes.'

'Exactly. But he should have thought of that before he almost certainly killed Sarah Morecambe.'

Arlene sighed. 'And what if he didn't kill her?'

'He still probably threatened to kill Jonathon and did enough bad things to be sent to prison. And, in the end, it'll be much harder for him to traumatise Jonathon from inside a prison cell.'

Arlene looked at Lance. 'I love the little guy,' she said, 'but I think you could probably traumatise him from the moon. And here's the big one: what if the murderer doesn't like being followed and lives up to his name and murders you?'

'We're calling him the uncle now, so he would have to uncle me – which, in my experience, means book tokens roughly every other year.'

Arlene gave him a look. 'How many times do I have to give you this exact look in this conversation?' she said. 'Am I doing it wrong? If it's not coming across, I am using my face to say, "You are ignoring some pretty obvious dangers here. Get real." I don't want you to wind up dead.'

'I think that might be the nicest thing you've ever said to me.'

'I just want it on record that you're risking your life because you have an unrealistically romantic notion of being a private investigator and you don't have any work.'

'That's true,' he conceded. 'But I'm being careful. I'm sitting in cars and public places quite a long way from a man who should have every reason to commit zero crimes. And if he isn't committing zero crimes then the person most at risk is Jonathon.'

Arlene gave him a softer look, and put her hand on his shoulder.

'Anyway,' said Lance, 'He's already up to no good. I followed him to Blackstock Road today.'

'I don't know it,' she said.

'It's not a major tourist destination. Basically every shop on the road looks like a front for something – there's this one painted red with poorly executed pictures of keys on it, and inside they sell only the cheapest things you can imagine, like a single nail for three pence, that kind of thing–'

'Maybe he needed a nail.'

'He didn't go in there. That was just corroborative detail so you'd know what kind of street it is. It also has London's scariest karaoke pub.'

'So he likes to sing.'

'He didn't go in there either. He went into a chicken shop – a cheap knock-off of Kentucky Fried Chicken.'

'He was hungry.'

'He went upstairs. I saw him look out of the window. And he had an expression on his face of … well, an almost unbearable rage tinged with regret – like you might expect to see just before someone murders someone else.'

'How did he look when he came out?'

'That's the weirdest bit: he didn't come out.'

Friday

14

The next morning, Lance waited till Arlene had left for work, then got ready and went out to the car, enjoying the feeling that this was his job. On his way, he stopped off for a takeaway coffee, a local paper and a copy of the *Financial Times*, in which he made little eyeholes. Then he drove once more to the murderer's car park and settled down to a bit of surveillance, the radio babbling quietly about a mayoral election and a missing set of prison keys.

It was a clear, bright day, and Lance looked at the windows near the top, wondering if he would again see the murderer looking out over London, in the general direction of Swiss Cottage. He took another sip of his coffee and the passenger door of his car opened with a pleasingly crisp click. Someone got in and closed the door.

'Hello.'

'Morning, tiger,' said Lance.

'Please don't call me tiger,' said Jonathon, amiably.

'Let me guess, Arlene told Piper and Piper told you.'

'Um, yes.'

'So?'

'So, thanks for watching the, um, uncle for me. There's really no need though.'

'No problemo, honcho. What's wrong with a bit of recreational uncle-watching? You wouldn't deny me that, would you?'

'Of course not. Is it recreational though? I heard you wanted to get the, um, uncle sent back to prison because he went to a chicken shop.'

Lance was about to deny this, but changed his mind. 'I do,' he said. 'I mean, if he's doing anything wrong, which I'm pretty sure he is. And if the chicken shop is a front for not being a chicken shop, which I'm pretty sure it is. It's on Blackstock Road,' he added, as though that settled the matter.

'I am a bit paranoid about him,' said Jonathon. 'But how much crime can he commit in a chicken shop? If it's serious, the police will get him. And if it's not, I don't want him to go back to prison just because of me.'

'Did Arlene tell Piper to tell you about his face?' asked Lance.

'I don't think so. Was it cold?'

'It was … *murdery*. I saw him at the first-floor window, looking out, and his face had an expression of almost unbearable rage tinged with regret, like you might expect a killer to feel. I didn't tell Arlene this, but I expected to hear screams afterwards. I reported it confidentially to a contact of mine in the police. And I bought the *Evening Standard* last night and the *Highbury and Islington Gazette* this morning, in case they had news of a killing.'

'Oh,' Jonathon looked alarmed. 'Did they?'

'Yes, of course. This is London. But none of them were at a chicken shop on Blackstock Road. Not yet anyway.'

'I think,' said Jonathon, 'we might be a bit paranoid about him. Would he really get out of prison and go straight to a chicken shop in the middle of the day and murder someone?'

'I don't know,' said Lance. 'It wasn't the public bit of the chicken shop: it was the first floor. And maybe that's the best time to do a killing: on your second day, when everyone expects you to be on your best behaviour.'

'But didn't you tell Arlene that he didn't come out again afterwards? Why would he kill someone on the first floor of a chicken shop and then just stay there?'

'Because he slipped out somehow, obviously. The fact that he didn't come out again makes the whole thing even more suspicious.'

'Oh god,' said Jonathon, his eyes widening.

Lance thought he might have alarmed Jonathon a bit too much, so he decided to try a different tack.

'Okay,' he said. 'Here's the thing. I'm mainly following him because I'm bored of trying to choose a camera and a font for my website. I've got MTV money saved up and no work has come in yet, so what I'm basically doing is pretending to work until real work arrives. How did you choose the font for your website, by the way?'

'I, um, hand-lettered mine in the style of John Tenniel, and then scanned it.'

'Oh, that must make it easier.'

'Not really. I did over seventy different versions. It took months. Websites are a nightmare.'

'They are. I'm not a details guy, but there's something about fonts. They're just so hard to choose.'

Jonathon nodded a grim nod, like a gnarled old sergeant listening to a new recruit complain about the shelling.

'Oh,' said Lance.

Jonathon looked at him and Lance pointed to the door of the block of flats, from which the murderer had just emerged, rubbing his face tiredly.

'He's probably going to get some milk,' said Lance. 'Shall we?'

'Shall we what?'

'Recreationally follow this uncle while he goes to the shop and buys milk,' explained Lance.

'Oh, right. Um, if you want. You know, I could help you with your website. You probably need–'

But what Lance would probably need was interrupted by a sleek roar as he started his engine and eased the car forward.

15

The murderer had not gone to buy milk. Instead, he had taken two buses, like the day before, and got off outside Finsbury Park. Lance once again executed a daredevil piece of parking-place theft.

'Arsehole!' shouted the other driver, simultaneously enraged and resigned.

'It's genetic!' shouted Lance, giving a helpless shrug.

Lance and Jonathon then hurried along Blackstock Road, hanging back as the murderer went once more into Ken's Plucky Fried Chicken. They exchanged looks, then pretended to browse flats in the window of one of the estate agents. When the murderer failed to emerge from the chicken shop, Lance led Jonathon into the cafe opposite.

Here, Lance executed a daredevil piece of table theft, taking the plum window position from under the nose of a chubby man hampered by a laptop, coffee and cake. Lance smiled pleasantly at the man, who forlornly adjusted his shuffling course.

'We can't take his table,' said Jonathon quietly, his face red.

'Of course we can,' said Lance. 'We're doing God's work.'

'But you said you were just doing a recreational follow so that you wouldn't have to choose a font for your website.'

'I am. God doesn't want me to suffer, especially from fonts.'

'But what about the man with the cake suffering from his table being stolen?'

'It's not his table. And he's got a cake. God's probably punishing him for his presumption in thinking he can have both.'

'Have you actually started to believe in God?' asked Jonathon. 'I mean, since our last ... sequence of horribly traumatic events?'

Lance paused for a second. Had he?

'I think,' he said, 'that God's basically comfortable with a degree of ambiguity about his existence. And I respect that.'

Lance was saved from a follow-up question by the arrival of a preternaturally slim middle-aged Mediterranean lady.

'What can I get you, darlings?' she asked in a possibly-Spanish accent.

'A cappuccino,' said Lance. 'Also, what do you know about that place?' He glanced out of the window, across the street.

'This is where you can place bets on horses and things like that. It–'

'No, I mean the place next to it: Ken's Plucky Fried Chicken.'

'Oh,' she said, as though she'd never seen it before. 'This is just a chicken place. It has been here for years.'

'Right,' said Lance. 'Is–'

'Oh!' said the woman again, as though struck by inspiration. 'I hear recently its chicken is not halal, though it says it is – see on the sign. My chicken is all halal, darling. It comes from the very good halal butcher up the road. You want maybe a chicken sandwich? I have very good focaccia bread.'

'Interesting,' said Lance. 'Any rumours of connections to crime, drugs, that sort of thing?'

'Could be,' she said, shrugging and gesturing around, as though to indicate that the Blackstock Roadiness of the environment made that almost unavoidable. 'But why you ask? You are an actor?'

'An actor?' said Lance. He'd been expecting her to ask if he was police, and hoping she might think he was a private investigator, which he absolutely was – the best in the business. But this actor thing caught him off guard.

'You look like an actor,' she said. 'You are researching for a role?'

This would be an ideal thing to claim to be, but it was difficult now to row back from his obvious surprise at her question.

'Kind of,' he said. 'I work in TV.'

'Oh, this must be a fascinating thing. But I hear it is very hard: long hours, and the drugs and carrying on …'

This was pretty accurate, he felt, so he did a little combined nod and shrug, to which she nodded back confidentially. She glanced over at Ken's, then leaned closer to him and said in a lower voice, 'You would like baklava? I have very good baklava.'

'Yes,' said Lance, as a matter of course.

'And you?' she said to Jonathon. 'You would like baklava also, darling? And what you would like to drink?'

The iron law of baklava is that, if it's been offered, you have to say yes. So Jonathon also had baklava, and a cup of tea.

When the Mediterranean woman had gone, Lance said, 'Well, you heard her: fake halal, and possible connections to crime and drugs.'

'She only said, "Could be."'

'Her whole manner indicated that there's something weird going on there.'

53

'Did it? I thought her whole manner indicated that she wanted us to buy some baklava.'

'You say potato,' said Lance.

'Wait, are you saying that those two things are essentially the same: selling baklava and telling someone about crime, drugs and halal?'

'They aren't incompatible,' said Lance.

'But then you're trampling all over the conventions of when you can say, "You say potato."'

'That's what I do with conventions,' said Lance, taking the baklava from the plate being lowered onto their table and, in defiance of convention, eating it whole, without breaking eye contact with Jonathon.

'Sorry,' said Jonathon to the Mediterranean lady, and also ate his baklava whole, in rebuttal of Lance's baklava-eating.

'So what's next?' Jonathon asked, when they'd both finished.

'If the uncle's not out in forty minutes, we go and ask around. Find out what people are saying about Ken's Plucky Fried Chicken.'

16

As Jonathon and Lance were eating their baklava, Teddy Robinson was bustling and sweating into a plush rented office near London Bridge.

'Most awfully sorry, Bolt,' he said. 'Meeting overran and then I got–'

'Ted, if you're ever late for another meeting with me, I'll knee-cap you and fly straight back to Australia.'

Bolton Lisby, his campaign manager, sat behind his desk, looking at Teddy with serious eyes. He was a fleshy, grey-haired man in an immaculate blue suit and perfectly tied tie.

'Understood,' said Teddy, running his hand through his extravagant copper-coloured hair. 'I promise it won't happen again, Bolton. Hand on heart.'

'It better not, Ted. Remember, while this election is on, I am the most important person in your life. This whole bumbling-toff-Billy-Bunter thing may go down well with voters, but it won't wash with me.'

'Absolutely. Absolutely, Bolton. Message received in the tympanic membrane and faithfully passed to the brain.'

'Good. Take a seat.'

Teddy sat, putting down his bulging briefcase and carrier bags, and smoothing his crumpled light tweed suit.

'God knows how you've got this far, Ted,' said Bolton, staring at him again with his unnervingly serious eyes. 'You've come from nowhere and narrowed Andy Sproat's lead to four points. But you've been stuck there for a month, and it's less than three weeks to polling day.'

'I fully understand the gravity of the situation, Bolt, and let me tell you, I–'

'Ted, it's not your turn to talk. This is the hard truth. You won't close the gap if you carry on the way you're going. You've got no discipline, mate.'

'Look, Bolton, I understand that I'm not the sort of conventional candidate that you're used to working with, but I will do *absolutely* anything to win this.'

'Okay. Well, you need to stop drinking, mate. You need to get to meetings on time. You need to read the briefings your team prepare for you, and stop just winging it. You need to get a haircut, maybe lose the tweed and get some proper suits.'

'But Bolton, that's my brand–'

'And it works, mate. For *some* voters. I heard a guy in a shop say, "I'm voting Teddy, me, 'cause he's a muppet." But you've hit the ceiling on voters who want a bumbling celebrity muppet for their mayor. And now you're finding out what I've been trying to tell you all along: that there are no shortcuts in this business. So you can either carry on trying to find one, or you can get serious.'

'Bolt, I–'

'This meeting's over, Ted. I want you to go away and take the weekend to think seriously about what I've said. Next time I see you I want you to have made your choice.'

17

'What do you think of the chicken?' Lance asked conversationally.

The teenager was perched on the low wall by the entrance to Finsbury Park, wearing a black hoodie. In his hand was a box of Ken's chicken. He glanced warily at Lance and said nothing. In fact, he put more chicken in his mouth – signalling that, as well as not wanting to answer, he was also physically incapable of it.

'Seriously,' said Lance. 'I'm thinking of getting some. Is it okay?'

The teenager gave him another wary look. He didn't seem entirely convinced that Lance was talking to him, or even that he was real. At length, he gave a minute nod, then forced in another bite of chicken.

'Is it halal though?' pursued Lance. 'People say it isn't really halal.'

'What the fuck do you care?' said the teenager, the words forcing themselves out involuntarily through the gigantic bolus of chicken in his mouth.

'I only eat halal,' lied Lance, deciding against explaining.

'It's halal, okay? It's good chicken.' The teenager stared furiously at the ground, trying to chew his way through all the chicken in his mouth. He checked his phone and looked around, as though hoping for someone to come and rescue him.

Lance said, 'Do you–?'

'Man, you say one more word to me, swear down I will call the police on you.'

18

Jonathon was standing unobtrusively beside a tree near the gates to Finsbury Park. He'd promised Lance he would speak to at least one person, but first he needed to give himself a pretty formidable talking to.

Approaching a stranger outside Finsbury Park was not going to go well. He would probably suffer a mild physical assault. But he'd been to school, hadn't he? He was great at being mildly physically assaulted. And maybe he would only be verbally assaulted, which was practically a walk in the–

'Yo, bruv, why's your mate going round asking about that chicken shop?'

Jonathon's pep-talk was interrupted by this question from a skinny man dressed in an immaculate white tracksuit and baseball cap.

'What? Um. He–'

'Is he an actor or something?'

'Oh, no. He … he used to be a TV presenter but now he's a private investigator. Someone we, er, know has started working there and Lance–'

'That the actor's name?'

Jonathon nodded.

'Figures,' said the man in the tracksuit.

'Lance thinks something, er, …'

'Shady? Something shady going down at Ken's?'

'Um, yes.'

'Man, there is *bare* rumours about that place.'

'Really?' Jonathon was appalled. He had been hoping they'd be able to go home and forget all about it, perhaps sort out Lance's font problem.

The man in the white tracksuit looked quickly around and said, 'Russian mafia. Trying to muscle in on London territory, you get me? Ken's is their first base. Bridge. Head. You get me?'

'I think so. You're saying the Ru–'

The man in the white tracksuit tutted. 'You think I'm chatting shit. But this is for real. *Think* about it, man. When you hear that shit, what is your first instinct?'

'Um, I–'

'You think, "No way! That is *bull*shit, man."'

Jonathon nodded.

'And right there, that is *exactly* what they want. If you are the

Russian mafia, what base are you gonna choose? One where people hear it and they are surprised, or one where people hear it and they are not surprised?'

'Um, surprised, I suppose. I mean, that's a good point. But the shop's so small–'

'It's not just the shop, man. It's the whole building over it. And underneath. And they are *big*, those buildings, you get me?'

'I think so. You're saying that the bu–'

'Plus, Kens are *everywhere*, man. All over north London. Must be a hundred of them.'

'Oh god. Really?' The idea was already sounding horribly plausible.

'Yeah, man. *Think* about it. You got people coming and going, all this space over the shop, vans and that delivering chickens and whatever they make the fries out of–'

'Potatoes?' suggested Jonathon.

'Yeah, right,' said the man with a smile, as though he almost envied Jonathon for being so naive.

'Not potatoes?' suggested Jonathon.

The man shrugged. 'Maybe it *is* potatoes, man. Maybe you're right. But I would be *very* surprised.'

'But what do *you* think they're made of?' pursued Jonathon.

'I don't know, man.' He said this with humility, as though hard-won experience had led him to recognise his fundamental ignorance on such matters – and to see that the question itself had so many false assumptions built into it that it could never truly be answered.

Jonathon was about to ask another question, but the man was now fist-bumping two others – one with a bandana and a little beard, the other in long denim shorts.

'Who's this?' asked the man in long denim shorts.

'Don't know his name,' said the man in the white tracksuit. 'But we got–'

'Jonathon,' said Jonathon.

They held out their fists, and Jonathon was proud of himself for remembering to bump rather than shake. He was relieved there were no high-fives for him to miss.

'We got chatting 'cause his mate over there is acting weird.'

They looked over at Lance, who was now nonchalantly drinking coffee beside a worried-looking girl.

'Is he a actor?' asked the man with the long shorts.

'Private investigator,' said the man in the white tracksuit, knowledgeably. 'Looking into Ken's.'

The man with the bandana nodded slightly and narrowed his eyes, as though to signal that he knew all about Ken's and there was *plenty* to look into.

'We gone Dick C's,' he said, indicating himself and the man in the long shorts.

'Dixie's?' asked Jonathon.

'Dick C's Fried Chicken. Round here you either eat Ken's or you eat Dick C's.'

'Why you gone Dick C's, man?' asked the man in the white tracksuit. 'There is something *wrong* about that taste – like there is too many spices.'

'It's halal, man.'

'Ken's is halal,' said the man in the white tracksuit. 'Don't believe that it ain't – that's just a rumour.'

'Oh, wait a minute,' said Jonathon. 'You think it's been taken over by the Russian mafia but it *is* halal?'

'Yeah. You saying the Russian mafia can't get halal chicken?'

'No, I would never say that,' said Jonathon, instinctively worried about hurting the Russian mafia's feelings.

They all looked at Lance, who had joined them.

'Are you a actor?' asked the man with the long shorts.

'I told you,' said the man in the white tracksuit, 'he's a private investigator.'

Lance looked pleased and nodded modestly.

'Are people meant to know that, though?' asked the man in the white tracksuit. 'If you're a good private investigator, don't you stay undercover?'

'It depends,' said Lance, looking at Jonathon.

'Sorry,' said Jonathon. 'It just slipped out.'

'It's because I said you was acting weird,' said the man in the white tracksuit. 'He was *protecting* you, man.'

'Thanks, hotdog,' said Lance.

'Hey, don't call him hotdog,' said the man in the white tracksuit. 'His name's Jonathon.'

'That's all right,' said Jonathon. 'I quite like it, really.'

'You sure?'

Jonathon nodded.

'Okay then,' said the man in the white tracksuit, and gave Lance a hard look that signalled he was not backing down but had just decided to leave it.

'So you two know Vince the journalist then?' said the man with the bandana.

They shook their heads.

'You need to talk to Vince the journalist. He's well into Ken's, Russian mafia, all that shit.'

'Really?' said Lance.

'What, you think I'm lying? You think I made up Vince the journalist?'

'We'll talk to him,' said Jonathon.

'Which paper does he write for?' asked Lance.

'I don't know, do I?' said the man with the bandana. 'He's just a old guy with a pen who comes round this area sometimes asking questions about Ken's. What, you want me to give you his phone number and address? You think I'm your secretary?'

They assured the man with the bandana that Lance didn't think he was his secretary. Then Lance got another hard look from both the man with the bandana and the man in the white tracksuit, with only the man in the long shorts abstaining, and the three of them strolled off.

After that, Jonathon had to go home to try to get some more work, so Lance debriefed him and continued the investigation alone.

19

'Are you Vince?' asked Lance.

He was talking to a distracted yet intense man in a half-untucked shirt and an old jacket, who had just walked out of the *Highbury and Islington Gazette*'s offices on Upper Street.

'Maybe,' said the man, narrowing his eyes.

'If you are,' said Lance, who recognised him from his picture on the website, 'I'd like to talk to you about Ken's Plucky Fried Chicken.'

'You'd better step into my office then.'

Vince didn't lead Lance back into the *Highbury and Islington Gazette*'s offices, but over the road and up a narrow street, to the Compton Arms – an old square yellow pub with baskets of flowers hanging outside.

They entered and were immediately at the bar. It was a small pub, with low ceilings, old beams and ancient wooden furniture. There were grainy black-and-white photos on the walls, showing Islington as it had been when it was full of horses and everyone wore a hat. In short, Jonathon would have loved it.

Vince was looking expectantly at one of the beer pumps, so Lance bought them two pints of Ridley's Rumpus, and followed Vince to a secluded snug in the back.

'First things first,' said Vince. 'I need you to swear you won't breathe a word of this to anyone.'

He looked seriously at Lance.

'Okay,' said Lance. 'I'm listening.'

'What?'

'I'm listening – to whatever you don't want me to breathe a word about.'

'No, I mean about this pub. Be a nightmare if people find out it's here. Best pub in London.'

'I promise I won't tell a soul,' said Lance, who didn't believe in souls, most of the time.

Vince looked at him again and narrowed his eyes: a hardbitten veteran journalist scrutinising a source.

'So,' he said, at length, 'what have you got to tell me?'

'I was expecting to ask you the questions,' said Lance.

'Well, you better adjust your expectations, hadn't you?' said Vince.

'It's just, if I tell you what I know, then you might just pocket that information and go home without telling me anything.'

It was vital that Vince did tell him something. If Vince could confirm any of the rumours about Ken's, that might constitute proof that the murderer was involved in illegal activity. Lance could then pass it to his police contact, left over from his last stint as a private investigator, and get the murderer sent back to prison. The adventure would be over before it had even begun.

That would be a shame, in a way, because Lance was enjoying the follows, the watching from cafes, the baklava, hearing the word on the street and talking to hardbitten journalists in secret pubs. But he would give it all up for the sake of sparing Jonathon further trauma.

Vince was, once more, regarding Lance with shrewdly narrowed eyes.

'Well then,' said Vince, 'this is where we play information poker. We take it in turns: you tell me something, I match it with something of equal value. You make sure what you tell me is valuable enough to keep me playing, but you keep back enough to flush out my high cards.'

'Okay,' said Lance. 'But isn't that more like snap: one card at a time, trying to match what the other person puts down?'

Vince looked at him again. He must have powerful facial muscles, thought Lance, to be able to keep his eyes shrewdly narrowed for so long.

'We are *not* playing information snap,' said Vince.

'Right,' said Lance. 'But for poker, we should put three pieces of information face down, shouldn't we? And then draw from a huge pile of pieces of information.'

'Just play,' said Vince, no doubt seeing that Lance was trying to wear him down with a preliminary metaphor barrage.

'Okay,' said Lance. 'I'll start with the fries: it's naive even to ask what they're made of.'

20

Dinner had been eaten, and they'd gone into the living room.

'Why don't I get some more wine?' said Piper, slipping off to the kitchen and giving Jonathon a significant look.

He was left alone with Rachel.

'Um, thanks for coming,' he said.

'No problem,' she said. 'Thanks for the invite.'

'Should we …' he said, his heart beating faster, 'um, talk about the … the elephant in the room?'

'If you like,' she said. 'Where did you get it?'

She nodded at a neatly carved wooden elephant that Piper had brought back from a holiday in India with her dad.

Jonathon looked at it, then looked at her and shook his head in mock disappointment.

'Sorry,' she said, 'I was totally pretending to take that literally.'

'I know,' he said. 'And it really–'

'Because,' she persisted, 'an elephant in the room can be something big that no one's talking about, or it can totally be just an elephant, inside a room.'

'You don't have to *explain* it to me,' he said.

And they smiled at each other, because giving unnecessary explanations was a thing they used to do eleven years ago. He hadn't expected her to remember it.

'But anyway,' she said.

'I,' he said. 'Um. I'm really sorry about … everything, all that time ago. I–'

'No, it was totally–' she began.

There was a loud knocking on the front door.

Jonathon looked from Rachel to the door, not sure which one he should concentrate on. Rachel flicked her head in the direction of the door.

'Pause,' she said, pressing an imaginary button.

'Sorry,' said Jonathon. 'One minute.'

The dog came with him, as though to protect him, but – as ever – stood shyly behind.

Jonathon opened the door and there stood Lance, his hair in its elegantly wasted mode, which signalled that he'd had a few drinks.

'Hotshot,' he said. 'I've got something I need to talk to you about urgently. Can I come in?'

'Urgently?' said Jonathon as his stomach lurched. 'Um, yes. Come in.'

They climbed the stairs to Jonathon's little office in the attic, and Lance said, 'I've got a smoking gun.'

'Oh, sorry,' said Jonathon. And then, 'Wait, what? What do you mean?'

'You've never heard that phrase before?' said Lance irritatedly, sitting in Jonathon's chair and picking up his pen.

'Only to mean that someone has a … smoking gun. Oh! Or direct evidence of a crime.'

'I'm using that second meaning.'

Jonathon perched awkwardly on the edge of the desk, wishing Lance would put his pen down. It was a present from Piper, and he was afraid Lance was going to break it.

'But what,' said Jonathon, 'are you using that second meaning to mean? Sorry, I've had some wine.'

'I've got direct evidence that the murderer's committed a crime.'

'The uncle,' corrected Jonathon.

'I've had five pints,' said Lance, 'so I'm going to call him the murderer. Because he murdered Sarah Morecambe, god rest her, back in our first adventure.'

'It was never proved,' said Jonathon. 'And it was a sequence of horribly traumatic events, not an adventure.'

'You say potato.'

'I don't though,' said Jonathon. 'I never say potato. And what is this direct evidence that the, um, uncle's committed a crime?'

'It's indirect,' said Lance, 'but highly suggestive.'

'You've got indirect direct evidence?'

'Something like that,' agreed Lance. 'Look, it's late and I'm a little bit drunk, so let's stop saying potato and I'll just tell you what Vince said.'

'Vince the journalist?'

'Uh-huh,' said Lance, nodding.

'That was quick.'

'Hey, if you don't want your information quick, don't come to Lance Ferman, PI.'

'Wow. So when I went off to do my unsuccessful marketing, you tracked down Vince, in an afternoon?'

'Rightarooney,' said Lance. 'How did your unsuccessful marketing go, by the way?'

'I managed to arrange a phone call with someone at HSBC. But then when I called no one answered. I'll try again on Monday.'

'You should just turn up at his office,' said Lance.

'Her office.'

'Potato.'

'Can we use the word "potato" on its own like that?' said Jonathon. 'I feel like–'

'Look, do you want me to tell you what I managed to get out of Vince the journalist in an epic game of information poker? And drinking.'

'Yes.'

'There's a war coming between north London's two biggest fried-chicken empires – excluding actual Kentucky Fried Chicken, obviously.'

'What are they?'

'Ken's and Dick C's. Only Vince says it's not a fair fight because Ken's now has powerful backers.'

'The Russian mafia! That can't really be true, can it?'

Lance looked at him sadly, as though he pitied him for being so naive. 'No. It's the Romanian 'Ndrangheta.'

'But that's even less plausible. And aren't the 'Ndrangheta from Corsica?'

'Sicily. But they've spread all over the Mediterranean. They reached Romania before Ceausescu took over, and managed to cling on while he was in power. And you had to be pretty vicious to survive Ceausescu. Plus, since the collapse of his regime, the 'Ndrangheta there has recruited lots of his ex-secret police and has been expanding really quickly. Now it's big enough to target

London.'

'Is it? I've never heard about that.'

'Well, that really surprises me,' said Lance, the five pints having turned his sarcasm gauge up a few notches, 'because you've been a subscriber to *Romanian Crime Weekly* for years, haven't you?'

'But I watch the news,' said Jonathon, feeling his cheeks go red, 'sometimes, when there isn't anything awful going on. And I read the papers, ditto. I thought I'd have–'

'Stuff like that doesn't really get covered in the mainstream media.'

'Is that what Vince the journalist said?'

'Think about it,' said Lance. 'Are the 'Ndrangheta going to take over a prominent, well-known international corporation, or are they going to start with a small chain of chicken shops no one's ever heard of?'

'But that's what the man in the white tracksuit said about the Russian mafia.'

'And it's true whether we're talking about them or the Romanian 'Ndrangheta.'

'But where's the proof?'

'Well, the fact the murderer has just started going there every day tells you something.'

'He's an uncle–'

'Potato!'

'And how does him going there prove it's been taken over by Romanians?'

'It's suggestive. There's also the fact that one of the senior people at Dick C's has disappeared.'

'Does a chain of north London chicken shops have senior people?'

'The owner's son, then. Look, obviously Vince didn't give me a load of photos and secret documents proving all of this. But he's been looking into Ken's for a while now – ever since he started coming across rumours about it online. He's a professional journalist, and this is the conclusion he's come to. Given that we're worried about the murderer, we'd be stupid to just dismiss all this stuff out of hand.'

'But what can we do? Get jobs at Dick C's Fried Chicken?'

'No one,' said Lance, 'is going to have to get a job in a fried-chicken shop. But what Vince says is that the 'Ndrangheta is smuggling crack in barrels of cooking oil and selling it on from Ken's.'

'We can't walk into a police station and tell them that we went and hung around at Finsbury Park because we'd got paranoid about an uncle, and then a man in a white tracksuit told us about Vince the journalist, who then drunkenly told you that the Romanian 'Ndrangheta is putting crack in barrels of cooking oil at a shop called Ken's Plucky Fried Chicken. It's ridiculous.'

'We don't have to walk into a police station,' said Lance, as though this was the problematic part of what Jonathon had just said. 'I have a contact in the police who I can discreetly mention it to. We've kept in touch since my Lenin & Plover days. If it fits with other information they're getting, they can follow it up. If not, what have we lost?'

Jonathon said nothing. Once again, something that had sounded insane just moments before was now beginning to sound perfectly reasonable.

'It's your choice,' said Lance, even more reasonably.

Oh god, a choice, thought Jonathon. If they did pass this on, it could mean that the woman downstairs – whose heart he had apparently accidentally broken many years ago, and who had indisputably utterly smashed his own heart – would see her uncle go back to prison. But if they didn't, the uncle might go back to murdering people, and the Romanian 'Ndrangheta might take over London.

'What would your police contact do, if you discreetly mentioned it?'

'Nothing big. Probably get a couple of detectives to have a nose around, maybe put someone in undercover for a bit. Just enough to finally get a few answers.'

'And will you,' asked Jonathon, 'stop following the uncle around if I say yes?'

'Mm-hm,' said Lance.

'Okay, well then ... just mention it to your police contact and see what she says.'

'He.'

'Potato,' said Jonathon, because if he was going to accept the rest of what Lance had said, he might as well also accept his new 'potato' thing.

21

Teddy Robinson switched on the sitting-room light, put down his briefcase and said, with no trace of surprise in his voice, 'Hello, Hooray.'

'Evening, Teddy,' said the black-clad man sitting in an armchair by the window. He picked at a fingernail with a vicious-looking commando knife.

'How long were you sitting in the dark,' asked Teddy, taking off his jacket and throwing it on the sofa, 'pretending to clean your nails with that knife and hoping to give me a heart attack?'

'Twenty minutes or so?'

Teddy nodded, and started pulling off his tightly knotted tie. 'Any damage when you broke in?' he asked.

'Teddy!' said Hooray, in mock-outrage but with a genuinely wounded note in his voice. 'I am a consummate professional.'

'One could wish,' said Teddy, 'that you might consummate your professionalism elsewhere.'

'Don't be like that, Tedders. It's my brand: the unexpected visit, the shadowy, menacing figure framed by the curtains.'

Teddy kicked off his shoes and said tiredly, 'Well come down to the kitchen and be a shadowy, menacing figure framed by the fridge.'

Down in the kitchen, Teddy took a bottle of wine from the overflowing fridge, opened it, and sloshed wine into a glass and a mug, passing the mug to Hooray.

'This place is an absolute tip,' said Hooray.

'What do you expect?' said Teddy, putting the wine back in the fridge. 'I'm in the middle of an election campaign and a divorce – I don't have time to look for a cleaner. To be perfectly honest, I haven't the faintest idea how one goes about such a thing.'

'There are ways,' said Hooray darkly, balancing his knife on one finger.

'What in the name of fuck are you talking about, man?' said Teddy, rifling through the shelves and trays. 'You can't murder your way to recruiting a cleaner.'

'What?' said Hooray. 'Sorry, I'm a bit distracted.'

Teddy pulled a pizza box out of the fridge, looked at the contents, grimaced, and put it back.

'I'm ordering a pizza,' he said, pulling out his phone. 'Want one?'

'Of course,' said Hooray. 'What are you having?'

'Salsiccia.'

Hooray wrinkled his nose. 'Do they have goats' cheese?'

'How am I supposed to bloody know? I'm not your concierge.'

'Well, you could ask, Tedders.'

'Hello?' Teddy said into his phone. 'Yes, I'll have two large salsiccia pizzas and two cannoli.'

'Fine,' said Hooray.

Teddy gave his address and ended the call.

'You're annoyed with me, aren't you?' said Hooray.

'Bloody right I'm annoyed with you. I wouldn't have ordered you a pizza at all, except I know you'd just eat mine.'

'It's this blasted journalist,' said Hooray, shaking his head sadly.

'You're lucky I'm too tired to be angry.'

'You've every right to be angry,' said Hooray. 'Seriously, I–'

'You specifically said you wouldn't seriously injure him. *Bruises*, you said. And there's me having asked around for his contact details just a week or so before. My mayoral campaign can survive a divorce, but it can't survive a murder.'

'It won't come to that, Tedders. Honestly.'

There was a pause.

'I'm waiting for you to tell me why not,' said Teddy.

'Well, for one thing, because it's us. We are Fortuna's favourites.'

'I see,' said Teddy. He took a large gulp of his wine, picked up the bottle and stamped back upstairs to the rearmost of his two adjoining sitting rooms, where he flopped onto the sofa, which was strewn with papers and surrounded by pizza boxes. Hooray followed him, sitting forward on the armchair in which he'd staged his dramatic entrance.

'When I asked you for that address, word of honour, I seriously intended just to rough him up a bit – to warn him off looking any deeper into my affairs.'

'But then you thought, "Fuck it, I'm going to stab him to death in his kitchen instead, and get the whole thing plastered all over the papers."'

'Not at all, Teddy. It was a calculation. In order for him to be effectively warned off, he'd have to know – or at least strongly suspect – that it was me giving him the beating. I mean, he's probably sticking his nose into hundreds of chaps' affairs. If he's beaten up by an unknown assailant, how does he decide which chap's affairs to stop digging into? And even if he gets the right answer, if he just has a few bruises there's a risk that he thinks, "Right, I'm going to get that bugger back," and sticks his nose all the deeper into my affairs.'

'Have you ever considered ordering your affairs in such a way that they don't constitute serious crimes?' asked Teddy wearily. 'I mean, if you make an insurance claim for the theft of some diamonds and then start hawking those diamonds around for sale five minutes later, is it any wonder a journalist gets wind of it?'

'Teddy,' said Hooray, with a shocked face. 'I expected better of you. For one thing, I was *extremely* discreet in my inquires about selling those diamonds. And for another, it was in the service of a greater good.'

'Not this idiot Chad scheme still.'

'It is not an idiot scheme. Chad is ripe for the taking. A few good men, a modest quantity of money and a bit of weaponry is all it wants. And then I shall have a country, while …' He caught Teddy's eye and ended the sentence there.

'While I'm still messing about trying to take a mere capital city?'

'That's not what I said, Teddy. In any case, to get back to this journalist, the ringing around he'd already done had got me interviewed by the New York police. I've had to leave the city where I'd made my home, until it all blows over. He took my *home*, Teddy. Does that mean nothing?'

'It's desperately sad, Hoo,' said Teddy, pouring himself some more wine. 'Desperately.'

'But what really swung it, Teds, is this: I imagined this journalist thinking, "How in blazes did this Horatio chap get hold of my address?" And then I imagined him starting to dig around into *that*. And if he suspected it was you, maybe he'd start to make *your* life difficult, even though he hadn't a *shred* of proof. *So* unfair. And this is a critical time for you, Tedders, and honestly I couldn't have lived with myself if he–'

'Found out I'd recently asked four separate people for his address? Oh god, I can't believe I've walked into this gigantic diplodocus trap.' He flung his head back against the sofa, his arm draped despairingly over his eyes. 'All out of loyalty to you, Hoo – entirely misplaced and unreciprocated, I now see.'

'Not at all misplaced and unreciprocated, Ted. Not a bit of it.' Hooray came over and perched on the sofa beside Teddy, on top of a report on rail transport. 'Teddy, I would *die* for you. Seriously. I absolutely love you. Ever since our first Michaelmas half we've had a bond. I take that very seriously. I don't have mystical bonds with every Tom, Dick and Harry. Well, I mean, Harry Cholmondeley, yes. He's like a brother. But you take my point.'

'Oh god,' said Teddy. 'This old shit again – after you've gone and ruined my bloody life.'

'Tedders, seriously, you're taking this far too much to heart. I *seriously* owe you for this. I know I'm in your debt and I'll do whatever it takes to repay it. I'll work night and day.'

'Hoo, I'm running for mayor of London. I need to be surrounding myself with people who have track records in policy and campaigning, not ones with long and illustrious careers in assassination, kidnap, fraud and international paramilitary freebooting.'

'Teddy!' said Hooray, giving him a look full of hurt and wounded pride.

'Oh god,' said Teddy. 'I'm sorry, Hoo. I didn't mean it. I'm just tired and angry, that's all. I had a fearful wigging from my campaign manager this morning, and then this journalist thing. I know you take your debts seriously–'

'I *do*, Teddy.'

'Exactly. And I'm sure we can find something useful for you to do, a man of your talents.'

Part Two

Cheese

The Weekend

22

The murderer was sitting on the bed in Gemma's room, his holdall on the floor next to him. He didn't know why he'd come in here. He should be off, really. But the flat was empty: Lisa had taken Gemma to practice. He didn't even know what she was practising. So, he'd found himself coming in and sitting on the end of the bed, just staring, while nearby the ghost of Jeremy Kyle confronted someone about something or other.

It looked like Gemma had never thrown anything away. The walls were full of pouting, fragile boys, but they were stuck on top of unicorns, princesses and ponies. Lurking at the back of her dressing table, surrounded by sprays and brushes, was a small family of plastic cows. He remembered buying them for her. They'd caught his eye in a corner shop – he'd only popped in for a packet of biscuits – and he'd taken a fancy to them. He didn't know why.

For a while it was the box that Gemma had loved, but then she'd discovered the cows, and took them everywhere. She'd brought them with her to visit him in hospital. He remembered that visit. She'd had a lot to tell him, but not many words to do it with. It got easier to understand when Lisa told him it was basically all episodes of *William's Wish Wellingtons*.

'And he go, and he go, and he go … splosh!' Gemma had said, looking at him with her big, serious eyes.

'He went splosh! No way! That's amazing, Gem. In his wellingtons?'

'Yes. In his … wellingtons. He go splosh in his wellingtons.

He did.'

'And did he make a wish, what with the title and everything? Did he make a wish?'

She'd looked at him with eyes wide. 'Yes. He make a … wish. He did.'

When had she stopped talking to him?

They had got on, when she was little, before he'd gone. She'd been a good mate of his. Much nicer to spend time with than most of his actual mates, who were solid blokes in their way, but also – every single one of them – a total nightmare.

She hadn't visited him for his last three months in prison. And before that she'd been coming less and less often, and saying less while she was there.

'And how you doing, Gem? You all right?' he'd said in that last visit.

'Yeah. Fine.'

'What you do after school these days?'

'Don't know. Hang out? Homework?'

He hadn't known what to say. She'd been looking at the floor. It felt wrong to ask who she was hanging out with, and he knew he'd be out of his depth asking about her homework. He'd just nodded and smiled.

'That's magic, that is, Gem. Great.'

And they'd hardly spoken since he got back. She was in her room all the time. Not even slamming doors and playing loud music. Just being quiet. When he saw her he didn't know what to say.

'Morning, Gem. Uh …'

'Oh. Hi.'

It was like they were ignoring each other. And he didn't know how to stop it.

Suddenly, he was on his feet. *Got to get off. Can't sit in your daughter's bedroom all day.* He needed to work off his anger. He was out, slamming the door. Down the stairs today. Too worked up for the lift.

On the bus, the only other passengers were an elderly Sikh man and a sick-looking child, but the murderer couldn't help scanning them for signs of a fight kicking off – a prison habit. At least it kept him sharp: he had a job to do.

Off the bus, down the street, into Ken's, where the clink of the bell reminded him of what had happened that Thursday, two days ago …

The murderer reached the top of the stairs, where Ken was waiting, a fresh white shirt stretched over his paunch, moustache neatly combed.

'Welcome, welcome,' said Ken.

'All right, Ken,' the murderer replied.

'Oh, it is you,' said Ken, smiling as the murderer came into the light at the top of the stairs. 'I am preparing myself for a troubling encounter, but now I see it is you.' Ken shook the murderer's hand in both of his own and added, 'You are most welcome. Please come into my office.'

The murderer followed Ken into a room at the front of the building. As Ken took a seat behind a desk, the murderer strolled over to the window and glanced down into Blackstock Road, suddenly feeling an almost unbearable rage tinged with regret at what he was about to do.

Then he turned, just in time to see two faces appear at the top of the stairs, through the open doorway. Ken had followed his gaze.

'Go away, Wilson! Go away, Anaya!' shouted Ken, storming out onto the landing. 'Can you not see I am talking to this gentleman?'

The faces disappeared, though not without some giggling, and Ken returned, carefully closing the door behind him.

'I have more of these rug rats, you see, even though the ones I had before are so vexing to me.'

Ken sat down behind a cheap-looking desk, and gestured for the murderer to take a seat.

'Vexing, yeah,' said the murderer, heart beating as he sank into an incongruous armchair on the other side of the desk. 'That's what kids are. How old?'

'Wilson is six and Anaya is seven. But I have already a daughter who is fourteen and a son who is seventeen. You see, I have these years where I was very sensible and had just two children, but then

I became completely crazy and had two more. Curse my loins. You have had more children? I remember at one time you come often to this shop with a very beautiful little girl with blonde hair and red cheeks like roses, who often carries a small cow.'

'Blimey, you got some memory.'

'Forgive me, you are a memorable man–'

The murderer gave a modest wave of his hand.

'... especially with your daughter. And we chat sometimes, as I was then always working in the shop.'

'I've still just got the one, Ken. My Gemma.'

'But forgive me,' said Ken, 'I have forgotten your name.'

'Colin. Colin Slater.'

'Welcome, welcome. And how can I help you, Colin?'

'Well, since you got a good memory, do you remember something you did, round about that time?'

Ken's eyes widened. 'I ... I hope it was nothing at all regrettable or unpleasant.'

'Well, it was a bit unpleasant for the bloke on the receiving end. You punched a fella.'

Ken was aghast. 'Me?'

'Yes. I mean, he was robbing your shop, so it wasn't totally out of order.'

'Oh this. Of course I remember this. I am being robbed. I hit him because he tries to take money from my till. But I already see you come in, and perhaps I would not have dared hit him otherwise.'

'Looked to me like you knew what you was doing. Good square punch it was.'

'This punch would not have been helpful at all if you had not put your daughter carefully back in your car and knocked out these two ruffians. I say, free chicken to you for life. This is still available.'

'Do you remember what else you said?'

Ken looked blankly at him, then smiled to cover it. 'Here my memory has let me down.'

'You said if I ever needed a job, I only needed to ask.'

'Oh. Oh, I was babbling. Of course a man like you does not work in a chicken shop.'

'All right,' said the murderer, standing slowly. 'Thanks for your

time, Ken.'

Ken stood too. *'But please, do not misunderstand me. Of course you may have a job. But it is beneath you. Please, sit.'*

The murderer sat again and Ken followed suit.

'There's not much beneath me right now,' said the murderer.

'Indeed?'

'I've been … away, if you know what I mean. Eleven years. Just got back.'

'I see. I see.'

'That change things?'

'Oh no. You may still have a job, if you would like it. I employ many people who have been away for a time.'

'I would like it. They want me to sign on, for benefits: Jobseekers' Allowance and that. I said to them, I'm what you'd call a small state man, like old Mrs Thatcher. I need to work, get back to supporting my family that way. I know you probably haven't got many hours and it probably don't pay millions, but there's not much around when you've … been away. I just want to get started somewhere, so I don't sit around all day in my pants.'

'I understand, I understand. Now, it is true, I don't have manager positions available, only kitchen and till. But I have lots of shifts, because it is very difficult to find reliable people and I have now twenty shops—'

'You got what?'

'Twenty shops,' said Ken, sitting back and smiling proudly. 'For years I have only this one. But after I buy the second one, the others come very fast. Now I have twenty shops all over north London. You know my secret?'

'What?'

Ken leaned forward and said conspiratorially, 'I am inspired by Kentucky Fried Chicken.'

'No!' said the murderer.

'But,' said Ken, smiling, 'I do everything one better. They have secret blend of eleven herbs and spices? Okay. I have secret blend of twelve herbs and spices. And I am halal. Though there are those who lie and say I am not, just because I personally am a Christian.'

'Twelve. Amazing.'

'So, yes. I have many shifts. But wages for these jobs are not high – only seven pounds seventy per hour.'

'You what?'

Ken held up his hands. 'Of course, this is just at the beginning, and when you are trained maybe there is some management vacancy – but by then you have found something better than chicken.'

'Ken, you got me all wrong,' said the murderer, his rage and regret at asking for a job in a chicken shop already subsiding. 'I've spent eleven years working for a pound an hour, maximum. Seven pound seventy's a bloody fortune.'

Ken looked shyly pleased. 'So, when you would like to start?'

'Sooner the better.'

'Excuse me. Let me look.' Ken pulled a keyboard over to him and said proudly, 'We have this now all on computer.'

He tapped irritably at the keyboard, chewing his moustache and craning forward as though he read by touching the screen with his eyeballs.

'Ah!' he said. 'Ah, ah, ah. One second.' He picked up a phone, pressed a couple of buttons and then talked for a while in a foreign language, sounding angry but also laughing several times.

'So,' said Ken, once he'd put the phone down, 'how about now? We have a four-hour shift which starts at half past. I have moved Teo over to a different shop, so you could start here. Asif will teach you.'

'Sounds magic,' said the murderer.

He'd picked it all up quickly. Now he had the rhythm, he could work out some of his anger and frustration on the fryers, weaving a furious dance of fillets, wings and drumsticks, punctuated by the occasional violent cha-cha-cha as he re-stocked the bun toaster. He always kept up with the orders, no matter how fast they came in. And Asif was there on the till, building the flimsy boxes and filling them, flipping fries into their little paper bags with the scoop.

'Add mix!' called Asif, then added 'boss' and 'please', as he remembered who he was working with.

'Gotcha!' called the murderer, pouring some more milkshake

mixture into the machine, then added 'cheers' and 'Asif', as he remembered he wasn't in prison.

Despite the mid-morning rush, the murderer soon built up enough of a buffer to take the black sack from the bin and lump it downstairs to the rubbish area. He brought up another couple of boxes of fries and left them on one of the benches in the scruffy back room while he went for a slash. Just as he'd started, he heard the shop door go *cling!* And then it went again, and again. Just his luck.

Why does everyone always come at once? he thought. *Bloody chicken telepathy around here.*

But there was something wrong. Some of the new customers were running heavily upstairs. He could hear muffled voices, and then a clear shout.

'Police!'

The murderer's urine turned to hot ice in his bladder. He stopped mid-stream. In one move he was out of the toilet, through the back room and out of the back door, into the yard behind.

He emerged into a pool of shadow cast by the steep flight of outdoor steps that led up to the first floor, where Ken and his family lived. Above him he heard a deep thud. He looked up to see boots disappearing through the doorway.

The murderer pulled off his apron, discarded his hat and made for the back gate, stopping just in time as he saw the blue flash of police lights in the access road behind.

Someone was saying, 'Foxtrot one-two, Foxtrot one-two, this is Papa Mike, over,' followed by a little crunch of static.

His heart was beating hard in his chest. He turned around. A man emerged from the doorway, machine-gun held at eye level.

'Armed police!' shouted the man. 'Place both your hands upon your head, now!'

———

23

'Oh, it's you,' said an impatient Cockney voice.

'Yes, it's me,' said Lance, edging down the volume on his phone. 'What are you sounding annoyed with me about?'

'We raided three branches of Ken's yesterday.'

'Right,' said Lance, 'but this is what I'm annoyed with you about.'

'Listen, sunshine,' said the impatient Cockney voice, 'you don't get to be annoyed with me. You're some dick just playing at being a detective, and I'm an actual bloody detective inspector.'

'I'm a serious private investigator,' said Lance, 'who passed on some concerning information to you in confidence. And you responded by immediately breaking a load of doors down.'

'Your information was a load of dick,' said the impatient Cockney voice. 'Do you know how much a bloody raid costs? Overtime, van rental, paperwork – you're looking at ten grand a pop. We–'

'Oh, that's actually less than I thought,' said Lance.

'Never mind what you bloody thought. What do we find? Dick all. No weapons, no crack in barrels of cooking oil, no underground dungeons or squads of Romanians, not even any fries not made of potato – just one prisoner on licence working in the kitchen, as notified to his parole officer.'

'Working in the kitchen?' said Lance.

His voice didn't tremble and he wasn't suddenly overwhelmed by the enormity of his misjudgement, but he recognised that this was the sort of occasion when a normal person might react that way.

'We go in there swinging our dicks around,' said the impatient Cockney voice, 'and come out with egg on our bloody faces.'

'Gross,' said Lance. 'But why did you order a raid? I thought you'd do a bit of digging, maybe put someone undercover in the kitchen …'

'Undercover in a Blackstock Road chicken shop? Any of our

lads would stick out a mile. Plus there's the paperwork and the cost – not to mention the bloody health and safety implications of working with hot fat etcetera. Believe you me, a raid was the only practical option. Plus, I've found the longer you wait before doing something like that, the more likely it is that the targets will get wind of it.'

'You mean your officers warn the criminals?'

'I'm not saying anything of the kind. I just have a healthy paranoia, that's all. Plus, rumours have been flying around for weeks about Ken's, so when you tell me that a former hitman – even if the bloody CPS couldn't make it stick – has started going there, well, it was now or never. There's no smoke without a fire.'

'Unless,' said Lance, 'you leave a chicken on an electric rotisserie grill too long.'

'What?'

'You know in London chicken shops like Ken's they always have a chicken in the window slowly rotating on a rotisserie machine with glowing electric cooking panels behind it – like a kebab machine.'

'I know what the front of a bloody chicken shop looks like. I just don't know why you're telling me about it.'

'Well the chicken gets crispy and starts smoking. So that's smoke without fire. I was just thinking, maybe in London chicken shops there is sm–'

'Give me strength. You know what, I am seriously not in the mood for you today, Lance. So I'll just say goodbye and fuck off.'

And with that, the call was over.

Lance immediately rang Vince, who answered by asking suspiciously, 'How did you get this number?'

'I called the *Highbury and Islington Gazette* and asked for it.'

'Right,' said Vince, again suspiciously, as though he knew there was more to it than that, but recognised there was no point pursuing it.

'Have you heard the police raided three branches of Ken's last night?'

'Course I have. I was there, covering it for the *High and I*.'

'How did you know about it?'

'Let's just say I have my sources. How do you know about it?'

'I read about it in the *High and I*.'

'Right,' said Vince again, with that same tone of having been told a lie, but it being pointless to probe it.

'Have you talked to the police about what they found?'

'Maybe. What did they find?'

'Nothing,' said Lance. 'Do you think whoever tipped you off about the raid also tipped Ken off? I mean, if there even is a Ken.'

'Oh, there's a Ken all right,' said Vince.

'Oh. What's he like?'

'Let's just say, "troubling" and leave it at that.'

'So, did someone tip troubling Ken off?'

'Listen, Lance, this thing is bigger than you could possibly imagine. I was tipped off in the normal way for police public-relations reasons. Ken, and the people behind him, are way ahead of that. They probably have cops on their payroll who they've groomed from childhood to go into the force.'

'Seriously?'

'Very seriously,' said Vince. 'Very seriously indeed.'

'But what makes you think that?' asked Lance. 'And why don't you go public with it?'

'Ever heard of Seddit?' asked Vince.

'The internet forum?'

'That's one way of describing it.'

'Yes, I ended up there the other day when I was researching cameras.'

'Well have a look on the UK chicken Seddit – there's an anonymous source inside Ken's posting there. I'm trying to make direct contact, but the source won't respond. Why don't I go public? Maybe because I don't want to end up in Ken's chicken.'

'What, they're putting people in–?'

'Never mind what they're doing or not doing. Just look on Seddit. I'm trying to sneak the truth out in my articles – there's a code built in to them, which is why it's taking me ages to do even relatively short features on the new swimming baths. The truth's too wild for my editors, but the truth wants to get out.'

'Why don't you just tell it to me?' suggested Lance. 'I mean, you know, without having to play information poker.'

'You'd like that, wouldn't you?'

'Yes.'

'Because, Lance, I don't know if you're one of *them*.'

24

That Sunday morning, Gemma finally found her voice. The murderer would have been pleased about this, except that she used it for some tearful shouting.

'So you've been working there five minutes,' she said, 'and it gets raided by the police. Are you telling me that's a coincidence?'

'I don't know, love, do I?' said the murderer. 'I don't know why the police do what they do. But I haven't done anything wrong. It's like there's a conspiracy against me or something.'

'What, like a conspiracy of people trying to stop you breaking the law? *Uh*, yes. Yes, there is. It's called *the justice system*.'

The murderer smiled. 'The justice system,' he repeated. 'You are clever, love.'

'Aaaaarrrrrggghhh!' said Gemma, producing a remarkably pure version of the sound of intense frustration felt by all teenagers throughout history at their parents' total inability to stop being their parents, even for a second.

'It's that sociology,' said Lisa. 'She wants to do a degree in it.'

'A sociology degree,' said the murderer. 'That's magic. It really is. But we need the money for it, and that's why–'

'Oh, better go and kill some people then, hadn't you!' shouted Gemma, bursting into tears and running out of the front door.

Rachel emerged carrying Gemma's rucksack. 'I'll go and …' she said gently.

'Yeah,' said the murderer. 'Thanks, Rach. If you could have her, just for tonight, till she calms down.'

'I want to go and talk to her,' said Lisa, with tears in her eyes. 'I don't know where all this has come from. She's always been such a good girl. All that time we been visiting you, she never said a word about … you know, what she just said.'

The murderer put a hand on her shoulder. 'Leave it, love. She just needs to cool down a bit. When she's ready, I'll be waiting for her. She can take as long as she likes.'

Rachel looked at them both and did that mouth-only smile that people do when there's nothing to be said and they know it. She turned and went after Gemma.

The murderer hugged Lisa and said, 'Better get off to Ken's. Get it over with. They won't want to keep me on now.'

'All right, love,' said Lisa, wiping her eyes. 'My shift starts in an hour, but I'll be back by six.'

'Okay. See you later.'

And then he left and walked down the many flights of stairs, so that Gemma and Rachel, who'd taken the lift, would be gone by the time he emerged. His heart was beating hard, responding to all this emotion like it was a really challenging set of deadlifts. God knows what it would do when he got to Ken's.

25

'Yo,' said Lance, pressing the answer button. 'J-Phone. Speak.'

'Um,' replied Jonathon, 'hello?'

'Hi. We've already covered this bit. Speak.'

'I was speaking. I was saying hello.'

'Right. So, what's on your mind?'

'I was just wondering if you … if you're around. This afternoon. There's a thing on at the Museum of London about detectives.'

'When you say *thing*, you mean …'

'An exhibition.'

'I see. Walking slowly around, looking at old things, reading tiny cards that tell you how old the old things are …'

'It's not really your sort of thing. I just thought the detective angle – if it is an angle – might make you …'

'… want to walk slowly around looking at dimly-lit old things in glass boxes? I'd love to – *love* to – but I've got stuff to catch up on, for setting up the agency, you know?'

'Oh, okay. Sorry, I–'

'Can't you take Piper?'

'She said that she hates detective stuff more than pestilence, injustice and cross-country running combined, and that she'd rather go to an exhibition about poo and have her legs pulled off.'

'Wow. That's what I should have said.'

'Plus, she's now busy with a …'

'With a what?'

'Um, an emotional crisis, I suppose.'

'Why are you going to detective exhibitions if she's having an emotional crisis?'

'It's not her emotional crisis.'

'Oh. Whose …?'

'Rachel's. A family thing. It seemed rude to ask.'

'Okay.'

There was a short pause, then Jonathon said, 'I think this is the point at which an American would say, "So that's happening." It would be quite handy to be able to say that.'

'You actually can, you know. I don't think they enforce the intellectual property rights on those things.'

'No, but you need their intonation, really. If that's the right word.'

'True,' said Lance. 'Listen, let's have a beer in the week.'

'Yes, that'd be good. Is–?'

'Oh, sorry, I've got to go. Call coming in from my accountant.'

Lance ended the call, adjusted his car seat to a more upright position and put his coffee in its holder. The murderer was standing in the block's main entrance, looking around – presumably to check that Rachel and the crying teenager had left. Having reassured himself on this point, the murderer set off with lowered head and heavy step across the car park.

Lance started the engine and eased the car forward at walking pace. If the murderer was going to persist in apparently not committing crimes, then Lance was going to persist in following him until he did.

26

Asif, manning the till, gave the murderer a sympathetic look and said, 'Ken's waiting upstairs, boss.'

'Cheers, Asif.'

The murderer made his way through the kitchen and up the stairs. At the top, waiting as he had been three days before, was Ken. This time his face was tense and serious.

'Please come this way,' he said, formally.

The murderer followed him into his office, where Ken carefully shut the door, sat down at his desk, and laid his hands neatly on its surface. He was very still, his face composed. He didn't say anything. Then his shoulders shook, his cheek twitched, a tear rolled down, and he covered his face, his body shaking hard. He was crying.

'They want to take from me everything I have built,' said Ken from behind his hands. 'All my beautiful chicken shops.'

Ken breathed out, wiped his face with his hands, and pulled out a chequered handkerchief. The murderer noticed that the computer was missing from his desk.

'I am deeply sorry that you see me like this,' he said, from behind his handkerchief. 'I apologise.'

'Don't you worry about that,' said the murderer. 'I saw it every day in … prison. Great big fellers, hard as nails – everyone does it.'

Ken nodded his thanks, took off his glasses and wiped around his eyes with his handkerchief.

'Who wants to take your shops then?' asked the murderer.

'Dick C's Fried Chicken,' said Ken, between his teeth. 'Why can they not compete in a proper manner? First they add a thirteenth herb or spice to their recipe, and now they have spread all these rumours about my shops, which have led to this raid, and now this article in the *Highbury and Islington Gazette*.'

Ken picked up the paper.

'An article? What's it say?' asked the murderer.

'It just says there is a raid and repeats all the rumours. But it does not say that these ridiculous rumours are totally wrong, or that the raid found nothing because there is nothing to find.'

'Give it here,' said the murderer, and Ken passed the paper over.

'Listen, Ken,' said the murderer, after reading the article. 'It's probably me. The cops probably raided just because I'm working here. They thought something must be off in a place that'd employ a big old ex-con like me – bound to be into all kinds of dodgy stuff.'

'Oh no. Everyone loves you, and these rumours started weeks ago – long before you work here. My weekly turnover has fallen nearly twenty percent in this time.'

'But what are these "persistent rumours"? It says "questions around the halal status of the chicken" and "ties to organised crime". There any others? Where do they come from?'

'There are many of them and they are totally false. I will tell you.' Ken turned his tear-stained face to the murderer. 'But really, what I have to ask you is, will you help me?'

The murderer sighed. For the first time, he missed prison, where – despite the frequent shankings over drug debts – the emotional drama was a bit less intense.

'Course I'll help you, Ken. What you want me to do?'

Ken wiped his face. 'I am most embarrassed that I put this demand on you. But this situation is very like this one many years ago when I am being robbed. In truth, I do not know exactly how I would like you to help me. But please come upstairs and hear what my daughter has discovered.'

'Your *daughter?* What, the seven-year-old?'

'No, not Anaya but Ranira, who is fourteen.'

'Okay,' said the murderer, thinking that fourteen-year-old girls are also not famous for defeating rival chicken-shop empires. Still, work with what you've got.

They went upstairs together. On the next storey up was a remarkably neat living room and the young children's bedroom, which looked like a Lego bomb had hit a My Little Pony convention. The storey above that contained the bedroom Ken and his wife shared, all crucifixes and floral patterns, as well as a small bathroom and a closed door with a missing handle.

Ken knocked on the closed door.

'Hello?' said a voice from inside, clear and confident.

'Hello, Ranira. It is me.'

'Come in.'

Ken pushed open the door and they walked into a room divided in two by an invisible wall that ran through its exact centre. One side was painted a deep red, almost black, and was festooned with posters of Lamborghinis and supermodels, the bed piled high with business-studies textbooks. The other side had clean white walls and one of those elevated beds with a desk underneath, at which sat a very small girl in a swivel chair, her legs tucked under her as though they were made of rubber. She was staring at the screen of a computer, which the police had, surprisingly, not taken.

'Ranira, this is Colin,' said Ken.

She waved a hand and said, 'Hi, Colin!' without looking around.

'All right, Ranira,' said the murderer.

'Ranira, please tell this gentleman what you told me.'

'One sec,' she said, sitting forward and clicking her mouse a few times. Then she swivelled her chair round, looked directly at the murderer and said, in a dramatic voice, 'I found an online *conspiracy* to *destroy* Dad's company.'

'Oh, right,' said the murderer, frowning. 'So, what … I mean, what is it?'

'Well, Dad said about all these rumours, so I just Googled his company, and I found some posts online, in a forum.' She looked at his face and added, 'A forum is a bit like an online *room* where people can go to discuss a given topic. And posts are like *messages* that everyone in the forum can see.'

The murderer bridled a bit at her tone, but had to admit that if she hadn't patronisingly spelled it all out for him, he would have had absolutely no idea what she was talking about.

'And tell him what these "posts" say,' said Ken, looking slightly proud of himself for using the word.

'Well,' she said, leaning forward in a gossipy way, her eyes wide, 'there are now *multiple* users posting on these topics, and they interject with multiple rumours, so I've printed a list …' She reached over, in her rubber-boned way, to a sheet at the corner of her desk, and passed it out to the class. '*But*, I then went back and located the first posts. They're from five months ago and originate with a user called ChickAn, who claims he works for you but definitely doesn't–'

'How do you know he does not?' asked Ken.

'He says you change the oil in the fryers every day.'

'Oh,' said Ken, 'then you are right, yes. He certainly does not work here. But this is a good thing he is saying.'

'The rest of what he's saying isn't so good – like you're smuggling heroin in fake potatoes.'

Ken gasped and put his hand to his mouth, like a prim Victorian lady.

'So then I replied to one of his posts,' said Ranira, 'with a link saying I had proof that your chicken isn't halal–'

'But it is!' wailed Ken.

'But he wouldn't have clicked on the link if I'd said that. I just sent him to an empty page I set up, which logs every visitor's Internet Protocol address. And then I used a few standard techniques to trace that address to a company.'

Ranira looked at Ken and the murderer. 'Are you wondering about those techniques?' she asked.

'No,' said Ken, 'I am not wondering this.'

'To be honest,' said the murderer, 'You lost me ages ago. This is all still something to do with the internet, yeah?'

'Yes,' said Ranira. 'I used the internet. And I found someone started spreading rumours about Dad's company five months ago. And then I found out where that person's computer is.'

'And?' said Ken.

'It's in the office of a company called Flock, based in Southwark.'

'Oh yeah?' said the murderer, feeling he was more on home ground here. 'Flock as in sheep? Meat-packing place, probably. I'll swing by, take a look.'

27

That Sunday evening found Lance standing in a dimly-lit alleyway beside St Christopher's Inn, smoking a cigarette and watching the murderer behave suspiciously.

After seeing the murderer leave his flat that afternoon, he'd followed him to Ken's and executed another daredevil feat of parking theft.

'What the fuck do you think you're playing at?' the other driver had shouted. 'You nearly drove into me, you wanker!'

'I'm completely unreasonable!' Lance had called back. 'And I have absolutely no consideration for other people!'

Then he'd waited in the cafe, eating baklava, before following the murderer on a bus journey to Borough High Street, south of the river. Lance was so curious about this departure from the murderer's routine that he'd left his car on a red line, knowing he would definitely get a ticket.

Lance had then followed the murderer up the road and nipped into a covered alleyway full of smokers from the pub. He'd accepted a drunken offer of a cigarette, even though he didn't smoke any more, and watched as the murderer stared in sad fury at a metal sign attached to the wall of an office building.

28

As the murderer had got closer to the address on Borough High Street, it had gradually dawned on him that Flock wasn't going to be a meat-packing place, as he'd imagined. He'd pictured himself hanging about in the shadows as men in blood-spattered aprons loaded freshly butchered beef onto refrigerated lorries, one of the men stopping for a smoke, and the murderer sauntering over.

'All right, mate,' the murderer had imagined saying, using his new chicken-shop affability. 'Know what's going on with this Flock company?'

'Ah, it's a right carry-on,' said the imaginary man in the apron. 'You knew where you were in the old days, but this lot are trying to put honest chicken shops out of business by messing about on the internet and that.'

'What if I said you could help me shut these jokers down and get things back the way they was?'

The imaginary man threw away his cigarette, looked the murderer in the eye and said, 'I'm in.'

But now that wasn't going to happen, because Flock wasn't a meat-packing place under the railway arches, but an office in an old four-storey brick building with a metal sign fastened next to the intercom.

The murderer stared at this sign for a while, but the words written underneath Flock's name were such a load of old bollocks that he couldn't work out what kind of company it was. How did anyone know what anything *was* these days? Probably Ranira knew more about Flock from looking at her computer than he did from looking at the place itself. He suddenly felt old and useless.

Well, he would walk around the block, see what there was to see, and then go home. He walked up Borough High Street, which was pretty quiet at this time on a Sunday. This was a funny area. Not so long ago it had been full of factories and warehouses, and a bit rough. Now it was all offices and sandwich shops, quiet pubs and suburban restaurants – as though someone had moved an Essex high street into the middle of London.

He turned right into Union Street, which was much quieter and narrower – mostly companies that were shut up for the weekend, plus a mysterious walled place called Crossbones Graveyard. Then he turned right again, into Redcross Way, which was a proper backstreet – dark, single lane, with an old wall at about head height. After a few yards this went under a railway arch, which was exactly the sort of place he'd pictured when Ranira had said where Flock was. At the end, he went right again, onto Southwark Street, a big road with four lanes. From there another right took him back onto Borough High Street.

It felt magic, in its way, just being out in the streets, in the cool air. He couldn't afford a drink at the St Christopher's Inn, but no one could stop him walking around. The murderer found himself doing a second circuit, down Union Street again, and then along the dark backstreet by the brick wall. He stood there for a bit. Over the top of the wall he could see the back of Flock's building, marked out by being a storey lower than the one next door.

He looked over the wall. Crossbones Graveyard turned out to be a big expanse of cracked concrete, with some graves, trees and plants scattered about. The murderer glanced around, then climbed over.

On this side of the wall the graveyard seemed bigger. He stuck to the shadows of trees and the bigger memorials, making his way across the concrete to the other side. When he reached the opposite wall he stood in the shadow of a lean-to, low and sturdy, with a flat roof. There was a bin next to it. They were making this too easy. He climbed onto the bin, then up to the roof of the lean-to. From here, he could easily get onto the next building, which also had a flat roof, and from there it wasn't too far to the back of Flock's offices.

'Did you find anything out, then?' Ranira would say, when he reported back.

'Yeah, I popped in,' he would say, nonchalantly. 'Had a look around.'

'You what?' she would say. 'You just popped in to a locked four-storey building. How did you manage that then?'

'Climbed up over the roofs,' he would say.

'You never!' she would say, her mouth hanging open.

'Then I just smashed a window.'

'Smashed a window? Didn't that set off the alarm?'

'It did, as it happens. What you do is smash the window, set the alarm going, and time how long it takes someone to get there and turn it off. Then that's how long you wait before you go back in. Didn't have long in there, but I found this.'

And then he would casually produce something from his jacket pocket and lay it on the desk.

'Magic,' Ranira would say. 'I'll just stick that in my computer and use the internet to put these jokers out of business. Nice one, Col.'

Only the murderer didn't know what that object would be. Things probably didn't work that way anyway. And why was he so bothered about impressing Ranira, a fourteen-year-old girl?

Gemma. It was because they were the same age, more or less. And he'd missed his chance to impress her, his own daughter. She was gone.

That was probably why he was standing on a roof in a graveyard at night, his heart beating too fast, thinking about climbing over buildings to break into an office, risking everything.

Best go home, he thought.

He wasn't coping well with being out of prison. Not well at all.

Monday

29

'Hotdog!'

'Oh, um, hi, Lance.'

'Can you come over?'

'I'd like to, but that HSBC work has fallen through, so I really need to do lots of work to get work.'

'Ah, shame. But if I turned up on your doorstep saying I urgently needed to talk to you about something, would you let me in?'

'What? Of course.'

'And if we then needed to go to my flat so I could show you something, would you come?'

'Yes.'

'Okay, well imagine all that's happened, and we'll just do the bit from when you arrive at my flat.'

And so Jonathon cycled over to Lance's flat, which was on the upper floors of a beautiful Georgian house on the other side of the heath, where Arlene answered the door and told him Lance was still in the bath. Shortly afterwards, Lance, wearing a kimono, joined Jonathon in his office, while Arlene dried her hair in the next room.

'So,' said Lance, brushing a speck of dust from his kimono, 'I followed our friend the murderer yesterday–'

'What? But you promised not to. You said if we told the police what we'd heard about Ken's Plucky Fried Chicken then you would leave it in their hands and stop following the uncle.'

'Actually, you asked if I promised that and I said, "mm-hm".

The "mm-hm" has no force in law.'

The hairdryer stopped.

'Hey, Jerk!' called Arlene from the next room.

'What's up?' Lance called back.

Arlene appeared in the doorway, also wearing a kimono, her hair half done and holding a brush.

'Are you giving Jonathon that whole "the mm-hm has no force in law" bullshit?'

'Mm-hm,' said Lance, leaning back in his chair.

'I'm sorry about this guy,' Arlene said to Jonathon. And then to Lance she said, 'Nothing you say has any force in law or in anything else. It doesn't even have any force in the limitless vacuum of space, because it is all bullshit.'

'That's a point of view,' conceded Lance.

'It's a stone-cold fact,' said Arlene. 'Practically a law of nature. You should pass out blank sheets of paper instead of talking, so people can just write in any old shit, because you don't take any notice of what you say anyway.'

'Hey,' said Lance, 'I kept all those promises I made to God that time I thought I was going to die, didn't I?'

'Did you?' said Arlene.

'Yes. I shaved my head–'

'And let it grow back.'

'I never promised to keep it shaved.'

'It's a shame. I think I kind of preferred it shaved. Actually, I like it both ways. These white darts are cute.'

'You think so?' said Lance, clearly delighted. 'I thought–'

'Are,' asked Jonathon hesitantly, 'we getting sidetracked? There's–'

'Yes,' said Arlene. 'We are. What else did you promise God?'

This was not really what Jonathon had thought they were getting sidetracked from, but he was terrified of Arlene, and so he let it go.

'I gave up my job at MTV,' said Lance, 'and left New York, just like I said I would.'

'After *two years*,' said Arlene, 'because I got offered a great job in London and you didn't want me to leave you.'

'You wouldn't have left me,' said Lance, as though stating a fact. 'And you being offered a job here was His will.'

'God's a he?' said Arlene.

'God's a she?' said Lance.

'Those aren't the only two options,' said Arlene.

'Is God non-binary now? Fine. I said I'd do anything They wanted.'

'You don't even believe in God.'

'Maybe not, but I've kept my promises to Them anyway, haven't I? That says something.'

'It says you only keep your promises to beings that don't exist. Anyway, didn't you also tell Them you would help the poor?'

'Yes, but God doesn't *seriously* expect anyone to actually do that. They recognise that it's just something people say. Besides, I'm helping Jonathon–'

'Um, I'm not sure that you are,' said Jonathon. 'It feels more like you're embroiling me in another seq–'

Arlene said, 'Jonathon is not *the poor*. The guy owns a cottage in Hampstead. That has to be worth over a million by now, right?'

'Well,' said Jonathon, feeling uncomfortable, 'sort of, but we got that by accident, because of that other sequence of horribly traumatic events. And it's in Piper's name, so I don't really own it at all.'

'Oh, really?' said Arlene. 'But I thought *you* were the one who was nearly–'

Jonathon, not wanting to be reminded of what had nearly happened to him, risked interrupting Arlene, which in itself was a small act of heroism. 'We both did stuff,' he said. 'Anyway, we're not breaking up – I hope – so it doesn't really matter whose name it's in.'

Arlene looked at him doubtfully.

Lance said, 'Wait, if you have a million-pound house, why are you both worried about work? Just sell it and retire to the countryside. You could never work again, just about.'

'But we were given a *house*, not an asset to sell. And it was a reward for … what we did. Anyway, I've met people who don't have to work, and it doesn't seem very good for them. They get really into expensive hobbies. And anyway, where would we go? We like it here. We like our lives. We just need a little push to make things a bit more solid, and then everything will finally be fine.'

'And that's why,' said Lance, with an air of quiet triumph, 'I'm following the murderer, so he doesn't get in the way of everything finally being fine.'

'Oh, this is where we started from. You said you'd stop doing that.'

'Okay,' said Arlene, 'you guys are going to have sort this thing out between you. I'm late for work, and half my hair is going to dry in a weird way if I don't work my magic on it.'

She looked at them both, added, 'Play nice,' and left the room, closing the door behind her.

'I didn't say I'd stop doing that,' resumed Lance quietly. 'I said, "mm-hm". It's a very different thing. Anyway, after the raid–'

'The *raid*?'

'Did you not hear about that?'

'No.'

'Don't you read the *Highbury and Islington Gazette*?'

'No. I didn't even when I lived in Highbury and Islington.'

'Okay. Well, I suppose I didn't either until two days ago. Anyway, after our tip-off, the police raided Ken's–'

'Oh god. Was the uncle there?'

'The murderer was there. But they didn't find anything.'

'But that's terrible. He'll know it's because of us, won't he? And then he'll–'

'They didn't find anything,' repeated Lance, 'which is why I followed him yesterday–'

'You followed him *because* they didn't find anything?'

'Of course. Not finding anything in the raid just means this thing is even bigger than we thought.'

'But what if it means this thing is smaller than we thought? Maybe nothing's going on at all? Maybe Ken's Plucky Fried Chicken is just a chicken shop, and the uncle works there selling chicken.'

'Well, he does work there selling chicken,' said Lance. 'But if that's all he's doing, why did he break into an office in central

London last night?'

'Did he?'

'No. But he looked like he wanted to.'

'What? How does someone look like they want to break into an office?'

'He stared hard at the sign, then walked round the block twice, and then climbed into a weird graveyard thing at the back and started to climb towards the office, as though he was going to break in. But then he stopped, as though he somehow sensed he was being watched – or someone tipped him off.'

'And then?'

'Then he went home.'

'Did you take a photo? Of him climbing, I mean.'

'I'm still trying to decide which camera to get – they're all so good. I did tell my police contact though.'

'What did he say?'

'Nothing immediately helpful. But I'm sure he'll be interested if we can find out a bit more. The question is, why did the murderer want to break into that company's office?'

'What's the company?'

'It's called Flock,' said Lance, tapping a key to bring his monitor back to life, displaying its website. 'Founder: Nikki Southall. It provides "full-spectrum marketing solutions" including "market-leading meta-influence methodologies".'

'Oh god,' said Jonathon. 'Why do we live in an age where it's impossible to understand what any company does?'

'It's the price we pay for not living in an age where we have to spend our lives growing wheat. Anyway, you're going to find out what's going on.'

'What?' said Jonathon. 'How?'

'You're a freelance illustrator. Just do some freelance illustration for them.' Lance gestured at his computer screen. 'See how bad the graphics on their website are.'

Jonathon laughed. 'It doesn't work like that. I mean, I'm trying to get new clients now, but it takes a long time. You do research and then get in touch with someone in the HR or marketing department, and they ignore you or tell you to get in touch with someone else, and you gradually–'

'Really?' said Lance. 'How long does it take to get a job, then?'

'Well, I haven't been doing it this new way for very long. I mean, I hate doing it, so–'

Lance gave him an 'answer the question' look.

Jonathon hung his head. 'I've never got any work that way.'

'So how do you ever have work?'

'People I've worked with before tell other people. Or people see things I've done and get in touch.'

Lance shook his head. Then he squinted at Flock's website, patted his lack of pockets, and held out a hand for Jonathon's phone, which Jonathon passed him.

'Hi,' said Lance, having dialled the number, 'this is Lance Ferman. I need to speak to … Nikki Southall.'

There was a pause, which Jonathon filled by waiting for Lance to be cut off, because what Lance was doing was not the way things worked.

'Hi, Nikki,' said Lance with a smile. 'Lance Ferman here. Listen, I'm sitting in the same room as the hottest young illustrator in London: Jonathon Fairfax. You need a new visual identity, right? Well, he can sort that out for you.'

This time, Jonathon occupied himself during the pause that followed by imploding with shame – as well as waiting for Lance to be cut off.

'Great,' said Lance. 'But maybe a bit later. Say three?'

Pause.

'Three hundred and fifty pounds a day. But he prefers to quote on a project basis.'

There was another pause, during which Jonathon stopped breathing, because this was quite a lot more than he'd ever actually charged.

'Perfect,' said Lance. 'He'll see you then. Ciao.'

30

Five hours later, Jonathon was standing outside a Victorian building on Borough High Street. And two minutes after that, he'd worked up the nerve to press Flock's buzzer.

There was a fizz of static and then a cheerful Lancashire voice said, 'Hello, Flock here. You all right?'

'Oh, um, yes, thanks,' said Jonathon. 'I'm here for an interview, or appointment – a meeting thing.'

The voice laughed indulgently. 'Lovely. And what name is it, sweetheart?'

'Fairfax, Jonathon Fairfax.' Why had he said it like that?

'Ooh, like Bond, James Bond – love it. Well come on up, lovely. We're on the third floor.'

'Righto, er …' He didn't know how to respond to being called 'lovely', so he settled for 'Yes.'

As he walked upstairs, he wished that he too could call people 'lovely' and 'sweetheart' in an authentic, unselfconscious, down-to-earth way. But he couldn't. He didn't even know how to carry an illustration portfolio up some stairs without painfully striking his legs.

On the third floor, the door was open, revealing a bright window, a colourful rug and a reception desk. At the desk was a young woman with a large friendly smile, glasses, and gingery hair. As Jonathon crossed the threshold, she looked up.

'Hello!' she said. 'Come on in. I'm Samantha. Fairfax Jonathon Fairfax, right?'

'Um, yes. I don't know why I said it like that.'

'No, I love it,' she said, laughing, and he believed her. 'You sit yourself down here.' She indicated a friendly green sofa beside her desk. 'And I'll tell Nikki you're here and get you a nice cup of tea. Or a coffee? Tea though, right?'

'Um, yes. A tea would be lovely.'

'I knew it was tea. I can always tell whether someone's a coffee or tea person.' There was something in her manner that implied tea people were better.

'Wow.'

'Let me guess: tiny bit of milk, no sugar?'

'That's amazing. How did you know?'

'Hot beverages are my superpower. I'd have preferred x-ray vision or, you know, flying, but you work with what you've got, don't you?'

Jonathon sat on the friendly green sofa and Samantha picked up a telephone and said, 'Hi, Nikki? Fairfax Jonathon Fairfax is here – your three o'clock.'

She smiled. 'No, like Bond James Bond. No, he doesn't mind. He's nice. Aren't you?' She addressed this last question to Jonathon, who thought for a second and then found himself nodding gravely. He *was* nice. It was easy for him to forget that when he was out and about, because the world wasn't totally full of people like Samantha.

She led him up to the fourth floor, through a big open-plan space full of sofas, and into a glass-fronted office. Inside, a robust, curly-haired woman with a tiny nose smiled up at him from a phone call.

'This is Nikki Southall, our founder and CEO,' said Samantha.

The curly-haired woman on the phone gave a little seated bow.

'And this is Fairfax Jonathon Fairfax, illustrator and international spy,' continued Samantha.

Jonathon found himself giving a little bow too.

'Sit down, Jonathon,' said Samantha. 'She won't be two minutes.' And with that she left, gently closing the door behind her.

'Exactly,' Nikki was saying, 'and that's why I had to take her to the *emergency* vet. Anyway, got to go, I–' she paused 'Yes, Mum. Bye!'

Jonathon sipped his tea and smiled shyly.

'Sorry about that,' said Nikki. 'One of my cats spilled fabric conditioner all over herself last night, so I had to take her to the emergency vet and then obviously give my mum a full account. So, what are we doing here? Illustration, visual identity, Fairfax Jonathon Fairfax, yes?'

'Um, yes,' said Jonathon. He fished in his huge portfolio and handed her a CV, as though it were a ritual gift.

'Okay,' she said, glancing at his CV, 'so I had a look at your portfolio online and I really like it!' She looked up and smiled, which hugely outweighed the damage he'd done his legs by unnecessarily bringing his portfolio. 'I think you *could* be just what we're looking for. We can probably all agree that our current visual identity leaves a lot to be desired.'

Jonathon pulled a face which he hoped said, 'I agree, but not rudely.'

'Okay, so … Actually, has anyone told you about our background and what we do?'

Jonathon shook his head. He was trying to minimise his chances of saying something really stupid.

'Okay,' said Nikki. 'Well, my background is in journalism. I used to work at *The Number* – remember that?'

'Yes,' said Jonathon. He remembered that all the intimidating students had read it when he was at university.

'Strap-line: *What's cool. What's now.* As you can see, I am neither cool nor now, and yet somehow they let me write for it. There were four of us in a tiny office with one computer, and it was *great* – until it folded.'

'Oh! Why?'

'The internet. And then I went to work for the *Mail* and got made redundant, also because of the internet.'

'Bloody internet,' said Jonathon.

'Indeed. I had two kids and two cats to support and I just thought, "You know what? I can make a *lot* more money with my skills." In the end, it's all just about influencing people. And you can either do that for a soulless press baron for a pittance, or do it for several soulless corporations for *significantly* more. So guess which I chose?'

'The, um, corporations?'

'Exactly. So at first I called myself Southall PR and churned out press releases. And then I thought a bit more about this influence thing, and I thought about how sheep in a flock influence each other. If you influence the influencers then your message goes a lot further, so I called that "meta-influence", which is exactly the sort of thing these corporate types love. And that's how I went from my kitchen table to spanning two whole floors of a medium-sized Victorian building near Borough Market, with a separate meta-influencing team that has its own room, through there.'

She waved vaguely through the wall, and Jonathon waved too.

'So, the website,' she said. 'I've let it get a bit *stale*, shall we say, mainly because they're such a pain to sort out.'

'It's the fonts,' said Jonathon.

'Yes!' said Nikki. 'That's exactly it. They're so hard to choose, and you do that and no one has any energy left to sort out the rest. So, it's way too stuffy and the graphics were done by a friend in a hurry. But I've been thinking for ages that I'd really like to use illustration to warm up our look a bit, and then your friend called.'

Jonathon couldn't help asking, 'Why did you take his call?'

'It's my *Number* instinct: if someone's that self-assured, they must be on to something. So, what do you recommend?'

'Oh,' said Jonathon, surprised to be asked such an open question. 'Um, I think' – he vigorously overcame an instinct to tell her that she should ignore what he thought, because he was an imposter and knew nothing – 'you should just make it clean and simple, with lots of space and a serif font, and some nice illustrations of different sorts of anthropomorphic animals dressed in business-casual clothes.'

Nikki thought about this for a few seconds, while Jonathon prepared to leave the room in disgrace. Then she said, 'Cool. I like it. Can you work on it in-house for a few days? When can you start?'

'Tomorrow?' suggested Jonathon.

'Okay, great. We're strictly normal human hours here, so nine till five thirty. We try not to stay late. Apart from anything else, it helps keep relationships together. Are you …?'

He nodded. 'I live with Piper, my, um …' He was always embarrassed about the world 'girlfriend' for some reason. Perhaps it was because she had become even more beautiful over the past couple of years. Now, when they were out together, he was slightly ashamed, on her behalf, that she was accompanied by an idiot like him. He secretly thought she should be with a proper man who has an important job and can fix cars.

'Piper?' said Nikki. 'Is she American?'

'Her mum is.'

'Well, if you want to keep her–'

'I definitely do.'

'Then make sure you don't ever work in journalism for several years – late nights, not coming home, etcetera.'

Jonathon nodded sombrely.

'Okay,' said Nikki. 'I'll get Samantha to show you how everything works.' She looked at her watch. 'I've got a call with a potential new client in a few minutes … Hold on, sorry.' She pressed a button on her phone and said, 'Sam, could you get the Teddy folder from next door?' Then she looked at him again and said, 'Anyway, I'd best say goodbye. Nice meeting you, Jonathon.'

They shook hands and Jonathon successfully left her office without falling over his portfolio. All in all, it was perhaps the most entirely successful encounter of his whole life.

How, he wondered, would he contrive to mess this one up?

Tuesday

31

Making your way through life, thought Jonathon as he made his way through London Bridge station, is very much like making your way through London Bridge station. There are many paths and many exits. But if you keep your destination clearly in mind, carefully follow the signs and persevere, then at some point you'll unexpectedly find yourself on Duke Street Hill – which wasn't what you intended at all – looking around in confusion as everyone tuts impatiently. Then someone will barge into you, drop an exotic coffee on your foot and angrily mutter, 'Fucking muppet.'

As Jonathon wiped the expensive froth from his shoe, he reminded himself not to come up with life metaphors on the Tube: it seemed to really interfere with his ability to navigate. Luckily, he was well prepared. He'd brought a spare handkerchief with him for his first day at Flock.

At the top of Duke Street Hill, London unveiled one of those sudden moments of splendour that it does just often enough to keep millions of people living there, despite everything. The sun dripped clean and gold down the fine old buildings in front of him, struck the picturesque old clock to his left, danced over London Bridge to his right, and generally did an excellent job of beautifying what was otherwise a huge and quite complicated traffic interchange next to a busy train station.

'Sorry I'm a bit late,' he said when he arrived in Flock's office a few minutes later. 'I never come out of the bit of London Bridge station that I mean to.'

Samantha smiled delightedly, as though this too were an endearing foible, rather than evidence of a general inability to deal with things.

'Don't worry about it,' she said. 'You're a creative, FJF. It's fine.'

No one had ever called Jonathon a creative before. Was he? The other companies he worked for called him a freelance, which seemed to be only half a step above a temp.

'I've set up a desk for you,' said Samantha. 'I hope it's okay.'

She led him through the office, which had large windows on one side, illuminating all the slightly quirky, good-natured people who worked there. They were chatting quietly and easily with each other, or eating biscuits as they stared thoughtfully into screens. Then Jonathon came to the largest desk he'd ever seen, which Samantha said was his.

'Nikki's booked you in for two weeks,' she said. 'But if that's not long enough, just have a word with us. It shouldn't be a problem.'

'This is amazing,' said Jonathon, marvelling at the vast expanse of desk. It was far bigger than the one he used at home.

'Let me show you the kitchen so you can keep yourself topped up with tea.' She glanced at her watch. 'I'd best be quick: Teddy Robinson's coming in today, so I need to be ready when he buzzes.'

'Oh,' said Jonathon. 'What are you doing for him?'

'Something to do with his campaign. I don't really know, to be honest, what with working more at the tea end of things than on the grand strategy side.'

At that moment, the phone on Samantha's desk went off, and she said, 'Oh, crikey, tell me that's not him already!'

She answered it, seeming almost as charmed and delighted with Teddy as she had been with Jonathon, then ran downstairs to welcome him in. Seconds later, he heard the great man's heavy tread on the stairs, his voice booming in the stairwell.

Jonathon's heart sank: he was going to have to tell Lance about this, and Lance was going to be interested.

32

Teddy was ushered into the glass-fronted office and instantly fell in love with the curly-haired woman who smiled up at him from her desk. He saw in that second that his two marriages and all those affairs had been mere passing infatuations. Here, at last, was the real thing.

She stood and said, 'Hello, Teddy. It's great to meet you. It's not often we get such famous people in the office. I hope they didn't all crowd to the stairs to get a look?'

The receptionist, Samantha, said, 'I told them not to and they were good as gold, weren't they, Teddy?'

'Didn't see a soul,' he said. 'And you're flattering me absolutely outrageously. I have the self-knowledge to realise that nobody in their right mind wants to see a tweed-clad heffalump such as myself bestriding the staircase.'

Nikki laughed and said, 'Please, take a seat.'

Samantha said, 'Can I get you a tea or coffee? Tea though, right? Earl Grey, squeeze of lemon?'

'Absolutely extraordinary. Yes, that's exactly what I'd like. How did you guess?'

'Hot beverages are my superpower. I'd rather have had the strength of a thousand men or death-ray eyes, but what can you do?'

When Samantha had left the room, Nikki leaned forward and asked, 'How can we help?'

Her dark curls charmingly framed a round face that housed the tiniest and most delicately modelled nose he'd ever seen. It was adorable.

'I'd like to be mayor of London, please,' he said.

She laughed a wonderfully earthy laugh. 'We'll do our best,' she said.

'And no one could ask for more.'

'Oh, I should have asked on the phone yesterday: where did

you hear about us?'

'Old school chum of mine. Knows General Grimaldi, who apparently speaks very highly of you.'

She smiled and gave a modest wave. 'He was an absolute treasure.'

'The fact is that Bolton, my campaign manager is not ... well, not quite up to the job, to be honest. So I'd like to supplement his efforts, discreetly – I don't want him to get wind of this, if I do go ahead and avail myself of your services.'

'We're *very* discreet,' said Nikki.

33

At the end of the day, Nikki came over and picked up one of Jonathon's drawings.

'Look at these!' she said. 'They're great. Simon! Come and have a look at these illustrations for our website.'

'They aren't finished yet,' said Jonathon.

'Aren't they good!' said Nikki to Simon, a smiley man with an unusually large head.

'I was admiring them earlier,' said Simon. 'Really good. I feel better about working here already!'

He laughed, Nikki playfully punched him, and Jonathon found he was smiling. He liked it here.

Afterwards, he walked down the stairs with Samantha, who also said how good his drawings were. When they reached the door she said, as warmly and familiarly as if they'd been working together for years, 'See you tomorrow!' and went off the other way.

Jonathon smiled and waved, then set off towards London Bridge station, past all the estate agents and sandwich shops, and also past the occasional tobacconist or dilapidated betting shop – marooned remnants of the scruffier, shabbier London that was being displaced. He felt it almost as a shadowy presence at his side. Then he realised, with a shiver of fear, that there was a real shadowy presence at his side.

'J-Mole,' said Lance, moving out of the shadows.

'Please don't call me J-Mole. I'm not working undercover as a mole. I'm just working.'

'Of course you are,' said Lance.

'Oh god. Don't say "Of course you are" like that.'

'Like what?'

'As though denying I'm a mole is a natural and essential part of my role as a mole.'

'Okay,' said Lance, again with the infuriating air that they were both colluding in pretending Jonathon wasn't a mole. 'So what did you find out on your first day?'

'I found out the brief for my illustration work,' said Jonathon.

'Nicely played,' said Lance, as though proud of him for sticking so thoroughly to his cover story.

Jonathon smiled in a long-suffering way and said, 'I sometimes wish I'd never met you.'

'Oh, that's standard,' said Lance. 'Everyone does. And yet, having met me, you don't wish you could stop knowing me.'

Jonathon thought this over. 'That's true.'

'It's a paradox,' said Lance. 'Anyway, since you're not working undercover but are just doing the freelance work I got you—'

'Thank you.'

'You're welcome. What happened on your first day?'

'Well, everyone was really nice. Samantha showed me the kitchen. Oh, and Teddy Robinson came in.'

'Ooh,' said Lance.

'Ooh?'

'Yes. What?'

'Just I've never heard you say "ooh" before.'

'We're investigating a company that the murderer almost broke into, and now it turns out that they're working with Teddy Robinson. I say it again: ooh.'

'I was afraid you'd take it this way,' said Jonathon. 'The Teddy Robinson thing.'

'I do,' said Lance. 'In fact, I need you to briefly accompany me into this pub.'

Jonathon hadn't even noticed they were passing one, but before he knew it, Lance had gently nudged him, like a human pinball, into a large wooden door, kicked it open at just the right moment, deftly switched sides, given Jonathon another very slight nudge so that he bumped into a huge polished wooden bar, nodded to a barmaid, laid a finger on one of the pumps, and then handed Jonathon a pint of London Pride.

'I should get home,' said Jonathon, automatically taking a sip of his beer. 'Piper–'

'You are getting home,' said Lance, taking delivery of another beer for himself and absently crumpling some money into the barmaid's hand.

'Am I? It seems like I'm being had a drink in a pub.' Jonathon thought this was the right grammar: no one had ever happened a pub drink to him before.

'This is speeding you on your way home,' said Lance. 'And it includes complimentary coaching on your freelance career.'

'Oh. Actually, I could do with that. How did you manage to get me a job with just one phone call?'

'Well, that's partly because I'm me, and there's a huge world conspiracy to make anything I want happen. But it's mainly because I'm not you. It's always easier to get work for someone else.'

'Oh. So then maybe I could help you get some investigative work.'

'You already have.'

'Have I?'

'Yes. We talked about this. You're helping me with a demonstration case which I can put on my website–'

'Oh, have you done your website now?'

'Not remotely. But once I've got this case finished and have chosen a font and caused my website to exist, every visitor will have an irresistible compulsion to employ me.'

'And the demonstration case is … working out what's going on with the uncle and the chicken shop?'

'The murderer and the chicken conspiracy and the mysterious company and the candidate to be mayor of London. Yes.'

'Could you,' said Jonathon, 'just allow it to remain a mystery?'

Lance laughed lightly, apparently taking this to be a joke.

'Luckily,' he said, 'I invited an associate along to this meeting to help us.'

'All right?' said Vince from behind, making Jonathon jump.

When Lance had finished buying Vince a pint, finding him a seat and explaining the situation to him, Vince nodded in his hard-bitten journalistic way, as though he came across exactly this situation all the time.

'Whatever it is,' he said, 'the cops are in on it.'

Lance narrowed his eyes and nodded, as though he too were a veteran journalist who'd been round the block a few times. Jonathon, not wanting to be left out, also tried narrowing his eyes in a grizzled way, but it made him sneeze.

'Gesundheit,' said Lance, possibly to show Vince that he'd lived in New York.

'Hanky-user are we?' said Vince to Jonathon, who was engaged in a post-sneeze nose-blow using one of the cotton handkerchiefs Piper had got for him.

'Um, yes,' said Jonathon, suddenly self-conscious about sneezing into a clean, washable piece of fabric instead of using his hands like a real man. He wondered what Lance sneezed into, and then realised he'd never seen Lance sneeze. It was probably on account of the genetic lotteries he'd won.

'But why do you think the police are in on it?' asked Jonathon, wanting to change the subject.

'Think about it,' said Vince. 'Lance calls his police contact when he sees this murderer about to break in to Flock's offices. A second later, the murderer changes his mind and goes home. The cops turn up, and Lance's police contact accuses Lance of wasting his time. Says not to bother calling him again.'

'Did he?' said Jonathon. 'You told me he just said nothing immediately helpful.'

'What he actually said,' Lance explained patiently, 'was that I should call him again when I've strangled myself with my own arsehole. It wasn't immediately helpful.'

'Exactly,' said Vince. 'Proves my point. He's already got what he wanted from you: an excuse to raid Ken's and say they've found nothing. Now he's warned this murderer that you're following him and he wants to wash his hands of you.'

Lance narrowed his eyes in a hard-bitten way.

'But why would the police be working with the murderer and whoever controls Ken's?' persisted Jonathon.

'Wouldn't you like to know?' said Vince, giving him a long, probing look. 'I've been working this Ken's story long enough to know the answer. I'm just trying to work out how much to share with Mr Handsome and Hanky Boy.'

Lance half-turned to Jonathon. 'I'm Mr Handsome,' he clarified. Then he said to Vince, 'We can help you. I've already told you about the murderer and the police. There's plenty more like that. I'm on this full-time at the moment. And Jonathon's working undercover in Flock.'

'Is he?' said Vince. 'How did you manage that?'

'Never you mind,' said Lance, narrowing his eyes again. Jonathon sneezed.

'Tell you what,' said Vince. 'I'll let you in on what I know if you tell me what Flock has on Ken's.'

'Oh,' said Jonathon, 'but I don't know.'

'I thought you were undercover there. You must have looked through their files.'

'He is undercover,' said Lance, giving Jonathon a hard look. 'But it's his first day. He's just getting his feet under the table–'

'It's quite a big table,' explained Jonathon.

'But that's exactly what he's going to do next,' concluded Lance.

Vince looked at Jonathon, who tried to work out how to tell him that he planned to just keep his feet under the table, where they were being paid, and not look at any files of any kind. He was increasingly feeling that if he had some good work with a nice company and the uncle wasn't currently killing him, then everything was basically fine and they should leave it all as it was. After all, apart from a slight shortage of work, his life had been pretty much perfect before all this had come along.

'All right,' said Vince, and downed the rest of his pint. 'When he's got something, give me a tinkle.'

Vince glanced over his shoulder in a hard-bitten sort of way, narrowed his shrewd journalistic eyes once more, and walked out of the pub.

Once Jonathon had stopped sneezing, Lance got him to relate everything that had happened while he'd been in Flock's offices, and Jonathon concluded by telling Lance where he stood on looking at files.

'I just can't do it,' he said. 'I absolutely can't look at their files.'

'Well then,' said Lance sympathetically, 'just have a *little* look at their files. Sometimes the only way to avoid a full-blown adventure is to have a pre-emptive micro-adventure.'

'Even a micro-adventure's too much for me,' said Jonathon. 'I can't cope with them any more. Why can't we just tell Nikki what we know?'

'It's too soon,' said Lance with certainty. 'We absolutely shouldn't do that until Vince has told us what he knows.'

'But everyone's so nice there,' said Jonathon. 'And Nikki has cats. I'm sure nothing bad's going on.'

'If everyone's nice and there's nothing bad going on,' Lance countered, 'there's no problem with having a peek in their files, if you happen to find yourself alone with them. You said yourself that when Nikki asked for the file on Teddy, it came from the mega-influencing department–'

'*Meta*-influencing department,' corrected Jonathon.

'*Whatever*,' corrected Lance. 'And you said it's right next door to her office. If you look under "K" in their filing cabinets and there's nothing there, then that tells us something. We could tell Vince, and that might be enough to get him to tell us what he knows. It would definitely stop him calling you Hanky Boy.'

Jonathon ate a pork scratching and, feeling that he should really make a gesture towards helping Lance, given that Lance had got him the best freelance job ever, he said, 'All right. If I happen to find myself alone with the files, I'll see if there's one on Ken's.'

'That's all I'm asking,' said Lance. 'And after that the pre-emptive micro-adventure is over.'

Jonathon, feeling reassured, finished his beer and went home, where he found a very quiet crisis was going on.

The murderer was sitting on a Ferrari-branded duvet, beside Ken and a pile of business-studies textbooks, facing Ranira, who was still in her school uniform. This was meant to be his break, but he was using it for a crisis meeting.

He said, 'I know you can find everything out on the internet–'

'Not everything,' said Ranira. 'I told you, it's only things that people have uploaded to the internet. Think of the internet as a shelf, and uploading is like "putting" things on the shelf. But I have made a bit more progress finding posts from computers based in Flock.'

'That's magic, that, Ranira,' said the murderer. 'But what I wanted to say was, I'm a real-world man, me. So I been there the last couple of mornings at Flock, before my shift, just watching: who goes in, who comes out, what they look like.'

'Please tell me the hours you spend on this,' said Ken, 'and I will add them to your timesheet.'

'I can't do that, Ken. But cheers.'

'What did you see?' asked Ranira.

'Well, I mean, all sorts of people – just normal, cushy-job-looking people. But then this morning I see a skinny kid go in there, smart clothes, carrying a bag thing, like he works there.'

'A kid?' said Ranira. 'Like my age?'

'What? No. Probably late twenties. A bloke, not a kid. But I know him. And if he's working there, this whole thing is even more complicated than we thought.'

'Who is he?' asked Ken.

'Our Rachel used to go out with him. Don't know his surname, but his first name's Jonathon. And he is trouble.'

Jonathon could tell as soon as he walked through the door that things weren't right. The cat was nowhere to be seen, and the house echoed with the sound of people suddenly not talking. Cess, the dog, put her head around the door from the living room, her brows set at a worried angle. She walked around Jonathon a couple of times as he took off his jacket, then she headed back in.

'Hello, Jonathon?' said Piper. Her voice was bright but a bit artificial, as though she had been given the role of herself in an amateur production of their lives.

'Hello?' he said.

'Come on in,' said Piper. She sounded like she was at the point in the amateur production where she no longer needed a script, but still wasn't quite sure who her character was. 'We're in here.'

He gingerly pushed the door open and looked in.

Piper was sitting in the armchair, holding a cup of tea. Cess stood beside her, looking with some concern from Jonathon to the people on the sofa.

'Hi,' said Rachel. Her hair was pulled back and she was wearing a fleece, looking as though she'd been teleported in from a French farm.

Beside her sat a pale, very young girl with red hair, freckles, and that intensely expressive absence of facial expression that only teenagers can do. She was wearing jeans and a hoodie.

'This is Gemma,' said Piper. 'Rachel's niece – or cousin. Her aunt's daughter.'

'Oh, hello, Gemma,' said Jonathon. His voice told him that he too had been enrolled in that same amateur production.

He flailed around for a way of easing Gemma of the awful burden of her adolescence. Being in the same room as her was reminding him of his own teenage years – the storms of violent and profound emotion that had howled through him, feelings totally unsuited to the life available to an underwhelming schoolboy in a smallish bleak town. He remembered how the only way of dealing with it seemed to be to try to pretend – utterly unconvincingly, he now saw – that he was feeling no emotions at all.

'Would you, um, like a …' He saw the cup of tea clenched in her hands, the plate of biscuits on the little table by her knee. '… a, er, piece of … fruit?' It was the stupidest thing he had ever said, and he blushed immediately.

'I'm good, thanks,' said Gemma, showing a mouthful of metal braces.

Like 'hey' before it, 'I'm good' had recently swept through the country, installing itself in everyone's brains without anyone ever saying a word about it. 'I'm good' always disconcerted Jonathon, because people found it impossible to say without adopting a slightly passive-aggressive tone, as though the thing he'd offered them would clearly have stopped them being good, and they just wanted to carry on being good, thanks, so perhaps he should just, like, have the thing he'd offered them himself, because he clearly didn't care about being good or whatever, yeah?

'Right,' he said, wincing. 'Sorry.'

Gemma looked stricken, and seemed to flail around for a way to ease Jonathon of the awful burden of adulthood.

'I mean, sorry,' she said. 'I had a banana in my packed lunch.'

'Come and make a cup of tea,' said Piper, getting up and giving his hand a quick squeeze. They went through to the kitchen, giving Cess a dilemma, as she instinctively wanted all animals, with the possible exception of cats, to be in a single group which she could then easily and unobtrusively guard. Cess cast a regretful look at the living room and hurried after them into the kitchen.

Piper closed the door, hugged him, put the kettle on and grabbed his arm all in one movement.

'Is it all right if Gemma stays here for a bit? Just for a few days?'

'Of course,' he said.

'Only, the thing is …' she continued in a quiet voice, 'well, you know what's going on. She's got all this anger at her dad for not being around when she was growing up, and now she's worried that he's gone back to crime. She was staying with Rachel, but

Rachel's got to go back to France because ... well, she lives there and has a job.'

'Yes. Of course she can stay here.'

'Only, the thing is,' repeated Piper, 'well, she feels a bit ... uneasy with men at the moment, because of her dad. So, would it be all right if you stayed somewhere – with Lance or something – just for a couple of days? Not tonight, obviously, but maybe tomorrow?'

'Oh. Right. Um.' He thought of Gemma's brace, and what a catastrophe that alone probably was. And he thought of how terrible he felt about his own dad, who had not even remotely been to prison for Jonathon's entire childhood. But then he thought of Gemma's dad, his possibly lethal nature, and how he'd gone back to crime, and Gemma's mum and her knowledge of where Jonathon lived. And he thought about what they might think of Jonathon taking in their daughter. It was a tricky situation. In fact, it suddenly seemed to Jonathon that the whole world was a vast conspiracy devoted to putting him in tricky situations.

'Um, yes. Of course,' he concluded.

Piper hugged him, gave him a kiss, and made him a cup of tea in one fluid move.

Wednesday

36

The next morning, Jonathon woke up slightly late, his hand having snoozed his alarm without bothering to ask his brain's permission. He hurried off for a shower, worried about not being on time for his second day at work, and found the bathroom door locked. This was impossible. He went back to the bedroom, where Piper lay unconscious beneath the living quilt formed by the cat and dog. His sleep-addled brain was seriously entertaining the idea that there were now two of her, when he remembered Gemma. Of course.

He went and stood anxiously beside the bathroom door. Then he tried a little cough, but Gemma seemed to be running every available source of water as hard as it would go. To distract himself from the worry that this might dissolve the bathroom, he went downstairs and used a spare dishcloth to wash himself in the thin trickle of cold water from the sink. Hurrying back upstairs, damp and in just his pants, he bumped into Gemma as she left the bathroom with a towel around her chest. They both jumped, turned red and fled. The only way in which Jonathon's reaction differed from an adolescent girl's was that he murmured 'morning' as he went. The door of his office, where she had slept, closed behind her with a bang.

After dressing quickly, he went and cleaned his teeth in the bathroom, which was now like a Turkish bath. Because the air was mostly composed of hot water, he soon looked like he'd had a small shower in his clothes.

'Hello, Johnny-boy,' said Piper tiredly, appearing behind him in a dressing gown. 'What did you do to the air?' She rested herself gently against his back, as though he were a kind of vertical mattress.

'It was Gemma,' he whispered, and then jumped, because Gemma was suddenly standing in the bathroom doorway, looking like she wished she didn't exist.

Piper must have seen her too, because he felt her jump a second later.

'Hello Gemma!' she said. 'Have you bread any hackfast? I mean … you know what I mean.'

Gemma coloured, looked at the floor and shook her head. 'Don't really do breakfast,' she mumbled. 'Sorry about the bathroom and everything. Mum's has a fan thing.'

'No need to be sorry!' said Piper, her hair sticking to her forehead. 'Would you like some coffee?'

Gemma blushed again and waved her head about in a noncommittal way. 'Think I'd better get to school. Thanks though and everything. Thanks for letting me stay.'

'Oh yes, school,' said Piper. 'I told Rachel I'd take you, just to show you the way.'

'I can do it on my own if you want. Thanks though and everything.'

'No, I'd like to,' said Piper. 'I often, um, go on the Tube … a bit … in the morning, don't I, Jonathon?'

This lie was too outrageous for Jonathon to convincingly back up, so he just smiled and stood on one leg. And so they all ended up walking to the Tube station together, having had no breakfast, him wheeling his little suitcase and Piper wearing her skirt back to front.

'FJF!' said Samantha, smiling hugely, as he wheeled his suitcase through the door. 'Good morning! How's it going?'

'Oh, hello, Samantha. Okay, thanks, except we've got a teenager staying with us and now I have to sleep in a strange hotel for a couple of nights. How are you?'

He didn't know why he'd told her about Gemma, except that her easy warmth had temporarily overwhelmed his certainty that no one actually wants you to tell them how it's going. She seemed interested, so he briefly told her what had happened, and she told him he was doing the right thing. Then she confided that – though it was only a Wednesday morning – she was quite hung over.

'… and that's why I'm never going anywhere near rich people and cocktails again,' she concluded. 'Look at me gassing on at you! You need to make yourself a nice cup of tea and ease very, very slowly into work. Have a Hobnob.'

It turned out to be her last one, but she insisted he have it.

In the kitchen a tall man with a little strap beard told him that he liked his jacket, which Jonathon was not at all prepared for. He tottered out, slightly shocked, and sat at his enormous desk, the excellent light pouring in through the huge windows, and got on with his fulfilling, well-paid work.

After a bit of sketching, Jonathon went to the toilet, which was on the next floor up. Coming out afterwards, it struck him that there was absolute silence beyond the door at the end of the corridor. This was intriguing, so he strolled over and looked through the window.

The big space with the sofas was empty.

He thought he might just see if Nikki was in her office. If she was, he could tell her how well the work was going. What could be less adventurous than telling your nice boss that your work's going well?

So he pushed the door open, sauntered into the big space with the sofas, and glanced around. Both Nikki's office and the meta-influencing team's office, with their glass fronts, were silent and empty.

At the end of the space, up a few steps, was a large meeting room. This did not have a glass front – in fact, its door had only a small window. Through it, Jonathon glimpsed Nikki in profile, making the sort of gesture that people only ever make when they're doing a PowerPoint presentation. She was probably talking about an uplift in performance indicators going forward, or something like that, talking to all the people who usually filled the meta-influencing team's office.

At that moment, Jonathon very quietly made a momentous

decision.

He decided to pretend to himself that he hadn't just glimpsed Nikki. After all, it could have been any curly-haired, tiny-nosed woman, couldn't it?

Maybe Nikki's in the room next to her office, he said to himself. He breezed over to the door of the meta-influencing team's room, opened it and stepped inside. *I'm just checking to see if Nikki's in here*, he said to himself. The room was empty. There, all along the opposite wall, nestled under the windows, were the filing cabinets – though of course these were irrelevant to him, because he was just looking for Nikki, just to tell her that all was well.

I'll just leave Nikki a note, he said to himself. *Perhaps there's a pen over there, on top of the filing cabinets?*

He was now, quite by chance, standing beside the filing cabinets in an empty office. He'd told Lance that if this happened, he would look under 'K'. And he happened to be standing by the cabinet marked 'K'. *Maybe there's a pen in it*, he said to himself.

There certainly wouldn't be a file on Ken's. That was all he had to confirm to Lance. He quickly flipped open the top drawer and glanced along the subject tabs. Nothing. No 'Ken', no 'KPFC'. It was fine. He eased the drawer closed. He took a breath. He glanced around the empty office. He could do this. He opened the next drawer down.

KPFC.

It was the first thing he saw. He almost disbelieved his eyes. He lifted out the folder in that compartment, just to check it was the right KPFC. That was all he had to do.

The cover of the folder was labelled 'Ken's Plucky Fried Chicken'.

Bollocks.

He froze.

Footsteps. On the stairs. Coming up. Were they just going to the toilet? He couldn't risk it. *Put it back.* He edged the drawer closed, then realised he still had the folder in his hand. The footsteps reached the landing. There was the sound of a door opening. Oh god.

The footsteps went to Nikki's office next door. Jonathon didn't move or breathe. In a split-second decision, barely conscious, he hid the folder behind his back, up his jacket, like someone in a children's television programme. If there had been a set of floor-length curtains in the room, he would undoubtedly have stood behind them, his feet sticking out incriminatingly.

Someone looked at him through the glass door: Samantha. She smiled broadly and walked in.

'Hello Fairfaxjonathonfairfax,' she said. 'How are you?'

'Hello,' he said. 'I am. Um. Fine.'

He moved his hands to his lower back, as though it was hurting, and surreptitiously pushed the edge of the folder down into the waistband of his smart-casual trousers.

At this point he remembered to smile at her. She jacked up her own smile a notch in return.

'How are you?' he now remembered to say.

'Hungry,' she said, conspiratorially. 'I was wondering if Nikki's got any more biscuits. Spoiler alert: she hasn't.'

'Oh, yes,' he said. 'I too came up here to find Nikki.' He really needed to work on the naturalism of his dialogue.

At this point Samantha frowned in confusion. 'Her office is next door.' She didn't add: *I took you there yesterday, and no one ever took you to this office*, but that general idea hung quietly in the air.

'Yes,' he agreed. 'I … er … wanted to leaven her a notes.' Oh god, why were there so many words to get right? 'So I thought I might be able to, um, pinch a Post-It from in here. I was just looking around for one.'

On the word 'pinch' he felt his face go red.

He looked around, as though resuming his fruitless search for a Post-It note. At that moment it became clear to him that he was standing in one of Western Europe's major concentrations of Post-It notes. The room was like an ammunition dump for a clerical army. There were several pads of them on every desk, plus some on a stand by the door, and even a few on the filing cabinets beside him. Samantha's gaze smilingly took them all in.

'I needed a pen as well,' he said, realising as he spoke that the room was so exaggeratedly full of the things that it was like a holy site for a pen-worshipping sect. In fact, almost everything in the room that wasn't a pad of Post-It notes was a pen, and vice-versa.

'I … I get a bit pen-blind sometimes,' he said. 'Do you ever get that? Where you can't see the thing you're looking for?'

'No,' she said, face expressionless. Then she laughed. 'I'm playing with you! Course I get that.'

He smiled with relief. They stood there smiling at each other, in this room brimming with pens and Post-It notes, while the folder crept stealthily down the back of his trousers.

'I'll just write that note,' he said. He selected from the dozen or so pens within an inch of his hand, and wrote on a Post-It note:

Hi Nikki, just wanted to say it's all going fine.

Oh god. Why would anyone leave a note saying that? He quickly added:

But let's have a chat.

Shit. Did that sound ominous? Peremptory? He added further:

Or not.

Ah, Jesus. It was like no note anyone had ever left in any circumstance in the whole of history. But didn't he always worry about things like this, and didn't they always turn out fine? He peeled the note from the pad with shaking fingers. His heart was pounding. Had he always been this bad at this kind of thing? He felt like he was getting worse at dealing with these horribly traumatic pre-emptive anti-adventure mini-adventures.

Jonathon attempted to linger, hoping to be able to quickly replace the folder, but Samantha was unmistakably waiting for him. So, he went next door and left the note on Nikki's desk, then he and Samantha walked downstairs together.

Samantha said nothing – he seemed to have temporarily overwhelmed her huge capacity for warmly setting people at their ease – so he tried his own hand at it.

'Are, um, you–?' he began, but was distracted by the shifting of the folder tucked precariously into the waistband of his trousers.

Samantha laughed. 'That's a pretty radical deconstruction of small talk there, FJF. Yes, I am, as it happens. Are you?'

'It's hard to say,' he replied. They were back through the door of the main floor by now.

'I know what you mean,' she said.

For a moment he was afraid she was going to put her hand on his back, but instead she lightly touched his shoulder. Then she gave him a look that seemed to combine camaraderie and concern, and went back to her seat at reception.

Jonathon walked to his desk, hands on his lower back, soothing his imaginary lumbago, then sat down and reflected on what a tragedy all this was. For the first time in his life he had a good freelance job in a company where everyone was nice, and he was risking it all. And for what? For the sake of possibly getting some information from a man who called him Hanky Boy, whose only positive attribute was the ability to narrow his eyes in a hardboiled and enigmatic way without sneezing.

He needed to cancel this pre-emptive mini-adventure. He'd done what he had said he would do: look in the filing cabinet to see if there was a folder on Ken's. There was. Now he just needed to put the folder back and continue living his life, hoping that at some point over the coming months his heart rate would go back to normal. If the uncle wanted to kill him for having sent him to prison and taken in his daughter, then so be it. After all, if you're not doing anything to stop them killing you then it can't be an adventure.

Jonathon continued with his work, keeping an eye out for opportunities to nip upstairs and replace the folder. At twelve, Samantha got her bag and said she was going to a sandwich shop nearby. This was his chance. There had been no way he could go back upstairs right in front of her eyes, but with her gone, the coast was clear. He waited exactly five minutes, then got up, pretending to wince in pain at his back, keeping a hand on the concealed folder as he walked the length of the office.

He quietly mounted the stairs, reached the top landing and was just stretching out a hand to open the door when it flew open. Nikki appeared, immediately followed by Teddy Robinson and the sound of a roomful of people suddenly released from a meeting.

'… really focused campaign,' Nikki was saying.

'… whack the blighter till he weeps,' Teddy Robinson was saying.

'… no one ever orders enough mini-croissants,' a voice was

saying from the post-meeting hubbub in the room behind.

Nikki smiled as she saw Jonathon.

'Hi,' she said. Turning to Teddy Robinson, she said, 'And this is our ace new illustrator, Jonathon.'

Teddy Robinson, a thin-yet-flabby, copper-haired, tweed-clad figure, turned his face to Jonathon, catching him in an unexpected charisma spotlight.

Jonathon noticed that, beneath the politicianly pallor, Teddy bore a surprising resemblance to David Bowie, and also radiated plucky good humour.

'Jonathon!' said Teddy, shaking his hand warmly, as though they'd been parted at birth and only just reunited. 'Absolutely marvellous skill to have, illustration! Brings an idea to life! Alice in Wonderland would be a tiresome farrago without Tenniel's illustrations!'

And then he was gone, down the stairs, and Nikki too. Jonathon felt as though a wave had burst over him and immediately receded.

The door opened again and the tide of post-meeting chat flowed back in. Amid the tumult, one clear voice spoke, saying, 'I wouldn't actually mind, but the samosas were a bit dry ...'

Jonathon quickly dodged into the toilet and locked the door behind him.

He was safe, for the moment.

He sat down on the closed toilet, realising that he could temporarily drop the pretence of being a man who didn't have something hidden up his jacket. The corridor outside was filling up with voices. Someone tried the door handle. For once, Jonathon was going to have to resist the psychological pressure to be rushed. He would have to stay here until everyone had gone, and then sneak back into the room and replace the folder in the filing cabinet.

But that would be so stressful. Could he really handle it? Or should he just leave the folder here in the toilet? But then what if someone was waiting outside and spotted it?

Maybe he should simply tell Nikki the truth about exactly what had happened. That would decisively cancel all traces of adventure.

He breathed a sigh of relief. That's what he would do.

And, when he confessed everything to Nikki, he could honestly say that he hadn't even looked inside the folder. This thought reassured him to such an extent that he leaned back and looked inside the folder.

37

Nikki had brought Teddy to the Fountain restaurant for lunch. It was in Fortnum and Mason, on Jermyn Street, and she hoped its soft green walls and delicate lighting would soothe him into signing the contract.

But it suffered from the standard problem with soft and delicate London restaurants, which is that the waiters – while charming and attractive – were also rising stars of fringe theatre or new-wave dance, and thus inclined to waft around smugly instead of bringing you your bloody food. She and Teddy had drunk a whole bottle of wine on an empty stomach, and Teddy had just ordered another.

'So, Nikki,' said Teddy, 'how does your company work, exactly?'

She couldn't help laughing. 'We did *touch* on that subject,' she said, smiling, 'in the presentation this morning.'

'Oh, come on,' he said, with his habitual poker-faced suppressed smile. 'What you gave me was the official version, for public consumption. I want the one-and-a-bit-bottles-in version. The juicy version. The one you tell your *friends*.'

He was confusing, his smile and manner making it very difficult to tell whether he was stupid and lazy or clever and deceptive. But it probably wouldn't hurt to begin with the story she actually did tell her friends.

'Go on then,' she said, taking another sip of wine. 'So basically I was on a date, and this guy started telling me how Chad Kroeger from Nickelback had been murdered by the other band members and replaced with a lookalike …'

Teddy gave her a look of studied blankness that said he'd either never heard of Nickelback or was pretending not to have.

'Rock band?' she said. 'Possibly Canadian? Quite famous? Anyway, it doesn't matter, because obviously no one has ever been murdered and replaced with a lookalike, at least not in possibly-Canadian rock.'

'Is that what you said to him?'

'No. I told him that Rice Krispies were invented by the KGB to undermine capitalism. And he believed me.'

'Doesn't surprise me,' said Teddy. 'You're talking to a hack who made up half his stuff for years. People will believe anything.'

'Exactly!' she said, pointing at him and putting a finger on her nose. 'So I just thought, basically, if someone's into conspiracy theories, that's the most valuable thing you can possibly know about them. Because these people are wandering around convincing themselves to believe in any old random shit. And if they're going to do that, why don't I make a massive fuck-off database of them and then get other people to pay me to funnel precisely targeted shit at them, in order to control what they buy and how they vote?'

'And so you founded Flock?' he said.

'No, I'd already set up Flock. It was just a normal marketing agency at that point. Because I'd already had the epiphany that journalism was deflating at exactly the same rate as London house prices were inflating. So if I was ever going to give the kids a proper home I needed to change career.'

'I see,' said Teddy. He fiddled with his napkin, then looked up with suddenly honest eyes. 'I suppose I had the same essential insight about journalism, and responded by moving into politics.' He smiled roguishly and added, 'I kept my newspaper columns going though.'

'I would have done that myself,' she said, 'except I'm a woman and I went to a normal school.'

She regretted it instantly. This was absolutely not the thing to say to someone whose money you want. But something about him – and half a bottle of wine – encouraged indiscretion.

He did his smile and said, *'Ignosce mihi pro educatione mea.'*

'What does that mean?'

'Latin. It means, "Forgive me for my education." I know how to say it because my parents spent an absolute fortune on sending me away to Eton in my formative years, turning me into the formidable scholar and statesman you see before you. And also, it goes without saying, wounding me deeply.'

She laughed, which seemed the safest response. But there was something wounded in his eyes.

'So,' he said, 'you have a database of people who'll swallow any old nonsense. Are there really enough of them to make a difference?'

'*Yes*,' she said emphatically. 'But you actually don't need that many. Often, just changing a few people's minds means that a lot of other people start to think, "Oh, there are probably points on both sides and it's all complicated and nuanced, so I don't know any more." That's real gold, if you can get a load of people to just give up having an opinion on something, then you can actually flip overall perceptions very quickly.'

'Really?'

'Yes, that's what we did with your friend General Grimaldi. Also, these conspiracists are people who like to talk, so things can spread quickly.'

'Can you measure it – the spread of an idea, I mean?'

'We're getting better at it. We're trying to get a sense of the true number of conspiracists by spreading a tracking rumour.'

'A tracking rumour?'

'A conspiracy theory we promote just to track its prevalence. We've tried a few, and the one we're using now is that dental floss causes schizophrenia. We're saying the dental deep state has known for years and is trying–'

'That was you?' he said. 'I read a piece in the *Telegraph* the other day debunking it.'

'Yes,' she said, blushing modestly. 'We were very pleased with that. Then we monitor the fall in dental floss sales around the country. It gives us a sort of heat map for conspiracism, area by area. In London, Shoreditch always comes out hottest, for some reason.'

'Amazing. And can you really just tell them what to believe?'

'Sort of. We know what result we want, but we have to try a lot of things before we find one that really takes hold. That's the art. For instance–' She stopped herself, suddenly wondering if she was going too far. 'No, I can probably tell you about this without giving too much away. One of our targets is a chain of north London fast-food shops. We tried all sorts of stuff about food poisoning and health scares, but what really took off was the idea that it had been taken over by organised crime, and its fries weren't made of potato. In the last two months its customer numbers are down twenty percent, and the police raided it at the weekend.'

'You know, you should really put some of this stuff in your presentation.'

'I talked to a lawyer about it. I sort of want to say it without saying it, if you know what I mean?'

'I suppose so. And yes, I still got the general idea that you could help me. But now I'm starting to think that this could be exactly what I need. It could, in fact, be electoral nitro-glycerine.'

'That's exactly what it is. I mean, we only have three weeks, but also you're only four points behind in the polls. It's absolutely doable.'

'You really think so?' he asked.

'Absolutely,' she said. 'Most people I talk to think Andy Sproat's a pretty good mayor and an okay sort of guy, but he's been around for a while and he's not all that exciting. So people would be up for a change. That's why we'll focus on changing perceptions of him.'

'Make people wonder what's in his fries, so to speak?'

'Exactly. I'll put my best people on it the second you sign the contract – which I just happen to have in my bag.'

38

Jonathon was wishing that he'd never looked in the folder, which detailed exactly what Flock had done to Ken's, at the instigation of Dick C's, including the conspiracy theories they'd tried to spread and how each had performed.

Confessing everything to Nikki was thus no longer an option. Instead he had tucked the folder more securely into the waistband of his trousers and gone back to his desk, where he spent the afternoon in ceaseless worry – and pain. It turned out to be extremely uncomfortable having a thick wodge of paper pressed against his spine and coccyx, and it made his belt cut into his stomach like a knife.

At half-past five, as people began to get up from their desks and go home, his worrying kicked into a higher pitch. He was going to have to make a decision.

The obvious solution – and the one which his brain presented over and over again – was simply not to have looked in the filing cabinet. He'd known he couldn't cope with it. Unfortunately, that was also no longer an option.

Of the options that were on the table, he preferred none of them. He wanted to crawl under the table and just hide there until everything was fine again.

After about ten minutes, he got beyond this, and realised he was doomed.

There was no way he could replace the folder in the filing cabinet: even if his nerves could stand it, his conscience couldn't. His conscience also had a big problem with stealing the folder. He still sometimes started with guilt when he remembered that he'd once shoplifted a packet of Chewits when he was fifteen. He couldn't go through that again. Also, he was the world's unluckiest man: he'd be spotted, arrested and instantly jailed, ruining his career, destroying his relationship and convincing Gemma that all men are criminals.

But what else could he do?

He could feel that his face had gone red, and he was unmistakably dithering, which would draw the attention of the people who hadn't yet gone home. He needed to act now.

Jonathon decided just to lie to himself. Lying was less wrong than stealing, and this was a white lie in any case – and he was its victim, so he wasn't hurting anyone.

He told himself that he hadn't got a folder hidden up his back.

Everything was normal. He just had some serious spine and stomach problems, that was all.

Jonathon waddled stiffly to the door, gave Samantha a tight little smile, and lurched out. Then he toddled rigidly down the stairs and along the corridor, his cheeks burning red, and finally emerged into Borough High Street, and freedom.

39

'Nikki?' Sam asked, putting her head around the office door.

'Yes, Sam?'

'I feel a bit weird about saying this …'

Samantha nervously stepped into Nikki's office.

'You all right, Sam?' said Nikki. 'Sit down. I've got some Hobnobs somewhere.'

'You haven't. Sorry. I pinched them. I was hungover.'

Nikki shook her head in mock disappointment. Then she scooted over on her swivel chair to a small safe, which she unlocked and withdrew the contents: an unopened packet of Hobnobs. She opened it with practised ease, and offered Samantha the two biscuits in the detached top section.

'Can I just say, I am in awe of you,' said Samantha, taking a biscuit.

'Now,' said Nikki, grabbing another biscuit, 'what do you feel weird about saying?'

'Well, you know Fairfax Jonathon Fairfax, the drawing person?'

'Yes.'

'It feels weird to say, because he's really nice, isn't he?'

'He's a sweetie. And I *really* like his drawings.'

'Well ... I think he's stolen a folder.'

'That's all right,' said Nikki through a mouthful of Hobnob. 'I'd be disappointed if people didn't steal the stationery – within reason, of course.'

'No, I mean ... well, he was in the office next door, by the filing cabinets ...'

'When?' Nikki looked alarmed.

'When you were in the meeting room with Teddy Robinson and all the MI people. I came up to pinch a Hobnob from you, and I thought I heard someone, so I looked in, and there he was.'

'What was he doing?'

'He said he was looking for a Post-It and a pen to leave you a note–'

'I didn't get a note,' said Nikki.

'Oh, he did leave you one. I saw him.'

Samantha looked at Nikki's desk, and pointed to the yellow corners of a Post-It peeking out from beneath a half-drunk mug of tea. Nikki picked up the mug and read out the note.

'"Hi Nikki, just wanted to say it's all going fine but let's have a chat or not." What the fuck?'

'Is that what he wrote?' said Samantha. 'That's weird.'

Nikki stared at the note and said nothing.

'I thought that maybe he was hiding something behind his back,' said Samantha, 'but, I mean, I also didn't really think about it, because people don't usually do that, do they?'

'No,' said Nikki. 'They don't.'

'But he's been behaving a bit strangely ever since,' Samantha continued, 'and then when he turned to leave he just ... I mean, he just blatantly had a folder up the back of his jacket. He was trying to walk really straight, so you wouldn't notice it, but ...'

'But it's difficult to hide a folder up the back of your jacket.'

'Yeah.'

There was a silence. Nikki stared again at the note.

Samantha said, 'Do you think he's ... I mean, he's a little bit kind of awkward, in a nice way, anyway. But do you think he's maybe ... having issues? You know, emotionally?'

'Maybe,' said Nikki. She frowned. 'Wait a minute, what am I saying? I don't *care* if he's having issues. I'm calling the police.'

40

Outside on the street, Jonathon instantly felt much better, apart from the pain.

It's over, he thought.

He started walking down Borough High Street, towards London Bridge station. He would go straight to Lance's flat and give him the folder. After all, it looked like it probably busted the case wide open. Lance would like that.

St Christopher's Inn was coming up. Jonathon was feeling so relieved at having got out of Flock that he considered having a celebratory beer. But no, there might be Flock people in there, and if anyone's going to pat you on the back–

Shit.

He stopped dead in the middle of the pavement, causing a tense, bearded man to collapse balletically over him, right himself and continue on his way, absent-mindedly apologising as he went. The thought that had stopped Jonathon was that he had left his wheelie suitcase in the office.

Should he go back for it? He dithered uncomfortably on the pavement. The idea of pressing Flock's buzzer filled him with such fear that he started walking again. He couldn't do it. He just couldn't. His heart would explode and his brain would collapse. His stomach would liquify and his central nervous system would burst into flames. His lungs would wither and his penis would drop off. He really, really couldn't face it.

The alternative was a night in the cheap Finsbury Park hotel that Piper had found, with nothing to read, no T-shirt to sleep in, no change of clothes for tomorrow and no way to clean his teeth.

He could deal with that. He would just buy another toothbrush. Actually, perhaps he should do that here, because the ones for sale in Finsbury Park would probably be made by strange companies with outlandish names that didn't necessarily specialise in making toothbrushes.

Jonathon started forward again, still shaken. It was probably best that he hadn't gone into the pub, because a couple of police had got out of their car and were walking purposefully towards it.

Once again he stopped dead. The police were looking not at the pub, but at him. They were coming to arrest him. He turned and took a step in the opposite direction. No, that would only make it worse. He'd never out-walk them, not with a coccyx as sore as his, and if he started running he would be in a police chase, which was an even more distressing idea than pressing Flock's buzzer. His whole body would fall off.

His face was bright red. He turned again, back towards the police. He was rooted to the spot, unable to take another step.

'Good evening, sir,' said the male officer. He was solid and fattish, with a big, open face. 'All right, are we?'

'Um,' said Jonathon.

'You seem to be having trouble there, sir,' said the female officer, who was slight and girlish, with large glasses. 'Are you feeling okay?'

She said it quite sympathetically, and reached out towards his shoulder. He flinched.

'Have you got something up the back of your jacket there, sir?' she asked, her tone changing slightly.

Wow, he thought. *That was on the nose.*

He felt the blood drain from his head and appear with an uncomfortable fizz in his aching stomach. He looked helplessly from the male to the female officer. She was wearing one of those strange caps with a little peak and turned-up sides, like no other kind of hat worn by any other category of people in the whole of history. How had they settled on that hat?

The female officer raised her eyebrows, and Jonathon realised he still hadn't answered.

'Um, a, um, shirt?' he said.

They looked unimpressed.

'Er,' he added, 'I mean, a ...' What was the point of pretending? They clearly knew. 'A folder,' he concluded.

'Could you show me this folder, please, sir?' said the male officer.

'It's actually really hard to take it out. Could I do it, um, in a ...?' He looked around, as though there might be a little changing booth somewhere on this crowded thoroughfare.

'Just here if you wouldn't mind, sir.'

Jonathon undid his belt and the top button of his trousers, untucked his shirt, and laboriously fumbled the folder out. It was a huge relief to his stomach and back, but the pain had now shifted to his psyche.

'Who does this folder belong to, sir?'

'Um, a company called Flock.'

The two officers exchanged a look.

'And how come it's currently in your possession, sir?'

'I was just ... I, um, wanted to look at it ... a bit? There's this company called Ken's Plucky Fried Chicken ...'

Jonathon had a sense that he was losing his audience.

'Did you remove this item without permission, sir?'

'I, um, I ... Yes. Sort of.'

'Sir,' said the female officer. 'I am arresting you on suspicion of theft of this folder from your employer. You do not have to say anything, but it may harm your defence if you do not mention when questioned ...'

41

The police led Jonathon to their affordable white hatchback, where he waited with the female officer, who introduced herself as Alice. The male officer – Mike – went into Flock and took a statement.

While they were waiting, Alice revealed that they'd actually been heading to Flock, and had only stopped and talked to

Jonathon because he was behaving so oddly. She also cheerfully revealed that they would never normally have attended such an insignificant crime, but they'd just finished dealing with a man smashing up a nearby pub and needed to relax a bit.

When Mike came loping back he gave Alice a thumbs-up and said to Jonathon, 'Okay, mate, what's going to happen now is that we're going to drive you over to a custody suite and get you all booked in, okay?'

'There's nothing to worry about,' said Alice, as though he might be worried about something other than the fact that she had arrested him.

'But what's going to happen?' he asked.

'Just a caution, probably,' she said.

'You won't take me to my house, will you?' he asked, anxiously. 'It's just that we've got someone staying and I don't want her to see that–'

Alice laughed. 'You'll need to get a taxi home. And we won't say anything to anyone, promise.'

Jonathon felt a bit better. He could get through this on his own, then talk to Piper about it once Gemma had gone. He'd lost the best job he'd ever had, and also the evidence Lance needed to bust the case wide open, but these were small considerations compared with Gemma not seeing him brought home in a police car.

They set off and immediately got stuck in traffic, because they were in London. Then, after about an hour – during which Mike and Alice pursued a long-running disagreement about Iggy Pop – the news came in that the custody suite was full, so they'd have to go to a different one, further away.

'If it was up to me, mate,' said Mike, making eye-contact in the mirror, 'I'd just give you a slap on the wrist and leave it at that. But unfortunately, these days, once it's called in and recorded as a crime, we have to take action to show it as a detection. In the old days we were given a bit more leeway with these things, to use our own discretion.'

'Oh,' said Jonathon. 'How come it changed?'

'Targets, I'm afraid, mate. Health and safety. Human rights. Cuts.'

Another hour later, they parked the car and walked Jonathon to a building with a thick grey steel door, propped open with a traffic cone.

Inside, the place was almost completely full of drunk, shirtless men. Were the police, Jonathon wondered, institutionally prejudiced against the shirtless community? Or had the men taken off their shirts to stay cool while they committed crimes? Whichever it was, Jonathon, Mike and Alice were suddenly engulfed in a sea of men who really should have kept their shirts on. Pigeon-chested men strutted about with their hands down the fronts of their trousers. Fat men with shaved heads shouted at each other. Men with tattoos raged and wept, perhaps still upset about the poor quality of their tattoos. There were some women too, but they managed to rage and weep with their shirts on.

When he reached the front of the queue, Jonathon found himself at a grey counter, behind which sat a uniformed middle-aged woman with blonde hair who somehow radiated both friendliness and severity.

'Good evening,' she said, smiling politely. 'Time of arrest, please.'

'Oh, I don't know,' said Jonathon, at exactly the same time as Mike said, 'Seventeen fifty-three.'

'And what is the offence?'

'Theft.'

'Circumstances, please.'

'Briefly, we received information that he had stolen an object from his employer, which was recovered from his person.'

'Okay,' she said, and turned to Jonathon. 'Do you understand why we have arrested yourself?'

'Because of the folder?'

'Was it a folder?' she asked Mike.

'Yes,' he said. 'Caution?'

She nodded and said to Jonathon, 'I'm going to authorise your detention so you can be interviewed and potentially cautioned regarding this information the police have received, which gives yourself the opportunity to give an explanation.'

She then got him to stand against a wall so she could see how tall he was, asked him how he felt, whether he wanted to read their code of practice and if he self-harmed. He seemed to harm himself all the time, but decided this was probably not the place to discuss it. After that, he said goodbye to Mike and Alice, handed over his wallet and keys, then went off to have his photo taken by a woman in a blue shirt, who put a cotton bud in his mouth and then dropped it in a little plastic tube. With this done, she walked him to a little room, through a small crowd of shirtless men arguing about cigarettes.

'They was my fucking fags, you wanker!' shouted one of the shirtless men to another.

'They was not your fags!' bellowed another shirtless man, investing the line with all the passion of grand opera.

'Would you like anything to eat?' asked the woman in the blue shirt.

Jonathon suddenly realised how hungry he was. 'Yes, please,' he said.

'I've got a menu, but everyone has the chicken curry.'

'Oh, yes. Chicken curry, please, if that's all right. How much is it?'

'On the house, love,' she said. 'We've got your wallet, remember?'

She locked the heavy blue steel door behind her, leaving him alone with a plastic mattress, a blanket, and a blue rectangle which was either a swimming float or a pillow. To one side was a separate section where a metal toilet lurked. It was, he had to acknowledge, a cell.

Once the chicken curry arrived, he sat with it on the plastic mattress and got down to a concentrated spell of feeling absolutely awful. How did he end up constantly engulfed by disaster, when he spent literally every minute of every day entirely dedicated to avoiding disaster?

And how could he have let such minor things – Lance's suspicion of a chicken shop, a local journalist calling him 'Hanky Boy', a desire to avoid telling a pleasant receptionist that he'd looked in a filing cabinet – get him arrested? Would the caution stay on his criminal record forever? Was he going to spend the rest of his life explaining it? Would he manage to conceal it from Gemma? Would Piper understand? Or was he going to have to start digging that shallow hole? He suddenly desperately wanted to see her. He wanted to be at home doing the washing up, chatting to her as he watched her unconsciously doing the head-and-shoulders part of a complex dance routine while she made them a cup of tea.

When the door opened about half an hour later, he was still sitting in exactly the same position, the plastic forkful of chicken curry poised halfway to his mouth. In walked the woman who'd been behind the counter, smiling in an apologetic way.

'Good evening, Mr Fairfax. You all right? Now, unfortunately, this one has come up as a Control Strategy crime, so–'

'What's a Control Strategy crime?'

'It's a type of crime that the Home Office has set as one of the current priorities for the respective area. In this case, theft from commercial premises. So, unfortunately, on this occasion, we will need to charge yourself.'

'Charge myself?' said Jonathon, flinching so violently that the uneaten chicken curry draped itself evenly over the whole of his top half.

'I'm afraid so, sir. I'm ever so sorry about this.'

'But Mike and Alice said I'd just be cautioned.'

Oh god. Now the nightmare scenario of just five seconds ago had become an unattainable Eden. He was a criminal.

'I do realise that,' she said, 'and like I said, we're really sorry. There's an anti-theft initiative on just now, so our custody computer says cautions are not to be issued – discretion's overruled in this case. And we do have to get the detection for our figures.'

'Oh.'

She took a step closer and put her head on one side sympathetically. Was she going to turn a blind eye? Perhaps she would say, *Just get out of here, you scamp, before I change my mind.*

'You've had a bit of an accident with your chicken curry,' she advised him, confidentially.

'I ... It ... Yes,' he agreed. He was wearing the chicken curry like a saucy shawl covering his entire upper body.

'Tell you what,' she said, 'let me get you a bag, and you can put your, er, soiled clothes in there. I'll find you something clean to wear from the box. Then you can see the magistrate in the morning and get everything sorted out.'

'But will I get a criminal record?'

'I can't lie to you, sir. You probably will. I mean, you have already admitted taking the folder, which you really shouldn't have done, and we have recovered the evidence. So just explain it all to the duty solicitor at the magistrates' tomorrow, and they'll advise you how to proceed. All right?'

'Um, right.'

'Lovely,' she said, and smiled a bright, tired smile. 'Someone will pop in with that bag in a minute or two.'

And then she walked back out of the cell, into the cream-walled reception area, where the shouting of the shirtless men continued.

About an hour later, after Jonathon had been given a plastic bag and a colossal striped T-shirt, a different policeman walked into the cell. Jonathon tried to adjust the T-shirt and the blanket around his shoulders to look more respectable, patted his bag of curried smart-casual clothes, and smoothed down the hair that stuck up at the back of his head.

'Mr Fairfax?' said the policeman, looking at a form on a clipboard. 'Theft?'

'Um, yes.'

'What's your living situation, then?'

'Um, I'm meant to be in a hotel tonight, just for–'

'Been thrown out, have we?' said the policeman, sympathetically.

'Sort of. I mean, not really. It's just for a couple of days. We've got–'

'What's the address of this hotel, then?' said the policeman, his attention diverted for a moment by a loud shout of 'You don't even smoke fucking Bensons!'

'I, um, I don't know,' admitted Jonathon.

'Okay,' said the policeman, glancing out through the cell door in the direction of some extremely distracting screaming. 'You have a rest here tonight, Mr Fairfax, and we'll get you in front of a magistrate first thing, see what he says. All right?'

'If you think that's best,' said Jonathon. His stomach seemed to drop out of him, as though it had been jettisoned at high altitude.

'No problem, mate,' said the policeman in his distracted way. He looked again in the direction of the screaming, muttered, 'Christ', then gave Jonathon a brief, tired smile and hurried out of the cell. The door clanked shut behind him.

42

Piper dialled the French number Rachel had given her and waited. She was sitting on the sofa, the dog's head resting in her lap. On the arm of the chair sat the cat, watching her like a television.

'Oui, allô?'

Oh, a French person. Piper hadn't expected that.

'Bonjour,' she said, trying to rapidly relearn French. 'Rachel est … là? S'il vous plaît?'

'Piper!' said Rachel. 'Nice emergency French. How's it going? How's Gemma?'

'Gemma's fine. I think. She's gone to bed. Or at least she's gone to Jonathon's office, where we set up the bed for her.'

'How are you? You sound a bit …'

'A bit what?'

'I don't know. Are you okay?'

'I'm sort of okay. Except probably not, because I'm a bit worried. Jonathon isn't answering his phone, and I feel really guilty about asking him to move out while Gemma's here. It's his house as well. And I don't think it was even a good idea for Gemma: it probably just reinforces the idea that men aren't to be trusted. And Jonathon isn't a criminal.'

'Yeah, totally. I've been thinking about that too, and I think I made a mistake. I should have just been, "No, Jonathon lives here." But instead I was, "Well, I'll ask them." It was just that Gemma had a proper, proper meltdown, which is just totally not her – or it didn't used to be. She called me in tears and just said, "Will you come and pick me up?" I was … quite flattered, really. And I thought it'd just be for one night.'

'You did the right thing,' said Piper. 'I mean, we were all playing it by ear.'

'I hope so. Thanks for taking her in. I'm totally still coming back on Saturday, like I said, and I've managed to get Monday to Wednesday off too, so I hope that's enough time to sort it out. Are we still taking her to the Notting Hill Carnival on Sunday? I can do it on my own, if you want?'

'No, I'd like to be there. It's just … is it okay if I ask Jonathon too? And I want him to come back home as well, tomorrow.'

'Of course. Yeah, do that. Where's he staying tonight? At a friend's?'

'No, he was too embarrassed to ask and he worries about getting in the way, so he booked an extremely cheap hotel next to Finsbury Park – kind of worryingly cheap, actually, now I think about it.'

'A *Finsbury Park* hotel? Yes, totally get him back.'

'I don't know why he isn't answering his phone. He's never done that before. I'm worried that he's really upset about the whole thing. I really shouldn't have asked him – I thought he'd stay with Lance and it might be quite fun. But, I don't know, he hasn't really recovered from … well, all the weird things that have happened to him.'

'I know why you're worried, Piper. But you do know, don't you, that he's probably just left his phone somewhere, or forgotten it's on silent?'

'That's true! He does that. He does that. That's probably what it is.'

'Everything's going to be okay,' said Rachel.

Piper felt a huge weight drop from her on hearing those words.

'It is, isn't it?' she said. 'Can you come and live in my head? I could do with hearing that about a hundred times a day.'

'Maybe. What's the rent like there?'

'Very reasonable. There isn't much room though. And the place is full of absolute shit.'

'Difficult commute to France as well, so I'm going to have to

144

pass.'

There was a little silence, then Rachel said, 'Hey, really, thanks a lot for taking Gemma.'

'Actually, one of the reasons … I mean, I wanted to help anyway, but also I've been thinking about … about whether to talk to Jonathon about maybe … having a baby?'

'Oh. Wow.'

'So I wanted to put it to the teenager test. Because babies turn into teenagers, I've heard. And so …'

'How's that looking now?'

'I'm not sure. I mean, I'm a lot younger than her parents. So, I thought she might see me as … well, as a cool and relatable young adult. But the more time I spend with her, the more I think she sees me as a slightly unhinged old lady. And she's probably right.'

'I'm sure she doesn't. And I wouldn't go by what Gemma's like right now anyway. If it's any consolation, *I* totally see you as a cool and relatable young adult.'

'Thanks, Rachel. God, I feel so much better for this conversation. Everything really is going to be okay, isn't it? It always is, and I always forget.'

Thursday

43

Jonathon sat awake all night, staring at the steel door as the voices of the shirtless ones dwindled and finally grew still. Silence filled the void, punctuated by the soft murmurs of the desk officers asking where the bloody keys were.

He had made a terrible, terrible, terrible mistake, and was an unbearably awful person. He owed it to Piper to get out of her life so she could be with the sort of man she deserved – the sort you see in adverts, with rolled-up sleeves and a ready smile, who could really handle a barbecue.

Eventually, the birds began their serenade, faint through the thick glass panels in the latticed window high on the wall, and the grey light stole in. Then Jonathon was put in a van by a pair of tired policemen, and – accompanied by many barely conscious shirtless men – driven to a different place, where he was locked in a different cell. They let him keep the blue blanket and T-shirt though, which was something.

After more sitting and staring, he eventually found himself in a windowless office with harsh strip lighting and old grey carpet tiles.

'Mr Fallfax,' said a greasy-haired man in a shabby suit, shuffling through a stack of papers.

'Um, Fairfax. Yes. Hello.'

'Fairfax, yes. Sorry. I'm Mr Last, one of the duty solicitors – actually, the only duty solicitor today. Now, I'm paid at public expense,' he continued, as though slipping into a script, 'but I work for you. I'm a fully qualified solicitor in the firm of Marshbank

Weakins Helmroyd. You're probably asking yourself, Mr Fairfall, what's the difference between a duty solicitor and a reputable high-street solicitor? Well, there isn't one! We're exactly the same people. And that's why my clients here often engage me subsequently on a private basis. Does that make sense?'

'Yes. Could I just–'

'Absolutely. Now, I see that you're up for, er, stealing a folder, so obviously you don't have much to worry about. However, even the smallest–'

At that moment the door opened and a harried-looking bearded man looked in, a security pass hanging over his crumpled shirt and tie.

'Mr Last, could you by any chance attend the waiting area outside Court Three? We've got a gentleman there kicking off somewhat. A Mr Deripaska?'

Mr Last looked at the bearded man, then down at the papers in front of him. He grimaced, stood, and started packing the papers into his briefcase.

'I do apologise, Mr Farfall. As I said, the other duty solicitor didn't turn up this morning, so I'm looking after the whole court on my own. I'll just be' – he looked at his watch – 'five minutes. And then you'll have my undivided attention.'

Mr Last hurried out of the room, and Jonathon was left alone with some muted shouting. After an indeterminate amount of time he was taken back to the cell, and then back up to a corridor, where he found Mr Last waiting outside a door.

Mr Last nodded at him, and said to the harried-looking bearded man at the door, 'Number twelve. Failfax.'

The bearded man consulted his clipboard and said, 'Hold on.'

They waited there while people milled around. Jonathon had no idea whether they were staff, witnesses, victims of crime, relatives or criminals. Everyone looked like they belonged in at least two of those categories. There was a black-clad security guard at the door with a strikingly villainous face. There was a kindly-looking woman in a blazer who kept smiling hesitantly at people. There was a chubby teenager trying out moody and aggressive slouching. There was a short, tough-looking woman with a neck tattoo and an air of authority. The only people Jonathon could confidently identify were the lawyers, who were either nervous and greasy, like the one standing beside him, or sleek and immaculately groomed, like living yachts.

The door opened and a sprightly, clean-cut young man in a smart suit and glasses came out, took off his glasses and burst into tears. After him came a woman in a floral skirt, then a sleek, suited woman, then a squat older man.

'Go on,' the bearded man told Mr Last. He held the door open and ushered them in, thereby outing himself as an usher.

The bearded man showed Jonathon into a wooden booth with thick glass windows, taking up one wall of a large room with ceiling tiles, strip lights and no windows. To Jonathon's left, by the entrance, was an area of tiered tip-up seats. Just ahead of him were three rows of desks that seemed to be a combination of office, meeting area and typing pool. And to his right, at the end of the room, raised a couple of feet above everything else, were two long benches. At the lower bench sat a nondescript middle-aged man, and at the upper bench sat an oldish man with short, white hair and a very pink face.

Jonathon was surprised that the pink-faced man didn't have a little wooden hammer, and that no one was wearing robes or wigs. The pink-faced man was peering at a computer monitor, apparently scrolling through a list, searching for something. Mr Last was hurriedly looking through some folders in his briefcase. A sleek, suited man with a magnificent head of hair was standing up, contemplating the desk in front of him. A woman sitting over by the far wall was typing something hurriedly and looking annoyed. Two beautiful suited women were having a whispered conversation at a table. And, among the tiered seats at the back, people were squeezing past each other, arriving and leaving.

Jonathon found himself staring at the British government's logo on the end wall, above the words *Magistrates' Court*. He quite liked it, though it wasn't what he would have chosen himself: a shield held by a lion and a unicorn, with a French motto underneath. It was as though some marketing experts had decided that the British government's branding should emphasise that it was obsolete, predatory, fanciful and alien.

The pink-faced man glanced up and said conversationally, in a pleasant Irish burr, 'Your name and date of birth?'

Jonathon told him, and the pink-faced man murmured, 'Thank you,' and resumed scrolling through his list.

'Address?' the pink-face man remarked.

'Do you mean the b-and-b?' Jonathon said. 'I can't quite remember the address.'

The pink-faced man nodded. After a while he added, in his pleasant conversational tone, 'May you be seated.'

Jonathon sat down.

The sleek man with magnificent hair said off-handedly, 'May I run through the facts, sir?'

The pink-faced man nodded at him with a sort of defensive gratitude, as though he simultaneously wanted to convey that he had all the facts, and that he was glad to be helped out because he'd completely lost his place in the document on his computer and had no idea what was going on.

'Theft of documents and intangible property,' said the sleek man. 'Police found them concealed beneath his clothing. No clear statement. No fixed abode.'

The pink-faced man peered and scrolled a bit more. Some people at the back of the room realised they were in the wrong place and squeezed out while some others squeezed in. 'What are you pleading?' he asked, in a tone of polite curiosity, glancing again at Jonathon.

'Um, I'm not quite sure yet,' said Jonathon. He would be able to work that out once the hearing started. Probably someone would bring in a small wooden hammer, possibly a wig or two, everyone would stand up, and then they could sort it all out. He would also be able to explain why he was wearing an oversized T-shirt and carrying a blanket and a small bag of curried clothes.

The pink-faced man said to the sleek man, 'To reappear at this court on August twenty-eighth, to enter a plea. In view of the flight risk presented by his residential status, in the meantime he will be remanded in custody.' He turned to Jonathon and said, 'Mr Fairfax, thank you.'

Mr Last packed his folders away and stood up. Jonathon stood too. It was only once he'd left the booth that he began to wonder whether the hearing might actually be over, instead of just about to begin. He looked around: everyone was doing exactly what they'd been doing from the start. People were squeezing in and out of the tiered seats, the annoyed-looking woman was finishing some typing, the sleek man was standing in a pose of concentrated ease and the pink-faced man was scrolling.

The court, it seemed, had only one mode – muted preliminaries – whereas Jonathon had been conditioned by television to expect clearly-signalled drama. Why had no one said, 'I put it to you, Mr Fairfax, that you did, on or about the afternoon of the ninth …'? Why hadn't an unconventional young defence lawyer shouted, 'Objection, your honour!' in an impassioned tone? Why hadn't there been a stern judge saying forcefully, 'May I remind you, sir, this is a *court* of *law*'? Instead, he felt like he'd just ambled into someone's office and sat quietly in the corner while they went about their business.

'Why on earth didn't you enter a plea?' said Mr Last, irritatedly. 'You could have saved yourself remand and–' Last was tapped on the shoulder by another harried-looking man with a pass round his neck, and hurried off.

'Nicely played,' said the bearded man. 'Bought yourself a few hot meals.'

Jonathon was ushered towards the door. It was all very bewildering, but at least he would now get to go home and have one of those hot meals the bearded man had confusingly mentioned. He would have a bit of time to think about his plea and find a lawyer. Did he get one free? Would he have to pay? He shuddered to think how much it might cost, and wondered whether he could extend his overdraft enough to pay for it. Piper and Lance would know what to do.

He felt awful. He would do whatever official things he needed to do here, then go home, explain it to Piper, eat, try to get a bit of sleep, and think about it properly later on, when his brain might be working a bit better.

Outside the courtroom door, a security guard rudely

handcuffed himself to Jonathon and took them both downstairs.

'Um, what do I need to do now?' asked Jonathon.

'Just wait in here,' said the guard, showing him into a cell with cream-painted brick walls and a wooden bench at one end.

After a bit, the door was unlocked and a harried-looking bearded man came in with some forms and asked Jonathon's name, age and weight.

Jonathon really wished he'd been taught how all this worked. At every school he'd been to, 'What to do when you're arrested' would have been a much more useful lesson than almost anything else on the curriculum.

About fifteen minutes later, the door was unlocked again and a woman casually handcuffed herself to him and walked him out to a long white van with little black windows. They got on, and she took him to a tiny cubicle with a single window and not enough room for a person's legs. Here the short woman detached herself.

'Do you need my address?' he asked, feeling nervous and confused.

'What for?' she said.

'To take me home?'

This struck her as amusing. 'You're dreaming, love. This is the bus for Flintwinch.'

'Flintwinch? But that's a prison. I haven't been sentenced. He let me out on remand.'

'You don't get *let out* on remand, you get *put in* on remand,' she explained patiently, locking him into his little cubicle.

'But–' he said.

'I can't stand around chatting,' she said, and got off the bus.

44

Nikki thought carefully about the way Teddy had been looking at her, and decided to put her feminist principles aside and play the damsel-in-distress card. On balance, it seemed the least risky option.

He answered on the first ring, which was a good sign.

'Nikki!' he said. 'To what do I owe this pleasure?'

'Hi, Teddy,' she said. 'This is a bit embarrassing, given that you're a valued client and all that. But, well, basically I'm calling to ask for your help. It's not a big thing, and of course feel free to say no, but you could be a real life-saver here.'

'I always leap at the chance to save a life – and I'd be honoured to save yours, Nikki. Of course I'd be delighted to help, if I can. *Delighted*. Though naturally it depends slightly on what the problem is.'

'Well, do you remember when you came in on Tuesday, I introduced you to an illustrator who's been working here?'

'Refresh my memory?'

'Thin-ish? Shy? Looks a tiny bit like the Cat in the Hat?'

'Oh yes, I do vaguely recall someone of that description.'

'The thing is that he's stolen a folder relating to one of our targets.'

'Is it about your work for me?' His tone changed in an instant. He sounded suddenly cold and suspicious.

Oh god, she thought. *Have I misjudged this? Maybe he doesn't fancy me* that *much.*

'No,' she said. 'I can categorically say it's nothing about you, Teddy. I came in early this morning, went through everything and worked out exactly what he took. It's one folder, dealing with one target. You're not involved.'

There was a moment's silence, and then he said, 'Nearly gave me a heart attack there. Go on.'

'I'm sorry, Teddy.'

'How much is he asking for?'

'It's more complicated than that. So, Sam – you remember Sam, on reception – she told me she'd seen him walk out the office with a folder hidden up the back of his jacket. And I just immediately called the police.'

'Well, quite right.'

'And then I was heading out to hunt him down, because you do *not* steal from me – except in small quantities from the stationery cupboard, but–'

'Fiery temperament: a good quality. You're a thoroughbred.'

Fine, she thought. *It's fine. If the price of his help is being compared to a horse, then so be it.*

'But on the stairs I bumped into a policeman, who said he'd come to take a statement. Said they'd already apprehended a suspect. I told him what had happened, he filled in some forms, and then he went off.'

'Excellent. Exactly the kind of efficiency you'd hope for in the Met.'

'Well, yes, but exactly *not* the efficiency you come to expect if you've ever dealt with them before. I mean, the policeman said they'd been dealing with an incident in a pub nearby, but still … they were there within minutes. And now they've got my folder, and I can't find out how to get it back. So I'm thinking, is something going on here?'

'What? Are you saying the police are in cahoots with this … illustrator?'

'I don't know what to think. I mean, I know I'm in the conspiracy-theory business, but stuff *does* go on.'

'Hmm. Which of your targets features in the folder?'

Should I tell him? she wondered. *It's a breach of client confidentiality, which is not a great thing to do, and maybe he'll see that as a bad sign. But then opening up to him might flatter his ego.*

'It was a chain of north London chicken shops,' she said. 'The one I mentioned at lunch yesterday, actually: Ken's Plucky Fried Chicken.'

'Perhaps they found out what you're up to and sent him in as a mole?'

'As in, an undercover agent? I can't believe he would do that. He just doesn't seem the type. He has this massive portfolio of animals wearing clothes: you wouldn't do that just to give yourself cover. Plus he's really good at it. I was looking forward to warming the brand up a bit with some illustration.'

'So what do you think's going on?'

'I don't know,' said Nikki. 'It doesn't make any sense. If I hadn't called the police, I'd have been able to talk to him and find out what's going on, or at least get a feel for it. I've got his mobile number, but he's not answering. So now I'm thinking, what are the options? I'm getting nowhere with the police ...'

'So what can I do?'

'Well, I was wondering if you could reach out to some members of your shadowy secret society ...'

She held her breath. She'd thought that making a joke of it would help, but now it seemed a risky move.

'By which you presumably mean Etonians?' he said, sounding not at all offended.

Nikki felt a wave of relief run through her.

'Exactly,' she said. 'And just see if you can find out, you know, where the folder is.'

Teddy sighed.

'Just say if I'm asking too much,' said Nikki. 'It's just, the last thing I need is this huge distraction when I'm trying to throw the kitchen sink at Project Teddy.'

She held her breath again and crossed her fingers.

'All right, all right,' he said. 'Leave it with me. I'll see what I can do. What's his name?'

45

Jonathon had only ever seen these streets as a free man. Now he was being driven through them, on a sunny August morning, in a prison van. He'd cycled this way only a couple of months ago, past these comforting old houses with their crumbling Victorian plaster scrolls, as though the builders had really wanted to make Greek temples and had only reluctantly agreed not to.

They passed a cafe where he'd stopped with a puncture, and he suddenly felt an overwhelming yearning for a time when his biggest problem had been the amount of air in a tube. Even his problems of two hours ago now had an aura of almost unbearable nostalgia. Two hours ago he hadn't been going to prison.

At length, they reached a high, featureless wall and drove alongside it until they reached a high, featureless gate, which eventually opened, swallowing them. They drove into a yard full of little temporary buildings. Above them loomed a colossal brick structure, like a Victorian fortress or factory – or prison.

Jonathon was last off the bus. He was taken to one of the little temporary buildings, which, like all little temporary buildings, looked like it had been there for several decades. Inside, the peeling cream walls were lined with benches. Most of the men sitting on the benches kept their heads down and stared at their feet. But three of them were leaning back in a relaxed way, as though they prisoned recreationally. Jonathon sat down quickly and tried to become one of the foot-starers.

'Yo,' said a voice.

Jonathon made himself not look up. After all, the voice could have been saying 'Yo' to anyone, even though he was certain it was saying 'Yo' to him. After four seconds, he heard the voice again.

'Yo, you with the hair sticking up and the giant T-shirt! What you in for?'

Jonathon looked up. The man had a huge black beard, short hair, glasses, and a lower jaw that was thrust forward in an aggressive yet relaxed way. He wore a bright white sweatshirt and a pair of very large, very thick and very new jeans, along with trainers so new and white that it seemed they could not possibly be on his feet, but must surely be still in their box, or perhaps even waiting in a sterile pre-boxing area in a very clean factory.

'Um,' said Jonathon, 'I stole a folder.'

'You stole a *folder*?' said the man, loading the word with the maximum possible amount of incredulity and contempt. 'That is *weak*, man. What you get?'

'Just, um, some bits of paper. I mean they've taken it back now, so nothing, really. Except I did find out–'

'No, how long is your *stretch*, man?'

'Oh, I haven't been sentenced yet.'

'Seriously? You're in here on *remand*, for *stealing a folder*? That is not how the system's supposed to work, bruv. My cousin's in on remand, but he's an armed robber and he never turns up at court.'

Another of the relaxed new prisoners – a solid man with a square head – chimed in. 'Mate, you do *not* go to prison on remand for stealing a fucking folder. What you really in for?'

This second man was performing confident, relaxed ease so thoroughly that he gave the impression of being in an invisible sauna, his legs wide apart.

'It really is just the folder,' said Jonathon, blushing. 'I didn't realise the hearing had started, so I've got to go back to court in three weeks to plead–'

'Wait, you haven't even entered a *plea* yet?' said the man with the huge beard, laughing exaggeratedly and shaking out one hand. 'Bruv, what is *wrong* with you?'

'I don't really know,' said Jonathon uncomfortably. 'Weird things just happen to me.'

The third of the relaxed men spoke up. He was relaxed in a twitchier way than the other two, and had blond-brown hair and waxy skin, like white chocolate. His eyes were open slightly wider than most people find comfortable, and he didn't blink.

'How come your top and bottom don't match?' he asked, moving his head in a disconcerting way. 'Bottom half office, top half homeless. You a spy?'

Jonathon tried to smooth down the hair at the back of his head, which, after a worried night on a blue plastic pillow, was doing its thing.

'No, I spilled, um, chicken curry on my top half, so they put it in this bag' – he held up the bag – 'and gave me a T-shirt.'

'An absolutely fucking massively gigantic T-shirt,' confirmed the man with the beard.

'Yes,' agreed Jonathon.

At this moment the door opened and a prison officer entered who could have been an end-of-level boss in a video game. He was wide and tattooed, with a shaved head and tiny eyes.

'Hamilton!' he called.

The relaxed twitchy man sat offensively still for three seconds, looking at the prison officer with his unnerving eyes, then got to his feet and walked across the room like a cowboy, hands six inches from his hips and shoulder blades well back. Just before he reached the door, he glanced back at Jonathon, opened his eyes even wider, and mouthed, 'Spy'. It was perhaps the scariest thing that anyone had ever mouthed at him.

After that, they were each called in turn, with Jonathon again being last. He walked fearfully through the door to the end-of-level boss.

'Right, Fairfax,' said the boss. 'You're here on remand until your next court hearing in three weeks. Do you understand that?'

'Um, yes. But I think there's been a mistake because–'

'Because you're innocent? Oh dear me. Seems like we've accidentally filled a whole prison with people who shouldn't be here.'

The boss gave him a sarcastic stare, then said, 'Look, just get on with it, all right? This your first time inside?'

Jonathon nodded.

'Then just keep your head down, trust no one and don't make any trouble. All right?'

Jonathon nodded.

'Good lad. And stay out of debt: it's all charged double bubble, which means you pay back twice what you borrow – or else.'

The boss took Jonathon's bag of curried clothes and put them in a storage box. Then he photographed Jonathon and gave him a prison number. After a few minutes in a holding cell, Jonathon was taken to a booth and told to undress, then immediately get dressed again, because they'd decided not to look up his bottom. For the first time in many hours, Jonathon felt a tiny bit pleased.

He had a very quick medical examination with a nurse, and then several prison officers in a row asked him about his mental health, any prejudices he might have, and how he felt about sharp objects and arson. After that, he was given a toothbrush, some toothpaste, an exhausted towel, a plastic bag with some tea and biscuits in it, and a piece of paper with a code number on it.

'This is your two-pound emergency phone credit,' said one of the officers, 'for calling anyone in the next twenty-four hours. I'd strongly advise you to use it immediately.'

There was a severely wounded blue phone clinging to the cream wall, so Jonathon went over and dialled the only phone number he knew by heart. Luckily, it was Piper's.

'Hello?' she said. It was her voice, her miraculous voice, sounding like she did when she answered the phone to someone she didn't know.

'Gub,' he managed, after quite an effort to speak. It wasn't at all what he'd meant to say.

'Jonathon?' she said.

'Hello, Piper. I–'

'Jonathon, why didn't you call me back last night? Where are you?'

'I'm in prison.' He instantly felt there must be a better way to say this.

'What?' she asked, quite sensibly.

'I'm afraid I've gone to prison,' he said.

'*How?*' she said. Packed into that one word was all her incredulity and care for him and his desperately unlikely and inconvenient nature.

'It's a bit difficult to explain. I got embarrassed about a folder, and one thing led to another, and then I got arrested. I'm on remand till my next court hearing in three weeks. I can have visits, if you'd like to come.'

'*If* I'd like to–?' He could hear tears building in her voice, but she calmed herself down. 'Yes, I'd like to come,' she said evenly. 'But this can't be happening. Has this got something to do with Lance?'

Some beeps sounded, which probably meant time was nearly up.

'I love you, Piper,' he said, glancing behind him in case anyone heard.

'I–'

And then there was that uncanny silence which happens when a phone reverts to being just a piece of plastic, inert and dead, no longer breathing the words and silences of another person.

He held it for a few seconds, then put it back on its peg.

After that he was taken to another room in which there was nothing, and he was told to wait there until someone was free to take him to the wing.

The wing. Oh god.

He was going to a wing. He'd never been to a wing before.

After a while standing in the nothing, thinking of Piper and wondering if he was going to faint, the door opened. A very young female prison officer appeared with a huge bunch of keys and led him into a corridor. She looked at him sympathetically. He saw in her eyes the impulse to say something reassuring and then draw a blank, as though there was nothing reassuring that could possibly be said. They walked in silence down the cream corridor. This was the last bit of the scruffy temporary building. At the end of it was a Victorian stone doorway leading into the fortress-cum-factory.

'Good luck,' said the officer, with a worried smile. Then she unlocked the heavy blue steel door and he stepped through.

46

'Teddy!' said Nikki, answering the phone. 'That was quick.'

'Right, well, I asked around. A man I KO'd in my youthful boxing days is now fairly senior in the Justice Ministry, and he looked it all up on their system. This Fairfax character is on remand in HMP Flintwinch, having been arrested for theft.'

'What? *Prison?* Already? Remind me what remand means.'

'It means he's being held there pending a trial. The indications are that he refused to enter a plea.'

'But isn't Flintwinch where they send murderers? I thought you went to a different place if you're just waiting to be tried.'

'Apparently Flintwinch is the local prison for a few magistrates' courts, as well as being a Category-B prison for pretty serious crimes. So that's where those courts send people, whether they're sentenced or on remand.'

'Bloody hell. I don't suppose he said anything about my folder, did he?'

'He said there's no way he'd be able to find out where it is. But the custody suite that processed him should have put it in a secure facility.'

'What's a custody suite?'

'No idea, I'm afraid. Part of a police station?'

'Did he say which one had dealt with Jonathon?'

'No. Sorry.'

'Okay. Thanks for all this, Teddy.' She made a rapid mental calculation of pros and cons and then added, 'You're my hero.'

'Oh, pish-pash. Anything for a friend.'

'I'm just trying to work out what it means.'

'Well, I suppose it means you don't have your folder, but neither do they – whoever *they* are.'

'Unless *they* are the police. This feels even more like something's going on, doesn't it? He takes the folder and now suddenly it's lost and he's in prison. The thing about making up conspiracy theories for a living is that it gives you a nose for the signs of a genuine conspiracy.'

'And what a nose it is. I still can't help wondering whether all this has something to do with me. I mean, the timing alone …'

Again, Nikki made a rapid calculation. If it had something to do with him, that might make him cautious about doing business with her. But it would also give him an extra reason to help.

'Maybe it has,' she said. 'I mean, how come he was there in the corridor when we came out of our meeting?'

'We should talk about this, Nikki. And after all this drama, you're probably in need of a bit of … comforting. Perhaps the highly strung thoroughbred needs a drink?'

47

The noise of the place slammed through Jonathon's body: it sounded like a huge swimming pool full of toddlers screaming with adult-sized lungs. Then the smell drove into his stomach: an oily-weedy fragrance with notes of stale sweat and powerful disinfectant. Finally, the look of it punched him hard in the eyes.

He was standing in a cream-painted brick hall the size of a large cathedral. The walls were dotted with recessed blue steel doors – on ground level and along the two storeys of open walkways above. There were nets in the spaces between the walkways, and the red floor beneath his feet stretched off towards a set of metal stairs at the end, where the organ would have been if this were a cathedral and not a prison.

'Fairfax!'

Jonathon spun around.

'Finally,' said a thickset middle-aged man in a tracksuit. 'I've said it three times. Didn't you hear me?'

Jonathon shook his head.

'Bit distracting, eh?' said the thickset man, gesturing at the brutal cathedral with a biro. He held a clipboard in his other hand.

Jonathon nodded.

'You on remand, yeah?'

Jonathon nodded.

'What for?'

'I STOLE A FOLDER!' Jonathon shouted, more loudly than he'd meant. It was difficult to judge what volume to speak at, with all the screaming.

'All right, mate. Keep your hair on.'

'Sorry.'

'Remand for stealing a folder though. That's not how the system's supposed to work.'

'I know. Everyone keeps saying. I didn't realise the hearing had started.'

'Anyway,' said the man, 'I'm Jason, your friendly local induction orderly. Let me see if I can find you a cell with someone who won't kill you on your first night.'

'Oh,' said Jonathon, 'thanks very much.'

Jason disappeared into a crowd of terrifying men – each approaching the business of being terrifying from a completely different angle. Some looked terrifyingly strong, others terrifyingly unhinged, and still others terrifyingly normal. Jonathon lost himself in a fearful internal debate about which approach was most effective.

'Fairfax!'

'Waagh!' said Jonathon, spinning around.

It was Jason again.

'Pay attention, mate. This is not a great environment for getting lost in thought.'

'Sorry,' said Jonathon.

'I've found you a berth. Follow me.'

Jason set off, moving through the terrifying crowd as though he were striding through a suburban shopping centre. Jonathon followed him all the way down the hall to the staircase, which they climbed, waiting politely at the top for a man to finish doing a set of tricep dips on the handrails.

When they reached a cell marked D3-27 a waiting prison officer unlocked the door and Jonathon stepped inside.

BANG! went the door behind him.

Jonathon flinched. His ears started to ring.

He'd been expecting Jason and the prison officer to come in with him. Instead, he found himself alone in a tiny space with another man.

The cell – about one Jonathon wide and two Jonathons long – was painted cream, flaking slightly and covered in a rash of graffiti, as though it suffered from an allergic reaction to prisoners. At the far end was a toilet with no seat and no privacy – exactly like the ones in Jonathon's anxiety dreams. Above it, high up, was a barred window composed of many small panes of thick glass, some of them missing. Against the left wall was a narrow metal bunk bed, and against the right wall stood a sink, a slim table, a plastic chair and a small set of shelves.

On the lower bunk was the cell's other occupant. It was the man with the big black beard and glasses who had talked to him in the waiting room. Or rather, it was a man with his face and body, but now hunched over and wearing a grey prison-issue tracksuit. The jutted jaw and aggressive crackle were gone. He looked up at Jonathon, muttered, 'All right,' and went back to rummaging in a big plastic bag.

'Oh, hello.' Jonathon didn't think he'd ever been so pleased to see a quite threatening man before. In this context it felt like he was an old friend. 'My name's Jonathon.'

'That's nice for you,' said the man, not looking up.

Jonathon stood there hesitantly, holding his bag of biscuits, his thin towel, his toothbrush and toothpaste. Somewhere nearby a person was kicking a cell door over and over again, someone else was using their cell walls as a subwoofer for an incredibly loud stereo, and another person was screaming angrily about something.

'Which bunk do you er …?' said Jonathon.

'Obviously I've got the bottom,' said the man, again not looking up.

Jonathon, who felt he'd had prison dropped on him from a great height, nonetheless felt a tiny glimmer of joy at this. Despite his age, he still felt a bit excited at the idea of sleeping in the top bunk, having only done it once or twice as a child, and remembering it as being like glamorously sleeping in the sky.

There was no ladder, so he awkwardly climbed the end of the bunk, and sat on the thin blue plastic mattress.

'Will we get sheets and blankets?' he ventured.

The black-bearded man didn't answer. He was putting the contents of his plastic bag on the shelves by the bed.

Jonathon sat there on the hard blue mattress, holding a gossamer-thin towel and staring at the blue steel door. It seemed strange that it had no handle.

And then, at that very moment, nothing happened.

And nothing happened. And nothing happened again. And nothing continued to happen, over and over. A hard blue mattress, the world's thinnest towel, a man he couldn't see who was no longer putting objects on a shelf, and nothing else. Nothing and nothing and nothing.

Time became a fractal, with each minute opening to reveal that it contained many minutes, each of which contained many, many more minutes, endlessly opening out into an infinity of empty time while the clock stood still. It made the most tedious Tube journey seem like a riot of excitement and interest – all those adverts to read, people coming and going, the stations!

His life had been on the verge of working perfectly, and then he'd bumped into Rachel on the Tube. How could he have mishandled an accidental meeting with an ex-girlfriend so badly that it had utterly destroyed his life within days?

Who would employ him now? How would he make money?

And how could he, in all conscience, carry on being with Piper? She clearly deserved to be with a man who couldn't turn an accidental meeting with his ex-girlfriend into a prison sentence. A man who spotted when his court hearing has begun. A man who didn't turn up uninvited in a murderer's car.

A normal man.

That's who she should be with. A man who washes his car on a Sunday, owns some power tools and knows how to make confident small-talk. Possibly a keen surfer.

Before coming here, Jonathon had the vague impression that prison was either a luxurious holiday camp or a hellhole in which people wearing brightly coloured overalls used metal dinner-trays to fight each other. Instead, it seemed to be just silently sitting in a small cream room with your thoughts, and this felt like the hardest thing it could possibly be.

The hardest thought of all was Piper, who he missed painfully.

Years passed.

Jonathon was an old, old man, blown hollow by the winds of time.

Then the door clanged open, and all those long years crumpled into minutes.

Outside, an official-sounding voice shouted, 'S and Ds!'

The man with the black beard and glasses stood up. 'Right,' he said, 'I'm going to find a toilet, because I am not doing a crap in front of a guy in a huge T-shirt holding a towel.'

'What are S and Ds?' asked Jonathon.

'Social and domestics. It's a tiny bit of time to do what needs doing, and I am going to take it. You stay here. I don't want to come back and find all my stuff gone, yeah.'

'Okay,' said Jonathon. He didn't know what he would have done anyway, and the alternative seemed to be a definite falling out with the black-bearded man, instead of being relatively benignly ignored by him.

'I'm Jamali, by the way,' said the the black-bearded man. Then he cranked himself up, put on his aggressive, jutted-jaw smile and swaggered out of the cell, calling, 'Yo, where's the toilet at?'

Jonathon got down from the bunk bed and stood on the floor. He'd had a vague notion of pottering about the cell, but he now saw that it wasn't potterable. He could go and stand by the toilet, if he wanted, or he could sit in the plastic chair, or he could continue standing where he was. Or he could just go and sit on the bunk bed again. There weren't really any other ways of interacting with the place.

He continued standing where he was.

Jonathon was dimly aware that people had published prison diaries, but he couldn't for the life of him think what could be in them. Wouldn't they just be an endless repetition of *I sat on the bed and then stood on the floor*? Maybe people also slept sometimes.

At that moment, a man put his head around the door. He had short hair in severe disarray, stubble and frightening teeth.

'All right, mate,' said the man.

'Um, hello,' said Jonathon. 'How are you?'

The man gave a microscopic nod and pushed the door further open. He stood there with his hands down the front of his tracksuit bottoms, as though perhaps he were nurturing a baby kangaroo in the warmth. He looked slowly around.

'They're my flip-flops,' said the man, nodding towards a pair on the shelf.

'Oh,' said Jonathon. This seemed strange, since Jamali had put them there just a few minutes before.

'Did you rob them off me?' asked the man.

'Um, no,' said Jonathon. The situation felt somehow familiar, as though perhaps he'd dreamed it.

'I want them back,' said the man.

'Right,' said Jonathon, in what he hoped was a casual and non-committal way.

'Pass them over then,' said the man.

'Um, I think they're Jamali's,' said Jonathon.

'You calling me a liar?' said the man, looking Jonathon in

the eye.

'No.'

'So they're mine then, aren't they?'

'No.'

'You what?'

'They're Jamali's.'

'So you *are* calling me a liar.'

'No. I think you honestly believe they're yours,' lied Jonathon.

This confused the man, just as Jonathon had been hoping. And he suddenly realised why the situation seemed so familiar: it was because he'd lived through it so many times at school. This was a textbook example of the genre, complete with the pre-violence opportunity to humiliate himself. And, all these years later, Jonathon's instinct was still to bog the man down in a conversation about the definition of lying.

He saw now that school had not been – as he'd always thought – a dreary waste of time, but instead a truly world-class preparation for prison.

The man visibly struggled to work out how to reply to Jonathon's claim, then narrowed his eyes and said, 'You know what, you're making me so fucking mad.'

'Sorry,' said Jonathon.

'So give me my flip-flops then.'

'I think they're Jamali's. They just look like your flip-flops.'

'*You* just look like my flip-flops,' said the man, suddenly very still.

This was it. The man had crossed the sense barrier. At this point violence was inevitable. Jonathon was now going to have to die to protect Jamali's flip-flops.

His body was flooded with adrenaline, and yet he felt strangely more relaxed than he had been in a long time. This was not one of those ambiguous social encounters that he so feared, where he might accidentally say the wrong thing and hurt someone's feelings or make them dislike him. There was absolutely no ambiguity at all here. Unlike everywhere else, his role was now completely clear: he just had to avoid actively assisting in the process of beating himself up. It was odd to find that, in a certain way, he was more comfortable being physically attacked than making small talk.

Something else Jonathon had learned at school was to duck and flinch early and often, just to manage his nerves. Of course, ducking and flinching would have been a terrible blow to the prestige of anyone who was good at fighting. But if you have no fighting prestige to maintain, there's really no penalty for it, so you might as well.

Jonathon ducked and flinched.

By sheer chance, he did this just as the man's fist shot out and punched a hole in the air where Jonathon's head had been a split second before. The force of the blow seemed to shatter the air.

In ducking, Jonathon's bottom hit the metal pole at the end of the bunk bed. He rebounded forward, staggering and off-balance, delivering an accidental head-butt to his attacker's stomach, which sent the man staggering backward a couple of steps, out of the cell.

'Sorry,' said Jonathon, automatically.

He regained his balance and stood up just as the man let fly another punch at where Jonathon's head had been and his midriff now was. Although Jonathon tried to jump back, the punch still had enough force to send a tunnel of sudden pain through his stomach, doubling him up.

'Ow,' said Jonathon, clutching his stomach – and his forehead, which had accidentally connected sharply with the bony bridge of the man's nose.

There was blood all over the floor. Oh god, he was bleeding: he really was going to die defending an uncommunicative stranger's flip-flops. Jonathon forced himself to turn his attention back to his aggressor, hoping to weather just one more attack.

But he was surprised to see that the man was now leaning heavily against the wall, swaying slightly and staring down at the floor, one hand over his face. There was blood all down his blue Nike T-shirt and grey tracksuit bottoms.

'Are you all right?' asked Jonathon, confused about who had bled on whom.

'You've broke me fucking nose,' said the man, pitifully.

'Oh. Have I? Sorry. I didn't mean to.'

The man didn't reply.

Jonathon wiped his hand gingerly over his own forehead. The blood was dark and congealing. He wiped it with his other hand, and was surprised to find it came away almost clean.

At this point Jonathon found enough spare brain-power to notice that a crowd was forming around them. Also, there was an alarm going off somewhere nearby.

'What you waiting for?' said a fat man who was suddenly at Jonathon's elbow. 'Crack him in the head.'

'I don't really want to,' explained Jonathon.

'Punch him, Gobber,' said a skinny youth beside the man with the bloody nose.

'Hold me back,' said the bloody-nosed man, but continued to prod tenderly at his face.

'All right, all right, excitement's over. Break it up. Everyone back to your cells.'

It was the voice of a middle-aged woman with bobbed blonde hair, pushing her way through the crowd, accompanied by four or five other prison officers.

'Oh, hello,' said Jonathon.

'He fucking attacked me, miss!' shouted the man with the bloody nose. 'He broke me nose!'

'Is that right, Mr Godber?' said the woman tolerantly. 'And what do you have to say about it, Mr ...?'

'Fairfax,' said Jonathon.

'Fairfax, *miss*,' the woman prompted.

'Sorry, um, miss.'

'I just went in to say hello, like,' said the man she'd called Mr Godber, 'and he went fucking mental.'

'I didn't go mental, miss,' rebutted Jonathon.

Mr Godber took his hand away from his nose, and Jonathon was shocked to see what a dark misshapen mass it now was.

'So what happened to Mr Godber's nose, Mr Fairfax?'

'It was an accident, miss,' he said. 'I don't really know how it happened. I tripped up.'

The woman sighed and shook her head. 'I don't really see that I've got any alternative but to put you both on a charge.'

'Ah, *miss*!' protested Mr Godber. 'Look at what the bastard did to me nose.'

'Oh,' said Jonathon. 'But he attacked me, miss. He was trying to steal Jamali's flip-flops. And what does being on a charge mean?'

'It means,' said the woman tiredly, 'that you need to go back to your cell, sit down, stop breaking people's noses, and wait for the paperwork to make its way over to you in its own sweet time.'

'But–'

'That's enough, Mr Fairfax. Now go back to your cell.'

Jonathon's nose began to run and tears pricked embarrassingly at the corners of his eyes. The injustice of it hurt far more than the punch in the stomach, though both were making him feel that perhaps he could do with sitting down for a bit on a wobbly bunkbed.

He had only just climbed up there when Jamali walked in. The door banged shut behind him.

Jamali looked at him for a few seconds, his face expressionless, then nodded and said, 'Folder Boy got some *moves*.'

Jonathon couldn't think of anything to say, though Folder Boy was a definite step up from Hanky Boy. The adrenaline had left his body and he was afraid to move for fear of showing how much he was shaking.

'I assume anyway,' said Jamali. 'I come back and see the guy in the Nike T-shirt with blood all down him, blood all over the floor, screws all round. I'm guessing he didn't just get a nosebleed.'

'He tried to steal your flip-flops,' said Jonathon.

'Thanks, man,' said Jamali. He stepped over and held out his hand, which Jonathon instinctively shook.

Jamali blinked and microscopically shook his head. 'Yeah,' he said, 'I was actually going for a fist-bump, not trying to initiate a game of rock-paper-scissors. Though, give you your due, that is a winning move. Paper beats rock.'

'Sorry,' said Jonathon, tiredly. 'I'm not very good at hand greetings. I can't do high fives either.'

'Look at the elbow,' said Jamali absently, rummaging in his bin liner.

'What?'

'Look at the elbow when you're doing it. Perfect high five every time.'

'Really?'

Jamali sighed and held up his right hand, face averted as though to avoid the embarrassment of taking part in this. Jonathon looked at Jamali's elbow and launched his high five, expecting it to slowly slightly miss, as usual. Instead, their palms connected perfectly with a neat clap.

'That's incredible!' said Jonathon.

'You know, I'm beginning to see how a person like you ends up in prison for stealing a folder.'

'Oh,' said Jonathon. 'Thanks.'

Jamali brushed a fleck of dust from his flip-flops on their shelf, then sat in the chair opposite and looked at Jonathon.

'So,' said Jamali, 'talk me through this outfit, bruv. You got a strong look going on here.'

'Um, I was wearing the trousers and shoes at work, but then I spilled curry all over my shirt and jacket, so the police gave me the T-shirt out of their box, and then the prison people put my shirt and jacket in *their* box. I wish I'd kept them now: the layer of curry might have helped keep me warm.'

'You cold?'

'A bit.' The cell had a bare concrete floor, and just the look and smell of the place seemed to embody cold, even without the involvement of the actual temperature.

Jamali put a grey hoodie on the narrow table.

'You spill curry on that, you're a dead man,' he said, pointing to it.

'Um, okay,' said Jonathon.

'Obviously I'm saying you can borrow it for a bit.'

48

'What was in the folder then?' Vince asked Lance. This was an emergency meeting at Lance's request, and they were again sitting in Vince's office, at his desk – which is to say, the table in the back bit of the Compton Arms.

'We don't know,' said Lance. 'All I know is that he told his girlfriend–'

'Hi,' said Piper, who was suddenly standing by their table, sweating slightly, cheeks flushed.

'Piper!' said Lance. 'What are you doing here?'

'What the massive fuck do you mean, Lance, what am I doing here? The question is what was I *not* doing here? Why aren't you involving me?'

Lance pulled out a chair and dusted the seat with his hand, as though to make it fit for her.

'I am involving you,' he said, nodding at the barman. 'I just … I didn't know how Vince would react to me bringing someone else along, someone he's never met before …'

Vince put his hands up and made a face, as though to say, 'Don't pull me into this.'

'And,' Lance continued, 'I didn't want to get your hopes up.'

'Don't!' said Piper, sitting down and holding up a finger in Lance's face. 'Don't you dare pull that … Don't keep me in the dark, and hide things from me and exclude me because you think I might hope too much. I'll manage my emotions for myself.'

'She's got a point,' said Vince. 'That's pretty patronising.'

Lance took a breath. 'I'm sorry,' he said.

A barman came over and put a beer in front of Piper. Lance handed him some money.

She closed her eyes, looking exasperated and impressed at the same time.

'How did you make that happen?' she said.

'Didn't you see me signal to the barman?'

'No,' she said. 'But most people have trouble getting served in pubs even when they're at the bar waving money and looking annoyed.'

'I just have a rapport with bar staff,' said Lance. 'By the way, I'm assuming Arlene told you where I was.'

Piper nodded and drank some beer.

'Just as I' – Lance began but, getting a warning look from Piper, changed tack – 'didn't anticipate.'

'I'm Vince, by the way,' said Vince, standing slightly to offer Piper his hand, which she shook.

'I'm Piper,' said Piper, not adding her usual explanation of her name.

'So,' said Vince, 'Lance here was just saying, "All I know is that he told his girlfriend …" Which is you. So what did Han– … what did he tell you?'

'You call Jonathon "Han"?'

'Yeah,' said Vince. 'After … Han Solo.'

'He's nothing like Han Solo.'

'It's short for Hanky Boy,' said Lance. 'Because Jonathon uses a hanky.'

Vince gave Lance a look.

'Fine by me,' said Piper. 'I don't care what you call him. And all he told me was that he got embarrassed about a folder and one thing led to another.'

'Didn't you ask him what he meant?' said Vince.

'No, that seemed perfectly self-explanatory to me,' said Piper sarcastically, holding Vince's eye until he made a face and looked at the table. 'The phone call got cut off.'

Vince looked up quickly, eyes gleaming. 'They were probably monitoring the call. He'd said too much.'

'Or they just didn't give him enough phone credit.'

Vince held up his hands again and looked away, as though to say, 'If you want to believe that …'

'But what do you think he meant?' Piper asked Lance.

'Well,' said Lance, 'since the … Rachel's uncle got out of prison, he's been working at a chicken shop–'

'Ken's Plucky Fried Chicken,' put in Vince.

'Sounds like a standard cheap chicken shop trying to sound a bit KFC,' said Piper.

'You'd think so,' said Lance, 'but there are lots of rumours about it. And Vince, who's an investigative journalist' – Lance couldn't resist giving him a promotion – 'has been looking into it for some time. He thinks it has links to the Romanian 'Ndrangheta.'

'That's not strictly true,' said Vince. 'I mean, it does, but that's the ultra-simplified, surface explanation of what's going on. It goes *much* deeper than that.'

'How much deeper?' asked Piper, with perhaps a hint of suspicion in her voice.

'Ah-ah,' said Vince, wagging a finger. 'First we get to the bottom of what Han–' Vince stopped himself.

'Hanky Boy,' prompted Piper.

'Of what Hanky Boy meant,' continued Vince, 'when he said he got embarrassed about a folder.'

Piper looked at Lance, who looked from her to Vince and back again.

'Okay, well,' said Lance, 'let me catch Piper up on a few things.'

He told her how he'd followed the murderer to Flock, watched him try to break in, then stop as though he'd been warned, leading him to get Jonathon a freelance job at Flock, on the principle that maybe his enemy's enemy was his friend.

'But then,' concluded Lance, 'the whole Teddy Robinson thing made me feel more suspicious of Flock–'

'So you guilted Jonathon into spying on them and got him arrested,' concluded Piper.

Lance made a face and briefly skimmed through his mental rolodex of charming diversionary tactics, rapidly concluding that none of them would work on Piper.

'Probably,' he conceded. 'And I have made a mental note to feel bad about it, when I've got a bit of time. But now that he's been arrested, I'm going to be pretty busy, because it means …'

Lance came to a halt, because it meant so many things, and he wasn't yet entirely sure how he would effortlessly solve them all. Meanwhile, Piper had buried her face in her hands and Vince had sat forward with an eager gleam in his eye.

'Want me to tell you what it means?' asked Vince.

Lance and Piper glanced at each other and nodded.

Vince leaned forward and lowered his voice. 'It means you're being played.'

Lance tried to think of some alternative to saying 'What?' in an incredulous voice.

'What?' said Piper, in an incredulous voice.

'Think about it,' said Vince. 'At every stage you've done exactly what they wanted you to do, and it's all gone like a dream, from their point of view.'

'Wait, who's *they*?' said Piper.

'I'm not ready to tell you that, not yet. But let's just look at what's happened so far. From what Lance told me, Hanky Boy bumps into his ex, who tells him about her uncle who – it just so happens – is about to be released from prison. Hanky's scared, so obviously Lance will start following the uncle and see him go to Ken's. Lance digs around for rumours and tells the police about Ken's. It's exactly what they want: a reason to raid. The police go in there. Now they can publicly say they found nothing.'

'They put out a statement,' Lance told Piper.

'So Ken's now has a clean bill of health,' continued Vince. 'The next step is for the uncle to lead you to Flock. Lance gets Hanky a job there. Hanky says he'll see if Flock has a folder on Ken's. That's the folder he tells Piper he's embarrassed about. I believe the contents of that folder were absolute dynamite: the truth, but in partially encrypted form.'

'What makes you think that?' asked Piper.

'Flock's a marketing company, right? What's one part of what marketing companies do? Competitor analysis. Who's known to be Ken's biggest competitor? Dick C's–'

'Dixie's?' asked Piper.

'Dick C's Fried Chicken,' said Lance. 'There's a turf war between them and Ken's, as the biggest fried-chicken places in north London – apart from actual KFC, of course.'

'So,' continued Vince, 'Flock's working for Dick C's and finds out something about Ken's. Hanky takes that information out of Flock. Next second he's arrested and in prison. So the folder

– and its incriminating contents – are now out of Flock's hands, and in the hands of the police – or elements within them. So, a few smart bits of manipulation and they've solved a lot of their problems. Everyone thinks Ken's is clean and has nothing to do with the 'Ndrangheta or the police. And the folder's no longer an issue. Best thing of all? You've done it all for them.'

'Wait,' said Lance, 'so you think Ken's is in league with the 'Ndrangheta *and* the police?'

'I do. And elements within the wider justice system – and beyond. *Far* beyond. If you want a clue, just look at Ken's logo. The good news is that there's someone battling against this force which has its tentacles' – here Vince paused slightly and looked at Lance and Piper – 'in so many places.'

'I suppose that's you,' said Piper.

Vince laughed. 'Me? No way. I'm just on the sidelines, piecing this together – occasionally trying to help people out by telling them the truth, smuggling it into articles about improvements to local parks, in the form of elaborate acrostics. No, the identity of that *someone* might just surprise you.' Vince finished his pint and stood up. 'One final thing: I learned a long time ago that there's no such thing as a coincidence. I advise you to learn that lesson yourselves. Fast.'

There was a short silence, and then Piper said, 'But even if all that's true, how does it help us find Jonathon and get him out of prison?'

'They'll never let you find him,' said Vince.

'Wait,' said Lance, 'won't they tell you where he is?'

'I don't think it's personal,' said Piper. 'There is a thing called the Prisoner Location Service, but you have to write to them – which I've done – and the website says to allow three or four weeks for a response.'

'Three or four *weeks,*' said Lance. 'That's outrageous.'

'It's just not set up for people who get embarrassed about folders and forget to mention which prison they're in.'

'Right,' said Vince. 'You just keep telling yourself that.'

'Anyway,' said Piper, 'I'm going to try ringing around and see if there's another way of finding out.'

Vince gave a hollow laugh. 'There won't be. They'll make sure of that. And it's not going to suit them to let him out either. They need him to disappear. So my guess is that he's going to have a nasty accident very soon. Best for them if it happens before you can find out where he is.'

'But don't you think there's *any* way of finding him?' asked Piper.

'Your best bet? Ask Teddy Robinson.'

'Why Teddy Robinson?'

'I'm not ready to tell you that. Not yet. Now, if you'll excuse me, I have journalism to investigate.'

And with that, he swept away, only spoiling the effect slightly by heading for the toilets.

After Vince had gone, Lance turned to Piper and said, 'Are you okay?'

'I'm fine,' she said. 'Except for having spent the last five minutes listening to a total load of bullshit.'

'Oh,' said Lance. 'You didn't …?'

Piper, at the same time said, 'Wait, did you actually …?'

'What?' he said.

'Sorry?' she said.

'You didn't think there was something in what Vince said?' he asked.

'No. Did you?'

The barman put another pint in front of Piper and Lance paid for it.

'I surreptitiously ordered it,' he confessed, 'because I thought you might be devastated by what Vince said … about Jonathon having an accident.'

'I am devastated, but not about what Vince said. And Jonathon might well have an accident, because he's the most accident-prone person in our dimension and he absolutely should not be in prison. That's why we need to do everything we can to find out which prison he's in, then visit him and get him legal help.'

'Well, yeah.'

'Please tell me that's what you want to do as well, rather than focusing on the gangster-folder-chicken-shop-Teddy-Robinson angle.'

'Of *course* that's what I want to do,' said Lance, switching into sincere mode. 'I mean, we should probably do a bit of both. It's not like I *believe* all that stuff Vince was saying, but is it *all* wrong? There's clearly *something* going on here.'

Piper looked at him. Her expression was the facial equivalent of one of those blank protest placards used when the problems are so obvious there's no point putting them into words.

She said, 'I'm going to phone all the prisons and police stations in London. And I'll try to get through to my dad – he's away on holiday – and talk to him about lawyers.'

'Great,' said Lance. 'That's a great plan.'

'What are you going to do?' she asked.

49

The cell door clanged open and a passing voice on the walkway shouted, 'Exercise!'

'S and Ds *and* exercise,' said Jamali. 'It's our lucky day.'

'What kind of exercise is it?' asked Jonathon, climbing down the shivering bunk bed.

Jamali stopped and looked at him. 'Are you for real?' he asked.

'I think so,' said Jonathon, who was regularly confronted on this point. 'Sorry. I just … haven't been in prison before.'

'So what are you thinking? Burpees? Squats? Cross-country?'

Jonathon raised his eyebrows helplessly. They all sounded perfectly reasonable.

'In prison,' said Jamali, 'exercise means standing in small groups eyeing each other aggressively. Or you can walk slowly around the outside of the yard, if you're an athlete.'

'Oh, well,' said Jonathon, feeling relieved. 'Have you been to prison before then?'

Jamali was on his feet, getting his shoulders into place and jutting out his jaw again.

'Look at me,' he said. 'Of *course* I've been to prison before.'

They left the cell, swinging the door shut behind them, Jamali glancing back to check his flip-flops were well hidden.

'This prison, in fact,' Jamali continued. 'Just not this bit of it. There's a smaller building next door.'

'Oh,' said Jonathon, distracted by the need to keep an eye out for Gobber.

'Weed and a knife,' said Jamali, answering Jonathon's unasked question. 'Which, where I live, is pretty much like wallet and phone. Don't leave home without them.'

'Really?' said Jonathon. 'A knife?' Jamali didn't seem the type.

Jamali shrugged. 'Is it sensible to be the only unarmed man in a *heavily* tooled-up neighbourhood? Specially when people want to kill you based on your postcode.'

'Your postcode?' said Jonathon, surprised.

'Yeah. You never heard of that? It's all over the news.'

'I, um, haven't been keeping up with the news lately. It's too …'

'Absolutely fucking horrible? I feel you.'

'But … when I was growing up all the violence was, well, personal. People decided whether to punch you really hard in the stomach based on a range of factors, but they were all about how you looked and sounded. I don't think postcodes came into it. That sounds really bureaucratic.'

Jamali gave a rare smile and nodded. 'That's fair. Yes. It is *insane*. But then you'd be surprised: there is one or two postcodes where *everyone* is a dick. So, go figure.'

They'd been making their way down the metal staircases and were now queuing to get into the yard. The doorway ahead was a rectangle of bright sunlight and clear blue sky, like a portal to another world. It didn't seem possible that such a day could have been going on while he'd been sitting in the chilly grey cell, or preparing to die for the sake of Jamali's flip-flops.

As Jonathon stepped through the door he was barged from behind by a powerful shoulder, so that he caromed along Jamali's back and collided with the doorpost. The barger, already moving out into the yard, turned and stared back at him with unnervingly wide-open eyes: it was Jonathon's other nemesis. This nemesis traced a line from his eyes to Jonathon's and again mouthed the word 'spy'.

How, Jonathon wondered, had he managed to collect *two* nemeses already? If they continued to double every three hours, by mid-morning tomorrow he'd be fighting two hundred and fifty-six men to the death over Jamali's flip-flops. He would never make it to his court appearance in three weeks, because by then they'd be busing in tens of thousands of fresh nemeses every day.

Luckily, the man with the unnervingly open eyes had accidentally walked into a similarly muscular and unhinged-looking man, and the two of them were now standing a couple of feet apart, wiggling their chests at each other and twitching their arms. That was a factor in Jonathon's favour: his nemeses might gather their own nemeses at the same rate, which he hoped might distract them from Jamali's flip-flops.

'Don't worry about it,' said Jamali, glancing at the stand-off and putting a hand on Jonathon's back to keep him walking. 'I mean, worry about it, yes: he could rip your head off. But also, don't worry about it, if you know what I mean.'

Jonathon walked on, nodding and flinching.

'Jesus,' said Jamali. 'Will you relax?'

Jamali set them on a course around the perimeter of the huge yard. Each side was about the length of the wing, giving it a total area of roughly one square cathedral. In this case it was an open-air cathedral surrounded by a high red-brick wall with razor wire roughly where the elaborate vaulting would begin. In the centre was a patch of scrubby grass, and around the edges were a few benches. Otherwise it was bare tarmac.

The wing loomed above them. At this distance it was clear that the outside was coated in unspeakable substances that the prisoners had managed to throw out of their cells. At one end was a hexagonal hub where this wing joined on to the others, and from the centre of this hub rose a tower in which Jonathon imagined the governor sitting, smiling a satisfied smile and perhaps peeling a grape.

A ring had formed around the two muscular men, whose wiggling and twitching could only dimly be discerned through the gaps between spectators. They had the air of a race-day crowd: some excited, some shrewdly observing, others debating form or placing bets.

'There's basically only a few different types of people here,' said Jamali. 'That guy who barged you is a proper psycho. Probably difficult to stay out of prison if you're that way, unless you get medication or what-have-you. So you get a few of them. Then there are the guys who are good at violence *and* have a bit of self-control: armed robbers, real gangsters, that sort of thing. There aren't many of them, but they're the people who run the prison – its aristocracy – so stay on their good side.'

'What about Gobber?' asked Jonathon, flinching and looking behind him.

'From what I saw, I think Gobber's just a bit of a dick, like he was born without a shame module in his brain, so he just tries it on all the time and cries when someone hits back. Plenty of people like that here.'

Jonathon felt relieved at that. 'And what about you?' he asked.

'Me? I was just … I started from the wrong place. Know what I mean? Like, "How do I get to a nice life?" Answer: "I wouldn't start from here." That's me. I'm just trying to make my way, and prison is an accident that's probably going to happen from time to time. But if the sentences are short and I keep up my front, stay out of trouble, maybe I can get through. Maybe I can make it.'

'I hope you do.'

'Thanks, man.'

They passed an old man with a sort of cartoonish pinched-up mouth that Jonathon had never seen in real life, only in illustrations – as though he had no teeth.

'That's a type right there,' said Jamali. 'Homeless guy who gets himself sent to prison every now and then so he can get a bed and a hot meal – even if it's a tiny and disgusting hot meal that's not even very hot. I mean, even if you're not trying it's pretty difficult to stay out of prison if you're homeless. And then there are guys coming out of the army, and people with learning difficulties – it's just like, people playing life with the difficulty setting on high. They all end up in prison.'

'Oh, so how many …?' Jonathon didn't quite know how to finish the question.

'… of the people here actually *belong* in prison?' suggested Jamali. 'Don't know. Most of the dicks, some of the psychos. The problem is, the people who really *deserve* to be in prison absolutely love it. It's all their favourite things: drugs, violence, bullying, twenty-four-seven, delivered to your doorstep.'

'Jesus shit,' said Jonathon. He was reeling, and the effect was heightened by the beautiful summer sun flooding the most dangerous place he'd ever been.

'Jesus, as you say, shit,' confirmed Jamali.

'What, um, what type am I?' asked Jonathon.

Jamali sucked his teeth and shook his head. 'You, my friend, are not a type. No one like you has *ever* been to prison before.'

Jonathon wasn't sure how to feel about this. Of course, it was good that Jonathons didn't just pile up in prison. On the other hand, he found it hard enough to fit in outside prison, where he had a key for his door and none of his neighbours attacked him for footwear.

'Oh!' said Jamali. 'There's Cheese – he was in my old wing. Come on, I'll introduce you.'

Jamali strode off across the yard, and Jonathon would have followed him but for an abrupt change in his circumstances.

50

It was their daily meeting, and the murderer – in his habitual place on the Ferrari duvet next to the business-studies textbooks – gave his report.

'The kid didn't go into Flock this morning,' he said.

Ranira, who was never knowingly undramatic, gave a little gasp and asked, 'What do you think that means?'

'No idea. But two of the women who go there looked troubled, like something bad had happened.'

'Anything else?' she asked.

'No.' He sighed. 'I know it's not really telling us anything, me watching the place like this before I come in for my shift, but it's all I can think of.'

'You never know what it might turn up,' said Ken. 'By the way, I would still like to pay you for this time that you spend watching.'

'Cheers, Ken. Tell you what, if it leads to anything, you can pay me then.'

'Will you pay *me*?' Ranira asked her dad hopefully.

Ken looked uncomfortable. 'Already I give you pocket money, plus this computer–'

She held up her hand to stop him. 'Just asking,' she said. 'But I *have* found out a ton of stuff.'

'That's magic, that,' said the murderer. 'Well done, Ranira. What you found out then?'

'Well,' she said, leaning forward in her gossipy way, 'the same people "posting" in "forums" about us' – she looked at Ken and the murderer to check they were keeping up with her terminology – 'are also posting about other companies and people.'

'Which ones?' asked Ken.

'The most interesting ones are Andy Sproat and Teddy Robinson.'

Ken and the murderer exchanged a look – Ken's surprised and the murderer's blank.

'Friends of yours?' hazarded the murderer.

'Deadly rivals to be the next mayor of London,' said Ranira. 'Don't you know that?'

'I'm not really into the news,' he said. 'Don't see the point.'

'But it's so important to be informed,' said Ranira. 'Anyway, they're saying Andy Sproat is strangling puppies in a basement beneath a refugee centre in Brent.'

'You're joking!' said the murderer. 'Really?'

'No, these are lies,' said Ranira patiently. 'Like the lies they spread about Dad's company.'

'Oh, right,' said the murderer. 'Got you.'

'And then today,' she added, leaning forward again, 'someone said that Sproat … eats babies.'

'Who would say such a thing?' asked Ken, looking horrified.

'This guy,' said Ranira, dramatically flourishing a piece of paper from her printer. 'He posts under the name Avid4Truth, and nearly all his other posts are about some old guy who used to do the weather on TV … Michael McKettle?'

'Oh, I remember him,' said the murderer, glad of a familiar name. 'Where did he get to then?'

'He writes big books with titles like *Secret Facts Are Being Hidden* and only wears yellow.'

Ken breathed a sigh of relief. 'So insane people are spreading these rumours. People will see this, and then the rumours will die down. This is good.'

'I don't think so, Dad. People don't respond like Avid4Truth is insane. And I mentioned him because he says that we're linked to Andy Sproat somehow – that we're both part of the same conspiracy.'

'But we are not,' said Ken. 'Except that I voted for Mr Sproat. But he cannot know this, can he?'

'Hold on,' said the murderer. 'Is this Sproat the one who's strangling puppies and eating babies?'

'Yes,' said Ranira. 'I mean, no. He's the one they're *saying* is doing those things.'

'Got you,' said the murderer. 'And what are they saying he's got to do with Ken?'

'I don't know exactly,' said Ranira. 'But it's got something to do with the logo on our shop sign, something about how the star on Dad's cowboy hat has eight points.'

'Is this unusual?' asked Ken. 'How many points should a star have?'

'Five?' said Ranira. 'Eight is a lot.'

'She's right,' said the murderer.

'Is this why business is so slow today?' said Ken. 'Because of this star?'

'Maybe,' said Ranira. 'This guy also says that there's one man who knows all about this conspiracy and is working to stop it.'

'Who's that then?' asked the murderer.

51

Jonathon was a man in a headlock, and had been for some time. His pre-headlock days seemed dim and distant. In his new life, his hands scrabbled at a sinewy arm and there were dark blotches in front of his eyes. The blotches were growing larger, and Jonathon had a vague idea that they had something to do with the fact that he wasn't breathing. This was a mixed blessing: it saved him from the cutting, milky smell of a prison armpit, but on the other hand he would soon pass out and die, unless he did something.

In the course of his last sequence of horribly traumatic events, Jonathon had received some specialist training, which he regretted having failed to keep up. All that remained was a lingering facility for shorthand – oh, and a knowledge of where a man's kidneys are and how hard to punch them.

With the last of his strength, Jonathon drew back his arm and, as hard as he could, punched the place where his assailant's left kidney should be.

'Ahyerbastard,' said Gobber, arching his back and neck in a way that allowed Jonathon just enough space to get his right hand around Gobber's forearm, and just enough time to take a breath, so that the dark blotches faded. He could feel the oxygen arrive in his brain, as though someone had opened a small skylight there.

That skylight, however, was immediately shut, and one of those surprisingly expensive Velux blinds drawn over it as Gobber renewed the pressure on Jonathon's neck. The man's strength seemed to be a built-in aspect of his general unpleasantness, independent of how neglected and out of condition his body was.

As Jonathon tugged desperately at Gobber's arm and tried to summon the energy to deliver another kidney punch, the dark blotches in front of his eyes returned, spreading, darkening and linking together like germs under a microscope.

Oh god, he thought, *I'm going to die here, in a stranger's armpit, because of a folder and a pair of flip-flops.*

Jonathon was slapped in the face by a nurse wearing an outdated uniform. He was covered in what looked like mucous and blood, and the nurse immediately added injury to insult by taking a pair of scissors and casually snipping through the long tube of skin that led from his tummy into the lady in whom he had recently been residing. The nurse then wrapped him in a towel and peer-pressured him into drinking some warm and slightly sour milk from the lady.

After that, Jonathon's life passed quickly but precisely, in great detail and yet all at once. His dad was typing in his study, his mum was on the phone, and he was playing with toy cars under the table, careful to give them all equal attention so as not to hurt their feelings.

He went to nursery, where someone put sand down his fire-engine shorts. Then he went to school, where someone put him in a headlock. And then he went to another school, where someone else put him in a different sort of headlock. He watched, school after school, headlock after headlock, as he evolved an infallible defence against them.

Ah, thought the observing part of him. *Was there really not an easier way to remind me how to get out of a headlock?*

Jonathon wrapped his left leg around Gobber's and leaned heavily into him. Unable to steady himself, Gobber crashed to the ground with Jonathon on top of him. The grip around Jonathon's neck slackened for an instant and he wrenched his head from the sickening armpit. He was careful to keep hold of Gobber's arm as he moved to sit on the man's upper back.

This move, though effective, was so clumsy, undignified and prestige-destroying that it had been unavailable to the boys who were actually good at fighting. In this it was typical of Jonathon's response to being attacked, which was so difficult to accommodate in a normal school hierarchy that he was gradually exempted from violence and moved over to the psychological bullying programme.

The move's major downside, as Jonathon now remembered, was that it meant sitting on top of an angry, violent person until the very last second of playtime – or, in this case, exercise hour, of which only about five minutes had elapsed.

'Punch him in the fucking head while he's down!' a fat man urgently advised Jonathon.

'I, um, don't really want to,' replied Jonathon.

That was when he noticed that the situation had attracted a crowd. There was a ring of men around them, laughing excitedly and shouting advice.

'Go on, Gobs, get up!' shouted someone.

'What's the matter, Gobs?' said someone else. 'Having a bit of a lie-down?'

Gobber's face was bright red. 'Get off me, you wanker. I'll fucking kill you!' he screamed – supplying, in the same breath, an instruction and the main reason for not obeying it.

By now Jonathon had managed to twist Gobber's other arm behind his back, so that it looked like he was preparing to row the man away. How, he wondered, was he going to sit here on this enraged human canoe, surrounded by screaming men, for another fifty-five minutes? Playtime had only been fifteen minutes, so even quite an early headlock had only meant sitting on someone for ten minutes. Now he had to do five and half times that. And the men surrounding him would soon work out that the only way to make the situation interesting again would be capsize Jonathon.

'You need to smash his head in,' said the fat man.

'But I really don't want to,' said Jonathon.

The fat man looked like he was trying to find a more compelling way of putting his argument, when suddenly Jamali was there. He was accompanied by a man with glasses and sandy hair in a boyish side-parting, wearing a polo shirt with a pastel-coloured sweater draped over his shoulders. Jamali was smiling, as though vastly entertained by the situation.

'Folder Boy got some *moves!*' he said, and laughed.

'What you call him Folder Boy for then?' asked the fat man

'He's in here on remand for stealing a folder,' said Jamali.

'On *remand?* For a *folder?*' said the fat man incredulously. 'That's not how the system's supposed to work.'

'I didn't realise–' Jonathon began.

'Remand is hugely over-employed by the courts,' said the man with glasses and sandy hair. 'Partly because they're so over-worked. There was a report on the subject last year.'

The fat man shook his head. 'The things they put people away for. I mean, take me. All I did was crack a bloke in a shop. Right cheeky bastard he was.'

The man with glasses opened his mouth to reply, but then seemed to think better of it. His presence seemed to have a calming effect on the ring of men, though, as they began competing to recall the most minor offence that had brought someone to prison. Meanwhile, the man with glasses squatted down beside Jonathon.

'I'm Cheeseman,' he said. 'Don't believe we've been introduced.'

'Oh, I'm Jonathon,' said Jonathon.

'This is more a surname sort of place,' said Cheeseman.

'Oh, then I'm Fairfax.'

'Pleased to meet you, Fairfax. So, what's your game plan here?' he asked, looking at Gobber, as Jonathon rode out another spasm of writhing.

'Well,' said Jonathon, 'I was planning to just keep sitting on, um, Gobber, till we go back inside.'

'I see. Tricky moment when you let him up.'

'Yes. I'm just trying to remember what I used to do at school. I think I'll just wait till the last second and then get up and run in.'

'Oh. Public school man?'

'No, just, um, normal … violent schools. There are a *lot* of headlocks in them.'

'Oh, well, that'll stand you in good stead here. I'm an Eton man myself, so this place is a home from home. I'm what's called a Listener, which isn't altogether different from my time as a prefect.'

'Do you work for the prison then?'

'Goodness me, no. Or only in a voluntary capacity. I'm a prisoner. Complex financial stuff, as you'd expect. Bit of a legal grey area. It's all being appealed by my lawyers.'

'Does anyone? Work here, I mean.'

Cheeseman laughed. 'There's a scattering of screws.' He gestured to a distant nervous-looking young man with a huge bunch of keys, standing by the door to the wing. 'But not enough. It's quite difficult to convince people to come and work in a prison when they could be doing anything else at all. And it's even more difficult to get them to stay once they've found out what it's like. As a result, we're guarded by a tiny number of saints, plodders and fascists. That's why nothing works and we end up locked in our cells most of the time. As for educ–'

There was another violent spasm from below.

'How remiss of me,' said Cheeseman. 'Afternoon, Mr Godber.'

'Fuck off, nob cheese.'

'Thank you. Just wondering about your plans for when Mr Fairfax here stops sitting on you?'

'I'm gonna rip his fucking head off,' Gobber said.

'The thing is that if you say that then he rather has to carry on sitting on you.'

'Just get this nob jockey off me!'

'Looks like this is going to be a tricky negotiation,' said Cheeseman. 'Worse than dealing with the Bank of England.'

'Maybe it's a prestige problem?' said Jonathon. 'What if someone forces me to get off him, but also forces him to go to the other side of the playground–'

'Prison yard,' corrected Cheeseman.

'Sorry, yes, the other side of the prison yard, and not attack me. That way we've both been beaten, so we're even.'

Cheeseman mulled this over and nodded.

'But who's going to do it?' said Jamali. 'You need someone violent but good-hearted.'

'I know,' said Cheeseman. 'If only Slater was still here.'

'What about McGill?' said the fat man who'd advised Jonathon to punch Gobber in the head. 'He just faced down that new psycho.'

Cheeseman approved, and asked Jamali to see if he could get McGill to come over, politely brushing aside the fat man's renewed suggestion of smashing Gobber's head in.

A couple of minutes later a muscular, bearded man appeared, still flexing and twitching slightly, the adrenaline of a near-fight in his eyes. Cheeseman took him aside, out of earshot, and they returned a minute later.

McGill gently pushed Jonathon, who stood up.

Gobber leapt to his feet and shouted, 'I'll fucking kill him! Hold me back! I'll kill him!'

McGill obligingly held Gobber back, and said, as though reciting a script, 'Leave it, mate. He's not worth it.'

Gobber theatrically struggled himself away, accompanied by McGill, and Cheeseman called after them, 'Thank you, McGill. The Haribo will be with you tomorrow, after canteen.'

Once Gobber was about half a cathedral away, Cheeseman said, 'Obviously it's none of my business, so please do tell me to fuck off, but are you really in here on remand for stealing a folder?'

'It's a little bit more complicated than that,' said Jonathon.

'I thought it might be.'

Jonathon told Cheeseman all that had happened, with many ums and enquiries as to whether he was boring him. But Cheeseman was not a Listener for nothing: he soaked it all up with interest, asking an astute question here and there.

When Jonathon had finished, Cheeseman said, 'When you said it was a bit more complicated than that, I assumed – and this is nothing personal, just the natural habit of mind one acquires here – that you must have stabbed someone for the folder, or filled it full of drugs, or woken up clutching it in a room full of dead dogs. But actually, in terms of the legal kernel of the case, you really are in here on remand for stealing a folder.'

'Um, yes.'

'That's really remarkably bad luck – though bound to happen, I suppose, with the justice system being so overstretched and you so mild-mannered. I never know why they don't just put a couple of pence on income tax and fund it all properly, like they do on the continent.'

'Oh, I thought …' Jonathon stopped himself from finishing the thought.

'That being a public schoolboy and financier I would never believe such rubbish?'

'Well, yes.'

'We're not quite as homogenous as we seem, Fairfax. Or at

least some of us aren't. Especially those of us who have actually encountered the justice system and seen what prisons are like.'

Jonathon took a breath and was about to relate his two contradictory opinions on public schools, but Cheeseman pre-emptively interrupted him.

'What's in your favour in all this is the fact that you only have to stick it out for three weeks, until your next court appearance. In the meantime, get a lawyer. Not the duty solicitor, but any decent local firm should do. I'd recommend my team, but it's not really their area and they're absolutely blindingly expensive. What do you do? For a living, I mean?'

'I'm, um, I'm a freelance illustrator. Yes I am.'

'There much money in that?' asked Cheeseman dubiously.

'Um, sometimes I make a normal amount of money,' said Jonathon.

'Well, raid your savings or get a loan and go for a standard local solicitor. Then do whatever they say, to the letter. They might be able to find some procedural step that the police missed and get the whole thing dismissed. More likely, they'll just tell you to plead guilty. If so, do. The court would never sentence anyone to more than three weeks for stealing a folder, and there's no evidence you intended to use the contents for personal gain. There could even be a public-interest defence. The point is, you are exceedingly unlikely to be sent back to prison. So look upon this as an educational experience. I can't imagine freelance illustrators are often asked about their criminal records, so it shouldn't hurt your career. You might even get a graphic novel out of it.'

'But how do I get a lawyer when I can't make phone calls?' asked Jonathon.

'Can't make phone calls?'

'No, my free credit didn't last long–'

'It doesn't.'

'And I've applied for a proper phone PIN number, but apparently it's taking four weeks at the moment. Also, my wallet's in a box somewhere and I can't remember my bank details, so I don't know how I'd get any money to put on it.'

'Tell your girlfriend, for heaven's sake, when she comes to visit.

I'm sure she'd be only too glad to arrange the legal stuff.'

'We got cut off before I could tell her which prison I'm in.'

'Oh dear. Phone credit is like gold dust in here: it comes out of your canteen money and is about as eye-wateringly expensive as calling Mars from an ex-Soviet republic. I'm an enhanced-level prisoner, so I get the maximum twenty-five pounds a week of my own money, plus nine pounds a week wages. But that has to fund a *lot* of phone calls, plus food, plus bribes, plus every other way of making life bearable. You can't lend phone credit; all you can do is tell someone your phone PIN, which means they can use all your credit whenever they want. I'm sure you're a trustworthy chap, but I can't let my lifeline to the outside world hang on so slender a thread. Your best bet is to go to the office when one of the nicer screws is on duty and explain the situation, hope they let you use the phone there. However, Baxter's on duty now, and he's more morally deranged than the worst of the prisoners. I'll try to get word to you when someone decent's on.'

'Isn't there any other way?' asked Jonathon. 'I'd really like to hear Piper's voice again.'

'Not really. You could use a mobile that a drug dealer's smuggled in up his bottom, but that would probably involve becoming a drugs mule in exchange, so I wouldn't advise it. I'm sure we can find some solution in the next few days. You have three weeks, after all, which is ample time to get all this sorted out. In the meantime, your girlfriend may be able to find out which prison you're in – if the prisoner database is up to date.'

'That's true.'

'*Courage, mon ami.* You can survive anything for three weeks, and after that you need never see the place again – which is more than anyone else here can say. You'll get through this.'

For the first time since his arrest, Jonathon felt the tentative warmth of hope ignite in the centre of his chest. He would get through this.

52

Lance had tried asking his police contact which prison Jonathon might be in, but the contact was adamant that Lance should fuck off, and seemed indisposed to compromise on this point during the course of their fifteen-second phone call. This naturally meant that Lance needed to find some other means of busting the case wide open before he next saw Piper.

He walked from the Compton Arms, along Upper Street and through Highbury Fields. Then he embarked on that extended thoroughfare which begins as Highbury Park, with its cute little restaurants and expensive cheese shops, and kept going as the street gradually became more and more Blackstock-Roady, until eventually the signs were forced to concede that it *was* Blackstock Road. By that point Lance was surrounded by chicken shops and Finsbury Park was just a nugget's throw away.

Now Lance's plan was revealed to him: he had come here to see KPFC with his own eyes, from the inside, rather than watching unobserved from behind a coffee and baklava in the cafe across the road. He was standing outside the door. In the window to his right was a display chicken on a rotisserie grill, and in the one to his left was a neon sign saying 'open'.

He looked up at the sign, suddenly remembering what Vince had said about the logo. It was a picture of a moustachioed man in an incongruous cowboy hat with a star on the front, gripping a fistful of feathers: pretty much exactly what he'd expected.

Lance pushed open the door and stepped nonchalantly inside, causing a little bell to go *cling* and a large man behind the counter to look up from the tabloid spread in front of him and say pleasantly, 'What'll it be then?'

It was, of course, the murderer.

'I'd like a job, please,' said Lance. He was mildly surprised to discover this, but his mouth had said it, and so it must be both true and an excellent plan.

The murderer looked at him for a second, then shrugged his eyebrows, indicating that this was fair enough and that nothing surprised him any more.

'One moment, squire,' he said, looking under the counter. 'Here you go.' He laid a piece of pink paper next to his tabloid. 'Here's the wossname. Form thing.'

'Coolio,' said Lance, taking a pen from his jacket pocket.

'I shouldn't say this,' said the murderer, 'but if you can fill in that form, you get the job.'

'Let's see what I can do,' said Lance. He filled in the spaces and ticked boxes, absently going 'badabadabada' under his breath, and then said, 'Done.'

'Magic,' said the murderer, glancing over the form. 'You an actor then, are you?'

'Yes,' said Lance immediately. He'd written it on the form, and found that it's a relief to embrace what the world says you are. 'Yes I am.'

'What you been in then? Anything I've heard of?'

'This and that,' said Lance. 'I'm between jobs at the moment.'

'Aren't we all, mate? Aren't we all,' said the murderer.

Lance nodded in what he thought was probably the right rueful, man-of-the-world sort of way, and stood looking expectantly at the murderer.

'Well,' said the murderer. 'We'll … be in touch.'

'Oh,' said Lance.

'What, did you think–?'

'Yes,' said Lance. 'I assumed you'd snap me up straight away.'

'Well, it's not me who makes the decisions, to be honest.'

'Really?' said Lance. He hoped he had injected just the right amount of incredulity, as though it were inconceivable to him that there might be a higher authority.

The murderer looked around at the absence of customers and said, 'Hold on, mate. I'll just go and check.'

He manoeuvred his shoulders through the restricted space, stepped through a doorway and called back, 'Anyone comes in, just write down what they're having, all right?'

'No problemo,' said Lance.

When the murderer returned, Lance had neatly written down three people's orders, stacked the money by the till, and was answering questions about his acting career.

'You got the job,' said the murderer.

53

It was ten past six, and Jonathon and Jamali were debating their contrasting answers to the question, 'If you had to have part of your body baked in a pie, which part would it be and why?'

It would be difficult to retrace the conversational steps that had led them there, but Jonathon was finding that you cover quite a lot of ground when you're locked in a room with someone and don't have anything to do. They had long ago exhausted all the more straightforward topics, such as where they came from, what they'd done before prison and which destination they would choose if they absolutely had to go on holiday with the pope.

'But you can't have just your ankle baked in the pie,' insisted Jonathon, who was a stickler in such matters. 'Your foot would fall off.'

'Fam, you seriously telling me that these people can selectively bake body parts in a pie, but they can't just keep a foot joined to the end of a leg while they do it?'

'You'd need an artificial ankle. You're changing the whole foundation of the question.'

'I don't need an artificial ankle, man. I've got a leg that goes down to the ground and, oh, what's this on the end of it? It's a—'

CLANK.

The door swung open and in walked Cheeseman, holding a clipboard.

'Evening, chaps,' he said.

'What are you—?' began Jamali.

'Good news,' said Cheeseman. 'I've got you into Alcoholics Anonymous.'

Jonathon and Jamali exchanged looks.

'But we aren't alcoholics,' said Jamali, reasonably.

'I'd change your position on that, if I were you,' said Cheeseman. 'AA gets you out of your cell for two hours on a Thursday evening, and' – he looked at his watch – 'we've got enough time before it starts to swing by the SO's office. Shaw's on now, and she's the most decent screw you'll ever meet. If she won't let Fairfax use the office phone, no one will.'

Jonathon leapt to his feet, Jamali following more slowly. Once they were out, a bored-looking officer locked the cell door behind them and wandered off.

As they followed Cheeseman along the walkway towards the stairs, Jamali said, 'How we gonna pretend to be alcoholics? Won't the real ones get suspicious?'

'There aren't any real alcoholics there,' said Cheeseman. 'In fact, most of them are Muslim. Really nice chaps, actually. You'll like them.'

'You do know that I'm not a Muslim, don't you?' said Jamali. 'I'm just an atheist with a big beard, like Karl Marx.'

'My dear Jamali, of course I know. I just think you'll like them. That's all.'

'Why didn't you invite me last time I was inside?'

'Because I hadn't thought of it then. I only added it to my little empire of official positions about a month or so ago. I'm also chaplaincy officer, so I'll put you down for C of E service on Sunday. Gets you out for the whole morning.'

'Hallelujah!' said Jamali, and Jonathon raised his hands in silent praise of the lord.

They reached the ground floor and Cheeseman said, 'Shaw's in the office just along there.'

He pointed to an open door in among a little cluster of other rooms that looked slightly less cell-like than most.

'We'll just put our heads round the door and–'

At that moment, a capable-looking middle-aged woman came hurrying out of the office, buckling on a heavily loaded utility belt. She headed for the staircase and pounded up it as two other officers – one from the ex-army tribe, another from the young-and-keen faction – came hurrying in through the wing's main door.

'Oh dear,' said Cheeseman. 'It looks like this probably isn't the best time to approach her. Come on, let's go and see what's happening.'

'But the phone's just there,' said Jamali. 'The office is still open.'

'Yes, but everyone can see us, and we're on camera. They'd find out, and then we'd all be in terrible trouble. I have a certain lifestyle to maintain, and you might lose your kettle.'

They were walking quickly towards the stairs, which the two newly arrived officers were now pounding up, the ex-army man panting loudly.

'Won't we, um, get in trouble for going to see what's happening?' asked Jonathon.

'I've got a clipboard,' said Cheeseman, waving it like a talisman.

'How,' asked Jonathon, 'can you tell what will get you into trouble?'

'One develops an instinct, through trial and error. And it must be said that experience of boarding school helps enormously. Did I mention I was at Eton?'

The three of them climbed the stairs, reached the first floor and cautiously followed the sounds. Just ahead was a cell with its door open. Cheeseman signalled them to stay back, like a sergeant on reconnaissance duty, and walked slowly towards the open door, clipboard at the ready. Jamali ignored Cheeseman's signal and walked directly behind him. Jonathon, not wanting to be left out, followed.

As he walked past, Jonathon glanced in and saw that it was actually two cells knocked together, with a television, a PlayStation, a rug, a toilet curtain, quite a lot of wall-mounted pornography, and an absolutely staggering quantity of packets of Haribo. It was like a certain type of teenage boy's ideal bedroom. However, the occupant was a large, fully grown man who was covered in thick white foam and prison officers.

'Get off me, you bastards! I'll kill him!' shouted the cell's occupant, who was on the floor by the bed, writhing.

'Calm down, Mr McGill,' said the capable middle-aged woman

in a surprisingly reasonable tone, given that she was sitting on him. 'We're just doing our–'

'Here, grab his wrist!' interrupted the former soldier, struggling to get a pair of handcuffs on the inmate. 'Where's the–?'

'Ow!' shouted the young and keen officer. 'Shit. Stay still!'

The inmate looked up: it was the man to whom Cheeseman had promised a packet of Haribo earlier. Jonathon smiled at him reflexively and the inmate fixed him with a furious stare, still for a single moment that briefly locked them together. Then Jonathon looked around, realised Cheeseman and Jamali were no longer with him, and hurried to catch them up.

As Jonathon fell into step, Jamali hissed, 'Don't stand there in the doorway, man. You want to see something here, you do a drive-by looking: just give it the side-eye as you go past.'

As they walked down the stairs, Cheeseman asked, 'Did anyone see you?'

'Only, um, the man on the floor.'

'It's McGill's new cell – was it him? Did you see? I couldn't make him out because of all the foam.'

'Yes, that's what they called him. It was the man you promised a packet of Haribo.'

Cheeseman looked troubled. 'Who could have foamed McGill in a locked cell and then disappeared into thin air? That's very definitely not a good development.'

Shortly afterwards they arrived at a cream-painted room full of plastic chairs and old official posters. There, Cheeseman's question was lost amid the business of running an Alcoholics Anonymous meeting attended almost exclusively by non-drinkers.

When they returned to their cell, they found Jamali's flip-flops had vanished.

54

As Teddy neared his grand Georgian terrace, he noticed for the first time that the two houseplants in the front window were dead. In fact, they seemed to have died deaths of almost Shakespearean extravagance, their mighty stalks bent in soggy agony, their noble fronds pale and withered. It was all rather like Aaron's end in *Titus Andronicus*: 'Set him breast-deep in earth and famish him'.

Inside, Teddy saw that the hallway's tiled floor was grubby. And in the front sitting room, the sky-blue linen sofa was now quite badly wine-stained. Perhaps he shouldn't have dug his heels in so hard over the house. He'd thought that Cassandra might give up on the divorce if she couldn't get her beloved Number Twenty-Eight. But, if anything, his intransigence in the matter seemed to have encouraged her. And the house was, frankly, much too big: impossible for him to manage.

The wooden room-divider was drawn aside, and in the back sitting room, sprawling on another wine-stained sofa, was Hooray, unshaven to the point of beardedness. He was watching television, his hand nestling in a large bag of upmarket crisps.

'Bloody hell, Hoo,' said Teddy. 'You could have done some bloody clearing up, if you're going to be hanging about the place all day. It's an absolute charnel ground in here.'

Hooray yawned. 'It's a bit infra-dig, Teds, to be scurrying about the place like a char-lady when one's descended from the house of Plantagenet. I can hardly run the hoover around, can I? I'd feel the eyes of my ancestors on me, coldly judging.'

'My bloody eyes are on you, hotly judging. I bet you haven't even looked into how one gets a cleaner, have you?'

'All right, Tedders,' said Hooray, clicking off the television and coming to his feet with an air of wounded dignity. 'You have made your point, and it has been well taken.'

Hooray took his crisp packet and pushed it hard into the overflowing waste-paper basket, displacing some other rubbish that had been orbiting its event horizon. He then carefully moved a dirty fork from the table to the mantelpiece. This done, he surveyed the room with an air of satisfaction, like a captain inspecting the scrubbed deck of his ship. He dusted his hands and sat back down.

Teddy sighed. 'Want a glass of wine?' he asked, gruffly.

'Thought you'd never ask,' said Hooray.

They trudged through the hallway and downstairs to the kitchen-diner that occupied the whole of the lower ground floor. Teddy opened the fridge, sighing as he noticed an open bottle of upmarket ketchup on the counter, fruit flies flitting daintily around its mouth.

'You haven't even put the white in the fridge,' he said.

'Sorry, Teds. Hundred and one things on my mind. Totally forgot. Huge apols, old man.'

'I get home from a bloody hard day and I'm expected to relax with a glass of piping-hot Chablis,' he grumbled, taking a bottle from the box by the fridge. 'Have you at least ordered more?'

'Yes!' protested Hooray. 'I have. I'll do it first thing tomorrow, I promise.'

Teddy sighed again, took two child-sized mugs from the very back of the cupboard and filled them with wine.

'This really won't do, Hoo. Things can't go on like this. They simply can't.' He propped himself on a stool at the kitchen's central island, elbows on the counter, hands in his hair.

'Put ice cubes in them,' said Hooray, opening the freezer. 'Look, there's still plenty of ice cubes. I've always found Chab's better with ice anyway. Gives it a freshness.' He put a handful of ice in each mug and closed the freezer. Then he carefully put the bottle of Chablis in the fridge, closing it quickly so that nothing fell out.

Teddy took a gulp and felt slightly better.

'Godawful day,' he said. 'Had to visit a leisure centre in the morning. Parent made an unholy row about my conduct towards her son in a basketball demonstration.'

'Dear, dear,' said Hooray. 'No good treating children like delicate butterflies. They *need* robust–'

'And that company, Flock, you put me on to. Turns out they

had a mole. He took a folder related to one of their targets, and now he's been spirited away to prison in rather suspicious circs. Almost like he's being sheltered there.'

'Really?' said Hooray, his ears pricking up. 'Did the folder relate to you?'

'Nikki said not. The target was a company called … hold on.' Teddy went through all the pockets in his suit before finding the scrap of paper in the breast pocket of his shirt. 'Ken's Plucky Fried Chicken.'

'I see,' said Hooray. 'So, no immediate damage done to you, but nevertheless concerning, security-wise. Any indication who this mole was working for?'

'Nikki seems flummoxed by it. Says he's an illustrator she took on just a couple of days ago. I met him very briefly.'

'How did he seem?'

'"Startled" is the word I would use.'

'So why did Nikki tell you about this mole? You weren't the object of interest, and his work didn't affect you. If I were in Nikki's position I would seriously keep it under my hat, not go round telling my other clients about it.'

'Well, Nikki says someone at the office saw this mole steal the folder and told her. She called the police and then charged out after him. Bumped into a policeman on the stairs, coming to take a statement and saying they had the suspect in their car.'

'And? She *had* called the police. What did she expect?'

'What most people expect: that it would take them a long time to arrive, if they ever did, and they wouldn't do much about it. She considers that they acted suspiciously promptly – almost as though they were spiriting him away before she could catch up with him. In any case, she wants me to use my extensive network of contacts to find out what's happened to him.'

'You mean, tap up chaps from school, like old Beaky No-Balls Smallcock?'

'Precisely so.'

'And?'

'He told me the mole's in HMP Flintwinch, on remand.'

'On remand for stealing a folder? Something going on there.'

'Exactly my thought.'

'But in the end, Teddy, what business is it of yours? I mean, assuming he's the only mole and you aren't a target.'

'The thing is, Hoo, Flock's work is already showing great promise – in a day and a half. Nikki's managed to link my name to a conspiracy theory that was already spreading well. Says she's never seen anything like it. And I was *so* close behind Sproat anyway. If I can win London, my *god*. National visibility. Everyone will hear about me all the time. Do a term of that, then hop back over to parliament, bag one of the great offices of state. One day, *the* great office of state. Who knows, a few constitutional nips and tucks, and perhaps … *king*. Why not? But certainly statues, crowds, fawning biographies. All the acclaim to which a great man is entitled.'

'Good for you, Tedders!' said Hooray. 'You'll be able to receive me on a state visit, once I'm president of Chad.'

'Of course, of course – if you have a shave. So I don't want Nikki distracted by all this mole stuff. The sooner it's cleared up, the sooner she's fully back on the case – and the more grateful she'll be.'

'Oh yes,' said Hooray, leering suggestively.

'Honestly, Hooray. Your mind. I mean grateful in the form of extra resources for my campaign.'

'I told you Flock was hot stuff, Teddy.'

Teddy went and fished a packet of crisps out of the cupboard by the fridge. As he sat back down he said, 'The fact is though, Nikki *is* rather a good sort. I feel a sort of spiritual bond forming between us.'

'Rather like our own spiritual bond, Teddy? Pure and enduring?'

'No, Hoo. Utterly unlike our own weird and dysfunctional bond, from which I reap only discomfort and disaster. Also, I'm afraid I have absolutely no wish to have sexual relations with you. Sorry to break it this way.'

'Shame. I could have paid off my debt of honour to you in a jiffy, given my sexual prowess.'

'Actually, Hoo, there is something you *could* do to start repaying your debt of honour to me – besides clearing up a bit and ordering some more bloody wine. The debt is, after all, ginormous.'

'Teddy, if it's in my power to do, I shall do it.'

'You might just look into this company.' Teddy looked at the paper again. 'Ken's Plucky Fried Chicken. Just have a discreet sniff around and see if it yields any clues. And, more importantly, track down this startled mole fellow in prison and find out who he's working for.'

'In prison? Flintwinch, didn't you say? Bit of a tall order, T. One doesn't have much of an in with these establishments.'

'There must be some–'

'Wait a second! Isn't old Cheeso in Flintwinch?'

'Is he? Whatever for? Being an oily little creep hasn't been criminalised, has it?'

'Didn't you hear? He robbed a couple of pension funds absolutely blind. Went *way* over the line. I'm pretty sure it was Flintwinch they sent him to.'

'Don't you get sent to open prison for that sort of thing?'

'I don't know quite how it works, but I gather one has to start at the bottom and work one's way up to open prison. I couldn't *absolutely* swear it's Flintwinch he's in. Could be Pentonville.'

'All sound like Dickens characters, don't they, prisons? Just put a "Mr" in front and they could be sadistic stepfathers: Mr Pentonville, Mr Strangeways …'

'Long Lartin, the sinister gravedigger.'

'The crooked law firm run by Messrs Wormwood and Scrubs.'

'Do you have the name of this mole, by the way?'

Teddy hunted around for another piece of paper. 'Fairfax,' he said. 'Jonathon Fairfax.'

'Is this seriously all you have on him, Tedders: a name scribbled on a bit of paper?'

'No, of course not. What am I thinking? Nikki faxed over some stuff. Got it somewhere.'

Teddy went upstairs and returned with a shopping bag full of papers, which he emptied onto the kitchen floor and began digging through.

'Teddy, you'll never–'

'I just have,' said Teddy, holding up a stapled sheaf of papers. 'Never doubt the power of my methods, Hoo. Never doubt it.'

'Give that here. What have we got?'

Teddy rose from the floor and resumed his seat at the breakfast bar, passing the papers to Hooray.

'That's his CV,' said Teddy, 'including home address. And Nikki's also written down everything she remembers from her interview with him.'

'This is more like it,' said Hooray. 'Hello! "Lives with his girl-friend, seems devoted to her. Called Piper." Strange she should have an American name.'

'Well, it's not the strangest thing going on here.'

'Agreed. Pizza?'

Friday

55

When Jonathon returned to the cell that morning, he was soaked through – his underpants, towel and huge T-shirt dripping wet.

'What happened to you?' asked Jamali.

'An old man punched me in the stomach because I accidentally used his towel and then I had to sit on Gobber again. He said he'll kill me if I go in the shower again.'

'What, Gobber?'

'No, the old man.'

'What did he look like?'

'A bit like, um, Neptune?'

'As in the planet?'

'As in the Roman god of the sea? He had a sort of, um, stern and terrible majesty. And a really hard punch.'

'Where are your trousers?'

'Someone stole them while I was sitting on Gobber.'

'At least we got no flip-flops for them to steal.'

There was a short silence, while they both decided, for now, not to think about the mysterious disappearance of Jamali's flip-flops.

Jonathon said, 'Sorry I used the whole of S and Ds.'

'If you keep apologising to me I'm going to have to punch you in the stomach and steal your trousers myself.'

'Sorry,' said Jonathon. 'I'll stop apologising. It's a bit late for the trousers though.'

He sat down on one of the white plastic chairs and stared glassily at the floor. His stomach felt awful, as though someone had opened a small rift in space-time inside it. The adrenaline was leaving his system, and he could feel all the bruises he'd incurred in his wet wrestling with Gobber. The sounds of laughter as his trousers were stolen rang in his ears. He was shaking.

'Jamali,' he said, 'what am I going to do? How am I going to survive till my hearing without trousers and Piper?'

Jamali took a deep breath. 'Here's what's going to happen. I'm going to turn my back and you're going to put your wet clothes in the sink. We can dry them later. Then you're going to dry yourself on my towel, which I will lend – not give – you. Be very careful not to make it dirty. Then put on my hoodie and gym shorts.'

'Thanks, Jamali.'

'Okay. For this, you can thank me.'

A few minutes later, Jonathon was dry, clothed in surprisingly skimpy prison-issue gym shorts, huge prison hoodie, socks and shoes, and wrapped in the orange blanket full of other men's hair. His T-shirt, towel and pants were wrung out and drying on the pipe that ran along the bottom of one wall.

He was drinking a substance that had been inspired by distant tales of tea. And he was eating a baguette, delivered by a very stoned skinny man. Like a delicate salad, the baguette seemed to have been freshened up by misting it with water. But damp, powdery bread encasing plastic cheese had never tasted so good.

56

'Hi,' said a man with a moustache and a waxed jacket. 'I'd like some fried chicken, please.'

'Well, you come to the right place. What'll it be?' The murderer pointed up to the illuminated menu above his head.

'Uh, make it a … Ken's Klassik.'

'Lovely jubbly. What drink? Coke?'

'San Pellegrino?'

'What's that then?'

'Sparkling mineral water with fruit juice. Has a bit of foil on top to keep it fresh. The blood orange flavour's *seriously* good.'

'Sorry, squire,' said the murderer, who had never said 'squire' in his life before he'd got this job. He didn't know who he was any more. 'It's Coke or Sprite.'

'I'll take a Coke then. Why not?'

'That's just three fifty-nine then, squire.'

The man handed him a fifty-pound note and looked with interest past the murderer, into the kitchen behind, where Lance was clattering chicken machinery.

'Got anything smaller?' asked the murderer.

'What's that? Oh, no. Forgive me. That's all I have.'

'No problemo,' said the murderer, who had caught this from Lance.

'Listen,' said the man, 'I don't suppose you have any jobs going, do you?'

The murderer stopped and looked at him. What in blazes was going on? Whatever it was, no way was he sharing a tiny kitchen with with some posh bloke with a moustache.

'Sorry, squire,' he said. 'The last one went to the star of stage and screen behind me.'

'Hi,' said Lance, weaving a languid wave into his juggling of the fry racks.

'Tell you what though,' said the murderer, 'give us your name and number, and the boss'll give you a bell if anything comes up.'

'Not to worry,' said the man with the moustache. He turned and headed for the door.

'What about your chicken?' called the murderer.

'Not to worry,' said the man with the moustache, and exited with a *cling* of the door.

57

In the exercise period that afternoon, the various ethnically segregated groups in the yard were so absorbed in debate that they completely forgot to eye each other in hostile silence. Jonathon exchanged a puzzled glance with Jamali as they wandered over to Cheeseman, who was addressing a small knot of other prisoners with pastel sweaters draped over their shoulders.

'Fucking hell,' said Jamali. 'It's the whole of Notting Hill.'

'Um, what?' asked Jonathon.

'The ground-floor cells in our Wing, where all the white-collar boys live. Most sought-after real estate in Flintwinch.' And then he stuck his jaw out, put on his aggressive smile, and said, 'Yo, Cheese! What's coming to pass?'

Cheeseman looked round at him and pushed his glasses back up onto the bridge of his nose.

'Jamali,' he said. 'We're discussing the curious case of the locked-cell foaming, and how–' He stopped, catching sight of Jonathon's pale legs dangling down below the prison hoodie. 'What happened to your trousers?'

'I, um … Someone stole them,' said Jonathon. 'Outside the shower, while I was sitting on Gobber.'

'I see,' said Cheeseman. 'Is that how you got the bruise?'

Jonathon put his hand to his cheek, which had swollen up over the last couple of hours.

'No,' he said. 'That's from when I was punched by an old man who looks like, um, Neptune.'

'*Not* the planet,' put in Jamali. 'I know what you're thinking.'

'Neptune?' said Cheeseman. 'Oh, you perhaps mean Anderson. Scottish chap? So high?' He put his hand to about five foot four.

Jonathon nodded. 'I took his towel by mistake.'

They all laughed. 'Important lesson learned,' said Cheeseman. 'So long as you don't do something foolish like that, Anderson's an absolute pussycat. Heart of gold.'

'Yeah, never mind that,' said Jamali. 'Let me tell you about my flip-flops. When we got back to our cell after AA they was gone. Got to be the same person who foamed McGill, right?'

Cheeseman turned to him with a penetrating stare.

'Your flip-flops?' he said. 'Do you mean to tell us that someone stole them from your locked cell?'

Jamali nodded.

'Then this is even more serious than I thought. There would be just enough time, after we left your cell, for someone to open your door, steal your flip-flops, then move further down the landing to where McGill was taking a nap in his locked cell, open the door and foam him with a fire extinguisher.'

'How did they get in?' asked Jamali.

'That's the mystery we were discussing when you arrived – a mystery made even more baffling by your news.'

'Most of us think it must have been a screw,' said a man with rimless glasses and a very precise bald spot.

'I guess,' said Jamali. 'If a prisoner had the key and had some beef with McGill, he would have done something *much* worse. I mean, you know what goes on, right? Why wasn't he plated? Why wasn't he jobbed? Same goes for me and my flip-flops.'

'What's plating and jobbing?' asked Jonathon.

They all turned to him with a look that said he was much better off not knowing.

Cheeseman said, 'But why would the screws foam McGill? It doesn't make sense.'

'Think about it,' said Jamali. 'Nothing here works the way it's meant to: constant bang-up, no education, loads of short sentences. It's designed to keep people in here and keep them coming back: the prison-industrial complex feeds itself. The more riots and what-have-you there are, the more money they get. So one of the screws or the governor has done it to rile everyone up, keep the cycle going, get more money.'

Cheeseman said, 'It's hardly the governor – much less the screws – who benefit from the current system.'

'Who does benefit then?' asked Jamali.

'Well, politicians,' said Cheeseman. 'They're the ones pushing for more prisons, harsher sentences, worse conditions. They know it doesn't work, but it wins votes.'

'Sells papers too,' said a pallid man with a Caesar cut, who looked like one of the more devious Roman emperors.

'So what you saying?' said Jamali. 'A politician and a journalist got in, foamed McGill and stole my flip-flops?'

'Of course not,' said Cheeseman.

'You're missing the obvious angle,' said the precisely bald man. 'This prison is in the process of privatisation. The screws are all unhappy about it, because they think their pay and conditions will get worse. *That's* why they're trying to create unrest by foaming one of the most influential prisoners.'

'Right,' said Jamali. 'And stealing the flip-flops of a charismatic newcomer. That's why they've let us out for exercise. This place feels like a powder keg.'

'And they *want* it to blow,' said the devious emperor, glancing about.

'I, um,' said Jonathon.

He was surprised to find that this coincided with a moment of silence. Everyone turned to look at him.

'I saw the, um, screws running to the cell. The blonde lady didn't have her belt on, and they all looked terrified. I don't think they can have done it.'

'They're *acting*,' said Jamali.

'But,' said Jonathon, 'I don't think most people are very good at acting. They can't even convincingly pretend they like your shoes. I mean, even quite a lot of actors aren't very good at acting.'

'So, what do *you* think happened?' asked Cheeseman.

'I have a friend who says that once you've eliminated the impossible, then whatever remains, no matter how insanely stupid, must be the truth.'

'Which in this case means …?'

'Um, that a prisoner's got a set of keys and used them to get some flip-flops and cover someone he doesn't like very much with foam, instead of doing anything clever.'

'Wait,' said the precisely bald man. 'Just consider for a moment if it *were* a prisoner. McGill being humiliated like that by another prisoner would be a devastating loss of prestige …'

'And if McGill falls,' said the devious emperor, 'what would that do to the value of …?'

They didn't stay around to finish the sentence, but dashed off – even Cheeseman, though he gave them an apologetic smile and murmured 'gentlemen' as he went.

Jonathon turned to Jamali. 'What …?' he said.

'No clue, bruv,' said Jamali, shaking his head and looking blank. 'Not a clue.'

58

Drink tonight? the text from Teddy had said.

Nikki had given him an excuse the day before, but it felt risky to fob him off again today. After all, she owed him. Besides, she didn't have the kids – they were at their dad's till Monday. And she was meant to be going to the pub with Dave and Eleanor, but much of their conversation these days was about juice recipes, which made her feel old and boring. It was much more exciting to spend the evening with someone who'd been on television.

She had replied, *At mine? Half eight.*

The question mark and the full stop balanced: accommodation and assertion.

His knock came at quarter to nine. She opened the door and he came bustling in, a riot of tweed, with his briefcase and two carrier bags full of documents. An expensive bottle of wine was jammed in his jacket pocket.

'Nikki! So this is–' He stopped, having seen her. She was wearing her famous blue dress, and she handed him a glass of wine. He instantly dropped his briefcase, kicked his carrier bags against the wall and took a gulp.

'Welcome to my humble abode,' she said.

'You look extraordinarily beautiful, Nikki.'

Over the last few years she had unconsciously drifted into

thinking of herself more as a mum and businessperson – perhaps even a nascent cat lady – than as a femme fatale. It was nice to have a corrective.

He didn't take his eyes off her. And, with his copper hair and vivid green eyes, he looked fairly extraordinary himself – a rock-star trapped in the body of a standard flabby politician.

He moved closer to her, dropped his voice an octave, and said, 'I should say, before I forget, that I would *love* to introduce you to some of my colleagues in the party. I also think we might be able to get you writing for *The Commentator*, if you still have a journalistic itch.'

'Wow,' she said, laughing. 'You really pay up-front.'

'Not at all,' he said – seeming, as with the Eton thing, totally unoffended. 'I simply happen to believe that you're a remark-able person. And I've thought a lot about what you said – about privilege and all that. Thought I'd strike a blow for equality. And I *seriously* believe in helping my friends.'

'Are we friends already?' she asked.

'I hope so,' he said. 'Nikki, I can't stop thinking about you. I really like you.'

'Teddy,' she said gently, 'this is quite a lot to take in while we're still standing in the hallway. Why don't we go to the kitchen and have something to eat? I've got a tagine on.'

'Splendid idea!' he said. 'I'm famished. Wasting away.'

Seeing his sudden joyful enthusiasm at the mention of food, Nikki thought she'd seen who Teddy really was. He seemed, in that moment, childlike.

And then his phone went off. He rolled his eyes, looked at the display, held up a finger and answered.

'Hoo,' he said. 'Hi. Listen, I–'

'...' said the phone.

'Wonderful,' said Teddy. 'Great. Very glad you're on the case with KPFC. Look, Hoo, I'm just about to go into a meeting with Bolton–'

'...'

'Bolton Lisby, my campaign manager. I was talking about him just last night. Honestly, Hoo, I sometimes wonder–'

'...'

'The place is sewn up as tight as a what?'

'...'

'Oh, a Harrovian's *arse*. I thought you said–'

'...'

'Fine. Yes. Take the direct route, if you think that's more in line with your skillset. What *is* the direct route, by the way?'

'...'

'Oh, I see. Fairfax's girlfriend. Well, whatever you think best, Hoo. I'm absolutely counting on you to pull something out of the bag here.'

'...'

'The address is on the CV I gave you. Now listen, Hoo, I really do have to go, because Bolton's just ...'

Nikki, standing in for Bolton, had just surprised both of them by kissing Teddy.

Saturday

59

For Piper, Saturday began as Friday had ended: at the kitchen table, on the never-used landline phone, working her way through a laboriously compiled list of all London's prisons, police stations and custody suites.

'I am sorry, madam,' said yet another polite but resolutely official woman. 'I can't tell you whether someone of that name has been arrested. All I can say is that if he has been arrested by ourselves then he hasn't given permission for the disclosure of that information to yourself.'

Piper sighed. 'Please,' she said. 'I'm going insane. Isn't there anything I can do to find out which prison he's in?'

'He's in prison?'

'Yes, but I don't know which one.'

'This is Woolwich Custody Centre. You would need to write to the Prisoner Location Service for that.'

'I did that yesterday.'

'Yesterday? Well, we do advise yourself to allow three to four weeks for a response. Will there be anything else at all?'

'Could it be any sooner?' asked Piper.

Someone yesterday had said it could be just a few days. She knew that it didn't matter what these people said, because her letter had gone to a completely different organisation. But she couldn't stop herself trying to haggle for an earlier reply.

'It could be,' said the official woman, dropping her voice and becoming a bit less official. 'Look, I know as much as you do, love. All you can really do is sit tight and be patient. I know it's hard.'

'Okay,' said Piper.

'Is there anything else I can help you with today, madam?'

Bock-bock bock.

Someone was at the door. Piper instantly knew that it would be to do with Jonathon.

'I've got to go. Thanks. Bye!' she said, and bolted breathlessly for the door.

The dog was waiting just inside the living room, looking on with shy interest. Piper turned the latch with shaking hands and opened the door.

She was right.

There on the doorstep stood a man with a moustache and a confident air. He had regular features, slicked-back hair, and one of those short, green waxed jackets that a person of a certain class is issued when they come of age.

Piper was so full of relief and trepidation that she couldn't speak. She just stood there and wobbled her eyes at him.

'Good morning,' he said. 'Piper?'

'Yes.'

'Name's Knight. With the Home Office. I'd like to talk to you about Jonathon Fairfax. May I come in?'

This was not absolutely the first time someone official had said roughly these words to Piper, so she replied, 'Yes, of course,' and ushered him in.

Cess, the dog, stretched her ears towards the ceiling as the man stepped over the threshold. She turned to look at Piper, as though checking she'd noticed that this man was walking into their house. Piper ruffled the dog's hair and showed the man into the living room.

'Would you like a cup of tea?' she asked.

'Earl Grey would be seriously appreciated, if you have it. No milk. Lemon if there's one started.'

'Let me have a look,' she said, and went to check.

She found some Earl Grey at the back of the tea cupboard: a forgotten present from Jonathon's dad. In the presence of this man, with his luxurious corduroys and thick checked shirt, she felt she really ought to like Earl Grey, so she made them a pot.

Then she dithered over whether he would approve of Hobnobs, or would see them as a déclassé indulgence.

'Sorry we've run out of lemons,' she said as she set the tray between them and poured his tea. Even as she said it, she felt annoyed with herself for trying to give him the impression that they usually kept a huge stock of lemons for all their lovely Earl Grey tea which they drank all the time because neither of them thought it tasted like someone had ruined normal tea by tipping perfume into it.

'Ah, biccies,' said Knight. 'You're a marvel.' He immediately ate both biscuits with a confident lack of consideration, slurped his tea, then said, 'It's probably best if you tell me everything you know from the beginning, and I'll try to fill in the blanks.'

He was sitting in the armchair, where she would usually sit.

'I don't know anything,' she said, perching on the edge of the sofa. 'Jonathon got a freelance illustration job at some company – I can't remember the name. Then yesterday morning he called me and said he was in prison because he'd got confused about a folder. But he didn't have time to tell me which prison before he was cut off. Please tell me you know where he is.'

'We're working on tracing him now,' said Knight. 'Surprisingly difficult to pinpoint a prisoner early on, antiquated systems and so forth. If you hear from him – or anyone else – about this, it's seriously important that you call me.'

He laid his card on the tea tray and tapped the phone number on it.

She picked it up. It was plain white, with nothing on it apart from 'George Knight' and a phone number. The back was blank.

Knight looked at her earnestly and Piper nodded.

'Make sure you keep that somewhere handy,' he said.

'I will,' she replied. She grabbed her bag from the foot of the armchair, rummaged through the rubbish for her wallet, and carefully filed Knight's card among the old receipts and long-expired loyalty stamps. He gave her a little smile, as though to say, 'Of course I wasn't judging you for the fact that your bag is essentially a portable bin with a wallet in it.'

'Now,' he said, dusting the legs of his corduroy trousers with his strong, clean hands, 'I shan't take up any more of your valuable time.'

'Oh,' she said, surprised he was going so soon. The fact was that her time wasn't valuable at all: she would just use it pointlessly phoning custody centres until Gemma got back from her music group, and then she would pretend to be fine until that exhausted her and she finally went to bed and didn't sleep for a moment.

'Don't you … I mean, don't you have any news?' she said.

'Forgive me,' he said. 'I've told you all I can for now. I'll be in touch very soon with more info, I promise. Okay?'

She nodded.

'Do try to find other things to occupy yourself, instead of fretting about this. Have you any plans for the rest of the weekend?'

'It's the Notting Hill Carnival. I said I'd take Gemma. She's never been.'

'Gemma?'

'A friend's niece who's staying with us – with me – for a bit. It's not ideal timing.'

'On the contrary. It'll help take your mind off it all. Tomorrow, is that, or the bank-holiday Monday?'

'Tomorrow. It's family day. We're going to try to get there early.'

'Good show,' he said, standing up. 'In the meantime, if you hear from Jonathon again, or from anyone else, give me a call straight away. We're here to protect you.'

Piper nodded.

They went to the front door, which she opened for him. Then she watched him walk down the little path, get into a rugged, military-looking Land Rover and drive off. Cess stood beside her in the doorway with surprised ears, bristling worriedly.

60

'I still haven't managed to get anywhere near a phone,' Jonathon said to Jamali, as they sucked their tiny sachets of morning jam. 'I really need to tell Piper where I am, and let Lance know what was in the folder that I stole.'

Jamali shook his head. 'That is *complicated*, man. If I was you, I'd just let it be. Concentrate on surviving. This place is going batshit. I can't believe they cancelled Kabbalat Shabbat last night.'

'I can't believe–' began Jonathon.

But what he couldn't believe must remain forever a mystery, because at that moment the cell door crashed open.

'Fairfax!' shouted a prison officer. 'Visit!'

Piper! Jonathon thought immediately. She'd found him. How many months had it been since he'd last seen her? He did a quick calculation and was surprised to discover that it was only three days. Oh god, how he longed for three days ago, when he'd had only one nemesis, and there had even been some doubt about whether that one wanted to kill him.

Piper's face appeared in front of his eyes, so real and solid he felt he could touch her. It seemed unbelievable that he'd ever felt her arms around him, heard her laughter, or watched her do a miniature elaborate dance routine as she made a cup of tea. She seemed like a dream, as did the cat, the dog, and their little house.

'Oy, bruv,' said Jamali, softly. 'Not an ideal environment for crying. Know what I'm saying?'

Jonathon wiped his eyes on the hoodie's sleeve, then hurried out of the cell. The door banged shut behind him and he flinched.

'Took your time,' grumbled the prison officer, a florid man with short, white hair.

Jonathon followed him along the walkway to the gates at the end, which connected the wing to the prison's central body. It was odd that the prison had wings, like a bird, because there were six of them, which would have hampered its flight terribly, even if its body hadn't been a towering hexagonal chamber.

But this was not the moment to be picking holes in the prison's avian character. Thinking weird thoughts such as this was yet another of the terrible failings that made him completely unworthy of Piper.

As he hurried to see her, he resolved that he would never, ever tell her that she should be with a better man. Instead, he would do everything in his power to make her stay with him, despite his many flaws, simply because he now saw that it was absolutely impossible that she would ever, in all the vastness of time and space, find anyone who loved her more than he did. What's more, he would not delay a moment in telling her how much he loved her. Even if she had brought snacks.

'There you go,' said the prison officer, waving Jonathon into a dingy holding area where he was given a purple bib to put on over the prison hoodie and small shorts. Then he was released, along with all the others, into the visits hall.

Jonathon was overwhelmed by the number of people, and some of the visitors were nearly as terrifying as the prisoners, so he didn't spot Piper at first. His eagerness to see her had made him face blind. But there! At the cafe counter, by the visitors' entrance, in the middle of the queue … was a woman with hair of a vaguely similar colour.

Where was she? Jonathon had come to a halt in the middle of the visits hall. He began to look at each person, one by one, confirming that each in turn was not Piper. His failure to see her would be embarrassing to explain, but she was used to his foibles. She would–

A wave.

No, false alarm. There was someone at a table who actually looked very much like the man from the adverts. Jonathon turned to see who the man had been waving to, but everyone in that direction was engrossed in conversation.

The man at the table waved again. Jonathon looked around again. His feet took him a step or two forward, understanding slightly in advance of the rest of him that his visitor was not Piper but this man. As Jonathon approached, the man stood and held out his hand, which Jonathon shook automatically.

'Fairfax,' said the man. 'Good to meet you.'

He gestured for Jonathon to sit. There was a cup of tea and Kit-Kat in front of the seat, and Jonathon found they were taking up a disturbing amount of his attention.

The man had an officer-class moustache and a square jaw set in an outdoorsy face, and he smiled to reveal even white teeth. He wore a luxurious checked shirt with the sleeves rolled up, and gave the impression of being able to handle a barbecue extremely capably.

'The name's Hooray,' he said. 'Short for Horatio, as in Nelson and the Roman chap who held the bridge.'

'Pleased to meet you,' said Jonathon automatically, though this remark could more accurately have been addressed to the cup of tea and the Kit-Kat.

'Please,' said Hooray, gesturing to them. 'I know what it's like to be separated from life's little pleasures. Doesn't take long to start missing them.'

Jonathon sipped the delicious poor-quality tea and snapped a finger off the Kit-Kat.

'Of course,' continued Hooray, 'one also misses life's larger pleasures, such as one's loved ones.'

Jonathon stopped midway through a bite of Kit-Kat. The intense chocolate coating had given way and the biscuity-wafery stuff inside was almost crunched through.

'Just thought I'd toddle over and reassure you on that point,' said Hooray. 'Piper's fine. Radiant, in fact.'

Hooray produced a neat little digital camera from a pocket, pressed a couple of buttons and held it up. There, on its small colour screen, was Piper in the kitchen, doing the washing up in a ray of sunlight and, he could tell, talking softly to herself. There was another of her at the kitchen table, on the phone, looking worried.

'I popped round,' Hooray continued, 'and Piper and I had ever such a lovely chat.'

'What?' said Jonathon.

This was how his mouth chose to interpret the emotion that

arose in his breast, which could perhaps more accurately have been rendered as *Take my woman's name out of your filthy mouth*. But it's difficult to overcome a lifetime's conditioning on the spur of the moment and actually say that.

Hooray reached across the table and snapped a finger off Jonathon's Kit-Kat. He popped the whole thing in his mouth and crunched it up, ostentatiously not savouring it at all.

'Brass tacks,' said Hooray, switching gear. 'Here's Piper.' He held up the camera again. 'Here's your address.' He slapped a photocopy of Jonathon's CV on the table. 'And here's you in prison.' He gave a slightly theatrical wave of his hand, taking in Jonathon, the prison officers, and the couples at the other tables industriously snogging and smuggling drugs. 'If you want to keep Piper safe, you need to tell us exactly who you're working for, what they're up to, who engineered your little stay in prison and why, and what Ken's Plucky Fried Chicken has to do with Teddy Robinson.'

Jonathon stared at him. 'But ...' he said, and then words failed him, because Hooray seemed to be starting from such mistaken premises that he had no idea how to answer his question.

'I don't *want*,' said Hooray, 'to kidnap your girlfriend. I don't *want* to harm her. But if you leave me no choice, then I shall. Simple as that. You see, we don't have all the time in the world. Clocks are ticking. We need answers. Now.'

Jonathon goggled at him.

Hooray leaned across the table and said, 'Whatever they're threatening you with here in prison, that's what I'm threatening Piper with. And I can send photos to prove I've done it.'

'But you've mis–, um, that's not what it's ...'

'So what is it then?' asked Hooray, taking another finger of Jonathon's Kit-Kat and crunching it aggressively.

Something about Hooray's absolute certainty in his completely mistaken ideas rang a small bell of recognition in Jonathon's mind.

'Are you a friend of Teddy Robinson? Did you go to Eton with him?' he asked, feeling that this might be the source of the problem.

'Oh, so you know that, do you? What of it?' Hooray looked at him with renewed suspicion.

'No, it just occurred to me, that's all. It's just that you're so cer–'

'I don't know what kind of game you're playing, Fairfax. But these sound like questions, or possibly statements, and what I'm looking for is answers. Who's sponsoring this plot against Teddy? Is it Sproat? Is it Ken?'

'Um, Ken?'

'Nice try, Fairfax. I–'

A bell sounded and one of the prison officers shouted, 'Time's up, ladies and gents. The visiting period is over. Please say your goodbyes and make your way to the exits. Do remember you are being recorded and that you can be sent to prison yourself for passing in contraband.'

There was a general murmur of disapproval at this.

'What?' shouted a woman. 'That was never half an hour!'

One of the prison officers shrugged and said, 'Staffing issues.'

'How very *convenient*,' said Hooray. 'You've got one chance, Fairfax. I'll be back tomorrow, and I'll expect answers. I shall be very disappointed if I don't get them. And so will Piper.'

Hooray looked deep into Jonathon's eyes, then knocked his tea over him, crushed his last finger of Kit-Kat, and strode off towards the exit.

61

That night, after Lance had mopped the floor, changed the fryer oil and scraped the rotisseries, he retreated to the little changing area and removed his KPFC-branded polo shirt. He was just buttoning up his own shirt when the murderer appeared in the doorway, leaving very little doorway for Lance to get out through.

'All right, Lance,' said the murderer. 'What's going on?'

'I'm about to change my trousers,' said Lance.

'You know what I mean,' said the murderer.

'What do you mean?' said Lance.

'I mean, a posh bloke visited the shop yesterday. A proper

posh bloke, with one of them wax jackets and cord trousers. And he wanted a job.'

'Probably an actor,' said Lance. 'Like me.'

'Probably not an actor,' said the murderer. 'Like you.'

After that they had a little holiday from their conversation, while each looked at the other.

Then the murderer said, 'When it was just you, I could accept it. I thought, "Keep your head down, Colin. He says he's an actor, he looks like an actor, he's an actor. End of." But then old wax jacket comes in and it's obvious something's going on. So, I'll ask again: what's going on? What's someone like you doing working in a chicken shop?'

'What's someone like *you* doing working in a chicken shop?'

'I've just got out of prison. My employment options are limited.'

'Okay, well, since when do out-of-work actors *not* work in chicken shops? We need flexible work so we can go to auditions.'

'That's right. No one's going to argue with that – until that bloke came in yesterday. I can buy one person who clearly shouldn't work in a chicken shop asking for a job here, because that's me. I can even buy two. But three? That's where I have to ask what's going on. I'm still waiting for an answer.'

'Wait,' said Lance, 'so you were fine with me working here until someone else who isn't me and who I don't know came in and asked about a job?'

'Yeah.'

'Well if him coming in here means there's now something suspicious about me, then surely it means there's now something suspicious about you. If me being an actor isn't good enough, then you being an ex-con isn't good enough.'

'What?' The murderer looked confused. 'Yes it is. I used to come in here when my Gemma was little. One day I threw out some blokes who was getting argie. Ken says free chicken for life–'

'Free chicken for *life?*'

'Yeah.'

'That's good. Generous. Sorry, carry on.'

'And he says, if you ever need a job just ask.'

'Nice.'

'And I had a tip from this bloke in prison called Cheese–'

'Cheese?'

'Yeah. Problem?'

'No. Go on.'

'He says, you want to get a job straight out, don't matter what it is. If you're working, you'll get used to life outside and you can find something better later. Main thing is it stops you sitting round at home in your pants. That's the big danger, he says.'

'Wait, did you not already know people who'd been to prison, before you went?'

'What you saying?'

'Just, hadn't anyone already told you that?'

'You mean, being a crim, didn't I hang around with a load of other crims? Not specially. And if I did they was successful ones, never went to prison. It's only rubbish crooks and people who need help who go to prison. I was embarrassed to be there.'

'Okay,' said Lance, nodding sagely. 'Actually, that all adds up, so we can leave it there. Sorry I doubted you.'

Lance tucked the rest of his shirt in, swung his bag over his shoulder and headed for the door. The murderer instinctively stood aside.

And then he stood not-aside.

'Hold on,' he said. 'Why have I just told you my life story? It's you who's got the explaining to do. Now, as the old saying goes, we can do this the easy way, or we can do it the hard way.'

'What does the easy way involve?' asked Lance.

62

'The cell's too small for pacing,' said Jamali.

'Sorry,' said Jonathon, taking another not-quite-two steps across the cell and turning back. 'I just can't stand still.'

'I understand. If someone threatened my girlfriend while I was in here I'd be fucking livid, but you been at it non-stop since you got back. You're going to do yourself an injury, man.'

'I deserve an injury,' said Jonathon, still pacing. 'I should never have …'

His words trailed off. He still didn't know exactly what he should never have done. In the end though, Piper was in danger because of him. And he was in prison, also because of him. The problem here was definitely him.

'Like I said,' said Jamali, 'we just have to hope the screw gave Cheese our message. If anyone knows what to do, it's him.'

At that moment, perfectly on cue, the door clanked open and a prison officer said, 'Fairfax! Listener appointment.'

'What?' said Jonathon.

'It's Cheese, obviously,' said Jamali.

'Of course.' Jonathon turned to the prison officer and said, 'Can Jamali come too?'

The prison officer looked at his piece of paper. 'It don't say so. Come on, look lively.'

'I'm ready,' said Jonathon.

The prison officer looked dubiously at Jonathon's large, tea-stained hoodie, his tiny prison shorts and smart shoes, then shrugged and led him out of the cell.

They went along the walkway, down the great metal staircase to the ground floor, and about halfway along the main hall until they reached a cell with many laminated signs tacked to the door, including *Handicrafts Co-ordinator* and *Deputy For The Zoroastrian Faith*. The officer unlocked it, ushered Jonathon inside, and closed it up again with a bang that made Jonathon flinch.

Inside, Jonathon saw instantly why this neighbourhood was called Notting Hill. Cheeseman's cell contained a linen lampshade, a challenging modern painting, a percolator, a rug, and a coffee table bearing a large illustrated book about Bauhaus architecture.

'Thank god Jamali's message got to you,' said Jonathon.

'What message?' said Cheeseman. 'I scheduled this Listener session because of your, er, rather difficult situation. Please, sit down.'

Cheeseman, who was sitting in a geometrical chair that had possibly been designed by Mies van der Rohe, gestured to the foot of the narrow bed, which was neatly made and covered with an embroidered duvet.

Jonathon sat and said, 'How did you hear about my situation?'

'It's all over the wing,' said Cheeseman. 'News travels fast here. I doubt there's anyone who hasn't heard about it.'

'Oh. Did someone overhear in the visits hall?' asked Jonathon. It had seemed at the time that he and Hooray had spoken rather quietly, and that everyone else had been shouting too loudly to overhear them.

'Visits hall?' said Cheeseman, looking blank.

'I had a visitor,' said Jonathon. 'That's what caused the difficult situation.'

'Go on,' said Cheeseman, plainly intrigued.

'A man called Horatio came to visit. He told me I have till tomorrow to tell them who I'm working for. And he showed me a photo he'd taken of my girlfriend, and threatened to kidnap her if I don't cooperate.'

Cheeseman raised his eyebrows, sat back in his chair, took off his glasses and nodded thoughtfully.

'Oh dear,' he said.

'Yes,' said Jonathon.

'I was going to talk to you about a quite separate difficult situation. McGill says he saw you standing in his doorway smiling as he was being handcuffed, and thinks you're behind the foaming. Also, quite a lot of people are blaming you for the collapse of the Haribo–'

'Sorry,' said Jonathon, 'I thought you said "the collapse of the Haribo".'

'I did say "the collapse of the Haribo",' confirmed Cheeseman.

'What?' said Jonathon, falling back on an old standby.

'There's no money in prison,' said Cheeseman patiently, 'so people use other things as currency. It used to be cigarettes, in the old days. And a while ago it was tinned tuna, because everyone needs extra protein. But Slater switched it to Haribo, because he wanted a currency he wouldn't be tempted to eat. When he left, he appointed McGill his successor and bequeathed him all his Haribo. When you suggested McGill's foaming might be the work of a prisoner, some associates and I decided we should hedge our Haribo positions, as its exchange rate against the tuna seemed likely to fall if McGill became less dominant. Unfortunately, some people then panicked, the Haribo collapsed, and people with Haribo-denominated debt are defaulting right, left and centre, which has caused a wave of credit-related violence. That's why Kabbalat Shabbat was cancelled last night, and visits are curtailed. It got around, somehow, that you're responsible for the collapse of the Haribo, so you're in quite considerable physical danger from that, as well as from McGill, whose Haribo fortune, incidentally, is now worthless.'

Jonathon sat there for a while, staring at a small Henry Moore sculpture. He was stunned by the scale of the trouble he was in.

'I just tried to avoid Rachel on the Tube,' he said weakly.

Cheeseman looked at him with concern but evidently decided against following this up. He thought for a while.

At length he said, 'As a Listener, I'm occasionally asked for counsel, and my advice is always essentially, "Calm down, do your time, don't try to escape." Uniquely, in your case, I would strongly advise the opposite.'

Jonathon immediately started work on the opposite of calming down. He put his face in his hands and began to tremble.

'Sorry,' he said at length. 'Do you mean I should try to escape?'

'Yes,' said Cheeseman, gently. 'Not to put too fine a point on it, if you remain here you're likely to be killed by either McGill and his faction or the victims of the Haribo crash – in other words, well over half the prison's population. Whereas if you get out, you avoid that and should be able to reach your girlfriend before this Horatio character realises you're gone. Even if you were ultimately recaptured, you'd be sent to a different prison.'

Put this way, escaping did actually sound like the sensible and responsible thing to do. There was only one problem.

'I don't know how to escape,' he admitted.

'Leave that to me,' said Cheeseman.

Jonathon renewed his trembling.

'I'm sorry,' said Cheeseman. 'I've just realised I haven't offered you a cup of tea.'

'Thanks,' trembled Jonathon.

'Would you mind making us both one? The pot's in the little dishwasher under the bed and the Earl Grey's in the caddy by the sink.'

'Right,' said Jonathon, trembling to his feet.

As Jonathon trembled the tea, Cheeseman went over to the little rectangular window in the cell door and peered urgently out. He banged hard three times with his fist.

A face appeared and Cheeseman said, 'Would you mind unlocking me for a few minutes, Barker? I have an urgent errand to run as part of my duties as Head Listener.'

There was an agonising pause, then the door gave a loud clang and swung open. Jonathon was shocked to find that he recognised the prison officer in the doorway, wearing a starched white shirt and perfectly pressed black trousers. It was Carl Barker, who had been a security guard at a company where Jonathon had worked, and who had been involved in one of his sequences of horribly traumatic events.

'Um, hello, Carl,' said Jonathon.

Carl Barker looked blankly at him.

'I'm Jonathon Fairfax. I used to work at–'

'It's not my job to remember your name,' interrupted Barker.

'No, but–'

'I'll just be one second,' said Cheeseman, stepping out of the cell.

Barker followed him, slamming the door closed behind them, leaving Jonathon alone.

By the time the door clanked again and Cheeseman returned to the cell, Jonathon had drunk so much of the pot of tea that he was beginning to think guiltily of making another.

'Sorry that took so long,' said Cheeseman. 'It took some time to convince our guest to accompany me.'

Cheeseman walked over to his chair, and another man stepped into the room.

'All right, dickweed,' said the new arrival.

'Oh, hello, um, Gobber …' said Jonathon, as his system flooded with adrenaline. He got up and retreated towards the sink.

The door had clanked shut behind Gobber, who was now standing at the foot of the bed, his hands down the front of his tracksuit bottoms, chewing gum loudly with his mouth wide open. The bridge of his nose was still swollen and cracked.

'Please, do sit down,' said Cheeseman, indicating the spot on the bed where Jonathon had been sitting.

Gobber dumped himself there, making the bed heave. Cheeseman resumed his seat and Jonathon loitered anxiously by the sink, ready to respond to a headlock at any moment. Then Gobber held out his hand and Cheeseman placed in it two tins of tuna, as though they were wads of banknotes. Gobber immediately opened one, allowing the liquid to drip onto the floor, and started shovelling the contents into his mouth, not troubling to take out the chewing gum first.

'What you got to say then?' said Gobber aggressively, spraying fragments of tuna from his mouth.

'Well,' said Cheeseman, 'not to be too Poirot about this–'

'What the fuck's poo-arrow?'

'Poirot. He's a fictional detective, created by Agatha Christie.'

Gobber rolled his eyes and shook his head.

'In any case,' said Cheeseman, 'what I have to say is this: I've deduced that you, Mr Godber, have a complete set of keys for this prison.'

'Dream on, you fat arsehole. What makes you say that?'

'What makes me say that?' said Cheeseman, steepling his fingers. 'Well, firstly, I happen to know that there *is* a complete set of keys at large in the prison.'

'Oh, really?' said Jonathon.

'Yes. One of the officers arranged for a set to be "lost" in protest at the upcoming privatisation, hoping to stick the new owners with a bill for replacing all the locks. But the governor announced he'd found them, and the officer couldn't prove the governor was lying without producing the keys himself, for which he would have been sent to prison – on the other side of the plexiglass observation panel.'

'You're doing my head in, you,' said Gobber. 'So some nob-end lost some keys. Who says I found them?'

'I do, Mr Godber. Only someone with keys could have got into McGill's cell and foamed him while he was locked up. Whoever found the keys did that. He also stole Jamali's flip-flops. As our cells have no keyholes on the inside, the perpetrator was still dependent on being unlocked himself, which is why the incident occurred during free-flow yesterday evening, when you were returning from your work in the kitchen.'

Gobber looked at him expressionlessly and continued to eat tuna.

'The perpetrator committed both crimes and then vanished, which tells me he did them while returning to his cell. I believe he intended to attack Jonathon while he was unawares and out of range of cameras. But finding Jonathon's cell empty, he took Jamali's flip-flops – flip-flops which you had attempted to steal earlier in the day, Mr Godber.'

'They was my flip-flops.'

'The perpetrator's aggression having found no outlet, he attacked his most recent grudge: McGill – the man who didn't hold you back convincingly enough during the exercise period, Mr Godber, damaging your prestige. Being impulsive, you used the first weapon that came to hand: the fire extinguisher.'

Gobber said, 'This is all fucking … conjecture.'

Jonathon was shocked that he knew the word.

Cheeseman, taking it in his stride, rose and gave the final peroration.

'Who, Mr Godber, among all the men on this wing, was returning from a job, on a route that would pass Jonathon's cell, the fire extinguisher and McGills' cell – in that order, thus demanding little effort and no capacity for planning? You, Mr Godber, uniquely of all prisoners.'

Jonathon gasped, feeling it was polite at this point.

'And so I put it to you again, Mr Godber, that you have a set of keys for this prison, almost certainly found on Thursday – in a sand bucket in the kitchen.'

'Fuck's sake,' said Gobber, rolling his eyes. 'You're a right fucking bell-end, you are. Yeah, so I've got the keys. I went to hide some bugle in one of them sand buckets in the kitchen and I found the keys there. So fucking what? Do you want to buy them off us or what?'

'No, Mr Godber. I want you to escape.'

Godber looked uncomfortable. 'Get fucked,' he said.

'You don't know how to use the keys to escape, do you?'

'Course I do,' said Gobber, chewing nonchalantly.

'I think you just recognise the master key for the cells on your own landing, having seen it used many times. But you have no idea what the coded labels on the other keys mean. You also naturally have no idea what route to follow.'

'God, you are doing my head in so much,' said Gobber. He reached up and took a small ebony bust of the philosopher Zeno from the little bookshelf above the bed. 'Nice this,' he said. 'Think I might keep it.'

'There is a prison officer outside the cell,' said Cheeseman.

'What, Dwarfy Barker? I could have him any day. Piece of piss.'

'Also, just to be on the safe side, I booked in a listening session with McGill. Apparently he has a lot to get off his chest.'

'When's that then?'

'Not long. I'm not going to tell you exactly when.'

'You're full of shit, you,' said Gobber. But he nonetheless put the small bust of Zeno back on the shelf.

'The fact is,' said Cheeseman, 'you can either do nine more years here – plus whatever they give you for having the keys, and in whatever state McGill leaves you when he finds out you foamed him – or you can escape tonight, be free again and live the life of an absolute legend.'

Gobber looked at Cheeseman and, for the first time, said nothing.

'This evening,' said Cheeseman, 'after free-flow, Fairfax will come to your cell–'

'That nob-jockey?' said Gobber.

'Um, hi,' said Jonathon.

'That's the price of freedom, Mr Godber. Besides, Fairfax will have a prison officer's uniform, and he'll have memorised both the route out and the code for the keys.'

'Yeah? So what happens when he gets to my cell?'

63

The easy way turned out to involve firing up one of the deep-fat fryers, making some nuggets and a couple of milkshakes, and then telling the murderer everything. After that, the murderer made drumsticks, fries and a couple of other delicacies and told Lance everything, which caused Lance to revise his views on a great many things, including onion rings. They then went upstairs and talked to Ken, who told them both everything, this time over some leftover butter chicken.

Lance then took the murderer with him to go and confront Vince the journalist – who wasn't answering his phone – in order to compel him to finally tell them everything he knew.

'Vince!' said Lance cheerfully, appearing at his table in the back bit of the Compton Arms, interrupting his conversation with an intense-looking man in a yellow tracksuit.

'How did you know I was here?' asked Vince suspiciously.

'You brought me here last week, remember? Where else are you going to be on a Friday night?'

Vince narrowed his eyes shrewdly, as though he knew there was more to it than that, but saw it was pointless to pursue it. 'What you here for then?' he asked.

'I've come to confront you,' said Lance, 'and compel you to finally tell me everything you know.'

'And what if I don't feel like telling you?'

'That's why I brought my intimidating friend with me. His name's Colin.'

Lance stood aside and the murderer put in an absolutely vintage performance of burly looming.

'Right,' said Vince, with an air of hard-bitten meekness – not an easy combination to achieve.

'On the other hand,' said Lance, 'I'm buying. So, budge up. What's everyone having?'

When Lance returned with the drinks, balancing the fourth

pint on top of the other three, the murderer had loomed his way to a couple of extra stools, despite the pub being as packed as everywhere in London on a Friday night.

'So,' said Lance, when he'd distributed the drinks and sat down, 'first of all, why did you tell me Colin's working with the police?'

'Because he is,' said Vince.

'Are you?' Lance asked the murderer.

'No,' he said.

Vince looked from one to the other of them. For a second, it seemed he was going to admit that he was wrong. Then the moment passed and Vince said, 'So you say. You telling me you're just out of prison but you don't go to see a probation officer every week?'

'No. Course I see one. I have to.'

'Well then,' said Vince.

'But probation isn't the police,' said the murderer, 'and I'm not working for them. I'd get some money if I did.'

'Oh, well,' said Vince, 'if you want to quibble about which organisations are formally part of which other organisations, of course you can prove anything you want.'

Vince glanced at the man in the yellow tracksuit, who shook his head as though he were disappointed at the way the murderer was trying to wriggle out of this.

Lance and the murderer glanced at each other, disconcerted.

'What I actually said,' continued Vince, 'is that he's working in league with elements of the police and wider justice system. And let me just add this: he can do that without knowing it. Just like you can, Lance.'

'Wait,' said Lance, 'so me and him are working with the police–'

'Elements within the police,' corrected Vince, 'and the wider justice system.'

'Right,' said Lance. 'Without knowing it.'

Vince nodded shrewdly and took a sip of beer.

'Like I said: you're being played.'

'By the Romanian 'Ndrangheta?'

'It's got that in it,' conceded Vince. 'But it's bigger than that.'

'So why isn't there any crack in the barrels of cooking oil at

Ken's?' asked Lance. 'Like you said?'

'Isn't there, though?' said Vince, narrowing his eyes.

'No,' said Lance. 'The police took them all away and analysed them. Ken had to order more at short notice.'

'Cost him a packet,' said the murderer.

'Police misinformation,' said Vince, 'to justify the raid, so they could give Ken's a clean bill of health – put it above suspicion so they can carry on operating together.'

'But the raid caused even more suspicion,' said Lance.

'Customer numbers have been well down since,' said the murderer.

'And if you know so much,' Lance said to Vince, 'how come you fell for the police misinformation?'

'I didn't fall for it,' said Vince. 'Like I said, maybe I'm not ready to tell you everything.'

The murderer gave him a look. 'Do you want me to make you ready?'

Vince looked at his friend in the yellow tracksuit, who said, 'Getting late. I'd better head off. Nice meeting you all.'

He stood up, but the murderer fixed him with his eyes, fractionally shook his head, and looked back down at the man's seat. The man in the yellow tracksuit sat down again.

'Maybe,' said Vince, relenting but taking on a patronising tone, 'it's best not to take everything *absolutely* literally.'

Lance frowned. 'What do you mean?'

'Have you seen how many fried chicken places there are on Blackstock Road? Why? Because people are *addicted*. There's your crack: it's not *in* the cooking oil; it *is* the cooking oil.'

'So this is metaphorical crack now?'

'Could be.'

'So is the real 'Ndrangheta supplying the metaphorical crack? Because it's quite easy to get hold of normal cooking oil without them.'

Vince looked at the ceiling and sighed in frustration. 'You're not getting the point, are you?'

'No,' said Lance. 'What is the point?'

'This little bit of it that you're focused on, that's irrelevant.

Whether he's working with probation or police, whether the 'Ndrangheta has taken over Ken's or Dick C's – it doesn't matter.'

'Wait, so now you're saying the 'Ndrangheta has taken over Dick C's? Because that would actually–'

'Look, let's move away from what I'm saying or not saying. I'm a journalist: my job is to *ask questions* – and to point out that the standard answers we're given by the so-called authorities do not add up. It's like they're saying one plus one equals two, and we've heard it so often we're just parroting it back.'

'But one plus one does equal two,' said the murderer.

'Sometimes,' said Vince. 'But it's not that simple. What if I take one pile of papers and put it on top of another pile of papers? How many piles have I got? One. So sometimes one plus one equals one.'

'Hang on,' said Lance, 'so now you're saying that because piles can be combined, that means it doesn't matter whether Colin actually works for the police, or whether the 'Ndrangheta has taken over Ken's or Dick C's?'

'Jesus, Lance,' said Vince, looking him dead in the eye, fury on his face. 'Are you *trying* to be blind? I'm saying, ask some serious, fundamental questions about the true nature of reality and your place in it.'

'O-o-okay,' said Lance. 'Such as?'

'Such as,' said the man in the yellow tracksuit, 'why are there so many swimming pools at Davos?'

'They're not ready for it, Michael,' said Vince.

'Michael?' said Lance. He squinted at the man in the yellow tracksuit, de-ageing him, tidying up his hair and adding a suit. 'Are you Michael McKettle? Who used to do the weather?'

The murderer also squinted at him, and said, 'Oh yeah.'

'I've moved on,' said Michael.

'Anyway,' said Lance to Vince, 'I thought you said you were trying to get the truth out?'

'Yes. To people who are ready for it.'

'I'm ready for it,' said Lance. 'I even tried to work out the acrostics in your articles.'

'*I'm* ready for it,' said the murderer, in a tone of finality. 'What's the story with these swimming pools? And what's Davos?'

'Don't you watch the news?' asked Michael.

The murderer shook his head. 'Don't see the point.'

'Exactly,' said Michael. 'It's all a pack of lies. There is no point, except to brainwash yourself.'

'And Davos is a resort in Switzerland where they hold the World Economic Forum every year,' explained Vince.

'In Western Europe,' said Michael, 'the average ratio of people to swimming pools is fifty thousand to one. Guess what the figure is for Davos?'

'Five thousand to one,' said Lance.

'Five hundred?' hazarded the murderer.

'Three,' said Michael quietly. 'Three to one.'

'What do they need so many swimming pools for then?' asked the murderer.

'Okay,' said Michael, 'we'll tell you. But I warn you: you're not going to like it.'

There was a dramatic silence.

'The world's ruled by octopuses,' said Vince.

There was another dramatic silence.

Lance recovered first, because Vince's statement made sense of one important detail.

'Is that why,' he asked, 'the acrostic for your article on Clissold Leisure Centre said, "UN are obtopukes?"'

'Did it?' said Vince. '*Bloody* subs,' he added with feeling.

'So you're saying the world's run by octopuses?' asked the murderer.

Vince and Michael nodded.

'And,' said Lance, 'you don't mean that metaphorically? Like they have their tentacles in everything?'

'No!' said Vince, looking offended.

Michael said, 'Look up "octopus" in any encyclopaedia and it'll tell you, plain as day: they are highly intelligent, capable of abstract thought and use of tools; they can radically change their shape and colour, even the texture of their skin; they can weigh north of two hundred pounds, and be six foot tall or more; they can use their rear arms to walk; and they can survive for long periods out of water.'

Lance and the murderer exchanged a look.

Vince, spotting this, added a crucial detail. 'One thing that is a bit different about the strain that rule the world: the encyclopaedia will tell you that the average lifespan of an octopus is three years.' He shook his head and gave a rueful laugh.

Michael leaned forward and said, 'Try *a hundred* and three years.'

'But,' persisted the murderer, 'what makes you think the world's run by octopuses?'

'Heard of the Knights of Malta?' asked Michael.

'No,' said the murderer.

'The Knights of Malta are supposedly a humanitarian organisation. They have embassies in various countries. They issue their own passports, coins and stamps. Guess how much territory they own?'

'Quarter of the globe?' suggested Lance.

'None,' whispered Michael, significantly.

'And yet they have a seat on the UN,' said Vince.

Michael said, 'You look into it and you'll see that everyone who's anyone is a Knight of Malta: Bill Clinton, Steve Jobs, George Bush. Nixon was. Kennedy *wasn't*. Look what happened to him. Churchill was and so was Hitler. Even Napoleon.'

'It stretches back into history,' said Vince.

'But what does it have to do with octopuses?' asked the murderer.

'The Knights of Malta rule the world. And the Knights of Malta are octopuses.'

'Wait,' said Lance. 'We asked you for proof of the octopus thing, and you've just told us another thing for which you have no proof.'

'Not true,' said Michael. 'I've got genealogical charts for hundreds of the most influential families in the world, tracing their links to the Knights of Malta through the generations.'

'But what about the octopuses?'

'The Knights of Malta *are* the octopuses,' said Vince, seeming puzzled that Lance was so slow on the uptake.

'But genealogical tables don't prove that the Knights of Malta are octopuses. Do they?'

'You want proof?' said Michael, earnestly. 'I'm writing a book right now to prove it beyond a *shadow* of doubt. It's this thick' – he held his fingers five inches apart – 'with evidence linking the octopus and the concept of power in human culture stretching back thousands of years. Heard of a little thing called Atlantis?'

'Yes, but–'

'I know what you're going to say,' said Michael. 'Atlantis sank hundreds of years ago. Typical small-minded objection. And wrong. Atlantis–'

'That wasn't what I was going to say,' said Lance. 'Atlantis doesn't exist, and–'

'Oh,' said Vince sarcastically, 'shame no one told *Plato* that. He wrote about it in not one but *two* works: *Timaeus* and *Critias*. But maybe you're cleverer than the father of modern thought.'

The murderer looked at his watch.

'Have you,' asked Lance, 'got a photo of a powerful person that incontrovertibly shows they are also an octopus?'

'Easy,' said Michael. He reached over and grabbed Vince's newspaper, which he put triumphantly on the table.

'That's Dick Cheney,' said Lance, 'shaking hands with a soldier.'

'For god's sake,' said Michael. 'You're telling me that you can look at him, knowing what you now know, and *not* see an octopus there?'

'I know what he means,' said the murderer, appraising the picture. He shook his head. 'But also this is a waste of time. You two are chasing yourselves round in circles in your heads. You've gone mad. Whenever anyone asks you for proof you just start talking about something else. It's doing my head right in.'

'I know,' said Lance. 'To think I was hoping that you would tell me what's going on, and which prison Jonathon's in.'

'I know where Jonathon is,' said Vince. 'That's easy.'

Lance and the murderer exchanged a look and then sighed.

'We've come this far,' said the murderer. 'We might as well.'

Vince looked from one to the other and then said, 'Your mate Ken, whatever you think of him, is one of *them*. The eight-pointed star on his shop front tells me that. You, Colin, were duped into leading Lance to Flock. Jonathon was duped into getting the folder out of their hands – whether to protect Ken's or Dick C's I don't know. Which prison's he in? He isn't. He's being held at Buckingham Palace. Dowsers report vibrations there that could only be consistent with a *vast* underground swimming pool. If you want to know more, ask Teddy Robinson. He's the only high-profile politician who isn't an octopus. He's leading the resistance.'

Lance and the murderer looked at each other and drank the rest of their pints.

'Let's go then,' said Lance.

'Do you know Teddy's address?' said Vince.

'We're not going to Teddy's house,' said Lance. 'We're going away to regret that my natural sense of intrigue, and the weirdness of most of what's certainly true about the world, ever led me to think that you aren't an absolutely huge waste of time.'

The murderer nodded at them, poured their pints solemnly over their heads, and walked away.

As Lance followed him, Vince said, 'I *told* you they weren't ready for it.'

64

The time came for Jonathon to leave his cell. He took off the prison hoodie and handed it to Jamali.

'I–' he began.

'If you're going to thank me for something or apologise, don't.'

'Oh. Okay.'

'It's been real, man,' said Jamali.

'Yes,' said Jonathon. 'Also pretty unreal.'

Jamali nodded. 'That's prison.'

He held out his fist and Jonathon shook it.

'Always with the rock, paper, scissors,' said Jamali.

'Always.'

'You be safe, okay?'

'You too.'

And with that Jonathon left, the cell door clanging behind him. He joined the sparse ranks of those on free-flow, Cheeseman's words still echoing in his ears.

'Both of you – Mr Godber, Mr Fairfax – will leave clothes in your bed to make it look like you're asleep. Jamali will have an early night, so as not to be implicated, and will raise the alarm in the morning, as late as he can.'

Jonathon followed the walkway to the staircase, and from there to a cell on the ground floor. Here he sat among the crowd of non-Jewish prisoners who chatted while Cheeseman performed a perfunctory Havdalah service, printed from the internet. Afterwards, they had tea from an urn and Jonathon – at a nod from Cheeseman – slipped out, taking a clipboard and a bag full of clothes.

'When Fairfax reaches your door,' said Cheeseman, *'you push the keys out and he–'*

'Do you think I'm fucking stupid or what?' said Gobber. *'I push one key out.'*

'Very clever, Mr Godber. Very well, you push out the master key for your landing. Then Fairfax unlocks you.'

Jonathon made his way back up, past his own cell, to Gobber's. He knocked quietly on the door. After a long pause Gobber's middle finger appeared in the observation panel. Shortly afterwards, a key appeared from under the door.

The escape attempt had begun.

'Now,' said Cheeseman, *'you both go to the gym at the end of the landing – closed since Slater left.'*

They went to the gym. Jonathon told Gobber which key to open it with.

'Once you're in there,' said Cheeseman, *'Fairfax changes into the prison officer's uniform and–'*

'What you talking about?' said Gobber. *'I'll wear the screw's clothes.'*

'Come now, Mr Godber. Fairfax will have memorised the map and the key codes. It'll be much easier and quicker if he–'

'No. He's not the boss.'

'But–'

'I don't care. I wear the screw's clothes. End of. Where you getting them anyway?'

'I've got a white, short-sleeved shirt and some dark trousers,' said Cheeseman. 'And then I'll cut up my spare pillowcase to make the shoulder tabs and tie. It won't work close up, but it should be good enough at a distance and on CCTV.'

Ultimately, Gobber had won the argument about who should wear the uniform by repeating everything Jonathon said in a stupid falsetto. Now, in the darkened gym, he changed his clothes and they waited.

'Sit quietly in the dark,' said Cheeseman, 'until after the final free-flow, when the night shift comes on and there'll be even fewer screws.'

The two hours Jonathon spent in the pitch-black gym with Gobber were the longest of his life. They were far longer than the decades of that first hour in prison, because in that first hour no one had been deliberately belching as loudly as possible, and nor had anyone been repeatedly attempting to give him a Chinese burn. But eventually, the luminous hands of Cheeseman's little travel alarm clock told Jonathon it was the appointed hour.

'At three in the morning,' said Cheeseman, 'you let yourselves out of the gym. The rest depends on Fairfax's memory of the route and his knowledge of the key codes.'

Jonathon opened the door of the gym and peered out. In the whole vast space of the wing, there was not a single person to be seen. He beckoned urgently to Gobber.

'All right, you fucking ponce,' said Gobber. 'I'm coming.'

'One more thing,' said Cheeseman. 'It is absolutely essential that you behave exactly like a screw escorting a prisoner at all times. If you give yourselves away by even the smallest detail, your escape will fail.'

Jonathon, being the prisoner, walked in front. He glanced back to check that Gobber was following, and was given the finger. Remembering Cheeseman's words, Jonathon resolved not to look back again. Seconds later, his ear was flicked in the most incredibly painful way. When he glanced back, Gobber did an upsettingly vivid blowjob mime.

The escape was doomed.

Jonathon was amazed that they managed to get to the door at the end of the first landing.

'Key D3-H,' he whispered.

'All right, twat,' said Gobber, fiddling for the right key.

Jonathon was glad Gobber's contempt for intellectualism made him see the keys' labels as a baffling cypher. That and a couple of details of the route were all Jonathon had over him.

'Now Gobber's gone,' Cheeseman said, closing the cell door, 'I'll tell you the way out. From your landing, get into the prison's central hub, then into A Wing.'

The lock opened. They were through their first door, into the hub. Gobber moved on.

'You'd better lock it again,' whispered Jonathon.

'You'd better lock it again,' mimicked Gobber in his high-pitched Jonathon voice. 'What's the point? You're just doing their job for them, guvboy.'

'People will see if we leave it open,' said Jonathon.

'You're a right pussy, you are,' said Gobber, contemptuously locking the door.

To Jonathon's relief, the central hub was deserted. He led Gobber down its staircase to the ground floor, past the visiting room and then to A Wing's door. Gobber unlocked it, revealing another vast space identical to their own. As Jonathon stepped through, his heart stopped.

There was a prison officer – only an eighth of a cathedral away, or barely ten Jonathons.

He was on the opposite side of the wing, walking away from them – an overweight older man with sparse grey hair. He had a shambling, heavy gait and he shook his head as he walked.

Gobber gave Jonathon a hard shove in the back and locked the door noisily behind them. The older officer glanced round. Jonathon's eyes did a spontaneous crash zoom on the man's face as it registered … nothing much. The officer shambled on again. Thank god Cheeseman could make a convincing tie from an old pillowcase.

'*A Wing's divided in two by a chain-link fence,*' said Cheeseman. '*There's a gatehouse not far beyond it with two doors. Get through both of them and you're out.*'

They walked on, past silent cells, till they came to the door in the chain-link fence. Gobber unlocked it without fuss, re-locked it behind them, and they marched on towards the gatehouse. Was it Jonathon's imagination, or was Gobber growing into his role? He glanced back.

Gobber was walking along with his trousers unzipped and his genitals hanging out. Seeing Jonathon's expression, he doubled up with laughter.

'Your face! That's sick! Ah, man, you are so *nesh!*'

'Shut up!' whispered Jonathon furiously.

'Relax, bell-end, there's no one around,' said Gobber.

Amazingly, given this colossal provocation to fate, Gobber's words continued to be true all the way to the gatehouse.

'This one,' said Jonathon. 'A1-G1.'

The gatehouse's inner door opened and they stepped through. Ahead of them, through the outer door's window, he could see the dark sky. As they strode across the gatehouse floor, footsteps sounded on the stairs above them, coming down.

'A1-G2,' whispered Jonathon as they reached the outer door. 'Quickly.'

'Get fucked, you twat,' whispered Gobber, attempting a flourish and dropping the keys.

He picked them up, fumbling for the right one. The footsteps were on the landing directly above. The key was in the lock. The lock clicked and the door opened. Fresh, cool air rushed in. Jonathon stepped through. The air on his face and in his lungs was the sweetest, freshest thing he'd ever felt.

Gobber locked the door behind them and they stood, backs to the wall, listening as the footsteps continued down the stairs. Whoever it was must have heard the keys drop, the door open. Would they come to investigate? Jonathon and Gobber exchanged glances. Jonathon was horrified to see Gobber's fist was clenched, keys protruding between the fingers like a cat's claws.

'*Whatever happens,*' said Cheeseman, '*it is absolutely essential that you do not use violence. It would guarantee you spending the rest of your lives in prison.'*

The footsteps moved from metal staircase to concrete floor. They stopped. There was a jingle of keys. A lock clanked. A door opened. But not this one.

Gobber unclenched his fist and Jonathon unclenched everything else.

They were in a concrete yard facing some windowless brick buildings that looked like storage sheds. To their left, in a corner where two high walls met, was a low wooden platform stacked with building supplies and covered in blue plastic. Jonathon pointed to it silently, his vocal cords still too tense to speak.

'Piece of piss,' said Gobber.

Jonathon gulped.

They walked to the overshadowed side of the platform, then climbed the lower part of the blue plastic sheeting, where it covered some timbers. This got them high enough to climb onto the wall. They then hung down the other side, noses to smooth brick and rough mortar, arms at full stretch, and let themselves drop the few feet to the ground below.

Jonathon landed, staggered backwards and tripped over the wooden side of a raised bed of soil, falling among broad-leafed plants. As he got up, he saw that there were six of these raised beds, arranged in a grid, as Cheeseman's map had shown. Beyond them were several arched greenhouses.

Jonathon moved at a crouch through the grid of raised beds, groping about in the last of them until he found a small weed fork and a pair of secateurs. Then they sneaked through a cluster of fruit trees, over a tiny lawn, and past some wooden portakabins, until they came to an old metal fence.

They turned left and followed the fence until – there it was: a little way ahead the metal fence was brand new. And, between the new fence and the old, there was a missing section.

'The screws regularly complain,' said Cheeseman, 'about the maintenance contractors. About a month ago, Barker was telling me that the fence was one of several things they still hadn't done–'

'About a month ago?' said Jonathon. 'Surely it will have been

fixed by now.'

'Absolutely not,' said Cheeseman. 'There are plenty of risks in this plan, but the maintenance contractors suddenly getting their act together isn't one of them. It's been like that for over a year.'

Jonathon had bitten his lip and allowed his stomach to turn inside-out in silence. After all, if he didn't manage to escape, Horatio would kidnap the woman he loved.

He and Gobber crept through the gap in the fence. There was now only a single obstacle between them and freedom.

'It's a twenty-foot high wall surmounted by razor wire, with an inward-facing net to prevent climbing, and powerful spotlights to illuminate anyone who tries,' said Cheeseman.

'Um, what?' said Jonathon incredulously. He dropped heavily onto the bed and covered his face with his hands.

'I realise it sounds impossible,' said Cheeseman, comfortingly. 'But, as in so much of this plan, the staffing crisis is your chief ally. That and the fact that no one has ever tried to climb it.'

'But that's because it's impossible, isn't it?'

'Partially,' conceded Cheeseman. 'But it's much less impossible than it seems. After all, if your job is to watch CCTV images of a very long, brilliantly illuminated wall that no one ever attempts to climb, you lose interest in it pretty quickly. Even the governor calls that job the sudoku shift.'

Jonathon reached under his absolutely massive T-shirt and untied the ends of the improvised rope concealed by its providentially capacious folds.

'I have some spare bedsheets,' said Cheeseman. 'And if there's one certainty about breaking out of prison, it's that knotting bedsheets works. Especially John Lewis bedsheets.'

Jonathon and Cheeseman had tried different methods of knotting sheets, testing each with a tug-of-war, in which Cheeseman showed himself to be extremely competitive. They'd ended up with a rope a little over twenty feet long. Jonathon now tied the end of it around the neck of the weed fork.

'What you gonna do with that, you spanner?' asked Gobber.

'I'm going to try and throw it up so the fork gets caught in the net at the top of the wall.'

'Dream on, cheese dick,' said Gobber, pushing him over and snatching the fork, just as Jonathon had hoped he would. This was where Gobber's playground skills would come into their own.

Gobber strutted out into the brightly lit strip of bare ground in front of the wall and threw the fork up with an easy looping motion. It described a graceful parabola through the air, soaring up to the top of the wall, striking just below the net, and clattering back down to earth.

'Practice throw,' said Gobber. Adding, as though he'd almost forgotten, 'You dicksplash.'

Gobber threw again. This time the prongs of the fork caught in the holes of the netting at the top of the wall.

'I'll climb it!' whispered Jonathon, just as he'd rehearsed with Cheeseman.

'The fuck you will, cumstain,' said Gobber.

Gobber grabbed the rope in both hands, put a foot against the wall and heaved. The netting gave way and the fork fell to earth, nearly hitting Gobber on the head.

'Can you throw the fork up again so it gets caught in the stanchion?' whispered Jonathon.

'The *stanchion?*' said Gobber with disgust. 'What kind of gaylord says *stanchion*?'

'This probably isn't the time to argue about what to call it,' whispered Jonathon.

'Oh, I'm a boffin, me,' said Gobber in his pantomime of Jonathon's voice, mincing about. 'I'll just hook this jolly fork over my stanchion. Bellend!'

'The metal thing at the top!' whispered Jonathon urgently.

Gobber looked at him. 'I've never met a bigger fucking rimjob than you.'

'They'll see us!' hissed Jonathon.

'Oh, we'd better get our stanchions out then, hadn't we?'

Oh god. Jonathon hadn't anticipated this. What could he do? Reverse psychology again. It was the only answer.

'I bet I could hook it over the metal thing better than you,' he whispered. 'You … stanchion, um, head.'

'Could you fuck, dildo. Come on then!'

To Jonathon's horror, Gobber held the fork out to him.

'You do it!' whispered Jonathon.

'No, you wanted to do it, helmet. So do it.'

Jonathon ran forward at a crouch, and took the fork from Gobber's hand. This was like being back in PE, except somehow even more stressful and high-stakes.

Jonathon looked up, hefted the fork in his hand, kept his eye steady on the metal stanchion, drew back his arm and was shoved violently forward so that he fell over and the fork clattered off the wall.

'This is how you hook a fork over a fucking stanchion,' said Gobber. He drew his arm back and threw, the rope ribboning out behind the fork as it flew up into the darkness of the night sky and hooked neatly over the metal thing at the top.

Gobber looked at Jonathon. 'Good, aren't I?' he said.

'You're amazing,' said Jonathon. And in that single moment he fully meant it.

Jonathon handed over the secateurs with the air of bestowing an honour, and Gobber put them in his back pocket. Then Gobber wrapped the rope loosely around his arm, grasped it tight in both hands, put a foot against the wall and hoisted himself up. He made the top in just a few hard tugs, climbing through the hole in the netting and cutting the razor wire with the secateurs.

They now reached another of the many moments Jonathon had been dreading: Gobber might pull the rope up after him and climb down the other side, leaving Jonathon alone at the foot of a brightly lit prison wall.

Gobber looked irritatedly down at him. 'Come on then, you wazzock,' he said.

Jonathon grabbed the rope as Gobber had done and hauled. At first his feet slipped. But then he got a grip. He hauled, moved his hand up, and hauled again. After an agonising effort, he joined Gobber at the top of the incredibly high spotlit wall, his whole body shaking.

For a moment, he and Gobber looked at the huge edifice they had left – the wings radiating from the hub like a big dead star-fish. Jonathon took in the rows of black windows, the deserted yards, all the intractable suffering concentrated there. And then he looked out the other way, over London, with its golden street lamps, its silver speckle of windows illuminated by people doing whatever they wanted.

Then Jonathon gathered up the bedsheet rope and dropped it down the other side of the wall.

'Ladies first,' said Gobber.

Jonathon rapidly and clumsily descended the other side, hoping that Gobber wouldn't think it was hilarious to untie the rope from the fork. At the bottom, in a narrow street between the high prison wall and a lower wall behind some houses, Jonathon looked up and saw Gobber still sitting there, apparently unconcerned. Then he gave prison the finger, swung himself over, and climbed easily down the rope.

They ran as fast as they could down the narrow street and into the road at its end, into a wide white glare.

Headlights.

The beep of a car's horn, the squeal of its tyres.

Jonathon ran headlong, crashing over a low hedge, falling, getting up, running again, across a lawn, over a wooden fence, over a steel fence, crashing down in undergrowth, running on, dodging trees, slithering down a slope, reaching a railway line, seeing the train, judging the distance, slipping over cold sharp rails, crunching over loose stones, the train almost on him, tripping on the last rail, throwing himself forward as the train pounded past, huge and shockingly fast, punching its way through the night air as he fell hard full length, Jonathon instantly getting up and running for the undergrowth, up among the trees, up a hill, turning left, still running, past the backs of houses, seeing a gap, scrambling over a wall, running up past flats, into a street and, finally, stopping.

His vision dimmed almost to black. His heart was a hammer. His body needed oxygen faster than he could breathe it. He felt himself sway. He put his hands on his knees, bent double. He felt as though his blood, brain and breath would all simultaneously implode and explode. It seemed as though he were rushing away from the world at infinite speed.

And then the moment passed. His vision started to clear. He was breathing hard but no longer gasping. His pumping pulse was ticking down.

He looked up. He was in a nice, normal London street. He almost cried at the sight. There were Victorian terraces with sleepy-eyed windows and yawning door mouths. There were knobbly trees, low hedges, little cars. It felt as though he had stepped into another dimension.

There was a loud whoop behind him.

'Fucking freedom!' shouted Gobber. 'Mint!'

Jonathon turned and looked at him.

'We did it, you daft streak of piss!' said Gobber. 'We fucking did it! We're out!'

They had done it.

'Thank you,' Jonathon said to Cheeseman. 'I feel guilty that you're making such sacrifices.'

'It's not much of a sacrifice, really, given that your girlfriend's life may well depend on it, as well as your own. I'm only giving up a bedsheet, a shirt, a pillowcase and two tins of tuna.'

'But what if they find out the sheets were yours? They know I came and talked to you.'

'Do you have sheets of your own?'

'Not really. The ones in my cell are–'

'Well, there you go. I'll tell them that I lent you my sheets because you couldn't sleep. Believe me, dealing with authority and bending the rules to suit me are my specialties.'

For about quarter of a second, it seemed they were going to hug. Then Cheeseman held out his hand and Jonathon shook it.

Jonathon, standing in a London street, free, felt suddenly chilled by a breeze on his sodden gigantic T-shirt and on the bloody privet scratches on his bare legs.

'Where we going now then?' asked Gobber.

'What? Now we split up and try to avoid getting caught.'

'Split up? After all that?'

'But that was always the plan. I, um–'

'Whatever, bumhole,' said Gobber, and stalked off.

Part Three

Chicken

Sunday

65

Jonathon often felt mixed emotions. But they were not often as mixed as when he finally opened the gate to his little front garden and walked the few steps to the door. There was the familiar comforting feeling of being home – where, as Paul Simon's song should perhaps have mentioned, no one gets you in a headlock and steals your trousers – as well as relief at having finished the huge journey across London, anxiety that the police might even now spot and arrest him, embarrassment at wearing these clothes in public, and hope and love and yearning at the thought of seeing Piper again. But the ice in this emotional cocktail was the fear that something awful might already have happened to Piper – and because of him.

The journey had taken all night: it was a long way, and he'd made it much longer by erroneously walking towards Peckham for quite a while. It was thus around nine o'clock – judging by the sun, the volume of traffic, and how awful he felt – when he pressed the doorbell.

Drrrkkkkhh.

It was an unimpressive sound, but Piper could hear it through anything. His heart thudded in his chest at the thought of hearing Piper's footsteps.

There were no footsteps.

Jonathon stood waiting in his huge T-shirt as there continued to be no footsteps. He heard people in the street and glanced back, his shoulders tensely creeping up towards his ears. Luckily there were no police arriving to arrest him.

He pressed the doorbell again.

Drrrkkkkhh.

There were still no footsteps.

Jonathon walked back to the front gate and looked up to the first floor. The bedroom curtains were open. So were the living-room ones on the ground floor. He approached the front window, squeezing himself behind the large bush that they used to discourage tourists from looking into their living room. On the little table there was, heartbreakingly, a plate with toast crumbs on it, beside a mug with the dregs of an extinct cup of tea – just as Piper always left them. At that moment, he would have given his life just to negligently leave a toast plate and tea mug next to hers one last time.

And then Cess, the dog, shyly nosed open the door from the kitchen, where she invariably hid whenever the doorbell sounded. Seeing a face at the window, she drew back. Then she peeped out again, and recognised Jonathon. She came into the middle of the room, tail wagging, and tried to get to the window by going first one way and then another, finding each in turn was blocked by a combination of plants, walls and sofa. Politely excluding the option of climbing on the sofa, she paced from one side of the room to the other, looking at him eagerly and glancing around to see if a passage to the window had opened up yet. Jonathon had never been more pleased to see his friend the dog.

But if the breakfast things were there and Cess was behaving like this – i.e. normally – there was a chance that Piper had not been abducted, but that she had simply and uncharacteristically got up early and gone somewhere. After all, even the most considerate abductor doesn't wait for the abductee to have a nice cup of tea and a slice of toast before getting the abduction underway. It was a comforting thought. But still, Piper getting up early on a Sunday was itself a profoundly worrying sign.

Gemma. He'd forgotten Gemma. That could be the cause of this odd behaviour.

If he could just get in, he could call Piper from the landline phone they never ever used, warning her of the danger and fulfilling the main purpose of his escape. He thought of the spare set of keys they kept in the small brass pot in the kitchen. If he could just get his hands on them, he would be able to get inside. But he couldn't for the life of him think how to get them without already being inside.

Cess continued her eager pacing on the carpet. Could she help somehow?

Jonathon squeezed back over to the front door, where he crouched down and opened the letter flap.

'Cess!' he whispered urgently.

Her nose and eyes appeared shyly around the door from the living room. She was delighted to find it was him who had called, and trotted excitedly over, smiling in her tonguey way.

'Cess,' he whispered. 'Keys! In the kitchen! In the small brass pot next to the sink!'

Cess panted happily and very gently licked his fingers.

'Cess!' he whispered still more urgently. 'Keys! Kitchen! Small brass pot!'

Incredibly, she turned and trotted into the kitchen. After a tense minute or two, she emerged again – with a small bunch of keys not at all in her mouth or anywhere near her, because of course she didn't know a small brass pot from a hole in the ground, although she would have been considerably more interested in the hole.

'Good girl,' he said anyway, because Cess was looking pleased with herself, and it was quite impressive that she understood the English word 'kitchen'.

'Rooooaw,' remarked someone behind Jonathon. He started and looked behind him. There was the cat, Hastings Banda, his tail in the 'hello' position, looking as pleased to see Jonathon as a genial academic might on bumping into a favoured acquaintance at a conference.

Jonathon stroked the cat with the hand that wasn't holding open the letterbox.

The cat flap! he thought. Of course. If he could just climb the wall into the back garden and get to the cat flap in the kitchen door, then he could … totally fail to get the keys that were several feet away from it, and waste a lot of precious time trying to explain the idea of a small brass pot to two species of animal that were utterly unequipped to grasp either the concept or the keys within.

He looked at the sturdy front door and the double-glazed windows, and concluded that he could not break into his own house. Nor could he ask the neighbours for help: the nicer ones were in Addis Ababa and the newer ones were too new. Besides, even with the friendliest neighbours, it's very difficult to be absolutely sure that you're on prison-break terms.

Jonathon suddenly realised how long he'd spent peering through his window and letterbox. The only remotely practical thing was for him to go to Lance's flat and get him to phone Piper. At least Lance was certain to be in on a Sunday morning. Jonathon just hoped that he or Arlene would hear the doorbell from their bed.

66

Teddy flung open the door to the guest bedroom and stamped in, sending a small pot of upmarket guacamole skittering away across the carpet.

'Fairfax has escaped!' he said to the dark form amid the crumpled duvet.

Hooray sat up and stared at Teddy with the urgent vacancy of the suddenly awakened.

'Come again?' he said.

'I said Fairfax has escaped!' said Teddy. 'I've just heard it on the radio. He and another prisoner – a hardened criminal, by all accounts – managed to get out somehow. Did you know he's homeless?'

'He isn't homeless,' said Hooray, scratching. 'I've been to his home. I told you.'

'More misinformation!' said Teddy. 'We're drowning in the stuff.'

'Did they say how he got out?'

'No. The prison authorities are looking into it, apparently. Clearly an inside job. What are we going to do?'

'Calm down, Teddy. I told you, I went to see Fairfax yesterday and applied a little pressure. This simply confirms that he responds to it – and that his weak spot is his nearest and dearest. So now I simply have to swing into action and kidnap her, as I told him I would.'

'What if he gets to her before you?' asked Teddy, running a hand through his tousled hair.

'Flintwinch is on the other side of London, whereas we're only five miles from the girlfriend's house in Hampstead. I can pull on some clothes, gather up the old cable ties and drive over there in half an hour.'

'But they said he broke out during the night! He could be there already!'

'Teddy, really. This unseemly panicking is quite unlike you. Is this the man who, from his bed, engineered history's most ruthless and effective Oxford Union presidential campaign?'

Teddy took a breath. 'I'm not panicking, Hoo. I am simply galvanising a response to a crisis.'

Hooray picked up a laptop from the floor by the bed, flipped it open, and said, 'Consider me galvanised.'

He clicked and tapped for a few seconds, then said, 'The girlfriend is outside Notting Hill Gate station – which means she's gone to the carnival, as planned. Not the actions of a woman who has recently been rescued by an escaped convict.'

Teddy relaxed very slightly. 'And you're sure he won't be able to call her?'

'Teddy,' said Hooray, shaking his head with hurt disappointment. 'This constant impugning of one's professionalism is wearing. The S140 combined GPS tracker and mobile-phone signal blocker is a robust and dependable piece of technology. What's more, it is discreet. I have sneaked it into jackets, I have sneaked it into coats, and on one occasion I sneaked it into a hat worn with considerable approval throughout Ladies' Day at Ascot. In this case, it is in a large and disorganised bag, where I'm confident it will stay until kingdom come – and certainly until I drive over to the Notting Hill Carnival and kidnap its owner.'

After Hooray had left, Teddy got a cab to the Notting Hill Carnival, where he wanted to be photographed pretending to enjoy the music. Ideally, he would be caught dancing in a dufferish but enthusiastic way and it would make the news that night.

Teddy felt so relieved at Hooray's calm response to the Fairfax crisis that he took the next step in his burgeoning relationship with Nikki, and propositioned her by text message. In fact, he was so full of optimism that he suggested she come to his house that afternoon. After all, he was fully capable of tidying a couple of rooms before she arrived: he had seen it done many times.

67

Jonathon ran all the way across Hampstead Heath, taking just over ten minutes to reach Lance and Arlene's flat on Dartmouth Park Road.

The flat was spread over the top two floors of a handsome and solid Georgian semi-detached house, made of golden sandy bricks and with a delicately flowering creeper curling picturesquely up one side. A short flight of steps led up to the front door, which was sheltered by a colonnaded portico that looked like a small and exquisitely tasteful Parthenon.

He climbed the steps to the front door, his huge T-shirt drenched in sweat, and pressed the doorbell for Lance's flat.

Di-ding! came a graceful chime from within.

Jonathon waited. The extraordinary pain of his feet had by this time become such an integral part of him that he couldn't imagine life without it. His smart freelancing shoes were only a couple of months old, and he'd never previously worn them continuously for three days, walked for an entire night and then sprinted across Hampstead Heath.

He couldn't help noticing that he was still waiting.

Oh god, were Lance and Arlene not in either? How had everyone turned into active Sunday-morning people while he'd been in prison? Life really does move on while you're inside.

Jonathon hid behind one of the portico's columns while he thought about what to do. Could he climb on top of the portico and use the creepers to get up to one of the windows, hoping it was unlocked? After all, he'd been going climbing for the last few months, believing it would probably be more therapeutic than the therapy Piper thought he should be going to. But so far they had mostly covered how to ascend walls that had clear, colour-coded hand- and foot-holds bolted to them; there had been little emphasis on porticos or creepers. Would trying to climb up to this flat really be more practical than attempting to explain the concept of a small brass pot to two uncomprehending quadrupeds?

Or should he just bite the bullet and knock on someone's door, asking to use their phone? It had made sense not to do that in the middle of the night when he'd just escaped from prison, but perhaps now it was his best option. People were bound to be suspicious, and he was shy, but he couldn't let those be the reasons Piper got kidnapped.

Footsteps.

He looked anxiously around the slim Corinthian column he was standing behind and there was Arlene. She was dressed in a fresh linen shirt, trousers and shades, and until about two-fifths of a second ago she'd been carrying a woven shopping basket, which she had dropped in order to launch the hard punch that was now heading for his face.

As he ducked and flinched, their eyes met. They stared at each other for an instant, Jonathon frozen in mid-duck, Arlene frozen in mid-punch. Then they both burst out laughing and Arlene hugged him as he remained in his ducked position.

'My god, Jonathon!' she said, breathlessly. 'What the fuck? What happened to you? Lance said you were in prison!'

'I, um, escaped.'

'You *escaped*? Jesus, you are a busy little guy.'

She looked apprehensively around the street, straightened her sunglasses, gathered her fallen basket and hustled him through the front door and up the stairs to her flat.

'So, what happened?' she asked, as soon as the door had closed behind them. She immediately interrupted her question with others. 'You want coffee? I'll make you scrambled eggs. What happened to your clothes?'

'Well,' he said, 'there have been a *lot* of misunderstandings, which sort of came to a head with me and a man called Gobber climbing over the prison wall.'

'Gobber? Wow. Where's he? He need help too?'

'He, um, no – he got upset with me. Oh! I need to phone Piper! To warn her. That's why I escaped. Can I borrow your phone?'

'Sure,' said Arlene, rummaging through her basket, taking out organic eggs and *Bonne Maman* jam until she found the phone.

He rang Piper's number.

There was a pause. Then, when there should have been ringing, there was silence followed by Piper's voice saying, 'Hello! This is Piper Palgrave, which you should know really, I suppose. Anyway, leave me a message and I'll call you straight back, almost. Promise!'

There was another silence.

'Piper!' said Jonathon. 'Listen, you're in–'

Beep.

'Oh god, is that the signal to start the message? I always forget there's a delay. Anyway, you're in, um, danger. A man called, well, Hooray has threatened you. Please go somewhere safe, like a police station or a ... fishmonger's? I don't know why I said that. Well, you know what's safe. And please call me. No, not me – I haven't got my phone. I've escaped from prison to, er, save you, if that's all right. So please call Arlene. This is her phone. Or Lance, except I'm not with Lance. Where is he? God I'm doing badly with this message. Sorry. I, um, I love you. This is Jonathon by the way.'

He looked helplessly at the phone in his hand, which now said, insinuatingly, 'If you would like to ... *re-record* ... your message, please press–'

Jonathon looked questioningly at Arlene and was about to

ask whether this was a good idea, but she gently took the phone from his hand and pressed the button to end the call.

'You need to sit down and have some coffee and scrambled eggs,' she told him.

'Can I call Lance?' he asked.

'I'm on it,' she said, pressing a button and tucking the phone in the crook of her neck as she did something to the coffee machine and got out a frying pan.

'Where is he?' asked Jonathon.

'He left early to go to work.'

'Work?'

'Did you not know? He has a job in a chicken joint now. He operates the fryers.'

She looked at him, mouth slightly pursed, as though the situation itself were a more eloquently sarcastic comment on Lance than anything she could say.

'Hey, Lance–' she said.

'...' said Lance, apparently – the phone was too far away for Jonathon to hear.

Arlene said, 'There doesn't have to be something *wrong*, just because I–'

'...'

'I don't *always* call you Jerk. Listen, let's not get into that, because there *is* something wrong–'

'...'

'Like I'm just about to tell you what, if you'd let me speak. Jonathon's escaped from prison–'

'...'

'That's what I said! But Piper's in danger. Someone wants to kidnap her or something–'

'...'

'I think he's called ... Gobber?' she glanced at Jonathon, eyebrows up.

'Hooray,' said Jonathon, suddenly embarrassed, as though the names were his fault.

'Hooray?'

Jonathon nodded.

'…'

'The Notting Hill Carnival,' said Arlene. 'Is–'

'…'

'Of course I've heard of it. I just didn't know it was today. Why didn't Piper–?'

'…'

'Gemma! Of course. I should have gone over. It was just all that Lagerfeld craziness, and–'

'…'

'Still, she could have asked me. I would *love* to go to NHC–'

'…'

'Well they should. It's way better branding than clunky old– You know what? My views on that can wait. How's it going over there?'

'…'

'Uh-huh. Sure, I'll pass you over.'

She handed Jonathon the phone.

'Hello?' he said.

'How do you do it?' asked Lance.

'I don't know. It just happens. I try to keep everything normal, but–'

'But then you go to prison over a misunderstanding about a folder and immediately escape?'

'Um, yes.'

'Are you okay?'

'I don't know. Sort of. Arlene's making me scrambled eggs.'

'On toast!' she put in.

'I probably won't be okay when all this is over,' said Jonathon. 'If it ever is. I just need Piper to be safe. I'll go to NHC' – Arlene worked a thumbs-up into her scrambling – 'as soon as I've eaten the scrambled eggs on toast. How are things with you?'

Lance sighed. 'When I heard you were in prison – we didn't know which prison, by the way – I assumed that Ken's had somehow got wind of what we were up to and had managed to get you put away. So I took the unbelievably brave step of going in there undercover–'

Someone with Lance said something Jonathon couldn't hear.

'Well, yes,' said Lance, 'I used my own name, because I was

going for a job, so I needed my National Insurance number and everything. Anyway, that makes it slightly less undercover but even more unbelievably brave. And then last night I confronted Colin–'

Again, someone with Lance said something.

'Whatever. Some confronting happened. And then me and Colin–'

'Wait a minute,' said Jonathon, 'how come you're not calling him the murderer any more?'

'Because his name's Colin, and he's a good guy. Anyway, we got talking, and then I talked to Ken, who owns the place, and his daughter. Long story short, I no longer think Ken's has been taken over by the Romanian N'Drangheta and become the centre of a vast conspiracy, involving Flock and threatening you by giving Colin an easy means of disposing of bodies–'

Jonathon gasped. 'Is that what you thought?'

'Yes. I didn't want to tell you all of it because I thought it would worry you. Anyway, last night me and Colin went and confronted Vince the journalist, and he ended up telling us everything.'

'Wow. Really? What did you find out?'

'Crack's a metaphor, there are too many swimming pools in Davos and something about the Knights of Malta. Oh, also the world's controlled by octopuses.'

'Wow.'

'So, that was a dead end. I'm still keeping an open mind about whether Dick C's has been taken over by the Romanian N'Drangheta and become the centre of a vast conspiracy involving Flock. But I guess there's no need to think about all that until we've made sure Piper's safe.'

'She didn't pick up her phone. Do you think Hooray's already got to her?'

'Relax. It's probably just that thing where there's so many people that you don't get a signal. Loads of people go to the Notting Hill Carnival.'

'Is that a thing?'

'Could you put him on speaker?' said Arlene. 'It's killing me not being able to hear.'

'This one?' said Jonathon, pressing a button. The phone crackled into life.

'I think that's a thing. Isn't it?' said speaker-Lance.

'What's a thing?' asked Arlene.

'Not being able to get a call if there are thousands of people around you.'

She waggled her head uncertainly and said, 'I guess that's a thing.'

'Anyway,' said Lance, 'thing or not, here's what we should do. You eat something, then take Arlene's phone and my bike–'

'You've got a bike?' said Jonathon.

'Yes I've got a bike.'

'How come you never use it? Or mention it?'

'I use it,' said Lance defensively.

'You've used it once,' said Arlene. 'You said it made you tired and messed your hair up.'

'Twice,' said Lance. 'And I'm going to start cycling regularly, as soon as–'

'Hell freezes over,' finished Arlene.

'Is this maybe not the time for this?' suggested Jonathon.

'Yes,' said Lance. 'You take my bike and Arlene's phone. Wear some kind of disguise, because there'll be a giant police manhunt and your photo will be everywhere. Meanwhile I'll take the tube to Notting Hill Gate–'

'Have you told the police about this kidnapping thing?' Arlene asked Jonathon.

'Um, I've just escaped from prison,' he said. 'And I've got no proof. There were no witnesses when Hooray threatened Piper.'

'Okay, well it looks like I'm the best person to call the police – though I guess I am now an accessory to a crime, since I've helped you. I know there's no evidence and she's in literally the single most difficult place to spot someone, but I am *great* at convincing people to do stuff on the phone. I'll use the landline.'

'Right,' said Lance, 'so you call the police and I'll meet Jonathon at Notting Hill Gate and we'll try to find her.'

'Jesus,' said Arlene, 'this is the most half-assed plan I ever heard in my life. Even Mugler could do better than this. But I guess it's all we've got.'

'Okay,' said Lance. 'Go!'

And with that dramatic invocation, they ended the call and Jonathon immediately ate some scrambled eggs on toast.

68

The murderer shook some fries into a bag, put them on a tray with the rest of the Ken's Klassik, and told the customer, 'You enjoy that, yeah? Lovely jubbly.'

Beside him, he heard Lance – who hadn't done any work all morning – say, 'Go!' dramatically into his phone.

'Finally,' said the murderer. 'Can you get some more fries on? We've only got about two portions.'

Lance stared at him vacantly, then shook his head and said, 'Nope. We need to shut up shop and go to the Notting Hill Carnival.'

The murderer sighed. You didn't get any of this stuff with Asif.

'Look, Lance mate, I get that you're worried about your mate John, but you *do* actually have a job–'

'Listen, Jonathon's escaped from prison and–'

'He's what? He's a busy one, isn't he? How?'

'That's what I said. And I don't know how. But the thing is that he's escaped because someone threatened to kidnap his girlfriend, Piper, who's gone to the Notting Hill Carnival with your daughter, which means she's in danger too.'

'Gemma?' asked the murderer, feeling his face go cold.

Lance nodded.

'Why's my Gem gone to the Carnival with John's bird?' asked the murderer quietly.

'You know Gemma's staying with a friend of Rachel's?'

'Yeah. Just for a couple of nights.'

'Well Piper's that friend.'

The murderer frowned and stared at the floor.

Someone at the counter said, 'Klassik, Coke, and nuggets, to go.'

The murderer loomed at him and snapped, 'Look, give it a rest for a second, will you?'

He turned back to Lance and said, 'So my Gem's in danger?'

Lance nodded.

The murderer felt again the gleam of tears in the corners of his eyes. His throat thickened. His little girl.

And then he felt a switch flick somewhere in his chest, and a warm red rage spread through his body. Maybe he didn't know how to talk to Gemma, but he did know how to hurt anyone who might even think about threatening her. For the first time in a long time, he felt useful.

'All right,' he said, ripping off his apron. 'We shut up here, go to the Carnival, find Gem and Pipe, get them somewhere safe, and then rip this someone's head off. And on the way you're going to explain all this again, slowly and clearly.'

'Done,' said Lance.

'Right then,' said the murderer with determination.

'Yo, mate, can I get that Klassik and nuggets now?' said the customer.

'I *said* leave it,' said the murderer, leaning across the counter, bringing his eyes to within an inch of the customer's. 'You've had enough chicken, all right? The shop's shut. If you're not happy about it, talk to the octopuses.'

69

The Notting Hill Carnival was exactly the sort of thing that made Piper proud to live in London, and also – inevitably – exactly the sort of thing she never went to. She would see some mention of it the week after and realise that she'd missed it once again. You have to be incredibly organised to have fun in London.

But this year she had spotted it coming and been determined to go. She had wanted to take Jonathon to the Monday, adults' day, after which the proper London people she knew would say, with a slight smile and a narrowing of the eyes, 'Yeah, things got pretty messy.' Piper knew she couldn't pull this off, but just for once she had wanted to fail to pull it off.

Like all Piper's plans it had been squashed flat – this time for the novel reason that she was living with a teenager. It had been a relief really, sitting in the living room with Rachel and Gemma on Tuesday evening, to abandon the idea of the messy adult Monday and instead suggest that they all go to the tamer family day on Sunday. They were meant to be meeting Rachel at the opening ceremony – the exact spot to be decided by text when they got there.

When they got out at Notting Hill Gate – remarkably close to being on time – Piper was amazed to discover how many other people had managed to get there already. She and Gemma came up from the bowels of the earth and emerged, genuinely blinking, into the light of day. After the crush underground, the crowds were standing in dazed clumps on the pavement beside the dual carriageway.

'Shall we get a cup of tea?' suggested Piper.

'I'm good,' said Gemma. There was a pause, and then she quickly added, 'But I'll wait if you want to get one. I'll come with you.'

Piper took a step towards the nearest branch of 'Sup.

'But,' said Gemma, 'do you really, really want one? Because there's a big queue and we're meant to be meeting Aunty Rach in twenty minutes at the opening ceremony. We don't want to keep her waiting.'

Piper hesitated.

'But I'm not your mum,' said Gemma. 'You get one if you want.'

It was true: there was a big queue at the branch of 'Sup they were standing outside, as well as at the two or three nearest ones. It was galling to be out-functioning-adulted by someone in their early teens, but Piper took it on the chin.

'You're right,' she said. 'Let's just go to the opening ceremony.'

They crossed the dual carriageway and began to walk down Pembridge Road.

'Oh!' said Piper. 'Retro Woman! I'd completely forgotten about that. It sells second-hand designer clothes. I used to be completely obsessed with it.'

'*Second-hand* designer clothes?' said Gemma, laughing. 'Doesn't that, like, defeat the *entire* point of designer clothes? Aren't they meant to show that you're really up on fashion and have loads of money?'

'Oh,' said Piper, taken aback. 'Is that the point of them?'

'What is the point of them then?' asked Gemma, intrigued.

'I was thinking it was a way of getting unusual, really high-quality clothes without paying too much.'

Gemma looked in the window. 'What, like a big orange skirt for … Oh my god, does that really say *two hundred quid?* Just imagine what you could buy with that!'

'I didn't buy any big orange skirts,' said Piper defensively. 'And I stopped going there after a bit because … well, I looked like someone who's wearing second-hand designer clothes. Which is to say, indefinably odd.'

Gemma glanced meaningfully at Piper's outfit, and Piper pretended to hit her.

They turned down Portobello Road, past little knots of drifting people, past closed antique shops and open shops selling flimsy Union Jack umbrellas, and then reached some attractive little houses.

'Is this actually the right way?' asked Gemma. She looked up at the sky, which was dithering between sunshine and rain, sending a few experimental droplets down to see how it felt.

'Oh,' said Piper. 'I don't really know. I suppose I was just drifting with the crowds and assuming they'd take us to the opening thing.'

Gemma gave her a little smile and touched her arm.

'Bless,' she said. 'The crowd's mostly going that way, where the music's coming from.'

'Do you know where the opening ceremony is then?' asked Piper.

Gemma nodded. 'It's this way, Mrs P.'

'You're calling me Mrs P now?'

'Yeah, it suits you.' Gemma laughed.

As they turned and began walking in the right direction, Piper imagined how it would have been with Jonathon, if they'd managed even to get this far. The two of them would have just drifted down the road, her blithely leading them the wrong way and Jonathon walking amiably beside her. He would have been absently watching the play of light on a magpie or something, or they would have been chattering about this and that, and then they might have stopped for a cup of tea. And they would have completely forgotten about the opening ceremony – in fact, it wouldn't even have existed, and nor would Gemma, or prison, or even Rachel.

And everything would have been fine.

70

Lance's bike, predictably, was the most desirable non-human entity Jonathon had ever seen. It was spare, elegant, purposeful, and painted a deep, vibrant blue that made him feel he was seeing through the dross of physical forms and into the essential fabric of the universe. It had sleek dropped handlebars and was unnaturally light, as though the manufacturers had perhaps needed to add a little ballast to prevent it floating away.

Jonathon bobbed it lightly from the beautiful shed in Lance and Arlene's half of the garden, through the flat, to the street beyond, like a child with a balloon.

'Maybe tuck it in?' said Arlene, as Jonathon struggled to manoeuvre his T-shirt over the saddle.

'What?'

'The huge T-shirt. Maybe tuck it in. Arms up.'

Jonathon put his arms up and Arlene dextrously tucked the T-shirt into his prison shorts, just so.

'And here's your disguise,' she added, installing a giant pair of sunglasses on his face and a velvet Balenciaga baseball cap on his head.

'Um,' he said.

'I like this look on you,' she said, raising her palms in a gesture of satisfaction. 'I'm not even being sarcastic.' Then she handed him a little gold rucksack, saying, 'That's got an *A-to-Z* in it, and a little cash, like fifty pounds.'

'Thank you.'

'And this is not a thing that I will *ever* do for anyone again, but here's my cellphone and hands-free. Clip the phone to your shorts and use the hands-free. But *do not* take any calls, unless it's Lance or Piper or someone. I've heard what you're like on the phone, and I do not want Lagerfeld to have to deal with that.'

'Okay.' He felt he ought to say something effusive, but all he could think of was to repeat, 'Thank you, Arlene.'

'You're welcome. Now, head down that road at the end, follow it down Kentish Town Road to Camden, get on the – what's it called: a path next to a canal?'

'Towpath?'

'Right. Get on the towpath heading right, which is west, and then just keep going till you hit Westbourne Park. Then south and you're at Notting Hill Gate.'

Jonathon nodded, convinced he could remember all this for Piper. Then he spurred his noble steed and galloped off towards Kentish Town Road, waving his thanks as he went.

Jonathon's own bike, though he loved it dearly, was a colossal pile of plodding steel. In comparison, riding Lance's bike felt effortless – he almost felt he had to work to keep the speed down. He hurtled along Kentish Town Road, his body humming with adrenaline, powered by a huge quantity of scrambled eggs.

He flashed past a newsagent's. A photo of Gobber stared out from the front page of a paper. Beside him was a blank-faced cretin. A couple of blocks later, Jonathon realised who that had been. There was no time to think about it. He just had to hope that the police were no better at recognising him than he was, and that the hat and sunglasses made their job even harder. He bent low over the handlebars and spurred the bike on.

London's narrow, winding, car-choked roads are utterly unsuited to cycling – and this is exactly what makes it so exhilarating. Jonathon joined the stream of cars, entirely in the moment as he precisely matched their speed. All his senses were trained on the road as it writhed through the city, a boiling mass of bollards, traffic lights, railings and drivers – bored, angry, distracted drivers.

Unfortunately, it's quite difficult to be entirely in the moment and navigate at the same time – a difficulty compounded by London's paucity of road and street signs. Jonathon was just beginning to worry that he was going in the wrong direction when a rare sign appeared: Camden. He reached a bridge and caught a glimpse of canal and towpath. His bike instantly leapt across the road in pursuit of it, like a horse after a fox, in exactly the sort of manoeuvre that makes London cyclists so hugely unpopular.

Now he was coming down the short ramp from the bridge onto the towpath. The clouds parted and the day was suddenly revealed in all its glory. He pelted along past a covered market, past some picturesque barges, past a sign saying 'cyclists dismount'. He found that he was smiling, despite himself, hurtling along by the beautiful canal in the sunshine, weaving around pedestrians, dodging occasional oncoming cyclists – all of whom were also riding as though they'd just escaped from prison and were on their way to rescue their girlfriends.

Around Camden Lock, the sky greyed over once more, his hat blew off, and he found himself suddenly worried about the sexual politics of what he was doing: was it in some way crass, regressive and patronising to be riding off to rescue Piper? Did it make her seem passive and objectified? Would she prefer to be rescuing him?

But then the sun came out again and he resolved to worry about all this later, much later, when it was all over.

Under bridges he flew, past majestic willows and well-tended boats, past small stately homes with gardens that ran down to the canal. And then, like a portent, some unprepossessing little brick flats appeared and the towpath ended, forcing him out onto a road. He carried on, still in sight of the canal. Then, suddenly, he was in Italy, surrounded by grand palazzos gleaming white. A palm tree flashed by. Had he cycled through some sort of portal?

But no: he went over a bridge and was abruptly back in London, surrounded by concrete tower blocks.

Soon, a huge motorway loomed overhead. Then there were graffitied walls and metal fences topped with barbed wire. He was riding more slowly now, dodging the people wearing flags and holding beers or children. He ducked under a low metal bridge and when he emerged, there it was.

Two huge faces – a weeping silvery moon and a grinning orange sun – were mounted together on a pole held aloft by dancers in a riot of purple and green feathers, becalmed and bored, surrounded by a huge crowd.

He had reached the Notting Hill Carnival.

He spurred the bike boldly forward, towards the parade.

71

At the opening ceremony, the parade was stationary. Piper and Gemma were standing in a thick crowd on the pavement. Nearby, in the road, was a small cluster of little girls, wearing glittering white tutus and standing glumly behind a lorry, its huge speakers silent, guarded by an excited-looking middle-aged woman who also wore a glittering white tutu.

All of them were looking at a man on a stage, politely tolerating the speech he was giving. The man wore glasses, a striped office shirt and a huge ceremonial gold chain. He was probably the local mayor, but he looked uncomfortably like an accountant who had re-trained late in life as a pimp.

'… and that is why we come together as a community to say …' the man said, in a voice that sounded more accustomed to reading out the tax code pertaining to permissible deductions than giving speeches.

'Are you sure this is the opening ceremony?' Piper asked Gemma. She had been expecting something more along the lines of spectacular dance numbers and celebrities leaping through hoops of flame.

Gemma turned and nodded reassuringly, giving her a small thumbs-up.

The speech continued to roll over them, the crowd maintaining its good-natured forbearance.

'… sure you are, like me, delighted to be present at this opening ceremony here today …'

Piper looked around for a convenient landmark so she could text Rachel to say where they were. That was when she realised that George Knight was standing next to her, still wearing his tailored waxed jacket and luxurious checked shirt, his moustache nestling softly amid his regular outdoorsy features.

'Good morning,' he said. He didn't whisper it nor strain to make himself heard. The words simply marched matter-of-factly to her ears.

She was too surprised to reply.

He glanced quickly at her and then, looking off over the heads of the crowd, said, 'Don't be alarmed.'

This is an instruction that it's quite difficult to obey, since it's one of the most alarming things anyone can say to you.

'Okay,' she replied unconvincingly, her stomach having instantly turned to lava.

'You're both in great danger,' he said, even more alarmingly. 'Do you understand?'

She glanced around. Off to the left was another, taller man, who also had tanned, regular features, a tailored waxed jacket and a commanding bearing. He broke off from scanning the rooflines to give her a small reassuring nod, then continued his vigilance.

'I understand,' she said.

'Good. We're here to get you to safety. Please follow me. Are you ready?'

Was she ready? What was going on?

'What's going on?' she asked.

George looked at her sympathetically and smoothed down his moustache.

George said, 'It's difficult to explain here. We're in touch with Jonathon Fairfax. He's in a tricky situation, but we're hoping to reunite you later today. I can explain in more detail once we've attained a safe distance.'

Piper had a brief inward tussle, in which her very mixed feelings about mysterious upper-middle-class men from the government vied with her desire to see Jonathon and find out what was going on.

'Okay,' she said. 'I'm ready.'

'Good. Please have a word with the young lady.'

Piper gently touched Gemma's shoulder.

'Gemma,' she shout-whispered into her ear, 'this is George Knight. We have to go with him. Jonathon's in a tricky situation. George is from the government, to help.'

Gemma looked at Piper and then at George, who stood four-square, his moustache bristling nobly.

'Are you ready?' he asked her, clipped but gentle.

Gemma nodded.

'Follow me,' he said, and moved off through the crowd.

Piper followed him through the thick crowd, glancing back to check Gemma was behind. After her came the other man, with his officer's bearing and his own tailored waxed jacket.

The man on the stage shifted one shoulder forward and said, '… and so without further ado, allow me to introduce the main event …'

72

Jonathon was neck-deep in people, wading through them, Lance's bike held above his head. Had there been a way of avoiding the crowds? Why hadn't he checked the *A-to-Z*? He'd already seen his face on newspapers tucked under arms and in bags. Someone was bound to recognise him. He was an idiot.

'I'm an idiot,' he couldn't help saying aloud, and the tutting crowd agreed.

How much more of this inconveniently huge street did he

have to push his way through? He glanced back and saw that he'd already inconvenienced his way through an infinity of close-packed people. Ahead lay another infinity of them, though a slightly smaller infinity, if that was possible, because in the distance he could see that this road terminated in a row of houses, which would mean he'd have to choose between going left or right at the end.

The crowd seemed thinner over to the right. He should probably try to cross the road, through the parade, before it started moving. He turned abruptly, stepping into the gap between two troupes.

'Oof,' he said. He'd collided the whole of his body into someone else's.

'Ow,' said the person he'd walked into. 'Look where– Jonathon! Oh my god, it's totally you!'

'What?' he said, disoriented by Rachel's sudden appearance.

'It's totally you!' she shouted above the boring speech and the mighty murmur of the bored crowd.

'Yes!' he shouted back.

'Why are you dressed–?' she began, and then seemed to think better of it. 'Are you meeting Piper here too? What's going on with her and those guys in waxed jackets?'

'Waxed jackets!' Jonathon's blood ran cold. 'Where?'

Rachel pointed across the parade route but Jonathon couldn't for the life of him see anything but thousands of faces waiting for a speech to end.

'I can't see them!' he shouted.

'They're moving away from us! Will we go after them?'

'Yes!'

They dashed across the parade route.

'Oy, mate!' he heard one of the T-shirted officials call, but he and Rachel were already on the other side, apologetically pushing their way through the crowd.

'Sorry!' he called back.

Just ahead of him, Rachel half-turned and seemed to shout, 'Miper's mop something her hone!'

'What?' he shouted, struggling to keep up.

'I said, Piper's not answering her phone,' said Rachel.

'Still? Oh god, I bet he's done something to it.'

'Who – the waxed-jacket guy?'

'Yes. His name's Hooray. He threatened to kidnap her and it looks like he's really doing it. Oh god.'

'What? Why?'

'It's a long story. Quite a lot's happened since you left. Can you still see them?'

'Just up there!' She pointed.

This time he caught the flash of Gemma's red hair, then the green of waxed jackets on square shoulders, and finally Piper's face, in profile, as she turned at the end of the road, heading right.

'PIPER!' he called.

It was the loudest he'd ever shouted in public. But his shout was swallowed in the sounds of the day: the amplified boring speech, the idling engines of the lorries waiting to parade, the distant boom and blare of huge speakers somewhere in the streets.

By the time Jonathon reached the end of Great Western Road, the crowd had thinned enough for him to put the bike down. He looked urgently around, but there was no sign of Piper. He grabbed the phone clipped to his shorts and called her number. As Rachel had said, it was still going to voicemail – but he should leave a message, just in case.

'Piper,' he said, after the beep, 'don't trust that man you're with – the one with the waxed jacket. He came to see me in prison and threatened to hurt you if I didn't co-operate. That's why I escaped, mainly. I mean, my trousers were stolen. But that's not relevant now. Oh god I'm bad at leaving messages. I'm at the corner of Great Western Road and' – he looked frantically around for signs – 'Westbourne Park Road. Lance is going to Notting Hill Gate. If you hear this, get away and call me, find one of us. Find a policeman – or woman – or one of the people in T-shirts. Um.'

He stared at the phone for a second, then pressed the button to end the call. It would have to do.

'Wow,' said Rachel. 'You're really not great on the phone, are you?'

'No. Listen, I'll give you a number for my friend Lance – who I just told Piper about – and for Arlene, his girlfriend who's trying to get the police to help us. Call her and tell her what's happened.'

Rachel got out her phone and Jonathon gave her the numbers.

He said, 'Now I'll try and catch up with Piper – I can probably just about use my bike on this bit. After you've called Arlene, try to get some police or, um, T-shirts to help, if that's all right.'

She nodded and said, 'Go!'

Jonathon got on the bike and looked helplessly around.

'There!' Rachel pointed, and again he saw Gemma's hair, far off down the incredibly long road. Keeping his eyes fixed on the hair, he weaved his way through the thinning crowd, going only marginally faster than he would have managed on foot.

Piper's group kept on along Westbourne Park Road as the swell of many competing sources of music grew. Jonathon gradually narrowed the distance, sometimes cycling almost at normal speed, often forced to stop as people pushed food carts in front of him or stumbled merrily across his path in huge groups.

At length, he saw that Gemma's hair had reached another part of the parade route, which cut across this road. The carnival had begun now, and the lorries were on the move, each bearing a gigantic sound system and trailing a swarm of dancers.

Gemma's hair plunged into the thicker crowd that lined the parade route. Jonathon put on a final burst of speed, narrowly missing a flag-draped man, then clambered from the bike, hoisted it over his head and waded in after them.

'PIPER!' he shouted.

DING-DA-LOO-DA! DING-DA-LOO-DA! DING-DA-LOO-DA! – *TAY!*

A lorry rolled in, slow as a cloud, loud as a storm, trailing dancers and music. Off over to the right, in front of the lorry and far out of reach, he saw Hooray raise the white cordon and lead Piper and Gemma across the road, with the other waxed jacket following – all done with such clear authority that no one protested.

And that was it: he had lost sight of them.

He had to get across. There was no point heading right: the lorry was going that way, so the distance would be growing even as he struggled through the crowd. He headed left, making for the cordoned dancers following the lorry.

As he rushed slowly through the crowd like a stick dragged through treacle, the lorry seemed to reload its music and unleash a fresh broadside.

BOOM-DA-DA-DEE-DOOM! *uwansumbadeenow!* BOOM-DA-DA-DEE-DOOM! – *TISH!*

The lorry boomed past, revealing the crowd of dancers in its wake. There were more of them than in other troupes, and their costumes were just white T-shirts with a pink logo. They were holding little balls or packets of some kind.

'PIPER!' Jonathon shouted, straining to see across the dancers and through the crowd on the other side.

A dancer – a tall man with sunglasses and a green neckerchief – turned to him, grinning broadly, put his arms in the air like Jonathon's, as though holding an invisible bike, and shouted, 'PIPER!'

A woman – wearing beads, her T-shirt artfully cut and torn – grinned, raised her own arms in the air, moving rhythmically, and shouted ecstatically, 'PIPER!'

It was as though the spirit of the carnival were working through them, amplifying Jonathon's shout – a miracle!

And then another dancer – a broad man with sunglasses on his head, his long hair in a bun – raised his hands and shouted in a truly huge voice, 'DRUMMER!'

This was a much more appropriate thing to be shouting, and soon everyone was throwing their arms in the air and shouting 'DRUMMER!'

The miracle was snatched away. Jonathon was going to have to do this himself, rather than rely on the mystical spirit of the carnival. He ducked under the cordon that separated the dancers from the crowd, determined to get to the other side.

'PI–!' he began.

And then the full force of the beat from the lorry's sound system hit him – this time from speakers directed at the dancers. There was no crowd to absorb it.

BOOM-DA-DA-DEE-DOOM!
BOOM-DA-DA-DEE-DOOM!

sumbadeesumbadeesumbadaaaaaaaaaaaaaaaaaay!
BOOOOOOM!
BOOM-DA-DA-DEE-DOOM!

Jonathon felt each wave of sound move through the cells of his body like ripples through water. He was water. He was surprised to find that he was moving in time to the music: it was dancing him. He was dancing totally unselfconsciously for the first time in his life. And yet it was also essential that he get through this clump of dancers and reach Piper.

A spray of purple erupted in front of him, like a brightly coloured bomb, then a plume of yellow. Jonathon looked wildly around. The dancers were taking the little balls they held and throwing them in the air and at each other. When a ball hit, it exploded in a shower of bright colour – they were bags of powder paint! One hit the bike, and a shower of bright red spurted up into the air. The sky was thick with colour. The world was a pounding rhythm, a helpless dance, grins and raised hands and flying powder paint, ecstatic cries. And then he was at the cordon on the opposite side. He ducked under it, dancing urgently on down the road, people melting away before him.

'PIPER!' he called, hurrying rhythmically on, the bike held like a totem above his head.

He looked around the corner of the nearest street – Elgin Crescent – and glimpsed that signature combination of red hair and green waxed jacket. There was Piper! Just disappearing around the curve of the crescent.

He gave chase, ran into the side of a mobile jerk-chicken stand, righted himself, and weaved through the crowd, which was thinner now. Lowering the bike to the ground, he saw that it – and his arms – were covered in bright red paint. Never mind. He wheeled the bike through knots of people, then climbed onto it and cycled to the end of Elgin Crescent. There! Down the first road on the right.

A regular-featured man in a green waxed jacked was climbing into a Land Rover. There was a flash of red hair as the back door closed and the Land Rover pulled off.

Jonathon gave chase.

73

Piper was sitting beside Gemma in one of those very serious Land Rovers beloved of the country elite's hardline element. They were in the back, on a bench seat, facing the taller man with the curly wire leading to his ear.

'Are you okay, Gemma?' she asked.

'Uh, yeah,' said Gemma. 'Where are we going?'

'Where *are* we going?' asked Piper.

'A safe place,' said the man with the curly wire. He had taken the idea of the stiff upper lip and run with it. The whole of his lower face was stiff, and the muscles of his square jaw were so clenched that he had to post his words out of his mouth in little envelopes.

Piper decided to introduce herself before asking for more detail.

'I'm Piper,' she said. 'What's your name?'

The man narrowed his eyes and looked out of the back window. Had he heard her?

'Sorry,' she said. 'I was just saying I'm Piper, and wondering what your name is.'

She looked at him directly. After a couple of seconds he caught her eye, then gazed out through the windscreen.

'Not strictly relevant–' he began.

'Come on,' said George from the front. 'Don't be like that. This is Stephen Dench, formerly of the Special Air Services.'

The man just outed as Dench tensed his jaw an extra couple of notches.

'Oh,' said Piper, 'like Judi Dench, the actress?'

'Oh my god,' said Gemma quietly. 'He's in the actual SAS. Don't mention *Judi Dench.*'

Dench narrowed his eyes still further. 'Like Sir John Dench, hero of the battle of Malplaquet.'

'Oh,' said Piper. 'Congratulations?'

A silence settled. Piper could feel herself tensing like Dench's jaw. She was suddenly conscious of having taken Gemma from a place full of people into a confined space with two strange men – albeit ones with expensive country-wear and received pronunciation.

'Where *exactly* are we going?' Piper asked after a while.

'A safe place,' repeated Dench, posting the words out one by one so that they landed on the metal floor between them. 'He'll tell you more when we arrive.'

'Don't mind Dench,' called George from the front. 'He's not used to talking to civilians, especially females. He'd be more forthcoming if you were Pashtun militiamen. Isn't that right, Dench?'

'If you say so, H.'

Piper tried not to frown at this puzzling change in George's name. She didn't want to alarm Gemma.

But Gemma seemed to read her mind, and whispered, 'Like Q in James Bond.'

'We're headed to a safe house in Islington,' said George. 'Best we could manage at short notice. A bit of a mess, but there it is. We work with what we've got.'

These specifics mollified Piper a bit. Silence descended on the Land Rover, apart from the aeronautical holler of its engine and the manly rattle of all its exposed metalwork. She slipped her phone from her bag and Dench's eyes were on it instantly. She waved it at him to show it wasn't a small plastic explosive. Dench's eyes flicked over to meet George's in the rearview mirror. George gave a microscopic nod, and Dench set his alert level down a notch.

Piper looked at the phone, hoping to be told of many missed calls and messages, but it just stared blankly at her, like a cat for whom a door is being held open. She unlocked it, scrolled cumbersomely to Lance's number, yet again, and pressed the big blue button.

Boop boop boop, it said, and relapsed into silence.

She tried Arlene, and got the same result. She thought of trying Jonathon's phone, just to hear his incredibly maladroit recorded message, but she felt she should keep that in reserve for when she really needed it.

'George?' she said.

George was absorbed in negotiating the complex lane structure at the roundabout next to Hyde Park, and didn't immediately respond.

'Hello!' she said. 'George!'

He glanced round at her.

'What's that?' he said.

'I was just wondering if I could use your phone, please? There's a friend I'd like to call. I'm not sure if mine's working.'

'Of course,' said George. 'Only I'm afraid I can't let you use my mobile. Security protocols and all that. But there's a landline at the safe house you'd be more than welcome to use. We'll be there in a jiffy.'

'Oh,' she said. 'Okay.' And then, unable to resist it, 'Is Jonathon out of prison?'

Gemma looked at her sharply.

'We don't know just now,' said George, 'but we have people working hard to secure his release.'

'You never told me he was in prison,' said Gemma. 'What for?'

'I don't know,' said Piper. She asked George, 'How did he end up there?'

'Not clear just at the moment. There'll be a full briefing later on, once you're safe and the picture's a bit clearer.'

'It wasn't his fault,' said Piper.

'Yeah, right,' said Gemma, looking unhappy.

George glanced at Piper in the mirror and added, 'Between us girls, I believe he was misunderstood by people acting more from mistaken assumptions than malice. But the system's complicated, so it's taking time to get the full facts and sort it all out. And people in other wings of the security services may have their wires crossed, so we need to be careful.'

This sounded like the truth. Jonathon was always being misunderstood, and victimised by misconceptions.

Gemma asked George, 'Are you in, like, MI5 or something then?'

Piper shook her head, knowing that George would never

280

answer a question like that. Last time she'd had anything to do with the British security services they'd always evasively claimed to be 'attached' to some innocuous-sounding government department.

But George called confidently back, 'MI6, actually. Heard of us?'

Piper held Gemma's hand, wondering how to keep her safe if, as she suddenly suspected, she had made a terrible mistake.

74

Lance and the murderer had drifted into a discussion of the best way to manage the fryers when Jonathon's call came.

'Lance!' said Jonathon breathlessly. 'Piper and Gemma. In a Land Rover. Don't know where they're going. Following on your bike. Thanks for lending it to me.'

'Where are you now?' asked Lance.

'Don't know this area. Wide street. Trees. Big Georgian houses.'

'What's the street name?'

'I don't know! I'm trying to keep up with a Land Rover and have a ph– … Oh, wait! There's Notting Hill Gate! Tube station.'

'That's great. Hold on. I'll just tell Colin what's going on.'

Lance turned to the murderer and told him what was going on, which caused the murderer's eyes to water unnervingly and his knuckles to whiten.

'Which direction's he headed?' asked the murderer urgently, a rasp of fury in his throat.

'Which direction are you headed?' asked Lance urgently, leaving out the rasp.

'I don't know,' panted Jonathon. 'There aren't really any compasses around.'

'Okay, but the road you're on goes east-west. Are you headed towards – what would it be? – Shepherd's Bush? Or away from it?'

'I don't know. Never go to Shepherd's Bush. Oh! Trees! Loads of trees. On my right. Big park. Lots of grass.'

'Okay,' said Lance. 'It's got to be Hyde Park. You're really close to us.'

'Am I? Oh, I'm on Bayswater Road. Just seen a street sign.'

'Okay, I should be able to see you soon.'

'Oh, it's all opening out. That big arch thing. Oxford Street up ahead.'

'What, Marble Arch? You've passed us! How did that happen?' Lance looked wildly up and down the street, and then a thought hit him. 'Hang on, you weren't that guy painted red and riding a red bike, were you?'

'I am, um, a bit painted red.'

'How–? Never mind. Stay on their tail. We'll get a cab and follow you. We need to be on the other side of the road.'

The murderer stepped into the road, eyes warding off the oncoming traffic, and they crossed. On the other side, Lance held up his hand, willing a taxi to appear. As is traditional in these situations, the traffic was a uniform series of non-taxis.

In Lance's ear, Jonathon said, 'On Park Lane now. So many car showroo– Aaargh!'

'Aaargh?' said Lance. 'Are you all right?'

'Yub, um, hup,' said Jonathon distantly.

'Jonathon?'

'I'm okay. A Toyota tried to turn left through me.'

The murderer said, 'Lance mate, lend us a tenner.'

'What for?' asked Lance.

'I feel like buying a selection of magazines and having a nice read,' he said sarcastically. 'I always get this way when my daughter's been kidnapped.'

'Sorry,' said Lance, pulling out his wallet and handing it to the murderer so that he could get back to listening to Jonathon and conjuring a taxi from base traffic with his mind.

'Where are you now?' he asked.

'Just coming up to the other arch thing, at the roundabout.'

'You mean the roundabout at Hyde Park corner?'

'Yes, there's an arch with a lady in a chariot on top, and she– Oh god! Holy shit! Aaaargh! Sorry! Jesus! All right! I'm indicating!

There's no need … Why is …? Fuck. Oops. Ack! I'm going left!'

'Are you okay? Jonathon?'

Jonathon was breathing heavily. 'I forgot how horrible. That roundabout is! All beeping me.'

'Do you think it's because you're painted red from head to foot?'

'No. I think that made. Them give me a bit more space. Than usual.'

By this time, things were looking more hopeful on the transport front: more and more of the cars that passed were squat and black, even if none was yet a taxi.

The murderer thrust Lance's wallet back into his hand.

'Come on,' said the murderer, who was now holding a plastic shopping bag.

'Where are we going?' asked Lance. 'I'm pretty sure I can manifest a full taxi in another five minutes.'

'I can get us a ride in two,' said the murderer. 'This way.'

Lance looked reluctantly back at the traffic, but the murderer had an air of grim certainty.

'Why do you need a bag of stuff to get a taxi?' asked Lance as he followed the murderer up the road.

'It's not exactly a taxi,' said the murderer. 'I remembered that a mate of mine who lives around here said I could borrow his car if I needed to.'

'Oh, really?'

'Yeah. Forgot all about it till I glanced up the road and saw it sitting here.'

The murderer had now stopped beside a two-seater sports car: an old black Alfa Romeo.

'What's your friend's name?' asked Lance.

'Mike,' said the murderer, fishing in his shopping bag. 'Mike Car.'

'I see. Doesn't he have a less conspicuous car for you to borrow?'

'He … Just put your hand on the car, will you? Like you own it. Now look off down the street … perfect.'

The murderer fiddled about with the door handle.

'All Mike's other cars,' continued the murderer, 'are brand bloody new because he lives on a posh street just off Bayswater

Road, so they have immobilisers, and Mike knows they came in after my time.'

Jonathon's voice sounded in Lance's ear, asking, 'Are you still there?'

'Yes,' said Lance. 'Where are you?'

'By Green Park. Coming up to Buckingham Palace. Aaargh! Oh!'

'What is it? Jonathon?'

'Oh god,' said Jonathon, breathing hard. 'Just overtook. A Fiesta. Bad idea. White van. Nearly hit me.'

'But you're okay?'

The murderer gave something a powerful whack with the flat of his palm, then turned it hard and opened the door. He squeezed himself inside like some powerfully built toothpaste climbing back into the tube.

The latch popped up, Lance got in and the murderer handed him the shopping bag. In it was a bread knife, an *A-to-Z*, a couple of screwdrivers and a bottle of Pepsi.

'How does the Pepsi work?' asked Lance.

'I'm thirsty,' said the murderer. 'How do you bloody think it works?'

'I thought maybe you pour it into that massive lock on the steering wheel.'

'No,' said the murderer, holding out his hand like a surgeon. 'Bread knife.'

Lance gave him the bread knife, which the murderer used to saw a neat section out of the steering wheel, slipping the metal lock off it.

'Won't Mike be annoyed that you damaged his car?' asked Lance, opening the Pepsi and taking a sip.

'He'll be annoyed that you didn't get the *A-to-Z* out of that bag and work out the quickest way to get wherever your mate John is now.'

Where was Jonathon? Lance had tuned him out, like a weather forecast.

'Where are you?' he asked.

'I turned left at the big Queen Victoria. I'm on that wide

straight road. Park next to it. Pelicans.'

'You mean the Mall, next to St James's Park? Why don't you know the names of any roads?'

'They hide the signs! Going– Aaaaarrrggghh!'

'Jesus, what now? Jonathon? Jonathon?'

'Swedish tourists. Big group. Hold on.'

There was silence except for the sound of Jonathon's regular breathing.

'I'm looking you up in the *A-to-Z* right now,' said Lance.

He started flipping through the pages. Meanwhile, the murderer was wiggling the screwdriver around in the ignition and banging the centre of the steering wheel with the palm of his hand.

Uummmmhhrrr, said the car.

'There we go,' said the murderer, slipping it into reverse and pulling smoothly out.

'This is a nice car,' said Lance, appreciatively, running his hand over some walnut and leather. 'How come people don't borrow it all the time?'

'It's twenty-five years since I was borrowing cars,' said the murderer, 'but I'd say people don't borrow these, as a rule, because they're hard to sell. And they're hard to sell because they're easy to borrow.'

'What?' said Lance.

'Which way?' asked the murderer.

'I don't know,' said Lance.

'What was you doing while I was starting this thing? Just having a nice old chinwag with your mate John?'

'Trying to work out where he is and where they're going. The last I heard he was on the Mall, but–'

'Still am,' said Jonathon breathlessly. 'It's really long.'

'He's still on the Mall,' said Lance.

'Then I'm going down Bayswater Road,' said the murderer, beginning a three-point turn. 'No point wasting time.'

The murderer roared the little Alfa Romeo down the street, swinging left into Bayswater Road and forcing a taxi – one had at last manifested – to brake sharply.

Lance, who had been taking a swig from the bottle, spilled

some Pepsi on his trousers: not a good omen. It was exactly the sort of thing that didn't happen to him.

'You know what?' said the murderer, 'we're not going to pick a better route than them. Everything I know about London's streets is eleven years old, and you're a right muppet. Your mate John's all we got. He needs to stay on their tail.'

'Stay on their tail!' said Lance to Jonathon.

The murderer turned to Lance. 'Where did he go next, from here?'

'Down to Marble Arch,' said Lance. 'Then right.'

'Slowing down,' said Jonathon. 'For that other big arch. The one with the nose.'

'Admiralty Arch?'

'I don't know. There's no sign. Why do we need so many arches?'

'What nose?' asked Lance.

'What?' said the murderer, resolutely refusing to budge for a Mitsubishi that was assertively trying to pull out from a side street.

'He said something about a nose,' said Lance, covering the phone's mouthpiece.

'Focus, mate,' said the murderer.

'Focus,' Lance told Jonathon.

'I'm in Trafalgar Square,' said Jonathon. 'Nelson's Column. Lions. That gallery. Oh, thank god.'

'What?'

'Red light, at last. God that was hard. My legs hurt.'

'We're at Marble Arch,' Lance told him. 'Just stay on them.'

'Okay. I meant the little bronze nose. Fixed to the wall inside the arch. There's a few of them in London. Just fixed to buildings. Don't know why.'

'Noted,' said Lance. 'Wait. The registration. What's the Land Rover's registration?'

'Oh, um … HA54 KCJ.'

Lance relayed this to the murderer, hoping that between them they might remember it.

'Green light,' said Jonathon. 'Going left, up towards St Martin's. Do you think they'll spot that I'm following? I'm trying to stay two cars behind. But, I mean, I'm painted red.'

'Relax,' said Lance. 'This is London. There are plenty more conspicuous cyclists than you.'

'We're off again,' said Jonathon. 'Going right just before St Martin's. Pizza Express. Oh, there's Charing Cross station. The Strand! We're on the Strand.'

'He's on the Strand, heading east,' Lance told the murderer. 'And we need to head left at the lady on the chariot.'

'Lovely jubbly,' said the murderer, forcing his way into a space only just large enough, and making a Porsche beep.

After this everything went smoothly for almost two minutes, until Jonathon reached Aldwych, where he remarked, 'Oop, traffic light. He's going– Holy ...! AAAAAAAAAAAARRRRGGGGGHHHHHH!'

75

At Aldwych, the Land Rover turned left and the traffic lights turned red, so Jonathon bumped up onto the pavement, cutting behind the people stepping out into the road.

'Oop, traffic light,' he said. 'He's going– Holy ...!'

A pushchair. A blond toddler.

He jammed on the brakes.

For a moment, there was equilibrium. His bike was perfectly still, his eyes were locked on the toddler's. She was like a tiny, cute old lady, in her smock dress and big floppy hat, sitting there and looking back at him with wide-eyed curiosity, holding a nonchalant toy giraffe. Behind her, her father, who had just stepped out from behind a big blue construction hoarding, had not yet seen Jonathon.

The moment ended.

Jonathon went awkwardly over the handlebars, toppling the bike and saying, 'AAAAAAAAAAAARRRRGGGGGHHHHHH!'

At the same time, the toddler turned bright red and burst into tears, saliva stringing in her wide-open mouth.

'AAAAAAAAAAAAAAAAAAAAAAAAHHHHHH!' she cried.

'I'm really sorry,' said Jonathon from where he lay on the pavement.

He had hit his elbow on the way down, and then pretty much the whole of the rest of his body. His sunglasses had come off and he couldn't see where they'd gone.

'Oh, love!' said the toddler's father, scooping her up. 'Aaaah, it's all right, little bean.'

The man shot a cold glance at Jonathon as he got to his feet and picked up his bike.

A passerby said, 'Should be ashamed of yourself, mate.'

A cloud of tutting engulfed Jonathon as the crowd projected its intense disapproval.

'Look at the state of him,' said someone.

'Remember, kids,' said someone else, in a cod-American accent, 'don't do drugs.'

'I'm so sorry,' said Jonathon again. 'Is she all right?'

The toddler was by now sounding like an air-raid siren, emitting a sound so high and loud he seemed to hear it in his bones. She had her head tipped back and was putting the strength of her whole body into it.

Someone shoulder-barged Jonathon from behind so that he stumbled forward. The father turned his body to protect the child from this lunge, and the toddler cried all the louder.

Jonathon, helplessly and unforgivably, climbed back onto his bike.

'My, um, kidnap's been … Piper,' he said nonsensically, and then pedalled off, pulling out directly in front of a blue Mondeo. The car stepped on its brakes and beeped its horn.

'Are you fucking blind?' screamed the driver. 'You red prick!'

Jonathon pedalled as hard as he could, trying to ignore the pain in his elbow, body, and psyche. He couldn't even see the Land Rover now.

'Jonathon?' said Lance again, in his ear. 'Are you okay? What happened?'

'I'm all right,' he said unconvincingly.

'Where are you?'

'That, um, wide road?'

'Which wide road? Kingsway?'

'I don't know,' snapped Jonathon, suddenly very unhappy. 'Why don't they ever have signs? It's so st–' He caught sight of a sign. 'Yes, it is Kingsway.'

'Great,' said Lance. 'We're coming up to Admiralty Arch, catching you up.'

'I've lost them,' said Jonathon despairingly. 'I went on the pavement and fell off and nearly hit a toddler and now I can't see them!'

Ahead was a four-way junction with traffic lights and every major coffee shop.

The lights turned red.

Jonathon knew that if he stopped here, it would be the end of his chase.

He stood on the pedals, putting all his strength and weight into accelerating, cycling diagonally right to avoid a cluster of crossing pedestrians, then veering crookedly left to avoid a taxi turning across his path, horn blaring.

'Wanker!' shouted the taxi driver. But Jonathon, having not – this time – noticeably endangered the lives of any young children, barely felt embarrassed.

The traffic was bunching up on the right but the bus lane on the left was clear. He cycled up it, clicking smoothly through the gears, sitting further back in the saddle to maximise the power of each push of his legs, sailing up past the cars.

'The Land Rover!' he said. There it was, up ahead, rolling smugly forward, slowing for the junction by Holborn tube station. For a second, Jonathon was almost level with it. He caught a glimpse of Hooray's face, before falling behind again. The bus lane ended and the Land Rover moved across in front of him. Jonathon looked at the little square back window, hoping for a glimpse of Piper, but all he saw was a brief vision of a weird, wired cyclist, soaked in sweat and covered in red as if for some awful ritual.

Jonathon followed as the Land Rover turned left by the big

Sainsbury's, then right into an unexpected little Georgian street full of neat window boxes, then right again. He accelerated with the cars, slotting through gaps between them as the Land Rover changed lanes. They came to a stop at a big junction, approaching Holborn tube station from a different side now. Jonathon was three cars behind.

He'd caught up again, but didn't know how long he could keep this up. His legs felt hollow, he was shaking, and his elbow hurt in a way that made him think he might have quite serious problems with it later, if he survived long enough. But there was no time for shaking or serious elbow problems, because they were off again, going straight ahead.

'What's happening?' Lance asked.

'I found them again. We're going past Holborn tube.'

'Street?'

'That big one, going east-ish.'

'If we ever do this again, I–'

'Theobald's Road!' said Jonathon. 'Just seen a sign.'

And now the road was a dream, wide and straight, with a big lane for buses and bikes, so that Jonathon could stay relatively safe, ducking around the buses and keeping the Land Rover in sight, catching up at traffic lights.

In this way, they traversed the whole of Theobald's Road and swung left down Rosebery Avenue, past a big pink building covered in lions. Here the road narrowed and ran up a very long, progressively steepening hill, past the ornate Victorian building where he'd first met Piper. From there, he followed the Land Rover along St John Street, and over Angel junction, keeping up his dutiful narration of the route for Lance, who was now about ten minutes behind.

This was a place where all London's eras smashed into one another: faded Victorian grandeur, tatty old Eighties high-street shops, and gleaming black-glass turbo-capitalist motherships. He bobbed up Upper Street and turned right into Islington Green, cycling beside a little triangular park and a bookshop, keeping the Land Rover three cars ahead, moving at an easy pace now, and–

'Oh!' he said.

'What?' said Lance.

'They've gone. They went right, through a gap in the traffic. Shit.'

'Can you follow them?'

Jonathon slowed, signalling. The gap in the traffic had closed. The flow of cars was almost constant. He launched himself through them anyway – right into the path of an oncoming Hyundai – and realised he was in the wrong gear. The pedals barely moved. Time slowed as Jonathon balanced motionless in the middle of the lane, directly in the path of the car. He pushed with all his might, yanking on the handlebars for leverage. He saw the driver's horrified, surprised face looking up from a phone screen. The car beeped. And then he was across, only just avoiding an old lady with a shopping trolley.

He was now looking down a narrow road beside a corner pub.

'I've followed it,' he said, 'but it's gone.'

'Which way did it go?' asked Lance.

This question annoyed Jonathon so much that he couldn't answer. He moved off along the narrow road.

'There's a fork in the road ahead,' he told Lance. 'It's a three-way split: left, straight ahead, or right. But the roads bend so I can't see which way the Land Rover went.'

'Just pick one,' said Lance.

'Which one?' Jonathon asked desperately.

'Go with your gut.'

Oh god, his gut. It strongly favoured all three, and also thought they were all terrible mistakes.

He closed his eyes.

Which way? he asked. *Please, it's important.*

There, faint within him, was an impulse: the ghost of a preference for left.

Okay, he thought, and immediately went right. There was absolutely no way his gut would be right about a situation as vital as this.

'I've gone right,' he said, losing confidence even as he said it. 'But I think I might have made a terrible mistake.'

'We'll come and find you,' said Lance. 'What's the street?'

'Oh, there's a sign: Melmotte Row,' said Jonathon.

The street began modestly, then turned a slight corner to reveal a long, wide expanse of large and handsome Georgian terraces, four or five storeys high, with smartly painted front doors, sandy-gold brickwork and gleaming white stucco.

He rode hesitantly along, looking around him.

'Oh god,' wailed Jonathon. There was still no sign of the Land Rover. He'd lost it at the last moment. He should have gone left after all. Why had he ignored the still, small voice within? And why was he continuing to ride down this huge road when there was absolutely no–

'Oh my god. It's there!' he said excitedly. 'The Land Rover's parked just over there! HA54 KCJ. Oh! Gemma's hair. They've just gone into a house.'

A smart Prussian-blue door closed behind a glimpse of red hair and green waxed jacket. The sun gleamed on the pane of glass above, picking out an elegantly stencilled number: twenty-eight.

'Number Twenty-Eight,' he said triumphantly. 'It's Number Twenty-Eight Melmotte Row. That's where they've taken them.'

Lance said nothing to this, perhaps writing it down.

'Did you hear that?' Jonathon whispered urgently into the mouthpiece. 'Number Twenty-Eight.'

Lance still said nothing. Was he upset? Or … Oh god. Surely not. Jonathon pulled up around the corner and unclipped Arlene's phone from his belt. The screen was blank and grey: dead. When had that happened?

76

'Ah, flipping sugar,' said the murderer.

Lance covered the phone. 'What?' he asked.

They were coming around a bend in Rosebery Avenue, a spacious tree-lined street on a slight uphill grade. The murderer slowed as they passed a freckle of chicken and kebab shops. Now he was indicating, pulling up outside the Wilmington Arms.

'This is really not the time,' said Lance.

'Blimming petrol's out,' said the murderer.

'What?' said Lance. 'But we're in the middle of a car chase. That can't happen.'

'Well you tell that to the blimming petrol tank.'

'Didn't you check it before we left?' asked Lance.

The murderer gave him a look which eloquently answered this.

'Sorry,' said Lance. 'But Jonathon's just found the house where Piper and Gemma have been taken.'

'Really?'

The murderer actually smiled. He suddenly looked like an absolutely huge little boy.

'Yes,' said Lance. 'Melmotte Row, just near Islington Green.'

'He got the house number?'

'Did you get the house number?' Lance asked Jonathon.

Jonathon said nothing.

'Jonathon?'

He was still silent. In fact, Lance couldn't hear anything on the line at all. He looked at his phone screen, which cheerfully told him the name of his network – as though saying, 'Oh, did you want to make a call? That would be fine because I've got no other calls going on at the moment.'

Lance told his phone it was an arsehole and re-dialled the last number.

'Hey! This is Arlene Drummond. Hit me up with a message.'

Beep.

'Jonathon. Lance. I heard you're on Melmotte Row but I didn't get the house number. Call me back when you get this. I hope Arlene gave you her charger.'

Meanwhile the murderer had taken the *A-to-Z* from Lance's lap and was leafing through it. 'We're about half-hour away, if we walk it,' he said.

'Too long,' said Lance. 'Do you think there's a petrol can in the boot?'

'I'll just use my key to open it up and find out,' said the murderer sarcastically, looking down at the screwdriver jammed into the ignition.

'Point taken.'

Lance got out of the car and smiled at the people who were sitting at the trestle tables outside the Wilmington, trying to pretend the weather was much nicer.

'Hi,' he said, 'has anyone got any petrol?'

Quite naturally, they fell over themselves in their boozy eagerness to pantomime checking pockets and bags, loudly saying things like, 'I'm sure I put my petrol down here *somewhere*' or 'Oh Christ! I think I left mine in my car.'

The murderer squeezed himself out of the car like a bison emerging from a teapot and shouted over, 'Oi, where's the nearest petrol station?'

'Oh yeah, that's the thing to ask,' said Lance.

The people instantly switched to arguing heatedly about the locations of petrol stations. No sooner had someone mentioned one than half a dozen people mocked and belittled the suggestion, offering new ideas that were shouted down in turn. Finally, a man with a shaved head and a polo shirt told them there was one on Clerkenwell Road, which he said was a five-minute walk.

'Cheers, mate,' said the murderer. 'Lance, you're driving.'

Lance got in the driver's seat and the murderer pushed him through a heroic U-turn and down Farringdon Road – towards petrol and, they hoped, victory.

77

Jonathon sighed deeply and took stock of his situation.

He had no idea whether help was on its way, and the only way to find out was to charge Arlene's phone. But, being Arlene's, it was far too sleek and exclusive to fit a standard Nokia plug. It had a delicately etched metal finish and snapped shut like a tiny high-end German car.

Could it possibly be true that the best use of his time, with

Piper in the kidnappers' lair, was to go knocking on doors, asking well-heeled Londoners to ignore the fact that he was painted red and charge an unusual phone? It seemed unlikely. He couldn't even ask if he could use their phone, because the only number he knew was Piper's, and that wasn't working.

So, what to do?

He could try to get the police to investigate, but they were very likely to just take him back to prison. Besides, that would mean going further away from Piper, which he couldn't bear to do.

He should absolutely stop standing in the street, painted red.

And he should watch the house – but not from the front – and see if he could find out more. He should definitely try to warn Piper and Gemma that they were in danger. If they just knew that, they might be able to escape – or at least summon help more effectively than a scarlet and skimpily dressed prison escapee such as himself.

He hoped all that made sense. He'd missed a lot of sleep recently, and had been making very poor decisions even before that.

Jonathon put Arlene's phone into her gold backpack and wheeled Lance's bike over to a little walled parking bay nearby. He was in one of the smaller streets running off Melmotte Row, around the corner from the block containing Number Twenty-Eight. The parking bay was carved out of the end house's garden, and held a Mercedes A-Class and a Jaguar. Jonathon hid the bike behind the Mercedes, so it wouldn't immediately be stolen by London's army of diligent and professional bike thieves.

He then climbed up the sloping face of the Mercedes onto its roof, and from there got onto the high wall that separated the parking bay from the end house's yard. Looking around anxiously in case anyone saw him, he crawled along the top of the creeper-covered wall. The weather was now looking drizzly and overcast, which he hoped would keep people indoors on what was officially a Sunday afternoon in the height of summer. He was going to have to get through three gardens before he reached the one belonging to Number Twenty-Eight.

The first garden was overgrown, containing only long grass

and a mossy trampoline. He jumped down from the wall into the long grass, scampered behind the trampoline and made for the next wall, which was also topped with creeper. Grabbing the wall where the creeper was sparsest, he dug the toe of his smart-casual shoe into the mortar, stepped up and flung his arm and head over, managing to follow them with his knee, until he was lying full length along the top of the wall.

Then he dropped down into the next garden, which had a pristine lawn and manicured flowerbeds, and climbed up onto the next wall, again lying full length, hidden by the creeper. He froze: there were people in the garden beyond – the last one he had to get through.

'Kitty! Have you seen my glasses, darling?' It was a man with a smooth, distinguished face, like an Edwardian statesman's – peevish, but with the suggestion that he might at any moment make a rousing speech about tariff reform. He had greying, swept-back hair and was wearing an immaculate pair of olive shorts.

'Where did you last have them, Rupey?' called a bored voice from inside.

'If I knew where I last had them they wouldn't be lost, would they?'

'They aren't lost. You just hamneeahumhumhay,' the voice seemed to say, as its owner took it somewhere inaudible mid-sentence.

'It's going to rain any second!' said the man, plaintively.

'Have you looked on your head?' asked the woman, suddenly appearing in the doorway. She had rather severely bobbed hair, and wore blue glasses and a black-and-white sundress.

'That happened o–' began the man, then said in an accusing tone, 'There they are! On the bench.'

'Well *I* didn't put them there,' said the woman, laughing.

'I never said you did, Kitty,' said the man, nonetheless conducting himself with wounded pride as he took the glasses from the bench.

Their garden was tasteful and well tended, with two large trees at the end, a carefully casual crowd of coloured bushes in the middle, and a lower paved area next to the house, with a bench, a table and two chairs.

It suddenly occurred to Jonathon that these people were unlikely to wrestle him to the ground, and they might even help him.

'Um, hello?' said Jonathon from the top of the wall. He intended to drop lightly to the lawn, hands spread in a peaceable gesture, but his foot got caught in the creeper on the way down, so he ended up doing a sort of suspended handstand.

'What?' said the man, peering down the garden. 'Is someone there?'

'Er, yes,' said Jonathon, still upside-down. 'Hold on.' He hopped closer to the wall and gave a yank on the creeper with his leg. There was a crash and Jonathon landed hard on his back.

'That's my trumpet vine,' said the man, who was now a few feet away, his eyes moving rapidly between Jonathon and the creeper. 'Look what you've done to it.'

'Sorry,' said Jonathon. 'It's just that–'

'This is a private garden, you know. You really shouldn't be climbing in here.' He held his folded glasses in front of him like a dagger. 'Kitty!' he called over his shoulder.

'My girlfriend's been kidnapped!' said Jonathon. 'By some people who've gone next door, to Number Twenty-Eight.'

'Has she?' said the man, sceptically taking in Jonathon's appearance.

'What is it, Rupey?' asked Kitty, from the paved area.

'Stay by the phone,' he called, 'and be ready to call the police.'

'Call the pleas?' said Kitty, walking down the garden towards them.

'The *pol-ice*,' said the man, with the gigantic annoyance of the long-married.

'Oh, hello!' said the woman to Jonathon. 'Who's this?'

'I'm, um, Jonathon,' said Jonathon. 'Fairfax. My girlfriend's been kidnapped and they're holding her next door. Actually, you don't have a really sleek phone charger, do you? Only–'

'At you-know-who's house,' said the man to Kitty. 'I mean, he may be a lot of things but I very much doubt he's a kidnapper.'

'Have you been to a *rave*?' asked the woman confidentially, taking in Jonathon's attire.

'No,' he said. 'I've, er, well, I've escaped from prison. Look, could you call the police, please?'

The man and woman exchanged looks.

'You don't *look* like you've escaped from prison,' said the woman. 'I mean, he's wearing a Michael Kors lamé backpack. And Loake shoes.'

'They were in a sale,' mumbled Jonathon defensively, 'and Arlene lent me the backpack.'

'And look at his pupils,' said the woman. 'Hugely dilated.'

'What have you taken?' said the man. 'Perhaps we should give him a glass of water.'

'A glass of water's no good if you're off your head on drugs,' said the woman.

'Well we can't just leave him here,' said the man.

'But I'm not going to stay here,' said Jonathon. 'I'm going to try to find a way into the house next door, where my girlfriend and a, er, friend of hers are being held against their will – though actually they might not know it yet.'

'I really don't think that's a good idea,' said the man. 'I promise you, she hasn't been kidnapped by Teddy Robinson. That's the drugs talking. Look, you've clearly overindulged and something's … well, gone not quite right in your brain. Just climb back out, have a lie down and you'll feel better in no time.'

'But …' began Jonathon. He was having difficulty knowing where to start in tackling this man's quite reasonable assumptions.

'Come on,' said Rupey. 'There's a good chap. Otherwise we really shall have to call the police.'

'But I *want* you to call the police,' said Jonathon. 'They need to rescue my girlfriend from that house.' He pointed.

Rupey and Kitty looked at him rather sadly, clearly now having no intention of calling anyone.

'WHERE DID YOU GO CLUBBING?' Kitty asked loudly and clearly, as though the problem might be that Jonathon was deaf or foreign.

'What did you take?' asked Rupey.

'Sorry,' said Jonathon. 'If you don't want to tell the police that my girlfriend's been kidnapped, could you just say there's a man in your garden who's escaped from HMP Flintwinch and is trying to break into the house next door?'

Rupey sighed and shook his head. 'Look, darling, maybe we should get him that glass of water. He could have a lie down on the bench, maybe get a bite of toast.'

'But it's starting to rain,' said Kitty. 'And we can hardly be giving glasses of water to people who climb into our garden, can we? Suppose he's just trying to get inside?'

'But I'm not,' said Jonathon. 'I'm trying to get you to call the police.'

'Maybe we should,' said Rupey.

'Honestly, Rupey, you're such a pushover.'

'I am *not* a pushover, Kitty. I'm merely saying–'

'Um, I'm going to go now,' said Jonathon. 'Please call the police.'

'Look,' said Rupey, 'if you climb another wall after that one, you'll be in the car park behind the flats. Turn left out of that and walk for five minutes and you'll be in Angel. Have a nice coffee, sit down for a bit, and then you can get a cab home. You'll be yourself again in no time. Really you will.'

Jonathon used a branch of the larger tree to swing himself sadly onto the top of the wall. He lay there for a second before dropping down into the garden of Number Twenty-Eight.

78

Despite Jonathon's worries, Piper was now in absolutely no doubt that she'd been kidnapped.

From the outside, the house had looked reassuringly grand and solid – so much so that Piper had dismissed her fears and walked in. The alternative had been to try to run away, dragging Gemma with her, down a huge and deserted street. She would have needed more than a vague suspicion to justify that.

But the moment Piper had stepped from the hallway into the

living room, she'd known something was seriously wrong.

It was full of discarded pizza boxes, empty wine bottles and the smell of men who have reverted to adolescence. George had warned her that the place was a bit of a mess, but the way in which it was a mess just didn't fit with it being a safe house operated by the security services. Not that safe houses couldn't, she was sure, get into a pretty terrible state. But this specific pretty terrible state had confirmed all her doubts.

Piper took a breath and got about quarter of a second into a shout for help when George punched her hard in the stomach, doubling her up and knocking the wind out of her. He grabbed her, she bit his arm hard, and the next thing she knew he was sitting on her upper back, forcing an absolutely disgusting sweaty sock into her mouth. This was tied in place with a tea towel that had been used to mop up white wine. Then, despite her struggles, he tied her at the wrists, elbows, knees and ankles with something tough and thin that bit uncomfortably into her skin.

Gemma, throughout this, had been out of Piper's sight. But when Piper did get a glimpse of her, she too was tied up, with a slightly cleaner tea towel tied around her mouth. She seemed to have retreated deep inside herself.

Dench remarked, 'Well, you've done it now, Hoo.'

There was a silence, and then George said, 'Where do we put them, Stench?'

'I dunno. Bathroom? Attic? Somewhere out of the way.'

A little fizz of hope stirred in Piper's brain. She thought of all the sharp things there might be in a bathroom, and what she might do there if left unattended.

Unfortunately, George seemed to be thinking along similar lines, because he said, 'They might find a way to flood the place if we leave them in the bathroom. Neighbours'll spot water pouring out. Soon people are knocking on the door and calling the fire brigade.'

'Fine. Look, this is your gig, Hoo. I'm strictly rank and file on this one.'

'Don't be like that, Stench. Is that the spirit with which we competed in the All-England Under-Sixteens Taekwondo

Championship?'

'Yes, frankly.'

'Well, that was never my intention.'

'Look,' said Dench, 'you just need to keep them out of the way, somewhere they can't make trouble. Put them at the back of the house so they can't do anything to attract attention from the street.'

'Good idea. I want to be able to keep an eye on them though – don't want them worming out or finding – I don't know – nail files or hairpins or anything.'

Hairpins! thought Piper. Wherever they put her, she resolved to find something to cut her bonds, however long it took. The painful ligatures on her arms and legs felt like the bits of plastic that had secured her new kitchen scissors to their packaging, and which had been almost impossible to remove.

'Hairpins?' said Dench sceptically.

'*Or anything*. I don't know, do I?'

'Well, look, there are shutters on the back windows, and a fold-out partition to divide the sitting room in two. Just close the shutters and fold the partition out. Then no one can see them but you can still keep an eye on them.'

'Me? You mean "we".'

'Let's not go into that now,' said Dench.

Dench seemed much less keen on all this than George. That was one thing in Piper's favour.

'Is there a key for the door into the hallway?' said George. 'I don't want them in a room with an unlocked door.'

'How would I know whether there's a key? You've been staying here for the last week, haven't you?'

So, the room wouldn't be locked. Also, if George had been staying here, this must be his mess. Somehow this upended her idea of who he was even more thoroughly than the punch in the stomach.

'Yes,' said George, 'but I never knew I'd end up doing this.'

'Neither did I, till you called me at nine and asked me to come to the carnival.'

After that, Piper heard the banging of shutters being closed and barred, and partitions being unfurled. Then she was carried to the back part of the long living room and laid on a dusty Persian carpet that might have been quite valuable if someone hadn't spilled wine all over it.

Because of the gag, her nose was running. The snot got into her hair, which had fallen across her face, and added to the awful embarrassment of the whole thing. The gag reeked of rancid, dried wine and she could taste both the cotton and the stale sweat of the sock. She was physically and psychologically more uncomfortable than she'd ever been in her life. And this was made all the worse by her guilt at having got Gemma into this, and her worry about what would happen to Jonathon.

How on earth was she going to escape and save them?

79

Finally, Lance got out and helped the murderer push the car up the slight slope into the Texaco petrol station, where a BMW immediately drove into it.

DOOF.

'Holy shit!' said Lance, jumping back.

'You are joking me,' said the murderer, steadying the car.

'What the fucking hell do you think you're doing?' shouted the red-faced BMW driver, leaping out of his car. He had a pink shirt stretched over his paunch, for which his tight jeans acted as a sort of belly bra.

'Why are you driving out through the entrance?' asked Lance, pointing to a large sign that said 'In'.

'You fucking idiots!' the man shouted furiously, looking with loving concern at his almost-unscathed bumper.

'You. Shut it,' said the murderer, looking the man in the eye and pointing for emphasis.

The murderer looked grimly at the Alfa's front wing, which had crumpled like cheap trousers.

'How are we going to sort this one out?' he asked.

Lance joined him in examining the damage, shaking his head. The murderer tried unbending the Alfa's wing, but it had buried itself in the tyre. And as it came out, the tyre deflated with a whooshing noise.

'We could just walk,' said Lance. 'It might not be much more than half an hour. Or I could manifest a taxi.'

'Hi,' said the BMW driver into his phone. 'Listen, some idiots have just ...'

'Or we could borrow this bloke's car,' said the murderer. 'He won't mind.'

Hearing this, the BMW driver looked up and said, 'Are you out of your fucking brain?'

'Yes,' said the murderer, catching up in one step as the man made for his car. The murderer grabbed him by the waistband of his jeans and the collar of his shirt, and then half-carried, half-walked him over to the Alfa, opened the driver's door and squashed him inside.

'Swapsies,' he said. 'You broke it, you take it.'

Then he took the man's phone, dropped it on the ground and stamped on it. The former BMW driver looked helplessly at his phone and his new car. His mouth moved but no words emerged.

The murderer climbed into the BMW, pushed the seat way back, and was joined by Lance. Then he reversed the car and drove to the correct exit, where they sat and waited for a break in the traffic.

'Sure this is a good idea?' asked Lance lightly, as though they'd met for a quick drink and the murderer had just ordered a second pint.

'No,' said the murderer. 'But I'm doing it anyway, because of Gemma. Why don't you give your bird a ring, tell her where we're headed for?'

'Good idea.' Lance took out his phone and dialled.

'Arlene Drummond,' she said.

'Is that how you answer our landline?' Lance asked.

'It is when I think it's the police calling.'

'Did you get through?'

'I got through. They're sending someone out to take a statement. Should be here any minute.'

'Is that it? A statement?'

'Hey, it's the best I could do.'

'I wasn't blaming you.'

'Well, all I've got is that someone named "Hooray" threatened to kidnap two females who are at a carnival with half a million other people. I didn't want to mention Jonathon because of the whole escaped-from-prison thing, to which I am an accessory after the fact.'

'That's true. But listen, things have moved on. Jonathon saw Piper and Gemma get into a Land Rover with two men. He chased them–'

'He *chased* them? On your bicycle?'

'Yes.'

'My god. He is such a *busy* little guy.'

'I know. And he managed to stay on their tail–'

'He cycled as fast as a car?'

'It's probably easier than you think in London, with the traffic lights and stuff. But actually, yes, it is pretty impressive. Anyway, he saw them go into a house on Melmotte Row, Islington.'

'Piper and Gemma went in there?'

'Yes.'

'Okay, that is huge. That is … *terrible*. Any idea what's going on in there? Wait, what's the full address?'

'I don't know. I've lost touch with Jonathon. I think his battery must have run out. Did you give him your charger?'

'Did I? … Nope. There it is, in the wall. That was dumb.'

'Anyway, all we've got is the street name and the Land Rover's number plate.' Lance repeated them, and Arlene wrote them down.

'So where are you?' she asked. 'In a cab?'

'We're in a stolen car. Our second, actually. We're just trying to get out of a petrol station.'

Lance looked over at the entrance, where a car was trying to turn in, and the former BMW driver was trying to explain that the car in which he was sitting, blocking the way, didn't belong to him. However, this had created a gap in the traffic, allowing the murderer to pull out at last.

Arlene, who had been silent for a couple of seconds, now sighed and said, 'Okay.'

'Okay?'

'Sure. It has to be, right? So, you take your stolen car, go to that street and see what you can find out. I'll call the police again, and I'll bend them to my will. I'll bend them double. I'll get them to that street.'

'Sounds good,' said Lance.

'Yeah. Stay safe, okay. It is a theoretical possibility that I love you.'

'Thanks,' he said. 'I ... I actually do love you. But I defy anyone to prove it.'

Lance ended the call and sighed.

'I'm going to prison, aren't I?' he said to the murderer.

'You? Nah. You're not the type. Listen, the police have got a lot on their plate. There's blokes all over the shop, committing crimes left, right and centre. Everyone's used to it. That's why there's not a blue light in sight now, even though we just nicked this BM. Remember: there's always someone doing a louder crime, always some bloke with his shirt off smashing up a pub.'

'What about kidnapping? Would the police leave a shirtless man in a smashed-up pub to deal with that?'

'Maybe. Our best bet is to find that house and make it the noisiest bloody kidnapping you've ever seen in your life.'

80

Jonathon hit the ground and rolled behind a large wood-panelled hot tub.

Peeking out from behind it, he saw an overgrown lawn with a canopied wicker seat in the far corner. Steps led down from the lawn to a patio and French windows. Beside the patio was a small two-storey extension with a flat roof and a small sash window just above it.

There was absolutely no sign of Piper and Gemma, or of the two men.

Jonathon could still hear murmured conversation from the next garden. Then Rupey's voice said clearly, 'The fact is, Kitty, that it doesn't matter whether or not he *wants* us to call the police – it's simply the right thing to do.'

Jonathon's heart surged. The police were coming!

But then he imagined the police knocking politely on the door and being met with a plausible Etonian assuring them that no one had broken in, and laughing lightly at the notion of anyone having been kidnapped. Piper and Gemma might even confirm that.

The only solution was for Jonathon to do what he had threatened, and break in. He needed to be in the house when the police arrived. Then he could warn Piper and Gemma what was happening. And if they'd been overpowered, he could make enough noise to get the police to come in and find them. As long as Piper left with the police, he didn't mind what happened to him. He would happily go back to prison – even back to Flintwinch, and face McGill, Neptune and the consequences of having crashed the Haribo, with all the platings and jobbings that would entail. At least they wouldn't be able to steal his trousers this time.

But how was he going to get in?

It looked like the only way was to climb from the canopied wicker seat onto the extension's flat roof and then sneak in through the small sash window just above it.

Jonathon checked no one was watching, then ran at a crouch down the edge of the garden, to the wicker seat. He put a foot on it, then painfully pulled himself up over the scratchy wicker canopy, and from there climbed onto the high garden wall. He balanced carefully, then grabbed the top of the little extension, pulling himself up over brick and creeper. At length, he found himself standing on a small flat roof surrounded by a low parapet.

Jonathon crossed to the house wall and stood flat against it, beside the window, so he couldn't be seen from inside. When his breathing and heart had calmed down a bit, he peeped through the window. There was no one there: just a half-landing with stairs leading up and down.

His heart still racing from the danger of that brief peek, he crouched and tried to look down into the two rooms below. In the upper room, all he could see was a pair of beautiful wooden shutters, and below that, through the French windows, some beautiful parquet flooring.

Jonathon went back to standing against the wall, his heart racing once more.

It was time to open the window beside him. He moved out of hiding, grabbed the edge of the top sash with his fingertips and pulled down.

It didn't move even slightly.

He tried pushing the bottom sash up, but this also had absolutely no effect.

Peering in, he saw there was some sort of beautifully made authentic brass catch locking the two finely engineered sashes in place. Could he slide something up between them? An incredibly thin yet strong blade would do it. But all he had was a gold rucksack, an *A-to-Z* and a dead phone.

Wait. Maybe he could put the leather rucksack over his fist, punch out one of the top sash's smaller panes, then reach in and open the catch. That would almost certainly work. But would Hooray and his friend hear it? Where were they?

At that moment his question was answered.

'Memmy! Uh-heen-hynuh heach hoo hor hayis!'

Although several layers of nineteenth-century building materials were filtering out all the consonants, it was still clearly a deep, confident Etonian voice, with the characteristic lack of volume control, coming from terrifyingly nearby. Jonathon ducked back against the wall.

'His haw hunuh hon–' *clack*, a door opened '–trol, I promise you, Teddy. Old Stench is helping out, and a few more of the Chad lads are on their way.'

It was Hooray, and he sounded like he was just down the stairs. His voice began to descend, still shouting into his phone.

'Well, Number Twenty-Eight of course, Teddy. Where else did

you hink we'd hay hem? Hi hiuh huhuhuhuhunun.' After that Hooray must have reached the basement and moved further away, because Jonathon couldn't make anything else out, even at Etonian volume.

Nonetheless, this told Jonathon several things. Firstly, Hooray was now definitely in the basement. And he'd gone there from the ground floor, presumably for privacy, which implied that the other man was still there, the one he'd called old Stench. It would be absolutely stupid to smash a pane of glass just feet away from a strapping six-footer with a waxed jacket and a martial air. And of course Hooray, who fit the same description, could come back up from the basement at any moment.

As Jonathon pushed himself flat against the wall, his right hand connected with the cool, bumpy surface of an original cast-iron down-pipe – one of those accidentally indestructible things people used to make in the old days. It ran the whole height of the house.

Oh, he thought. Then, *Oh no*.

He looked up at the three storeys above him. The nearest window was closed, but the large sash windows on the top two floors were partly open, each an easy distance from the down-pipe. The pipe's thick cast iron was secured to the wall at regular intervals by sturdy brackets, all rust-free and neatly painted. There were also two large cast-iron junctions, presumably where the toilets were, concreted firmly into the wall. The nearest was about twelve feet above him – not far below the first of the partly open windows.

God no, he thought, and shuddered.

And yet, compared with the alternative, the idea did have certain advantages. If he could get to the nearest open window, two storeys above, there would be an empty floor between him and the Etonians, so they'd be much less likely to hear him come in. And it wasn't *that* far up: if he'd encountered it on a climbing wall, composed of colour-coded hand-holds, he would have considered it fairly easy. Unless, of course, he'd had to start from twenty feet above a stone surface, with no rope or crash mats.

So, this new idea wasn't dangerous in quite the same way as smashing the window, but it was still insanely, insanely dangerous.

Was there a way to not do this?

There probably was, if he could just sit down somewhere with a cup of tea and think things through. But he couldn't do that without leaving Piper in the clutches of an unhinged Etonian with profoundly mistaken ideas, and missing the chance for her to be rescued by the police.

So, he could either be a man abandoning the love of his life in order to skulk off and have a cup of tea and a think, or a man heroically scaling a house in order to rescue the love of his life.

I'm going to heroically scale this house, he thought. *Let's go.*

His body's response to this was to stay exactly where it was and pump sweat out of his palms.

He wiped his hands on his T-shirt. Then he knelt and tightly re-tied his shoelaces.

I might just go for that cup of tea after all, he thought. *I'm really tired and scared.*

He wiped his eyes and his nose.

Maybe I'll just climb up a bit, then skulk off.

He turned, stepped onto the low parapet, then reached up and grabbed the nearest of the pipe's brackets, just above his head. He walked the tips of his shoes up the edges of the brickwork, until his feet were flat against the wall, legs bent, hands gripping the pipe just above the bracket.

He really hoped that the pipe hadn't been weakened by the centuries of effluent that had flowed through it.

From this position, about six feet up, he lunged his left leg awkwardly over, as climbing instructors tell you not to do, and managed to get it onto the first window ledge. This supported some of his weight as he inched his hands further up the pipe. Then he lunged his right foot up onto the bracket where his hands had been.

He was now about nine feet higher than when he'd started out, and both his feet were on solid holds. Already, trying to skulk off seemed more difficult than just carrying on.

He brought his feet together on the bracket and slowly straightened his legs, inching his hands up the pipe until he was standing up. On tiptoes, Jonathon grabbed the junction pipe above him with both hands, and tried to haul himself up. For a second he was a man clinging on by just his hands to a toilet pipe far up in the air – absolutely not a recommended climbing move. His feet scrabbled for purchase, then got a toehold between the rows of bricks. He walked them up, then lunged his foot onto the smaller window ledge to his right, so that it took the weight off his arms.

He was splayed against the wall, his brow sweating like no brow had ever sweated before, his body trembling all over. When his arms had recovered a bit, he moved his hands up the pipe again, and got his feet onto the junction where his hands had been.

Another horrible bit was coming up. He needed to do it before he ran out of strength or fully realised how high up he was. He stretched his leg up, uncomfortably high, as though he were in a mid-air ballet class, his foot only just reaching the ledge of the open window to his left.

He shifted his weight over onto that foot, hanging from the pipe with one hand, the other reaching out. His fingertips hooked the edge of the window, drawing the top pane slowly, painfully down, till it was fully open.

Now for the worst bit of all. He swung his right hand over to the top of the window – hoping it would take his weight – and lunged up, getting his head in, wedging a hand onto the wall inside, stepping over the window, onto the windowsill and then down onto the tiled floor inside.

He was safe, from gravity at least.

He was also violently shaking and sweating, suddenly over-whelmed with terror at what he'd just done.

81

'Hi, Mum?' said Nikki.

There was the sound of a phone being fumbled with, followed by the hiss of a tap.

'Hold on, love!'

Nikki sat back on her sofa, blowing on her tea and stroking the cat, who'd come to say hello.

'There now,' said her mum. 'Sorry about that, love – my hands were covered in jam.'

'Jam? You're not …?'

'I'm making another batch. Gooseberry.'

'But I've still got four jars of the last lot.'

'Well you'd better get on and eat them up then, hadn't you? What else am I going to do with all the gooseberries from the allotment?'

'I don't know, Mum. Stop growing them? Just an idea.'

'You've got no idea what you're talking about, young lady. You and the kids will eat the jam and you'll like it. You know nothing else grows in that bit by the shed.'

'This isn't really what I was calling about, Mum.'

'Oh, what are you calling about then?'

'I've had a text from you-know-who.'

'Ooh! Juicy. What's it say? Hold on, I'll put the kettle on.'

There was the scoosh of a kettle being filled and the click of a switch.

'There we are,' said her mum. 'All ears now.'

'It says, "I need you. Please come over this pm. To no 28."'

'No 28?'

'Number Twenty-Eight. It's his house: massive palace in Islington.'

'Well? Are you going to go? You can always tell him you've got the kids.'

'Actually, I can't. He knows Dave's got them this weekend.'

'What did you tell him that for?'

'Well … I might have … slept with him?' said Nikki. 'A tiny bit? On Friday night?' She cringed and laughed at the same time.

'You didn't! With Teddy Robinson!'

There was a silence, then her mum laughed and noisily made herself a cup of tea.

'So?' said her mum. 'Are you going to go? What are you thinking?'

'Do you think the text's a tiny bit ambiguous? I mean, maybe he needs me for something to do with his campaign, instead of …'

'Instead of what?'

'Covering me with ice-cream again.'

'Is that what people do now?'

'Some of them.'

'Well,' said her mum, slurping her tea. 'Shows how out of touch I am. Do you like him?'

'I don't know. He's better in real life than on the telly. And he is sort-of good looking, if you look at him in the right way.'

'If you say so, love. He's not my type, I can tell you that much.'

'I've got myself in a bit deeper than I meant to.'

'Sounds like it.'

'The thing is, I do want to get Flock into this market. You've got no idea how much money the big parties have to spend on getting people elected. It's a really good space for Flock to be in.'

'Is it a good idea though, love? Getting people like him elected, I mean?'

'Well, realistically, how much difference is it going to make if he does become mayor? He won't have *that* much power. And he doesn't really plan to do anything anyway. He just wants the fame. So no, I'm not really worried about that. I mean, maybe the best thing would be if we made a big difference to his campaign but just not quite enough to win …'

'I don't know, love. I mean, I think you've done really well with that company. And you're right: if people are going to believe a load of old cobblers anyway, why shouldn't you get paid for making it one lot of old cobblers instead of another? I'm a hundred percent with you on that. But Teddy Robinson? I'm just not sure, love.'

'Maybe you're right.'

'What did the cats think of him?'

'They never like men.'

'Well that tells you something right there.'

'I suppose.'

'You'll make your own mind up, love. I'm not going to tell you what to do, apart from to eat up that jam, because there's more coming whether you want it or not.'

82

Jonathon looked around. He was standing in a luxurious but disgracefully dirty bathroom. It was lined with golden stone tiles and discarded towels. A degenerate toilet lolled with its mouth open near a large shower enclosure and a beautifully restored but horribly besmirched claw-footed bathtub.

There was a mirror facing him. It showed a man he barely recognised, with wild red hair reaching for the sky, huge white panda eyes in a streaky red face, and a massive red-and-black striped T-shirt, still tucked in just so. He instantly forgave Rupey and Kitty: he looked like he lived in a nightclub in Hell and ate three square meals of drugs every day.

Jonathon moved over to the door and listened for a few seconds. There was only the shouted murmur of Hooray's voice from somewhere in the lower floors, so Jonathon turned the handle and eased open the door. Before him was a landing with a beautifully restored wooden balustrade and stairs leading up and down. To his left was another door, slightly ajar, revealing a patch of soft cream carpet.

Jonathon crept forward, eased the bathroom door closed behind him, and then carefully peered around the edge of this other door. There was no one there, so he stepped inside.

The room was painted an expensive shade of not-quite-white. The soft cream carpet was marked by a grubby trail leading to a beautiful antique bed with a scroll end, on which were piled wet towels and a scrunched-up duvet. Another trail led to a set of finely carpentered wardrobes, with trousers, jackets and ties draped over their doors. Sunlight fell obliquely through the windowpanes, forming a glowing grid on the carpet. Jonathon stole softly over to the window and looked out.

A police car! In the street, white with blue and neon stripes and a code painted on the roof. One police person was just getting in and another was walking towards it, taking off his hat and ruffling his hair as he went.

Hooray must have been talking to them just now, despatching them with his plausible Etonian manner. Could Jonathon still stop them?

He tried to open the window, but it was shut with a beautifully crafted brass catch that he couldn't work.

'Hey!' he shouted through the glass. 'Police!'

Jonathon wrestled off the backpack, emptied it onto the floor, put it on his hand like a glove and punched one of the panes of glass. He tried again, harder, and his arm went right through the pane. The shards of glass fell away, and the bag slipped off his fist and dropped to the street below.

He put his mouth to the empty pane and shouted, 'Help! Police! My kidnap! Um!'

But the car was already pulling away. He fumbled again with the high-quality catch, shouting through the missing pane, 'Police! Police! Police! Hello! Come in! Police!'

From behind him came the sound of footsteps running upstairs, two at a time.

'Bedroom!' he heard someone say.

The door burst open and there stood a strapping six-footer with a waxed jacket and a martial air. Behind him was Hooray, equally strapping, moustache bristling.

'Crikey!' said Hooray. 'It's Fairfax!'

Jonathon, displaying an uncharacteristic burst of quick thinking, ran at them headlong, shouting 'Errrr!' – because it's difficult, on the spur of the moment, to come up with the right thing to shout when charging Etonians.

The strapping man in the doorway instinctively drew back into a terrifyingly competent fighting stance, and Jonathon slammed the door shut in his face. Despite the circumstances, he felt a surge of pleasure at having – for once in his life – immediately executed an effective plan, with no hesitation or overthinking. Perhaps he was self-growing after all.

Jonathon grabbed the door handle just as the strapping man tried to turn it. Then he spotted that the beautifully restored Georgian door had a thumb-bolt beside the handle. He snicked it into place and stood with his shoulder to the door.

Bam!

A boot crashed against the door, shaking Jonathon's whole body. It was a sturdy oak door, from a time before people had invented the technology required to make things truly flimsy, but nonetheless Jonathon knew it wouldn't survive much Etonian kicking. He needed another immediate and effective plan.

His body's response was, once again, to pump sweat out of his palms.

Bam!

A weapon, that was what he needed. Where could he find one? He needed to attack the Etonians when they were still off-balance from having just kicked their way through a sturdy oak door.

Jonathon looked around the room, hoping to see a beautifully restored antique sword. Instead, his eyes fell on a beautifully restored antique chest of drawers. Could he use it to barricade the door? He rushed over and tried to pull it out, but it was too heavy. Could he make it light enough to move by pulling out the drawers? He removed the bottom one, which was full of upper-middle-class knitwear.

Bam!

The door shook. There was no way he could do it in time. He looked desperately around. The curtain pole! There was a beautifully crafted metal curtain pole over the window. It was attached to slim wall brackets, and its curtains looked delightfully lightweight. He stood on the windowsill, shaking and twisting the pole until the brackets broke and it came off the wall.

BAM!

The frame split and the unnecessarily excellent door flew inwards, hitting the side of the bed and rebounding. This gave Jonathon time to brace himself and heft his new weapon in both hands, the curtains forming a hand guard and protective apron. The pole had a surprisingly satisfying balance and weight.

The Etonians entered, Hooray looking warily at Jonathon's weapon. The position of the heavy scroll-ended bed forced them to approach on a narrow front, directly into the curtain pole's range, like the Persian army advancing into the narrow defile at

Thermopylae.

Jonathon struck, amazed by the swift elegance of his stroke as the metal bar arced through the air to make contact with Hooray's outstretched hand, which caught it easily. Hooray surged forward and Jonathon stumbled, hampered by the fact that he was holding a curtain pole and standing in a knitwear drawer.

Jonathon felt Hooray's hands clutch his throat, pinning him to the top of the chest of drawers, his head striking a tasteful lamp and a Greek figurine on the way down. Jonathon's hands were trapped by the curtains. He tried to kick but someone grabbed his leg.

There was a brief moment when they formed a tableau, Jonathon's face pinned to the top of the chest of drawers, one leg in a drawer, one suspended in the act of kicking, his hands immobile and wrapped in curtains.

'Unk,' he said.

'Count of three and we move him to the floor,' said Hooray. 'One, two, *three*.'

Jonathon found himself transported to the floor, between the beautifully restored Georgian fireplace and the bed.

'Roll him over.'

He was now on his stomach, with someone's knee in the centre of his back. He felt his arms being pulled behind him, and something thin and uncomfortable was cinched around his wrists, pinning them together.

This had not gone to plan at all.

83

Lance and the murderer cruised slowly up Melmotte Row in their swapped BMW, looking out for Jonathon. They'd already cruised slowly down the street without seeing a trace of him.

'You sure he'll be here?' asked the murderer.

'I'm sure,' said Lance. 'He wouldn't just wander off. And what else could he do? He'll have found somewhere unobtrusive and be looking out for us.'

'Maybe the kidnappers spotted him, nabbed him in,' said the murderer.

Lance made a face. 'Just go up to the top and we can walk back d–'

'Wait. What's that?' the murderer pointed to something on the pavement.

'What?'

'That bag. And look, there's a bit missing from that window up there. Why didn't you spot that?'

'I was probably still distracted by that police car that drove past us. Stop here. I'll get out and have a look.'

The murderer stopped and Lance sauntered over to the pavement. He pulled out his phone and dialled.

'Arlene Drummond,' came the answer.

'I still can't get over how that's the way you answer our landline.'

'Stow it, Jerk. What's up?'

'Did you give Jonathon a gold Michael Kors bag?'

'Yes. It's not really my thing, but it was free and it's *such* a great size. Why?'

Lance got back in the car, holding the bag.

'I think he's used it to send us a message. It's lying outside Number Twenty-Eight Melmotte Row. Looks like he smashed a window pane and posted it out.'

'Oh god, I hope the little guy's okay. I'll call the cops again and tell them – they just left. I wish we'd had the full address when they were here. And I guess the window and bag count as evidence.'

'You've talked to them? What did they say?'

'They were just *British* about the whole thing: very polite but I have no clue whether they plan to do anything. I'll call them again.'

'Okay. You do that. Me and Colin will try to find out more.'

'Stay safe, okay?'

'I was born safe,' he said, ending the call, then added, 'But things have really gone downhill since then.'

Lance turned to the murderer.

'That his?' asked the murderer, pointing to the little gold bag.

'Yes. Well, Arlene's, but she gave it to him. It looks like he's used it to tell us where he is, since his phone's out of battery.'

The murderer nodded. 'He must've got inside somehow. Or been taken in, like I said.'

Lance winced at the suggestion.

The murderer, meanwhile, moved the car on, turned right at the next corner and braked suddenly. He pointed and said, 'Look at that: car park for them little flats, right next to the house. We could get over that wall.'

Lance nodded and opened his door. As they got out, he noticed the single yellow line on the road and said, 'We'll get a ticket.'

'Lance mate, it's a stolen car.'

'Good point.'

They ducked under a sturdy metal gate into the little car park. The murderer grabbed a bin, pushed it against the wall and climbed up, moving from there onto the flat roof of a little extension built into Number Twenty-Eight. He signalled to Lance, then took cover by a window. Lance followed him, panting.

'What now?' asked Lance, looking dubiously at a sturdy cast-iron down-pipe that ran all the way up the wall, passing close to two open windows.

'Not on your life,' whispered the murderer, seeing the direction of his gaze. 'You'd have to be a right nutter to climb that. Anyway, Gemma and Pipe are in this room.' He nodded down towards the one with the shutters closed.

'How do you know?'

'It's not going to be one with the windows open, is it? Too risky. But it'll be at the back, so no one can see them from across the road. So then, shutters or no shutters? Shutters. And the kidnappers'll be in the room next to it, at the front.'

'Makes sense,' whispered Lance.

'Thought you was supposed to be a detective,' whispered the murderer.

'Me? I work in a chicken shop,' whispered Lance. 'So do we climb down to that window? Or try to force the French windows?'

'Neither. I'll tell you what we do. But first I need to use your phone.'

'Who are you going to call?'

But before the murderer could answer, there was the sound of a heavy step on the stairs leading down to their window. He put his finger to his lips, and they flattened themselves to the wall.

84

Teddy crumpled a twenty into the cabbie's hand and hurried to his front door. A broken window! Up there at the top. Fortuna preserve him. There was a muffled crash from somewhere inside.

Teddy had been hurrying back even before Hooray's call, because of the text from Nikki. He'd thought he might be able to clear up a bit of the mess before she arrived. But now it seemed there was an even messier mess to deal with.

Still, it wouldn't be the first time Teddy had cleared up one of Hooray's messes. There'd been that awful time at Oxford when Hoo had turned up in his room at three in the morning, roaring drunk and carrying a dead bulldog belonging to the dean of Trinity college. *I have slain him, Teddy,* he kept whispering. *I have slain the beast.* Teddy had sacrificed an excellent suitcase and several volumes of a valuable (but usefully weighty) set of Oxford Classical Texts in disposing of the corpse, in the pouring rain too. But he had done it, and made it back in time for his tutorial.

He let himself in and headed to the stairs.

'Hello?' he called. 'Hoo?'

'Teddy!' said Hooray, putting his head over the upstairs banister. 'I hoped that was you! Good to see you! How are you? Good morning?'

'Never mind that. What are you doing, you godawful wretch? And how did you break my window?'

'Window?' said Hooray.

'Afternoon, Tedders,' called a familiar voice.

'Who's that?' called Teddy.

'I told you!' said Hooray.

'Dench!' called the voice.

'Stench!' shouted Teddy. 'Thank god there's someone sensible involved in this fuck-awful imbroglio. What are you doing up there?'

Teddy began to ascend the stairs.

'Coming down!' said Hooray.

Teddy reached the half-landing and looked up to see Hooray and Stench carrying a body with bare red-painted legs and badly scuffed Loake shoes.

'Oh god,' groaned Teddy. 'Please tell me he's not dead.'

'Teddy!' said Hooray, offended. 'As if I would! In your house!'

Teddy backed down the stairs as the two men descended, lumping the unconscious figure between them.

'Who is it?' he asked.

'Fairfax,' said Hooray, and flashed a smile. 'I told you going after his girlfriend would work. He's come right to us. Open the door, would you?' Hooray gestured with his eyebrows to the door leading to the back portion of the living room.

Teddy opened it and stood back, allowing Hooray and Stench to pass.

'Why's he … painted red?' asked Teddy.

'Do you know, I have no idea,' said Hooray.

'Some sort of war paint?' suggested Stench.

'And what's he tied up with?'

'Cable ties,' said Hooray. 'You know, plastic things meant to keep your wires and whatnot in a nice neat bundle. They work a treat – all the rage in Jo'berg. So light! But fiendishly difficult to get out of, if they're done up nice and tight. Oh, hope you don't mind, but we borrowed one of your socks and a cravat to gag him with.'

Teddy followed them into the darkened room.

'You can't keep him here,' he said. 'What if he's called the police?'

'He's hardly going to have called the police, is he?' said Hooray. 'He's escaped from prison. Besides, the police have already been.'

Teddy, who had just lowered himself onto the arm of a sofa,

stood up with a start.

'What!' he said. 'What happened?'

'What do you think?' said Hooray, lowering the unconscious body to the floor. 'They politely warned us that someone had threatened to break in, and one of their social betters – AKA me – told them in a suave and charming way that all was well and there was absolutely nothing to worry about. They went off tugging their forelocks in a satisfied fashion.'

Teddy clasped his forehead and his stomach. 'Oh, by the living shit of Christ. I can't have police coming here, Hoo. I can't. The election's only a couple of weeks away!'

'And the police have gone away and this conspiracy against you has been, I should say, absolutely thwarted,' said Hooray, standing now with his hands on his hips.

'Gah,' said Teddy, beginning to calm down.

Hooray made a courtly gesture. 'You're welcome. And I shall conduct his interrogation when he comes round. Debt of honour: repaid.'

Teddy slumped down onto the sofa, then jumped back up again, giving a small scream.

'It moved! There's a leg!' He looked more closely. 'Oh, fuckballs. There's a whole fucking person. And she looks about ten!'

'Collateral damage,' said Hooray. 'Regrettable. She was with Fairfax's girlfriend, so …'

Teddy, his eyes starting to get used to the gloom, followed Hooray's gaze. Lying on the floor next to Fairfax was a young woman, a tea towel tied around her lower face. Her eyes were fixed on his own and expressed, to put it mildly, profound irritation.

'You've got to get them out of here, Hoo,' said Teddy. 'Debt very much not repaid, until you've done that. Did anyone see you bringing unconscious females into my house?'

'Teddy, this constant impugning of one's professionalism …' said Hooray. 'Naturally, they weren't unconscious when I brought them in. As far as they knew they were seeking refuge in a safe house operated by the secret services and I was the dashing and dependable George Knight. And even then, no one saw us, I swear. Honestly, this place is dead, T. You'd expect to see at least *someone* in the street on a summer Sunday.'

'Can you vouch for this, Stench?'

Stench said, 'I know Hoo's usually as full of bollocks as a school sausage, but in this case it's all just as he says. We waited until we were inside before we overpowered them and broke out the old cable ties.'

Teddy nodded. At least you knew where you were with old Stench. He looked at Hooray and said, 'You've *got* to get them out of here, Hoo.'

'And I shall,' said Hooray, with dignity. 'How big are your suitcases?'

'Oh god,' said Teddy, ruffling his hair. 'Not this again. Do you want my Homer and Virgil again too?'

'Just the suitcases will suffice' said Hooray. 'We can hardly carry them out to my Land Rover as they are, can we? Even in the dead of night.'

'*Especially* in the d. of n.,' said Stench.

'And what will you do with them after that?' asked Teddy.

'Well, kill them, obvs,' said Hooray. 'And then disappear the remains.'

Teddy sighed and ran his hand fretfully through his hair.

'I don't *like* killing people, Hoo,' he said. 'Isn't there any other way?'

'Fraid not,' said Hooray.

Teddy looked at Stench.

'Fraid not,' said Stench, shaking his head.

'Oh god,' said Teddy. 'What a wicked web, etcetera.' He sighed.

'Look,' said Hooray, heading for the door, 'let's pop down to the kitchen and have a quick glug of Chab. Get our breath. Then we can work out next steps.'

Stench shrugged and followed. Teddy ran his hand through his hair, looked around in distress at the immobilised people nestled among the pizza boxes on his rug and sofa, said 'Oh god' again, and followed.

A thought struck him. He called, 'By the way, Hoo, I'm absolutely *not* having them pre-killed here. You'll have to do it in a ... I don't know, forest or something.'

85

Once the Etonian voices had descended to the basement and grown muffled, the murderer dialled.

It was answered almost immediately. 'Hello, emergency services operator. Which service do you require?'

'Police,' he whispered.

'I'll just connect you now.'

There was a click, and then a different voice – a woman's – said, 'Hello, where are you calling from?'

'Twenty-Eight Melmotte Row, Islington,' whispered the murderer.

'What is the nature of your emergency?'

'A big old ex-con, just out of prison, is breaking into the house.'

'Is anyone injured?'

'If no one's injured now, they will be soon. I can tell you that.'

'Are there any weapons involved?'

'Yes, there are weapons.'

Lance raised his eyebrows and the murderer shrugged.

'What is your own name, address and phone number?'

The murderer gave his name and address.

'Thank you. I'll send someone along.'

'Cheers, love. Make sure you send them soon. There's a right scene going on in there.' He ended the call. 'Will be, I mean,' he added.

He handed the phone back to Lance, who whispered, 'Calling the police on yourself? Aren't you worried they'll arrest you instead of the kidnappers?'

'They're going to arrest me whatever happens. As long as they get Gemma out – and Pipe – I don't care what else happens.'

'Okay.'

'Now, I'm going to break one of these panes with my elbow, open that catch, get in and we'll rush down into the back room, the one with the shutters. We'll barricade ourselves inside with the girls and make as much noise as we can till the cops turn up. Okay?'

Lance nodded. The murderer stood up, braced himself … and the doorbell sounded.

Bing-bong.

'That's never the cops already, is it? Bloody hell. Okay, soon as that door opens, we're in. Same plan.'

Lance nodded again.

Footsteps came up from the basement and traced a path along the hallway. There was the sound of the front door opening, and the murderer was about halfway through his swing when he heard a loud voice saying, 'Ponky! Trout! What a delightful surprise!'

'Teddy!' said two equally loud voices. As they came into the hallway, one said, 'Hooray called, asked for reinforcements. Spot of guard duty, he said. What's the sitch?'

'Shit,' whispered Lance. 'More Etonians.'

'Come downstairs,' said the first loud voice, 'and we'll fill you in. Rather a sticky situation but eminently fixable, especially for chaps with your experience.'

The footsteps receded downstairs to the basement, where they were loudly greeted by the two men already down there.

Flip, thought the murderer. The odds against them had pretty much doubled. It was now five against one. Or one and a quarter, he thought charitably, glancing at Lance.

Still, now or never.

The murderer put his suede-jacketed elbow on one of the window panes and leant on it hard until he felt it give, then he pushed the fragments of the pane until they fell to the carpet below. He reached in, turned the catch and yanked the bottom sash smoothly up. Then he squeezed his body through the opening, emerging as a clumsy mass on the half-landing. He reassembled himself and crept downstairs as quietly as he could, hoping that the school reunion downstairs would drown out any sound.

The murderer turned the handle of the back-room door and stepped inside. It was dim, illuminated only by what light crept in around the edges of the wooden shutters and from the doorway where he stood. Soon Lance joined him, closing the door behind them and making it even darker. As the murderer's eyes began to adjust, he saw a movement from the sofa.

It was her. She was tied up and had a tea-towel over her mouth, but he'd have known those eyes and that hair anywhere.

'Gem?' he whispered, moving over to her. 'You okay, love?'

She nodded, and he pulled the tea-towel down. There was a multicoloured Fair Isle sock in her mouth, which he pulled out like a magician producing a string of flags. As the sock kept on coming, he glanced around the room. There was a woman on the rug, next to a man in shorts, both tied and gagged. *Must be John and Pipe*, he thought.

'Dad,' whispered Gemma, when he'd finally removed the huge sock. 'You came.'

'Course I did. That's what I'm for.' He kissed the top of her head and looked around the room again, forcing himself to think about what came next.

'Ah, flip,' he whispered.

'What?' whispered Gemma.

'It's been knocked through. There's a flipping long door thing, wossname.'

'Room divider?' she suggested.

'That's the one. You are clever, love.'

Lance crept over and whispered, 'What's the problem?'

'We can't barricade ourselves in here, because of this room-divider thing. We'd never keep it shut. So, new plan: I'll guard the top of the stairs, stop anyone coming up; you cut everyone loose and get them out. All right?'

Lance nodded. 'I'll ungag Piper and Jonathon first, then cut them free. Did you bring the breadknife?'

'No. Did you?'

'No,' said Lance. 'How am I going to cut them free?'

'I don't know. Improvise.'

The murderer stopped and listened. There was the sound of a basement kitchen full of Etonians suddenly not talking.

'Flip,' he muttered. 'Okay, I'm off.' He looked at his daughter. 'Love you, Gem.'

He rose and moved as quietly as he could to the hallway, easing the door closed behind him. He looked down the stairs. Almost immediately, a moustached face appeared. It was the man who'd tried to order a San Pellegrino in Ken's.

'Cripes!' said the man. 'Someone's got in. Bloody big beggar too – the chap from the chicken place.'

'I told you I heard something!' said someone else.

'How did he get in?' asked another voice.

'How should I know?' said the man with the moustache.

He was soon joined by the three other faces, peering up the stairs.

The murderer said, 'The cops are on their way. You boys better give yourselves up.'

'Rush the beggar!' shouted the man with the moustache, and launched himself up the stairs.

The murderer braced himself between the wall and banister, and aimed a perfectly timed kick, catching the man just under the chin so that his momentum served to flip him neatly backwards, one foot sailing up into the air. His friends instinctively dodged, so that he landed in a heavy heap at the bottom of the stairs.

'Christ!' said one of the others. 'Hoo? Ted, come and see to him!'

'I've got a whole rack of kicks in the teeth up here!' called the murderer. 'Get them while they're hot!'

He laughed, suddenly elated – lit up with energy. He'd spent so much time in prison stopping fights happening that he'd almost forgotten how good they felt.

Another of the men took advantage of the laugh to come haring upstairs, passing the halfway point before the murderer had time to adjust his stance. The man's hands were reaching out to grab the murderer's ankles. The murderer jumped back, unsteadily, only just in time, and the man's hands flailed at where his ankles had been. The murderer managed to brace himself again, and flashed out a kick which – by pure luck – planted itself right in the middle of the man's face. It wasn't as clean and precise as the first, but it nonetheless sent the man slithering back to the foot of the stairs.

'Bloody hell!' said someone. 'Stench too! Teddy, come and get him, would you? Recovery position, and get water!'

The two remaining men disappeared for a few seconds. When they re-emerged, one of them held a dining chair, its four legs facing up the stairs. The second man was sticking close behind, supporting the first up the treacherous steps.

The murderer wondered if there was a spare chair in the front room, but in any case there was no time to get it. The men were advancing steadily upwards, the chair legs coming closer.

The murderer kicked at them but missed. They advanced further, almost reaching the top of the stairs. He grabbed two of the legs and pushed. The two men behind the chair pushed back. For a few moments they were evenly matched, feet slipping on tiles and wooden stairs.

'Now!' called one of the men behind the chair.

They yanked it back, pulling the murderer down – one step, then three, off-balance. He let go, and the chair instantly jabbed him painfully in the stomach and thigh. He fell back, sitting down hard on the top step. They jabbed again, hitting him in the centre of the chest. He vainly tried to grab their weapon, then kicked out and managed to get his foot against the base of the seat, pushing back against them.

A hand grabbed his ankle. He wrenched it up, rolling onto his back, his hands braced against the wall and banister post. A face appeared and the murderer kicked desperately, heel connecting with the man's forehead – a fumbled blow, but enough to knock him back, off balance. This gave the murderer just enough time to plant both feet on the chair's base and shove, sending them back down the stairs. Then he was up and managed to grab their weapon by one leg, ripping it from their grasp.

The two Etonians were standing at the bottom of the stairs again, sweating and eyeing him warily. One had a dirty shoe mark on his forehead, the Nike swoosh dimly discernible.

The murderer had now regained his position in the hallway. He briefly turned and hit the chair against the wall, smashing one leg away from the seat. The man with the Nike forehead rushed up to take advantage of the murderer's brief distraction, arriving in perfect range just as the murderer's elegant hardwood club was ready for use. The blow hit him smartly on the side of the head, sending him staggering into the wall and down the stairs, where he collapsed in a heap.

'Had enough yet?' called the murderer, as someone dragged away the latest casualty.

'Not on your life,' said the remaining man, advancing slowly and warily up the stairs.

And then the murderer saw it: the man was holding a chef's knife. He held it in his fist, blade downwards – the way people who know how to fight with knives hold them. When the Etonian reached two thirds of the way up the stairs, he lunged, the knife flashing out towards the murderer's legs. The murderer skipped backwards and struck with his club, but the man dodged back just in time.

The man struck again, the murderer skipped back, struck downwards, missed again. They repeated the dance twice more, and then the man said, 'There!' looking behind the murderer. He knew it was just a diversion, but it nonetheless impaired his concentration just enough that he failed to skip back swiftly enough.

The knife stuck in the side of his calf.

'Ow,' said the murderer, registering the blow but not yet feeling it. And then he brought the chair leg down with the full weight of his upper body and his anger – on the Etonian's head.

The Etonian crumpled and dropped, going *bub-a-dub-a-dub* down the stairs and arriving in a heap at the bottom.

'Oh Christ! Ponky too!' said a man with copper hair, rushing to attend him. It was the politician Lance had told him about – Teddy Something.

The murderer pulled the blade from his calf, paying no attention to the blood.

'Never bring a knife to a chair-leg fight!' he called downstairs, dropping it disdainfully to the floor.

He looked down at the copper-haired man at the foot of the stairs. Their eyes met. The man's mouth was working but no words came out.

'You coming up or what?' said the murderer.

The copper-haired man vanished.

'Thought not,' said the murderer.

He moved towards the front door, but his calf was bleeding quite a lot. He should probably put a tea-towel around it, he thought, so he went into the back room instead.

He stood in the doorway. Everyone turned. As they saw him, relief spread over their faces.

'That's all dealt with,' he said. Then, 'Why they all still tied up, Lance? What you been doing while I've been fighting half of Eton? Having a nice little breather?'

Lance was sawing desperately at the woman's wrists with a bit of metal he'd taken from the binding of a dismembered official document lying nearby.

'These plastic things are impossible to break!' said Lance.

The murderer sighed. Leaning on the handle of the open door, he glanced around for something to use on the cable ties.

'Oh my god, Dad!' said Gemma, looking at him from the sofa by the wall. 'What happened to your leg?'

'Cut myself on a posh boy. Can I borrow your tea towel?'

Gemma actually smiled. 'Course,' she said.

It isn't much, perhaps: your kidnapped daughter allowing you to use her discarded gag as a bandage. But nonetheless a swell of pleasure flooded his heart.

'Wait a minute,' said the murderer. 'I know where there's a—'

'What?' said Gemma.

'Knife?' suggested Lance.

But the murderer didn't answer, because someone had grabbed his shoulder and was punching him in the back.

'Oi,' he said.

He was hoping to add something smart, for Gemma's benefit, but he suddenly felt incredibly tired, like all his energy had left him at once. He tried to whirl around, but lost his balance. His legs were useless. He was on his knees. Whoever had punched him had also poured a warm cup of tea down his back.

Oh. He suddenly remembered people in prison describing what it was like to be stabbed. Exactly like this.

Flip.

'Dad!' called Gemma. And her voice echoed around and then rushed over him, with the darkness.

86

The huge man in front of Teddy sank to the floor, revealing a room full of shocked faces.

Instinct took over, and he found himself saying, 'Look, I promise you, that was not me. Hand on heart.'

He would have put his hand on his heart for emphasis, but he found he was still holding the bloody knife.

The giant toppled forward onto his face, and a handsome man in a nice jacket – the only other person in the room who wasn't tied up – moved towards him.

'Colin!' said the handsome man.

'I strongly advise you not to move,' said Teddy, brandishing the bloody knife he'd so recently disavowed.

The handsome man ignored him, kneeling beside the giant, effortfully shifting his head and one arm so that he was in the recovery position, putting his fingers on the giant's neck.

'Oh fuck,' said the handsome man. 'I still don't know how to feel someone's fucking neck! What does a neck like this *mean?*'

'Chaps!' Teddy called over his shoulder. 'Chaps! I've beaten him!'

The handsome man got up and sprang forward. Teddy jabbed out clumsily with the knife. The handsome man stopped and looked down.

'My shirt,' he said, in disbelief.

His shirt was, Teddy had to concede, ruined. It was cut, for one thing, and there was a huge and ever-growing red stain on it.

'Oh Christ,' said Teddy. 'Oh Christ.'

There was a noise so high and pure that at first Teddy thought it was coming from the panic centres of his own brain. But then he was shoved aside by Hooray, who rushed over to the girl on the sofa and pressed a cushion to her face until she stopped screaming and lapsed into coughs.

'Try that again,' said Hooray, brandishing the cushion, 'and I won't stop nearly so quickly.'

Teddy exchanged a look with Hooray, who had a little strap-beard of dried blood under his chin. Then he surveyed the room. The handsome man was lying on the floor, pressing a tea-towel to his shirt-wound. The red-painted man and the young woman, both tightly bound, were looking on with helpless shock.

Bing-bong! went the doorbell.

'Oh Christ,' said Teddy.

Hooray rose and took the knife from Teddy's shaking hand.

'If,' he said, holding up the knife like a combat instructor and looking around the room, 'any of you makes even the smallest whisper then … Gemma was it?'

The girl on the sofa nodded dumbly.

'Gemma,' continued Hooray, 'gets this.'

He perched on the sofa arm against which her head was propped, holding the cushion in one hand and the knife in the other.

'Understand?' he asked.

'Yes,' said the woman.

'Um, yes,' said the red-painted man.

Bing-bong! said the doorbell.

'Teddy,' said Hooray, 'be a good chap: see who's at the door and get rid of them.'

'Of course,' said Teddy.

'And for Christ's sake, keep your hand in your pocket. There's blood all over it.'

Teddy hurried along the hallway, trying to move soundlessly, and pressed his eye to the spyhole.

Nikki! He'd completely forgotten about her. Could it really be just half an hour ago that he'd been hurrying back, kidding himself that he could tidy up before she arrived? It seemed another world.

He glanced back. Stench had appeared at the end of the hallway and was mouthing, 'Get rid of them.'

There'd be no fobbing Nikki off. He'd just have to stay quiet and wait for her to go away.

DAH-DA-DA-DAAA-DA! DAH-DA-DA–

His phone! He jumped an inch or two into the air, then hastily silenced it.

The letterbox clacked open.

'I can hear your phone, Teddy,' said Nikki's voice through the letterbox. 'And see the front of your trousers. What are you doing?'

'Nikki!' he said. 'I–' He thought of the giant's bloody back. 'Listen, I–' He felt the sticky blood drying on his hand. 'S-something, er–'

'Why are you stuttering?' she said. 'Oh my god, you're not having a stroke, are you?'

The last thing he needed was for her to call an ambulance. He scrabbled the door open with his left hand, keeping his right in his pocket.

He'd only meant to open it a crack, but she stepped confidently in, unbuttoning her coat.

'What was all–?' she began, and then stopped, seeing Stench standing at the end of the hallway, a grubby footprint clearly visible on his face, wearing a little moustache of congealed blood beneath his nose.

'What's going on?' she asked in a different tone.

'Let me explain,' said Teddy. 'You were right: there is a conspiracy against us – both of us – and this Fairfax fellow was part of it. He broke into my house–'

'Where is he?' she said fiercely.

Teddy realised that he must have glanced in the direction of the back sitting-room, because Nikki spun on her heel and was at the end of the hallway in a second. Stench blocked her way, but she had evidently already seen into the room – the stabbed people being inconveniently clustered in the entranceway.

'Oh. My god,' she said.

'They broke in!' said Teddy. 'We had to stop them.'

'Have you called an ambulance?' she asked, her phone in her hand.

Stench snatched for her phone, but she flinched away from him. He grabbed her around the middle, pinning her arms to her sides, and carried her squirming into the back sitting-room.

Teddy followed, saying, 'For goodness' sake, Stench!'

Stench wrestled Nikki to the ground in the last spare body-sized space. One of his hands was over her mouth, one knee between her shoulder blades.

'This is no time for sentimentality,' said Stench.

Bing-bong! went the doorbell.

'Listen, Nikki,' said Teddy, 'I'll explain later. You'll see that it's not how it looks – I promise.'

Bing-bong! went the doorbell again.

'Ignore it!' said Stench.

'What if it's the police?' said Teddy. 'The giant said he'd called them.'

'Well, go and see,' said Hooray. 'And if it is, send them on their way.'

'And don't let whoever it is come swanning in this time!' called Stench as Teddy hurried up the hallway.

Behind him, he heard Hooray say, 'I remind you that if any of you makes a noise, Gemma gets it.'

Teddy looked through the spy hole. It was the police, two of them.

Poc-poc-poc. The sound was shockingly loud and close as the police knocked on the door.

Teddy took a deep breath, smiled, ruffled his hair with his clean hand and put his bloody hand in his pocket. Then he opened the door as Teddy Robinson from television.

They stood neatly on his doorstep. One was a very young, rather weedy-looking man with a serious air, the other a slightly older woman who looked like she might be happier as a teacher.

'Afternoon, officers,' he said, ruffling his hair. 'You're no doubt here to assure me of your support in the forthcoming election.' He did his poker-faced suppressed smile, and they looked politely back at him. *Tough crowd*, he thought.

'Good afternoon, sir,' said the woman. 'I'm Constable Hesp and this is Constable Blaine. Would you mind if we popped in and had a quick chat?'

'Ah,' said Teddy, 'I see what's happened here. A couple of your esteemed colleagues were here a short while ago. All cleared up now. Must have been some sort of miscommunication – double-booking and so forth. Happens in my team all the time.' He chuckled ruefully and ruffled his hair again.

'We are aware of our colleagues' prior visit, sir. However, we have received subsequent information of concern, and we're here just to follow up on that, so if–'

'I do apologise. Inspector Hesp, was it?'

'Constable, sir,' said the woman, without the little smile that Teddy had hoped would result from his deliberate slip.

'Dreadfully sorry – no doubt foreseeing a future promotion. The Proteus of politics, I'm often called. As I was saying, I do apologise: I've had a few school chums round and things became somewhat boisterous – you know how it is.' He ruffled his hair again and pulled a face. 'I assure you we've calmed down now, and I shall be personally taking each of my neighbours a bottle of something cold and expensive to express my regrets.'

'To my knowledge, sir, we haven't been in receipt of any noise complaints–'

'Oh? Well, that's wonderful. So, to what do I owe this honour?'

'It might be easier to do this inside, sir.'

'Ah, sorry. It's just that I *am* in the middle of something …'

'Of course, sir. We received an emergency call advising us of a violent break-in at the premises by a prison-leaver, potentially armed.'

'You mean someone's breaking into my house to attack me?'

'Yes, sir.'

'Bah, ha-ha. I think I'd have noticed if anything of that sort had happened. And if he's yet to try, well, my good friend Dench in there is a former captain in the SAS, we have an ex-major in the Guards, a couple of rugger props, and there *was* a time when I was rather a handy boxer, so I think we should manage to stick up for ourselves.'

'I do understand that, sir. However, we are concerned about this in light of that previous information received, concerning an attempted break-in by a thin man wearing shorts and … painted red.'

'Painted red? I would most definitely remember such a thing. Look, I'm not trying to say "Don't you know who I am?" but I *am* a reasonably well-known politician running for mayor, and it is possible that some people are attempting to express their displeasure at that prospect by making frivolous calls and wasting police time.'

'We are certainly aware of that possibility, Mr Robinson. What we–'

She was interrupted by a shout of 'Hey!'

Teddy turned to see, marching down the pavement towards them, a young woman in a rather fetching linen outfit, with an expression on her face of incandescent anger.

87

Arlene, marching towards the address Lance had given her, could not believe it when she saw Teddy Robinson standing in the doorway, laughing pleasantly as he chatted to a couple of cops.

'Hey!' she shouted. They turned to look at her, and even in that split second Teddy managed to leer at her disgustingly.

'Why in the hell are you not arresting him?' she said to the police, who looked like they'd much rather be doing some filing back at the station than dealing with this situation. 'How long have I spent on the phone to you guys, telling you about all the kidnapped women in this guy's house?'

The male officer turned towards her, showed his palms, and said, 'Let's lower our voice and calm down, shall we, madam?'

'Let's maybe stop kidnapping women first, *shall we?* Maybe that should be our priority here.'

'These are extremely serious accusations, madam,' said the female officer.

'Damn right they are! That's what I've been trying to tell you guys on the phone all day!'

'Oh look,' said Teddy, 'this is clearly a put-up job. Nothing better to do with her time than conspire to ruin a politician's Sunday afternoon.'

The female officer said, 'Madam, if you have specific

information in regard to kidnappings at this address, I would be more than happy to arrange for a colleague to take a statement–'

'I just gave a statement! A pair of cops finally came and took my statement – but I didn't know the house number then, only the street. So I called again and gave the house number and they said "Thank you very much, madam". And I thought, "These guys are gonna do nothing." And my husband was around here and now he isn't answering his phone. So I came here myself. And I'm glad I did, because I find you shooting the breeze on his doorstep instead of going in and rescuing all the people he's kidnapped!'

Both officers blinked at her, reeling. They looked at Teddy.

'Look,' he said, 'the press will have an absolute field day if I let you search this house, and she knows it. That's exactly what she wants – and her bosses at the *Guardian*.'

'Hey, I work in fashion, buster. I am a concerned citizen.'

'Absolute nonsense,' said Teddy. 'Not even a citizen of this country, by the sound of her.'

The female officer took a breath, clearly trying to work out what to say to all this. But Teddy spoke instead.

'Look, I've been jolly patient about all this, but I'm sorry, enough is enough. I don't have to be bullied into letting my house be searched. So, unless you have a warrant–'

'Come on!' said Arlene. 'You guys can go in without a search warrant – you have probable cause *and* exigent circumstances here! I watch cop shows!'

'Madam,' said the female officer, 'these things work a little bit differently here than in America. We do make every effort to secure the house-holder's permission before entering and searching a property.'

'Exactly,' said Teddy. 'Thank you, officer.'

'And,' continued the female officer, 'while we are allowed to enter without permission, we can only do so if we're in close pursuit, there's a disturbance taking place, we hear cries for help or distress, or if a del–'

'Well if you guys won't go in there, I will, and then you'll have to closely pursue me!' said Arlene, making for the door, which Teddy slammed shut and bolted.

'You heard that, officers!' Teddy called through the letterbox. 'I strongly suggest you arrest this woman. I simply will not have people threatening to invade my home!'

'See how desperate he is to avoid anyone looking in there!' shouted Arlene.

'Let's all just calm down, shall we?' said the male officer, deploying his palms again.

'Either you calm this down by arresting that woman,' called Teddy, 'or I'll phone the Deputy Commissioner and he'll calm you all down.'

88

Back in the living room, Gemma could vaguely hear the man with big hair shouting through his front door. But most of her attention was on the man with the moustache, who sat on the arm of the sofa, listening, his eyes fixed on Piper and Jonathon across the room. Specifically, her attention was on the huge kitchen knife, encrusted with blood, that he held just above her heart. There was a slight smile on his face.

She knew her dad was lying just a few feet away, but she couldn't see him. She would have had to raise her head, and she daren't move. She was willing herself to scream, despite that knife, because there must still be a chance that her dad could get to hospital on time. But she was frozen by some deep instinct, barely breathing.

Gemma's dad had been walking for a long time towards a bright light. He was now close enough to see within it his nan and granddad, his cousin Phil, and a few other relatives.

'Come on in, Col,' called his nan. 'It's magic in here.'

'Right you are, Nan,' he said. 'Lovely jubbly.'

'I was watching that barney you was having,' said his granddad. 'Beautiful job you did there. I was shouting at the end, "Behind

337

you!" Not that you took no notice.'

'Cheers, Granddad. Did you see who it was?'

'That one with the hair who's on the telly all the time.'

'You're joking! Didn't think he had it in him.'

'Put a cup of tea on for him,' said his Auntie Enid.

'What you on about, you lot?' said Phil, who'd died only a few months ago in a hot-tub accident. 'It's not his time.'

'Yes it is,' said his nan, indignantly. 'I should know.'

'Hear Phil out, love,' said his granddad peaceably.

'And since when do you say, "Lovely jubbly?"' Phil asked.

'I'm changing, all right?' said the murderer. 'I work in a customer-facing role now.'

'But why do you say it's not his time, Phil?' asked Auntie Enid.

'Well, he's got to look after Gem, hasn't he?' said Phil.

This set them off bickering, just like they used to at Christmas, leaving the murderer watching in a curiously detached way from just beyond the circle of light, unable to get a word in.

Then Phil broke off from the family argument, looked straight at him and said, 'You need to open your eyes, mate.'

Lance was lying very still, clutching to his stomach a couple of discarded tea towels that had been used as gags. He was thinking about all the films he'd seen in which the hero battles on, despite all manner of wounds. In reality, all those heroes would have lain very, very still, staunching their bleeding and trying not to think about how thirsty they were.

He should probably be trying to make a new deal with God, but somehow his heart wasn't in it. Besides, the only element of their last deal that remained unfulfilled was helping the poor, and there was no realistic prospect of him ever doing that.

It was probably best to just keep on lying very, very still.

Piper was on her side, watching Hooray and also lying very, very still. In her case this was cover for an attempt to use Lance's blunt bit of metal to cut through the cable ties on her wrists. Her mind felt overwhelmingly clear and sharp, dispassionate and detached, as though the huge responsibility she felt for Gemma had switched her into an entirely new mode that she'd never known existed. It was somehow even stronger than her desire to save Jonathon.

Piper didn't know what she would do when her wrists were free, since her arms were still bound just above the elbow, and her legs were fastened in two places. But she had to do something.

She was clearly aware of everything in the room. She saw Hooray's relaxed readiness, the eager gleam in his eye, his hand on the knife. She saw Stench's ruthless absorption in the task of keeping Nikki subdued, his hand over her mouth. She saw Gemma's frozen shock. She saw Lance, over by her feet, adjust his grip on the tea towels he held to his stomach. Between Lance and the sofa, she saw the man they now didn't call the murderer, whose eyes were fluttering, as though he were trying to open them.

And behind her, where they'd put Jonathon, she sensed that he was gearing himself up to say something stupid.

89

Out in the street, the tense stand-off between Arlene and the police was interrupted by another car rocking to a halt. Two officers got out and walked over.

'You here for the kidnapping, yeah?' said one of the new officers, pushing his hat back on his head. He was a big, spongy man with a confident, open face and a broad accent.

The female officer looked confused and said, 'We were directed to attend a break-in reportedly conducted by a prison-leaver, in the course of which this' – she cast around for some way of referring to Arlene – 'member of the public–'

'I'll take that,' said Arlene.

'–appeared and alleged a kidnapping.'

'What's that? said the second new officer. He was almost identical to the first, but with less hair.

'Says there's been a break-in by an ex-con,' said the officer with his hat on the back of his head.

'Blimey, it's all kicking off here. Is he the one who put that window through?' The officer with less hair pointed up to a top-storey window missing one of its panes.

'We don't have specific intelligence on the missing window pane,' said the female officer.

'Oh dear me,' said the officer with less hair, catching his friend's eye. 'No specific intelligence?'

'Weird place to break in,' said the officer with his hat on the back of his head. 'Front top. They usually go for bottom back.'

'I'll go and have a shufty round the back, see what's going on there,' said the officer with less hair.

'Okay, I'll catch up on the specific intelligence here,' said the officer with his hat on the back of his head.

Between them, Arlene and the female officer, whose name turned out to be Hesp, told the new officer what had happened so far.

'So that's Teddy Robinson's gaff?' he asked.

They nodded. He pushed his hat even further back on his head.

'What?' said the officer with less hair, returning from looking round the back.

'It's only bloody Teddy Robinson's house, innit?'

'Bloody hell. Someone's put a window through at the back an'all.'

'Apparently Mr Robinson says no one's broken in.'

'Do you reckon *he's* been kidnapped? Maybe denying it under duress and that.'

At this point a third police car rocked to a halt and another officer got out.

'Threatened break-in?' asked Hesp hopefully, as he approached.

'Alleged kidnapping,' said the new arrival, a tall man with grey hair and his hat pulled down low over his eyes.

'It's Teddy Robinson's house,' said the officer with less hair.

'Bloody hell,' said the new officer, pulling his hat down even lower.

A young woman with exactly mid-brown hair, who had been delayed by seatbelt problems, got out of the car and joined the new officer.

'Hi, I'm Rachel,' she said to Arlene. 'Are you …?'

'Arlene!' said Arlene. 'Yes! Thank you so much for calling me!'

'No problem. Thanks a lot for giving me the address.'

'I can't believe you got a cop in like five minutes. It's taken me all day.'

'There were quite a lot at the carnival.'

'You come from the carnival?' asked the officer with the tipped-back hat.

'Yeah,' said the officer with grey hair. 'I'm not really supposed to be here. Only I don't like dancing.'

'Let me get this straight though,' said the officer with the tipped-back hat to Arlene and Rachel. 'Neither of you actually saw the girls get in the car?'

They shook their heads.

'And neither of you has talked to an eye-witness who saw it?'

'Not directly,' said Arlene.

The officer with the tipped-back hat was about to say something when a burst of unintelligible static on their police radios made them all look at each other.

'Ah, bollocks,' he said. 'Sorry, love. We've been told to clear out.'

Hesp cleared her throat. 'And I hereby caution you that your recent behaviour was in violation of Section Five of the Public Order Act 1986 …'

90

Jonathon was desperately trying to think of something that might improve the situation, however fractionally, when Teddy came bustling back in.

'Floreat Etona!' he announced, raising his blood-stained fist in triumph. 'We have prevailed! Dreadful Moros on his black steed has fucked off and Fortuna smiles upon us once more.'

'Meaning?' asked Hooray, the knife in his hand still poised just above Gemma's heart.

'The Deputy Commissioner's had a word, and the police outside are packing up. They're reading that infernal American woman her rights.'

Arlene! thought Jonathon. It could only be Arlene. If she was here, there was still hope. Even if the police were trying to arrest her.

'Thank heavens for that,' said Hooray.

'Thank *me* for that,' corrected Teddy. 'And this shocking case of police victimisation could even help me in the polls.'

'Give me a bloody hand here, would you?' said Stench, who was still struggling to cable-tie Nikki while keeping one hand over her mouth.

'One moment,' said Teddy. 'I just need to call Bolton while the police are still in the street. He'll know how to play this. Back in a second.'

Teddy put his phone to his ear and left the room, saying, 'Bolton! Awfully sorry to trouble you on a Sunday …'

Jonathon wondered if he could shout loudly enough to bring the police in before Hooray could carry out his threat. But he couldn't risk it, not while Hooray had the knife poised in his hand, and while he was watching them so intently.

Surely there was something he could softly say, something that would make Hooray look in his heart.

'Um, Hooray?' he heard himself softly say. 'Could you look in your, er, heart?'

'What?' said Hooray, with irritation.

'Um, I was just wondering if you could look in your heart?'

'I thought I told you that if you don't shut up, Gemma here will get it. Gag them would you, Stench?'

'Gag them yourself,' said Stench, wincing as Nikki bit his fingers again. 'I've got my hands full here.'

Hooray sighed, looked around the room, and spotted the tea towels and socks beside Lance.

'Don't make a sound,' he told Gemma, holding the knife up to her face, 'or you get it. Understand?'

She nodded fractionally, eyes wide with terror.

Hooray stomped over to the pile of tea towels and Gemma

screamed.

Like the child in the pushchair, Gemma put her whole body into the scream. She screamed her grief, her anger, her fear. She screamed not just her own distress, but the primordial distress of everyone who has ever been totally fucked over by a bunch of self-serving, over-privileged nobheads for the sake of their empty ambitions.

As her scream washed over Jonathon, he suddenly saw that this whole situation had always been a logic puzzle, like the one with the boat, the fox, the chicken and the other thing. And Hooray had got the answer wrong – possibly because the boat had popped out to call its campaign manager and the chicken had irritated him by suggesting he look in his heart.

Then Piper joined in the scream, and so did Jonathon. Like the dance, it seemed to pick him up and scream through him.

Hooray froze, tea towels and socks in one hand, knife in the other.

Stench gave a grunt as Nikki got one of his fingers fully in her mouth and bit down hard.

Teddy appeared in the doorway. Jonathon dimly heard him say, 'Awfully sorry, Bolton, the … smoke alarm's going off.'

Hooray sprang back to life, trying to smother Gemma's scream with his bundle of socks and tea towels and shouting, 'Shut them up, Teddy!'

Teddy hurried over, but before he could do anything, there was a loud bang from the front door.

Two police officers were in the room, holding frail-looking telescopic batons and what looked like little spray cans.

Hooray raised the knife but a blow to the wrist from one of the batons knocked it from his grasp. Then he got a burst from the spray can and started coughing, and then the officer was on him, wrestling him to the floor.

Stench got off Nikki to face the other officer but she was up in a second and kneeing him energetically in the genitals. He shoved her across the room, then took a baton blow to the side of his head. He grabbed the officer's hand and they grappled. Another, older officer came into the room, carrying a riot shield and a long wooden truncheon, which he brought down hard on Stench's head.

'Thank god you've come, officers,' said Teddy. 'I assure you that I had nothing …'

And then Nikki, with a terrible shriek, was on Teddy, punching, kicking and scratching him as he howled and wept.

As sirens filled the air, the room filled with black-clad officers carrying machine-guns and shouting, 'Armed police! Everyone on the floor! Now!'

The last thing Jonathon thought, before he passed out, was that only the police would shout this at a room full of people who were already on the floor.

Later

91

The next day, Gemma went with her mum to visit her dad in hospital. He'd had emergency surgery and been given quite a lot of other people's blood.

They found him propped up in a heavy-duty mechanical bed, attached to a drip and a couple of machines, with a clip on one finger and an inflatable armband on one arm. When he saw them he didn't move, but tried to smile.

He looked like an old man who'd been packed into a fake muscle suit and given an incongruous polka-dot nightie. His face looked grey and ill. In fact, he looked quite a lot like Gemma felt.

She was extremely tired, despite having slept for nearly twelve hours, and she felt unnaturally calm and blank, as though she'd had all her emotions removed. Everything felt like a dream, except for the occasional memory of the day before, which felt like scenes from a film she'd watched.

'Oh, love!' said Gemma's mum, hurrying over to him.

She held the hand that didn't have a clip on it, and kissed him on the top of his head, like a baby.

'Hello, love,' he said in a quiet, tired voice. 'Hello, Gemma. Thanks for coming.'

Gemma said nothing, but her mum said, 'They told us you was doing ever so well. Said you'd probably be out next weekend. I says, are you serious? They says yes. Won't be going to the gym for a few months, but he'll be home, they says. You look great, love.'

'I do not look great,' he said, smiling with just the corners of his mouth, as though the rest of it was too heavy to move. 'Tell her, Gem.'

'He don't look great, Mum,' she said, honestly.

Lisa looked at her, then back at him. 'Well, I suppose great is pushing it a bit,' she conceded.

Her dad's shoulders moved fractionally up and down, and he coughed weakly.

'I shouldn't laugh,' he said.

Gemma and her mum sat down in the two plastic chairs by his bed, her mum leaning forward so she could carry on holding his hand.

There was a silence, and then he looked at Gemma and said, 'Thanks for saving me, love.'

'You what?' she said. 'You saved me. Saved all of us.' Then she added, 'Thanks,' and then, 'Dad.'

He smiled and closed his eyes. 'That's not the way I remember it,' he said.

They were silent again, and then he opened his eyes, looked at his wife and said, 'You couldn't get us a cup of tea, could you, love? There's a machine down the corridor.'

'Course, love,' said her mum.

'I'll get them,' said Gemma, getting up.

'Not you, Gem,' said her dad.

Her mum got up, kissed him on the head again and left the room.

'I'm sorry, Gem,' he said, when her mum had gone.

Gemma didn't say anything. No words had arrived to speak.

'Listen,' he said, 'what you said, last week: you was right. I have, you know … killed people. A few of them. Even a bird once, a woman.'

'How?' she said.

'A knife, mostly,' he said.

'No, I mean, how could you?'

'Well … it's always been like I've had a sort of circle around me, and you're either in the circle or you're out. When I was your age, and for years after, there was hardly space in it for anyone except me. And my mum, of course – your nan. Pretty much everyone else, I didn't care whether they lived or died. *Really* didn't care.

And then your mum came along, and then you. And that started to change things. You opened my heart. Slowly. The circle started getting bigger. I found the blokes from the gym were in it – even idiots like Velcroman. Nowadays I can hardly keep people out of the bloody circle.'

'How you going to make things right though, Dad?' she asked.

'I don't know, love. I don't know. But I've been given a second chance, and I want to try. Start with you. That okay?'

Gemma nodded. Her eyes filled with tears.

And then from the corridor outside she heard her mum's voice saying, 'It's a right palaver though, innit? I mean, you don't come to hospital with a load of change in your pockets, do you?'

'Tell me about it,' said a familiar voice. 'I haven't even got any pockets.'

Her mum walked back into the room, doing her laugh. With her was the man who'd removed Gemma's gag the day before. He was now barefoot, stooped and walking with tiny steps. He was also wearing a big, short-sleeved polka-dot gown, which he held closed at the back. Nevertheless, he somehow had the air of this being an ironic fashion statement, and one he was carrying off pretty well.

'You met Lance, didn't you, Gem?' asked her dad.

'Sort of,' she said. 'Hello, Lance.'

'Hello, Gemma,' he said. 'Nice to meet you properly – and you too, Lisa.'

Gemma's mum put three little plastic cups of tea on the table by her husband's bed.

She held one out to him, but he said, 'Sorry, love. Just remembered I can't have hot drinks yet. Memory like a wossname, hole-thing.'

He looked conspiratorially at Gemma, who found herself laughing, somehow.

'Sieve?' she suggested.

'That's the one. You are clever, love.'

'Yeah,' she said. 'I'll sail through my GCSEs, knowing what a sieve is.'

Gemma's mum politely offered Lance the spare tea, but he said,

'I'm more a coffee person. Plus I've been stabbed.'

'Well,' said her mum, looking a bit flustered. 'You look well on it though. Don't he look well?'

And they all agreed that Lance looked well – which, he modestly explained, was on account of having won several genetic lotteries.

92

By the time the charges against Jonathon were officially dropped, Lance and Colin were out of hospital and on the mend, so they had a modest celebration at the Flask.

As each person arrived, Jonathon and Piper bought them a drink and Cess gave them an excited tonguey smile and sniffed them politely.

There was Lance and Arlene, bickering affectionately about the legal status of the expression 'uh-huh'.

There was Piper's dad Gus and his new girlfriend Jenny, who thought the whole episode would have turned out much better if they hadn't been on holiday in Guadeloupe while it was going on.

There was Ken and his daughter Ranira, who was carrying the largest and most expensive phone anyone had ever seen – a present from her dad for saving his company.

There was Jamali, who'd finished his sentence and was wearing a pair of trainers so new and white that it seemed they must surely be the conceptual ideal of a pair of trainers, and not any actual pair that has ever existed.

There was Rachel, visiting from France, whose divorce from Fabien was on hold, and who, in fact, had brought him along with her.

And finally there was Colin, Lisa and Gemma, who seemed to have been brought together by the experience. It is, after all, difficult to maintain a frosty silence with someone who has stolen two cars, broken into a house and been put in intensive care in order to rescue you from murderous bumbling Etonians. And nothing opens up opportunities for talking to your daughter like having your life saved by her well-timed scream.

They pushed tables together and drew up stools around them, in the time-honoured way.

'Oldy-worldy, this pub, innit?' said Lisa, looking around in her good-natured way and clearly regretting it wasn't more modern and plush.

'Mum!' said Gemma, laughing. 'It's really nice,' she told Jonathon, who had clubbed together with the rest of them to buy her a saxophone, which was what she'd always wanted to play.

'Thanks,' he said. 'I like old pubs.'

'Me too,' said Colin, raising his pint. 'You know where you are with them.'

They clinked glasses and Jonathon asked, 'Do you know what you're, um, going to do? Now that you're ... better.'

'You're looking at the new manager of the Blackstock Road branch of Ken's Plucky Fried Chicken.'

'Oh, congratulations!'

'Cheers,' said Colin, holding up his pint again and taking a drink. 'Listen. About ... all that business, all them years ago.'

'Um, yes?' said Jonathon.

'Well, there's no hard feelings from my side. Just wanted you to know that. And I'm ... sorry, about what I done.'

'Oh,' said Jonathon, deciding not to ask him about all the murders. 'That's all right.'

'So if anyone gives you any trouble, just let me know. All right?'

'All right. Thanks. And if you need any drawings of animals in old-fashioned clothes ...'

'I'll know where to come. Cheers, mate.'

Colin drifted over to join Lance at the bar, and Arlene came and sat beside Jonathon.

'I keep meaning to ask you,' she said, 'who was that woman the police had to drag off of Teddy?'

'That was Nikki,' said Jonathon. 'She owned Flock, the company that was spreading misinformation to get Teddy elected ... and, um, put Ken's Plucky Fried Chicken out of business. And other stuff.'

'That was her? But she seemed so nice. If she was a bad guy why did they let her sit with us when we were all hanging around afterwards, wearing silver blankets and having tea and biscuits?'

'The Etonians turned on her at the end – that's why they gave her the tea, I think.'

'But what about all the bad stuff she did with her company?'

'I … don't think any of it was illegal. It was just really *bad*. But there was an article about her in the paper the other day: her mum persuaded her to close down her company and train as a teacher.'

'Okay! Well, that's one good thing to come out of all this. I mean, apart from Teddy and his buddies.'

'And there is that bill,' said Gus, 'which parliament has just passed, forcing Eton to live up to its charitable status and use its huge wealth to educate only people from ordinary or disadvantaged backgrounds, all on full scholarships.'

'I just hope it doesn't make them arseholes too,' said Lance, who had acquired an unshakeable prejudice against Etonians, for understandable reasons.

They all clinked glasses and drank to that, hoping it would be so.

A while later, after Colin, Lisa and Gemma had gone home, and the rest of them had drunk several beers and had something to eat, Jonathon found Lance sitting beside him at the ancient zinc-topped bar.

'I'm sorry,' said Lance, 'that I didn't manage to prevent an adventure breaking out, like I promised.'

'That's all right,' said Jonathon, whose state of relief had only intensified now the threat of incarceration had gone. 'Thanks very much for trying.'

'It's difficult to know what moral to take from this one,' said Lance.

'Oh, that's easy,' said Jonathon. 'It's that if you see your ex-girlfriend on the Tube, you shouldn't try to hide, because it could lead to prison.'

'That's the moral you're taking from it?' said Lance.

'Yes. I think so.'

'But, from what I understand, the problem wasn't trying to hide, but doing it badly. None of this would have happened if you'd successfully hidden from her.'

'Oh,' said Jonathon. He walked his way through the sequence of horribly traumatic events. 'Oh, yes.'

'I'd say the moral is that you should on no account ever call your ex-girlfriends,' said Lance.

'But then I'd never have made friends with Rachel again,' said Jonathon, looking over at a nearby table, where Rachel and Piper seemed to be talking animatedly to the ceiling. 'And I'd still be terrified of the uncle–'

'Colin,' corrected Lance.

'… of Colin, if I heard he'd been released – or if I'd bumped into him walking on the heath, if Colins go for walks on heaths.'

They were silent for a while as they both racked their brains for a moral.

'Maybe it's about the difficulty of getting the police to storm politicians' houses?' said Lance. 'Or that only teamwork and screaming can stop Etonians ruining everyone's lives?'

'They're both a bit on the nose,' said Jonathon.

'Okay then, you suggest something.'

'Maybe it's something about conspiracy theories?' suggested Jonathon, tentatively.

'That's something I never understood,' said Lance. 'I mean, you've been caught up in actual conspiracies; how come you're so reluctant to believe in conspiracy theories?'

'I don't know. I never really had a theory about any of the real conspiracies I was involved in. I think maybe if you have a theory, you've already missed the conspiracy.'

'You mean only people who don't have a clue what's going on have any chance of being right?'

'I just mean, maybe it's best to stay confused. It seems like most of the really big conspiracies are right out there in the open. If it came out that all our worst politicians were secretly members of the Illuminati, there'd be mobs torching Whitehall. But as they all openly went to the same school, it somehow seems too complicated and boring to do anything about.'

'Are Illuminati – and shapeshifting baby-eating octopuses – really a more straightforward problem?'

Jonathon hesitated, then said, 'Well, sort of. I mean, they're comparatively straightforward: you just have to stop them somehow. Whereas, god knows what you do about … prisons, say.'

'Just don't think about them,' said Lance.

'But–'

'*Dup!*' said Lance, holding up a warning finger. 'Definitely not today. This is your moment of triumph. I don't want you ruining it for yourself by spending all day coming up with a really detailed prisons policy.'

'Oh!' said Jonathon. 'I've got it!'

'What, a prisons policy?'

'No, the moral. It's that when a sequence of horribly traumatic events–'

'An *adventure*,' insisted Lance.

'Well, whatever you call it, when one of them's coming to get you, there's nothing you can possibly do about it. You just have to get through it as best you can.'

'And maybe even enjoy it along the way?' suggested Lance.

'What? No. That's impossible.' Jonathon shuddered. 'Just get through it, and when it's over, go to the nicest pub you can find and try to forget all about it.'

93

The next morning, in Flintwinch…

'What on earth happened to you?' asked Hooray.

Teddy closed the cell door and leaned against it, breathing hard and shaking. His prison T-shirt was soaked through and his legs and feet were bare.

'An old man punched me in the stomach, then Gobber stole my trousers and both of them said they'll kill me if I ever go in the shower again.'

'You let yourself be bested by an old man, Teddy?'

'You don't understand, Hoo. He had a sort of stern and terrible majesty. And a really hard punch. Looked very much like Poseidon.'

'As in the ship?'

'As in the Greek god of the sea.'

Teddy slumped into the white plastic chair and stared glassily at the floor.

'This place is awful, Hoo.'

'Well, Teddy, I don't mean to sound callous, but it strikes me as poetic justice – fitting punishment for your failure to prevent Gobber stealing my flip-flops yesterday.'

'He stole mine too!'

'That's your business. Mine were not yours to give away.'

'Don't be like that, Hoo. We're stuck in this godawful place together.'

'Your appeal for solidarity is a touch late, Teddy, after your sordid attempts to offload the blame onto me in our trial.'

'You did the same!'

'I was simply repaying you for the appalling ingratitude you displayed when I'd defeated all your enemies. Did I hear a word of thanks? I did not. And then you go off and call your campaign manager at the crucial moment.'

'Oh, I see. So it's all my fault, is it? Is that why you haven't lifted a single tiny finger to keep this cell habitable?'

'I have already explained, Teddy, that my ancestors' exalted rank makes it highly–'

'Oh, bugger your ancestors. The place is an absolute charnel ground after barely a day – there are blood-soaked socks in the sink!'

'That is because, Teddy, I have no flip-flops with which to protect my feet from all that lurks in the showers. At least I can manage to return from them *avec* trousers.'

Teddy looked down at his bare legs. His lip quivered.

'Oh god. I wish I'd bothered to turn up to prisons debates, when I was in parliament.'

Hooray sighed. 'Now then, Teddy. None of that. No doubt old Cheeso will lend you the requisite tuna to buy more trousers – and some flip-flops for me.'

'But you heard him! He says he'll charge double-bubble and that arrears will be dealt with by McGill.'

'Well you'll just have to jolly well scrape the tuna together and make sure you don't get into arrears, won't you? Otherwise my blood-soaked socks will pile up in the sink, and with them my ire, Teddy. You would do well to remember that I too am a man of violence.'

'Oh god,' said Teddy again, head in hands. 'What have I done, that I should end up a bloody trouserless convict with a tuna deficit? Why did I ever go into politics?'

94

Meanwhile, in an improbably beautiful little cottage in Hampstead ...

Autumn sunlight poured into the bedroom, illuminating the cat who sat on the window ledge, watching the street and rotating his ears.

Jonathon and Piper were sitting up in bed, warming their hands on mugs of tea and their feet on the dog, who lay utterly motionless, as though she'd been darted by a passing park ranger. They were taking it in turns to do 'hot-tea hands' – holding their warmed palms to the other's face.

'I don't think I could be happier than this,' said Jonathon.

And he meant it. Being in prison had made him profoundly grateful for every moment he spent not in prison. It was almost worth having an adventure for this total relief now that it was all over.

'Really?' she said, resting her head on his shoulder. 'Not even if the bedroom radiator worked properly?'

'Then we wouldn't be able to do hot-tea hands.'

'That's true,' she said, and kissed his shoulder.

And then the dog groaned contentedly, and the cat turned and slow-blinked his eyes in what could almost be construed as a smile.

A note from the author

Like many people, I've always found the world quite a difficult and confusing place. So, ever since I learned to read, I've been escaping into books. I've read and enjoyed lots of different sorts of books. But there's a particular kind that has really helped when the world has been at its most baffling and intractable.

I was nine or ten when I read *The Hitchhiker's Guide to the Galaxy* by Douglas Adams. It immediately made me think, 'Oh, maybe it isn't all my fault. Maybe it's just that nothing makes any sense.' It was a huge comfort and relief.

And then when I was in my mid-twenties and had a horrible corporate temping job, I found a 1932 *Jeeves Omnibus* by PG Wodehouse in a second-hand bookshop. I read it to soothe myself when I woke in the night, dreading the next day. Since then a few other books have worked the same magic. They include *Augustus Carp By Himself*, by the excellently named Henry Howarth Bashford, *Three Men in a Boat* by Jerome K Jerome, and *The Understudy* by David Nicholls.

There aren't many of these books, but I love them. To me it feels like the authors are whispering reassuringly that, if we're finding things difficult, it may well be because the world is senseless and absurd.

I would like to convey the same thing, however incompetent my whispering technique may be. I just want to write something that would have made me feel better if I'd read it when I was twenty-four and sitting full of dread on a District Line train.

I hope it worked for you. But in any case, thank you for reading.

Christopher Shevlin

To get in touch or sign up for my newsletter, please visit:
www.christophershevlin.com

What to do now

If you have enjoyed this book and are at a loose end, please:

1. Write a review on Amazon or Goodreads – each one makes the author feel like he isn't a complete idiot for up to 24 hours, and convinces 11 more people to give his books a try.
2. Sign up for the author's newsletter (at christophershevlin. com). You'll get a free copy of *The Deleted Scenes of Jonathon Fairfax*, and other things too.
3. Tell everyone you have ever even vaguely liked to get a copy of *The Fairfax Redemption*, as well as all the other Jonathon Fairfax books.
4. Leave a note on your fridge, reminding yourself that this book is attractively priced and, for the right person, makes a supremely adequate gift.
5. Sit back and bask in the author's gratitude and admiration. You are a good person, if somewhat misunderstood. Cup of tea?

Thank you again.

Also by Christopher Shevlin

The Perpetual Astonishment of Jonathon Fairfax

Jonathon Fairfax Must Be Destroyed

The Spy Who Came in from the Bin

The Fairfax Redemption

The Pursuit of Coconuts (a novella)

Printed in Great Britain
by Amazon

43005769R00209